VIRGINIA ANDREWS®

INTO THE WOODS

POCKET
BOOKS

LONDON • SYDNEY • NEW YORK • TORONTO

First published in the US by Pocket Books, 2003
a division of Simon and Schuster Inc.
First published in Great Britain by Simon & Schuster UK Ltd, 2004
This edition published by Pocket Books, 2004
An imprint of Simon & Schuster UK Ltd
A CBS COMPANY

5 7 9 10 8 6

Simon & Schuster UK Ltd
Africa House
64–78 Kingsway
London WC2B 6AH

www.simonsays.co.uk

Simon & Schuster Australia
Sydney

A CIP catalogue record for this book is available from the British Library

ISBN-10: 0-7434-6142-8
ISBN-13: 978-0-7434-6142-9

This book is a work of fiction. Names, characters, places and incidents are
either a product of the author's imagination or are used fictitiously. Any
resemblance to actual people living or dead, events or locales is entirely
coincidental.

Printed and bound in Great Britain by
Cox & Wyman Ltd, Reading, Berkshire

Virginia Andrews is a worldwide bestselling author. Her much-loved novels include RAIN, LIGHTNING STRIKES, EYE OF THE STORM and THE END OF THE RAINBOW. Virginia Andrews' novels have sold more than eighty million copies and have been translated into twenty-two foreign languages.

The Dollanger Family Series
Flowers in the Attic
Petals on the Wind
If There Be Thorns
Seeds of Yesterday
Garden of Shadows

The Casteel Family Series
Heaven
Dark Angel
Fallen Hearts
Gates of Paradise
Web of Dreams

The Cutler Family Series
Dawn
Secrets of the Morning
Twilight's Child
Midnight Whispers
Darkest Hour

The Landry Family Series
Ruby
Pearl in the Mist
All That Glitters
Hidden Jewel
Tarnished Gold

The Logan Family Series
Melody
Heart Song
Unfinished Symphony
Music in the Night
Olivia

The Orphans Mini-series
Butterfly
Crystal
Brooke
Raven
Runaways (full-length novel)

The Wildflowers Mini-series
Wildflowers
Into the Garden

The Hudson Family Series
Rain
Lightning Strikes
Eye of the Storm
The End of the Rainbow

The De Beers Family Series
Willow
Wicked Forest
Twisted Roots
Into the Woods

My Sweet Audrina (does not belong to a series)

INTO THE WOODS

Prologue

Goodbye, Sailor Girl

My last memory of my daddy was watching him walk out to his helicopter at the Norfolk Naval Base, where his student pilots waited respectfully at attention, their helmets under their arms.

They saluted him, and he saluted back. Then he turned to smile at me the way he always did whenever Mommy brought me to see him take off in a helicopter. He and I called it putting sunshine in our faces. In the years to follow, that smile would fade slowly like an old photograph until my imagination did more for it than my memory.

His face would always brighten with a fresh, happy surprise when he looked back at me standing beside Mommy. The specks of hazel in his otherwise light blue eyes would become more prominent. He used to call me Sailor Girl, and we would salute each other with only two fingers. He did it one last time that day. I responded with my salute, and then he turned back to his men.

My eyes drifted to a sea gull that looked lost, confused, even a bit frantic. It did a quick turn and dipped before shooting off toward the ocean as if it had seen something that had terrified it. I watched it until the sounds of the helicopter motors ripped the air and pulled my attention back to Daddy.

I stepped closer to Mommy. Something dark had already put its cold fingers on the back of my neck. My heart sank, and my stomach felt queasy. I had to feel Mommy beside me. Even at fifteen, I needed to be within the walls of her security. She and Daddy were my fortress. Nothing could harm me when I was with them.

"How he stands that noise is beyond me," Mommy said, but she looked so proud and so beautiful with her shoulder-length apricot brown hair dancing about her chin and cheeks. She was five feet ten and always stood with an air of confidence, regal. Anyone who glanced her way stared at her for a few moments longer as if he or she were hypnotized by her beauty.

Mommy's eyes were almost navy blue, which Daddy said proved she belonged with him, a navy man. She was as loyal to him as he was to the flag, her devotion and her admiration for him unflappable. My eyes were more turquoise, but I wished they were more like Mommy's so Daddy would think I, too, was meant to be always at his side.

"C'mon, Grace," she said. "I have errands to run, and you have studying to do and a guest for dinner."

She nudged me, and I followed along reluctantly. Something was telling me to stay as long as I could. I looked back only once as the helicopters lifted. I didn't see Daddy, and that disappointed me. They whirled off toward the ocean, following the sea gull.

A cloud blocked out the sun, and a long shadow fell around us as we continued toward our car.

I would remember that.

I would remember it all for a very long time.

And then, like the sea gull, it would all disappear into the distance and leave me standing alone, yearning for just one more smile, one more salute.

1

The Life

When I was very little, I thought everyone lived the way we did: moving frequently from one place to another. Houses and homes were like way stations, scattered not only across the country but across the world. School would always be interrupted and changed. As soon as a new neighborhood became comfortable or even before, I would be taken to another, and the process would begin again. Friendships weren't meant to last long, and so it was always better not to get too friendly or too dependent on anyone. It was hard to keep from doing this, especially when it came to my teachers. I remember growing so attached to my third-grade teacher that I cried until my stomach ached the day Mommy came to take me out of the school and load me along with our luggage and other cherished belongings in our car.

Daddy had been talking about the new naval base

and our new living conditions for days, trying to make it sound as if everything would be nicer for all of us. As a naval helicopter pilot, he was away often on his aircraft carrier. Occasionally we would get phone calls from him, and lots of letters, always with a separate one for me inserted in with Mommy's. Mine always began "Dear Sailor Girl," and he would go on and on about how much he missed me. He wasn't permitted to tell us where he was, but we knew that wherever it was, it was far away.

So whenever he was being stationed at a base for what looked to be a prolonged period of land time, Mommy was the happiest and more than willing to pick up everything yet another time, load our car, and be off. The women she knew as friends were all like her, naval wives, and were just as accustomed to the nomadic existence as well as the short friendships and months without their husbands.

Mommy was also happy because Daddy was succeeding. Almost every move we made was, in her words, a "vertical move." He was climbing in rank and in importance, and I thought there was little doubt in her mind that someday he would become an admiral. They joked about it all the time, with her calling him Admiral Houston. Once, when I was only seven, I even told my classmates my father was already an admiral. I had heard it so often at home, I believed it. Of course, the older boys and girls made fun of me.

"The only fleet your father is admiral of is an enema," a much older teenage boy said, and I ran home and told my mother, who surprised me by laughing. I know I looked as if I was going to cry.

"That's all right, Grace," she said. "Don't pay any attention to anyone. Someday your father *will* be an admiral, and they will have to swallow their jokes whole or choke on them."

"But why do you call him Admiral if he isn't an admiral?" I wanted to know.

She sat me down in our small living room in a house situated in what was the married naval officers' housing complex and explained to me how, when two people are as in love as she was with Daddy and he was with her, they often teased each other affectionately.

"When I first met your father, in fact, he pretended he was already a captain. I didn't understand the stripes and ranks then, so I believed him."

"He lied to you?" I asked, astounded. Daddy was my straight arrow. Lying, deception, betrayal could never be any part of who and what he was to me. He was perfect, a model for a navy poster, incorruptible, unadulterated, pure, and forever strong.

Physically he looked the part, too. He was six feet two and weighed 180 pounds that were always trim. Gym training was as much a part of his daily routine as eating, and I loved to sit and watch him play tennis or even half-court basketball with some of the other junior officers. Whenever he did something good, he would turn my way and give me that salute. It was almost as if his smile and mine were connected, his laugh becoming my laugh. I could no more take my eyes off him than a moth could stop circling a candle flame.

Mommy scrunched her nose and shook her head at my question and surprise.

"It wasn't a lie exactly, Grace. It was a little embellishment which he later described as part of his effort to win my attention. He was afraid I wouldn't give him the time of day if he wasn't an officer, but I was young and foolish, and nothing mattered but what I saw in his eyes."

"Why was that foolish, Mommy?"

She sighed. "You can't help being a little foolish when you're young, Grace. You're almost supposed to be a bit reckless." She thought for a moment, and then her eyes narrowed the way they did when she became very serious or very sad, and she continued with, "You know what love really is, Grace?"

Of course, I shook my head and held my breath. I knew it was something special, but I had no idea how to put it into words, especially the love between a man and a woman.

"It's an investment, taking a chance, and any investment involves some risk, and some risk means being somewhat foolish. In my heart of hearts I knew your father was going to be a big success. Every part of me believed it, so I wasn't afraid even though we were married and lived on a shoestring, and I had to be willing to send him off time after time, willing to contend with great loneliness until . . ." She smiled. "Until we had you, and I would never be lonely again," she said.

She hugged me.

And everything was all right. Everything would always be all right. Even if it was raining or snowing, the sun always shone when either she or Daddy beamed their broad, happy smiles on me. How I miss that feeling, that faith in our lives being one everlasting summer's day. Yes, we weren't rich, but if we lacked something necessary, I was unaware of it. Mommy was always buying me new things to wear, especially if we moved to a different climate. We always had a late-model automobile, and my room, no matter where it was, was decorated with all sorts of dolls and pictures and mementos Daddy brought home from each and every sea duty.

So much of that is buried in trunks now. I don't even look at them anymore. Memories can be very painful, each like a separate needle piercing your heart, bringing tears to your eyes and an ache into your chest. Better to keep them out of sight and out of mind.

Be careful about whom you permit to touch you deeply, a voice inside me warned and continues to warn even to this day. Your heart hardens around their words, their promises, and their touches like hand- and foot-prints in cement, and you carry them within you until you die and maybe even afterward. *The more you love someone, the deeper the pain is when they are gone, and they* will *be gone,* the voice insists. It makes me tremble every time someone tries to be close.

A few weeks before my fifteenth birthday Daddy came home with what Mommy would say was the best possible present he could have brought. A year before, Daddy had been transferred to San Diego. We were living in what was a little smaller house than the one we were in previously. Nevertheless, I had my own room, and I was in it doing my homework because I wanted to be free to watch a music special on TV. I also had an English test the next day, but I was confident about it.

As soon as Daddy greeted Mommy when he came home, he boomed a loud "Where's my Sailor Girl?"

"That sailor girl is nearly fifteen, Roland. You are going to have to stop treating her as if she was five," Mommy told him, but Daddy shook it off.

"She'll always be five to me," he declared, his arms waiting for me. Then he held me out with his hands on my shoulders and said, "Take a seat, Gracey."

"Oh, no," Mommy cried, her hand to her forehead. "Whenever you call her Gracey, Roland Stemper Houston, that means anchors aweigh."

"This is good, it's good," he insisted, waving her into a seat as well. Then he stood back with that cat-ate-the-mouse grin.

"Well?" Mommy asked. "Don't keep us sitting here like steamed-up ships in the harbor. Launch or drop anchor, sailor."

Daddy laughed. "First," he began, "I've been assigned to HC-8 in Norfolk, Virginia. That's Helicopter Combat Support Squadron Eight, the Dragon Whales."

"What do they do?" Mommy asked quickly, her eyes narrowing with concern and worry.

"Well, HC-8 flies the Ch-46 Sea Knight helicopter and performs search and rescue and vertical replenishment in support of the Atlantic Fleet," he replied proudly. "However," he continued before Mommy could ask him how dangerous it all was, "HC-8 also operates Heliops."

"What's that?" I asked first.

"That, Sailor Girl, is the Atlantic Fleet Helicopter Operations School, and yours truly is to be an instructor, which means," he continued without taking a breath, "as permanent a location for us as is possible. Maybe as long as three years!"

Mommy just stared at him. She looked as if she were afraid she had dreamed the words and if she said anything or interrupted him, it would all pop like a bubble of dialogue in some cartoon.

"Of course, this means a promotion," he said, and stood at attention. "You are now looking at Lieutenant Commander Houston, pay grade zero-four."

He turned his shoulder down to be sure we both saw his new shoulder board with its thick band, narrow band, and thick band. Then he flipped out a packet of pages and handed them to Mommy.

"Our new digs," he declared.

She looked at the pictures of the housing on base.

"Nice, huh?"

"Yes," she said after taking a breath, leaning back, and turning to me.

She could see it in my face: I knew it was to be goodbyes again, the departing words spoken practically in mid-sentence. Daddy caught the look on both our faces.

"Sailor Girl will be fine," Daddy said. "Shipping out is in her blood by now, right, Sailor Girl?"

"Right, Daddy."

"I'm sorry, honey," Mommy said. "I know you've made some friends."

"It's all right. There's no one with whom I'm that close." The truth was, there wasn't, but I also knew it was my fault more than anyone else's.

"You'll have a bigger room," Daddy promised. "It's going to be a very nice house and a good school and . . ."

"She knows the drill by now, Roland," Mommy said. "Save your breath."

He nodded. She stood up and kissed him.

"Congratulations, Roland."

"I'm closing in on that admiral," Daddy said proudly. "What do you say we celebrate and go out to dinner?"

Mommy looked to me.

"It's all right. I've almost got all my homework done," I said.

"My sailor girls," Daddy said, and hugged us both.

I looked at the house I had barely grown to know, the house we were now deserting like a sinking ship. *Someday,* I thought, *I will live in one place for a long time, and I will get to know people and have real friends, and all this will seem like a dream.*

Would I be happier?

I longed to discover the answer.

We were going clear across the country, from California to Virginia. Daddy decided we would sell our car, ship what we wanted to take with us, and fly. We would buy a new car in Norfolk. His orders required a very fast departure anyway, so if we didn't, he would fly, and Mommy and I would have had to drive across country ourselves, not that we hadn't gone long distances ourselves in the past. This time more than any time, however, they both wanted to have the sense of a truly new beginning with as much of it as fresh as possible. Possessions were more temporary for us than they were for most people. We had no furniture we had to take with us. Any pictures and decorations Mommy had bought for the present house would be either given away or sold.

Most of the children of naval personnel whom I have met and known seem almost numb to being ripped up and out of their "digs," as Daddy liked to call them. The faces of my current girlfriends were stoical, neither sad nor happy for me exactly. There was some curiosity about where we were going and what my father was going to do, but almost before I finished describing it all, I could see their eyes shifting, their attention moving off me, their mental erasers working, scrubbing my name and face from the pages of their memories. I had yet to actually walk out of the school and leave our house, but I was gone as far as they were all concerned. I couldn't blame them.

The phone didn't ring the day we were scheduled to

depart. No one called to say goodbye or promise to write or ask me to write. We naval children floated by one another like faces on balloons, caught in some wind over which we had no control. We were ribbons tied to the rear bumpers of cars and had just as much power and say over where the car would turn and go. At least gypsies moved in a small community, remaining together as if the world moved under their feet and they never left. Occasionally, I had run into someone I had known from a previous naval base whose father had been transferred shortly after or even before my father, but I found this more of an exception than a rule, and, besides, it didn't result in any tightening of any relationship. I think we were all afraid of the same inevitable goodbye.

It couldn't have been a more beautiful May day for our arrival in Norfolk, Virginia. The sky was my favorite shade of turquoise, close to my eye color, with clouds of whipped cream that looked dabbed onto a canvas, seemingly unmoving. It was warm with a soft breeze, and I remember how everything looked so new and crisp to me.

Daddy was right to be enthusiastic about our new home. It was in a gated community, and each home had beautiful landscaping. As soon as we arrived, the wives of other naval officers were on the scene to greet Mommy. One of them brought her daughter along. Her name was Autumn Sullivan, and she was just two months younger than I. We would be in the same grade and have the same classes. I could see she was anxious to tell me all about the school, the teachers, the other students, and activities.

Autumn had hair the color of amber fall leaves and tiny rust-tinted freckles spotting the crests of her cheeks. She immediately told me that was not the reason her parents had named her after the fall season of the year.

"It has always been my mother's favorite time of the year, and she would have named me Autumn even if I had black hair. She's from upstate New York, and when the leaves turn, she says it's the most beautiful sight. I've seen it a few times. We've gone back to visit my grandmother and my aunts, and my mother always tries to time the trips about mid-October," Autumn said.

Right from the start she was eager to talk and tell me as much about herself as she could in a single day. I think we were all like that, insecure naval brats, afraid that if we didn't get everything out quickly enough, we would not only forget but would be moved on before we had a chance to do it. Our friendships, which we knew would be short, had to be crammed full of events and information almost as if we were fast-forwarding our lives on a television screen.

Autumn's father was a lieutenant and an instructor in Heliops, too, teaching in the Landing Signalman Enlisted School. They had already been at Norfolk for nearly a year. Autumn had an older sister, Caitlin. She was a senior in high school, and Autumn let me know immediately that her sister's boyfriend, Jarvis Martin, was Vice Admiral Martin's son. He had already been accepted to Annapolis.

Just a little over five feet one, Autumn was plump and more chesty than I was. She had dimples in both her cheeks, deep enough to hold a nickel, as Daddy would say. I liked her immediately because of how bubbly and excited she was. Before I could get a word in, she rattled off a list of her CDs and made sure I knew exactly who were her favorite singers and groups.

"Can you come over to my house for dinner tonight?" she asked, gasping for a breath at the same time.

Mommy overheard and smiled. "Don't you think you should ask your mother first, Autumn?" she asked her.

"Oh, Daddy makes us dinner. He's a gourmet cook," she declared.

Mommy laughed and looked at Autumn's mother, who was talking with two other naval wives in the kitchen.

"I still think you should ask first," she said with a soft smile.

"Right. I'll ask," Autumn cried, and leaped off my bed where she had been holding court.

Mommy and I looked at each other and laughed.

"It's okay for you to come," Autumn cried, returning. "Daddy loves having another mouth to feed. That's what my mother said."

I looked at Mommy.

"It's all right. Go on. Enjoy yourself, honey. There's not much to do at the moment since you've already put your clothes away," she told me.

She knew I would want to take my time organizing my dolls and other important possessions. Daddy would have to put up some more shelving, too, I thought.

Mommy returned to talk to the other women, and Autumn and I left the house so she could show me around. The streets and the other houses looked remarkably as they were depicted in the brochure. Often the brochures were older and no longer as accurate, but these homes were still sparkling with a new sheen, the lawns and flowers rich and healthy.

I saw other officers in their crisp, sharp uniforms getting in and out of automobiles or talking to one another. Some gazed our way and smiled, others nodded, never losing their military demeanor. I was so used to men and women standing firm and straight, I thought most civilians were sick or deformed, slouching, moving with slower, undetermined, and insecure steps.

As we walked along, Autumn rattled off the names of the families in each home, which ones had children close to our age, and which didn't. Although there were two other girls who would be in my class at school, Wendi Charles and Penny Martin, I had the distinct sense that Autumn was not very friendly with them. Wendi Charles's father was a captain, a fighter pilot, and, of course, Penny was Jarvis's sister and the daughter of Vice Admiral Martin. She made them sound as though they were very snobby girls who let everyone know how important their families were in the naval community.

Autumn had been living in San Diego, too, only from what she told me, this was the first time her family was living on a naval base. We walked until we were at a small park where some mothers were supervising their small children on slides and the merry-go-round. We sat on a bench and watched for a while.

"I bet you're tired," Autumn said. The way she said it made me think she was saying I was tired of "the life," as Mommy sometimes called it. Some of the Navy wives she had known thought of their husbands' enlistment as they would a prison sentence, looking forward to discharge and their entry into the civilian world just as someone who had finished serving a sentence would.

"A little," I said. "You know how hectic it is to pick up and move so much."

"Did you have a boyfriend back in San Diego?"

"No," I said quickly. She nodded as if that was what she had expected to hear.

"Wendi Charles told me boys who know you are a Navy girl think you are more promiscuous. Do you know what that means?"

"Yes," I said, smiling.

"I bet you're a good student. I bet you're smarter than I am. You just look like you are," she said, and I laughed.

"I like to read," I admitted.

"Me, too, only I'm sure not as much as you. So?"

"So what?"

"Do you think what Wendi says is true?" she asked. "Are we more promiscuous?"

She couldn't be more obvious about fishing for personal information, I thought, or was she trying to confirm something in herself?

"I don't know. No," I decided. "Why should we be?"

"Because we're moving so often, Wendi says, they think we don't care about our reputations."

"That's stupid," I said, and she nodded.

"I thought so, too. Have you had any boyfriends, though?" she followed, raising her brown eyes toward me quickly in anticipation.

"No, not anyone I would call that. How about you?"

She shook her head. "I like this boy, Trent Ralston, though," she confessed. "You're the first person I've told."

"So Trent Ralston doesn't know, either?"

"No," she said, raising her eyebrows and widening her eyes as if that would be outrageous. "Wendi says once a boy knows you like him, he gets more aggressive. She says you have to keep them in doubt all the time."

"I guess she thinks she's an expert when it comes to boys, huh?"

"I suppose she is. She's very popular. She didn't actually tell me these things," she confessed. "I was just nearby when she was telling them to her friends, and I overheard."

"What about your older sister, Caitlin?"

"What about her?"

"Don't you ever ask her questions, get advice about boys from her?"

"No," she said quickly. "She thinks I'm still too immature to talk to me about such things." She shrugged. "We've never been that close."

"That's too bad."

"You never had a sister or brother?"

"No, but I wish I had," I said. "People never appreciate what they have when they have it," I added, a little bitterly, recalling the way some of my friends resented or argued with their brothers and sisters.

Autumn nodded.

One of the mothers started to chastise her son for being too rough with the others on the slide. She shook him hard, and he started to cry as if she had rattled something in him and caused something to break. His feelings were shattering, I thought. No one likes to be punished so vehemently in front of his friends. His mother looked so enraged, I could see she frightened even the other children, who cowered back to watch.

"I'm so terrified of becoming someone's mother," Autumn said, watching the scene before us.

"Why?"

"I'm sure I won't be a good mother. I'll be too permissive. I could never do that," she said, nodding at the way the mother was still reprimanding her child. "My children will become wild animals, and my husband will hate me and leave me out of frustration."

"My father says you never know what you will really do until you have to do it. Everything else is just talk. So don't be so quick to condemn yourself," I told her.

She smiled. "C'mon," she said, jumping to her feet and seizing my hand. "Let's go to my house to listen to some music and talk some more before it's time for dinner."

"I'd better go home one more time first and be sure there isn't anything my mother needs me to do," I said. Her eyes drooped with disappointment. "If there isn't, I'll come," I said, and she beamed again.

"Good, because there is so much I have to tell you. You should know who to trust and who not to trust, what to believe and what not to believe. It's so hard when you have to discover all these things yourself. No one is going to be a better friend to you than I will, because we come from the same world," she emphasized.

Her face filled with worry as she waited for my reaction. *I bet she has no friends,* I thought to myself, *not even a strong acquaintance.*

And for the first time, I realized how terribly lonely and afraid girls like us could be. I wondered why I hadn't felt it before. Was there something wrong or right with me? Shouldn't I have cared more, been as hungry for social life as Autumn obviously was? Why hadn't I ever been concerned about not having a steady boyfriend?

A butterfly passed close by as we started away, and I thought of myself as a butterfly still in its cocoon, its wings just starting to flutter, emerging but with fear more than excitement. Every new feeling, every new hunger, surely must first fill us with terror. What if we don't ever satisfy ourselves? What if we tremble like Autumn does and see ourselves as failing to find love, to find meaning?

How long can we continue to fly without it?

Mommy insisted she didn't need me for anything, so Autumn and I headed for her house. As we walked along, a flashy red convertible pulled alongside with two girls and a boy who was driving.

"It's Wendi Charles and Penny Martin," Autumn quickly whispered, her voice rattling a bit with trepidation.

"Hi," the girl in the front seat said, leaning over the door. "Are you the new kid on the block?"

"I suppose so," I said, and the girl in the backseat laughed.

"I'm Wendi. That's Penny giggling stupidly back there, and this is Ricky Smith, who enjoys being our slave. What's your name?"

"Grace Houston."

"Well, Grace, I see Autumn has pounced on you. What did you do, Autumn, wait at the gate all night or something so you could get to her first?"

"No," Autumn said quickly, but she couldn't look directly at Wendi, who had steely, cold, dark brown eyes. "I don't pounce on people," she added, but kept her eyes down.

"No, people pounce on you," Wendi said, and Ricky and Penny laughed again. "Isn't that right, Autumn?"

"C'mon," she said to me. "We have to get to my house."

"What's the hurry, Autumn?" Penny asked. "You doing something exciting again, or do you just want to tell Grace here your war stories?"

"Boom, boom!" Ricky bellowed, pumping his right arm like a cheerleader.

The other two laughed again. *How cruel and sarcastic they are to Autumn,* I thought.

"C'mon," Autumn urged.

I began to turn away to walk with her.

"Did you tell her about your secret abortion yet?" Penny asked, practically shouting it.

"What?" I said, pausing and turning back to her, not sure I was hearing right.

The girls and Ricky laughed.

"I guess you were building up to it, huh, Autumn?" Wendi said. She turned to me. "It's not exactly something you wear on your shoulder board."

I looked at Autumn. Tears were streaking down her cheeks, and her chin was down, almost touching her chest.

"I don't understand," I said.

"No, not too many of us do," Penny quipped. "Stop by and visit us later, Grace. We'll fill you in on what you really should and shouldn't know around here. If you hang with her, you'll get a reputation before you even unpack, and you'll be sorry. Unless, of course, you want that sort of reputation."

They all laughed again.

"Home, James," Wendi cried, and waved at the front of the car.

"Aye, aye, Captain," Ricky said, and they started away.

Autumn looked as if she was having trouble breathing. Her face was so white, and I could see her hands trembling, even as she clutched her elbows tightly, embracing herself as if she were keeping herself from toppling forward.

"What are they talking about?" I asked her.

She lifted her head slowly, her eyes now bloodshot.

"It's a lie. It's all a lie. They hate me!" she screamed, and shot ahead of me.

"Autumn!" I called after her, but she kept walking. I looked back. The convertible had disappeared around a corner. For a long moment, I was totally confused and couldn't decide which way to go. Was it a lie? How could she sound and be so innocent before and have had such a thing happen to her? I hadn't been in my new home and community more than a few hours, and already I was enmeshed in a grand drama, I thought.

Autumn had slowed down about a block ahead of me. I hurried after her and caught up as she started to turn the corner toward her house.

"What's going on? I don't understand," I said. "Why did they say that?"

"They're just mean, vicious."

"They are mean and vicious to do that. Even if it was true, no one should just come out with that when meeting someone new," I said, and she stopped, ground the tears from her eyes, and looked at me. "Are you all right?" I asked.

"No," she said.

I stood there silently, not sure what else to do or say. I looked down, up the street, and then back at her. She was staring at me so strangely now.

"Autumn?"

"Oh, what's the difference? You'll find out anyway. It's true," she said in a dry voice, just a little above a whisper, and then she started away again, moving at a normal pace, her head still down, her arms still embracing herself.

It was true?

I felt as if I had been dropped into a world of madness, unable to distinguish what was real and what wasn't. It made my heart pound. The roar of two fighter jets passing by was so loud it even drowned out my thoughts for a moment. I saw Autumn walk to her front door, open it, and go inside.

Feeling more sorry for her than confused and frightened now, I continued toward her house.

I pushed the door buzzer and waited. Moments later, a man with short hair so golden blond it was nearly buttercup yellow answered the door. He was wearing a full apron with a picture of Frank Sinatra on the front. I could immediately see the resemblance to Autumn in his face. Both had round, full cheeks and brown eyes and freckles. Her father didn't look to be much taller than five feet eight or nine. He wiped his hands on the apron and smiled at me.

"You must be our dinner guest," he said. "Marjorie called to warn me just a little while ago. You're not a gourmet expert, are you?" he kidded, pretending to look frightened.

"No, sir."

"Good, good. Well," he said, stepping forward and looking past me, "why did Autumn ring the doorbell? Where is she? Wasn't she with you?"

"She came home already," I said, surprised he hadn't heard her enter. She must have been walking on pussy willow feet.

"Oh, has she? Well, then, come on in. I'm Lieutenant Commander Sullivan," he said, offering his hand to me.

"I'm Grace Houston."

"Welcome to the base. I'm looking forward to meeting your father. You guys just came from San Diego, right?"

"Yes, sir."

"Well, we've been there, too. You'll like it here, even though the winters aren't as warm."

I nodded. *We are always supposed to like the new place more than the old,* I thought.

"Well, then," Lieutenant Sullivan said, "come along. I'll show you to Autumn's room." I could see he looked a little puzzled about our separate entrances but didn't care or want to ask any more about that. "I bet you girls have a lot to talk about. It's exciting but nerve-wracking to land on a new beachhead, huh?"

"Yes, sir, it is."

He smiled at me and then knocked on Autumn's bedroom door. When there was no response, he glanced at me again and then knocked again.

"Autumn? Your friend is here," he said. When she still didn't reply, he turned to me. "Are you sure she came home?"

"Yes, sir. I saw her enter the house," I said.

His face filled with concern, and he tried the door knob. It was locked.

"Autumn!" he said sharply. "What are you doing in there?"

We heard the front door open again, and we both turned quickly and looked down the hallway. One look told me it was Autumn's sister, Caitlin. I could see the resemblance even though Caitlin took after her mother more and was taller, slimmer, and more striking, with more defined facial features, a narrower jaw, and higher cheekbones. Following behind her was a tall, dark-haired boy who looked like a junior officer, his posture firm, his face, especially those bright, sharp hazel eyes, full of self-confidence. He had a military-style haircut and wore jeans and a button-down, light brown, short-sleeve shirt.

"What's going on, Daddy?" Caitlin asked immediately.

"This is Grace Houston," Lieutenant Sullivan said, "Lieutenant Commander Houston's daughter. They just moved to Norfolk, and Autumn invited her to dinner tonight."

"Oh, great. Welcome," she said with a friendly smile.

"However, your sister has apparently locked herself in her room. Again," he added after a beat.

Caitlin's eyes filled with both embarrassment and concern. She turned to the boy I already knew had to be Jarvis Martin, and he tucked the right corner of his mouth into his cheek and shook his head.

"Let me try," she said, and approached the door. We both stepped back. "Autumn, what are you doing? You have a guest here. Open your door," she said firmly. "You're embarrassing everyone, including Daddy," she added. She tapped on the door. "Autumn?"

A few moments of silence passed. I looked to Jarvis, who had turned away to pretend interest in a framed print of an old whaling vessel he surely must have seen many times.

"This is ridiculous," Lieutenant Sullivan said. "Step away from the door, Caitlin."

Jarvis turned quickly and drew closer.

"Autumn, if you don't open this door instantly, I'll break it down," her father threatened.

I felt frightened and awkward standing there and took a few steps back.

"Maybe I should go," I said softly to Caitlin.

She just shook her head. "I'm sorry," she said.

"Do you need any help, sir?" Jarvis asked Lieutenant Sullivan. He looked excited, even pleased with the call to action.

Lieutenant Sullivan gazed at him, the fury now so intense in his face I could see it swirling in his darkened eyes. Without reply, he stepped back and then lunged forward with his shoulder, smashing at the door. I heard wood splinter. Jarvis stepped closer and did the same, this time the door opening so fast he tripped forward, barely catching himself to keep from falling to the floor.

I moved closer to the front door, feeling almost as if I should run away from the scene. My instincts were lifting their heads out from under the dark places where they slept and screaming all sorts of horrid warnings. My heart was pounding. I think I even whimpered at the sight of the two men charging into the room, Caitlin walking slowly behind them.

I heard her scream and Lieutenant Sullivan cry, "Oh, my God!"

I didn't wait to see why. My bones had turned to ice. I turned and ran out of the house, down the walkway to the sidewalk, and then continued running, confused for a moment and passing the corner I should have turned down to get to my new home. I realized it almost immediately and doubled back. As I headed down the street, I heard a car engine roar and saw Autumn's mother drive past me, her tires squealing as she made the turn behind me.

I broke into a fast walk and hurried to my house. The front door was open. Daddy and Mommy were standing just inside talking when I stepped into the house. They turned to me. My whole body was still shaking, and tears were streaming down my face and falling from my chin.

"Hey, don't cry, Sailor Girl," Daddy said, rushing to me.

"Oh, poor Grace, did you see her do that?" Mommy asked quickly.

I shook my head. "I don't know what she did, Mommy!" I replied, and quickly told them both everything.

"That poor girl," Mommy said.

"What did she do to herself?" I finally had the courage to ask.

"She cut her wrists," Mommy said.

It took the wind from my lungs, because that was the image I had imagined and feared. It was a strange thing to me that we were a military family, and I had seen and heard guns go off and men prepared for war, yet I never had witnessed a single act of violence in my life, except what I had seen on television or in the movies. When I was a little girl, I used to think my father was just pretending, that it was all just one big adult game. Even stories about terrorists attacking naval vessels in distant ports seemed unreal. None of it, fortunately, had come close to touching us.

But this morning, almost immediately, I was so close to an actual attempted suicide.

"Will she be all right?" I asked.

"Yes, she will, I'm sure," Daddy said.

"Physically, maybe," Mommy said, her eyes turned to him.

He looked back at me quickly. "She'll be fine," he insisted.

Mommy shook her head.

I told them both what Wendi and Penny had done and how that had upset Autumn.

"They were so mean to do that," I added.

"What a welcome to a new community for you, honey. I'm sorry," Mommy said.

It's not your fault, I wanted to say, but then I thought, *Of course it is. It's always your fault when you're a parent and you're the one in control of everything. You make the choices, and what follows is always the result of those choices.* She made the decision to marry my daddy and be a Navy wife, and that meant I would be here today, on this very spot, having this very experience.

If only we could know what our decisions could mean before we made them, I thought. Maybe that was wisdom, but it seemed to me it came to us too late, or we wouldn't listen when older, wiser people were generous with what they knew and what they had learned. We would have to make our own mistakes almost as if we had to own them along with our own successes. It was how we achieved our own identities, our own names.

Poor Autumn, I thought.

Look at what she owned.

Look at what her name was now.

2

My Personal
Radar Screen

It wasn't any easier to keep secrets in our world than it was in the outside world, although there was something of an unwritten rule that whatever happened to anyone in the naval community was to be kept within that community. Neither Wendi nor Penny showed any remorse over what they had done to poor Autumn, but they did keep what they knew locked away from the civilian girls in our school. At least, that was what I thought.

They cornered me the first day I attended my new school and brought me into the girls' room so no one else could hear us talk about Autumn.

"You were there, too," Penny said, her eyes flickering with excitement. "My brother told me. Was there blood all over the place?"

"I didn't see anything. I went home as soon as they entered her room," I said quickly. I saw they were dis-

appointed that I wouldn't be giving them a blow-by-
blow description of the horrid event.

"She must have read about how to do it," Wendi said.
Penny nodded. Both of them looked mostly impressed
about that. "You know, putting your wrists in warm
water and all to keep the blood flowing."

"That means she really was going to kill herself,"
Penny declared with exaggerated eyes. "She wasn't
simply trying to get attention. How embarrassing for
her family. I know Caitlin is afraid my brother will stop
seeing her because of it. You know, once there is madness in one member of a family, there's a good chance
it's in another."

"It wasn't madness," I insisted. "She was just embarrassed and ashamed because of what you told me. Why
did you do that so cruelly?"

"We were just trying to protect you," Wendi replied.
"It was the least we could do for a new girl."

"You would think you would show some gratitude.
She could have gone around here telling everyone you
were her new best friend or something," Penny added.

"I don't need anyone to tell me with whom I can and
cannot be friends," I snapped back at them.

"Well pardon *moi*," Wendi said. "That's the first and
last time we'll do anything to help you."

"And another thing," Penny said, moving closer to
put her face into mine, "if you go around telling people
Autumn did what she did because of what we said,
we'll make you sorrier than Autumn.

"You know," she added, stepping back with her
hands on her hips and wagging her head, "families that
can't get along with other families in the naval community usually get transferred to another base and one not
as nice. My father has a lot to say about that."

I felt the blood rush to my face. The last thing I wanted to do was to make trouble for Daddy.

"Just watch yourself," Wendi warned, and they both turned and left me trembling in the girls' room.

I avoided them for the rest of that day and most of the week that followed. I made some other friends, none of whom was in the naval community. Some wondered what was wrong with Autumn and why she wasn't attending school, but I pretended I was too new to know who she was. By the end of the week, however, Mommy told me she was doing better, and her mother had said that if I wanted to visit her, I could. Her parents had decided to keep her home until her wrists had mended and she had undergone some therapy. However, a visit by me was fine.

I wasn't all that anxious to do it. I wasn't sure what I would say to her. Daddy sensed it and told me that if I didn't want to go, I didn't have to.

"I do feel sorry for her, though, Daddy," I told him.

He nodded. "I'm glad you're a compassionate person, Grace. It's a nice quality to have. Your grandmother Houston was like that," he said, and told me more about her, her involvement with charities, her volunteer work helping the homeless. She had even been written up in newspapers, and I had seen the articles with the picture of this kindly-looking, elderly but elegant lady serving food in a makeshift kitchen on some city street, but I had never met her. She had died before I was born. My grandfather had also been in the Navy. He was a chief warrant officer. He had served during the Korean War and just recently had passed away, too.

Like me, my daddy had been an only child, but I knew he and Mommy often talked about having another child. The moving around had made Mommy nervous, and from the little I had garnered from their conversations, I understood that she had been unable to get pregnant and they had stopped trying for a while. What made it difficult for one woman to get pregnant while another got pregnant the first time she and her husband tried was still a bit of a mystery to me. I also thought it was ironic that someone like Autumn, who shouldn't have been pregnant, was, and someone like Mommy, who should have been and had wanted to be pregnant, wasn't.

Daddy made me feel less nervous about visiting Autumn, assuring me that she was probably hungry for some company her own age, so after dinner, I walked over to her home. Her sister greeted me at the door.

"Oh, you," she said. "I thought we'd never see you again after the last time," she said. "Not that I would blame you," she added.

"I didn't want to come until your mother said it was all right," I said.

"Right. Like it will ever be all right. Come in. She's in her room staring at the ceiling and feeling stupid, I'm sure," she said. "I don't mean to sound hard and unfeeling," she added when she saw the expression on my face, "but when you do something like this, you should think about the people you are hurting beside yourself. I mean, like, this sort of thing doesn't help my father's career and doesn't make things easier for my mother or for me!"

All I could do was nod, thinking this was a home in which sympathy was a rare guest.

"You know where the room is. There's a new doorjamb," she made sure to tell me as I headed for it. Then she returned to her own room.

I knocked on Autumn's door.

"Who is it?" I heard.

"It's me, Grace," I said. I held my breath when there was a long pause. Would she refuse to see me? A part of me hoped so. I looked back to see if Caitlin was watching, but there was no one in the hallway, and the house was quiet. I wondered where her mother was and how she was able to take all this sadness.

"Come in," Autumn finally said.

Just as Caitlin had described, she was in her bed. I saw the television remote by her side, but the television was not turned on.

"How are you?" I asked.

"Fine," she replied, as if she had suffered nothing more than a bad cold. She sat forward quickly. "What do you think of the school? Who did you make friends with? Did you see Trent Ralston? Don't you think he's good-looking? Who's your favorite teacher? I like Madeo. He is so dramatic in English class, right? Oh, and don't you just hate Mrs. Couter, the principal? Everyone calls her Mrs. Cooties, right?

"Well?" she concluded, finally taking a breath.

"I don't know what to answer first," I said, laughing.

She scrunched her nose and pulled in her lips. "Are they talking about me? I bet Wendi is, and Penny, right?"

"No, not really," I said. She looked skeptical. Then she looked down at the bed and turned her hands palms up. Her wrists were still bandaged. "It's more my mother's fault anyway," she said.

"Your mother's fault? Why?"

"She had to go and tell Claudia Spencer, the base big mouth. She just had to confide in someone; she just had to. It was festering inside her like a big boil in her heart.

That's what she told me. Would your mother do that? Well, would she?"

I shook my head.

"I don't know," I said.

"Yes, you do." She flopped back against her pillow. "It doesn't matter anymore. I'm not going back to that school. They are talking about sending me someplace else."

"Where?"

"A private place for disturbed teenagers like me," she replied. "I don't care. I'll miss Trent, though, even though he doesn't even know I exist."

"Maybe they won't send you away. Maybe you'll get better and you will return to our school," I said.

She looked like a deflated balloon that needed hope blown into her. She pressed her lips together and then slid down farther in her bed and looked up at the ceiling.

"I bet you want me to tell you about it, don't you?"

"About what?"

"About how I got pregnant, silly."

I shook my head. "No, you don't have to do that. I don't really want to know."

"Yes, you do. That's all anyone wants to know. How could I have let this happen?"

She stared at me a moment and then sat up and nodded at the wall on her left.

"My sister, especially, asks that, my perfect sister who was prom queen and who has never done anything wrong her whole life. She's the perfect student with the perfect boyfriend.

"And I know my father hates me, hates me and wishes I was never born."

"I'm sure that's not true, Autumn," I said.

"How can you be so sure? You just met us," she fired back at me.

Her hopping from one mood to another and then back again was a little frightening, but I didn't flinch.

"A father can't hate his own child, his own daughter," I said. I meant it. I couldn't imagine my father ever wishing I wasn't born.

"A naval officer father can," she insisted. "He would throw me overboard if he could."

I started to smile, but she turned away.

"It wasn't my fault. It wasn't! I couldn't help it. I didn't even know I had done anything bad," she said, still looking at the wall.

The air between us seemed to grow so still. It felt flammable, as if I could snap my fingers and start a fire.

"How could you not know that?" I asked despite my fear of treading on that ugly ground.

"They gave me Roofies," she wailed.

"Excuse me? Roofies? What's that?"

She pulled herself up a bit and swallowed. "It's something called Rohypnol, a drug that is illegal. You can't taste it in drinks, and part of the effect of it is it causes amnesia. I didn't even know anything had happened to me. I couldn't remember!"

"Who did this to you?"

"Some boys at school. Their names are being kept secret because they're not considered adults," she said bitterly. "They were having a party!" she cried. "And no one ever invites me to a party, so I went with another girl, Selma Dorman. It happened to her, too, only she was lucky. She didn't get pregnant. We were the only two girls there," she revealed. "And there were five boys. We should have known something wasn't right as soon as we got there, but they kept telling us more girls were coming soon."

"Where did this happen?"

"One of the boys had his house free. His parents had gone to New York City for the weekend. It was a big house with a gigantic television set and sophisticated sound equipment. It had a room just for parties with a bar as long as a destroyer. All I remember is I drank what I thought was just a harmless soda, and about four in the morning I woke up naked in one of the bedrooms. They had hidden my clothes for a joke, too.

"My father was on a special assignment at the time, or he would have gone over there afterward and killed them all," she said. "They finally gave me my clothes and drove me home. My mother was furious at me for coming home so late, so I didn't tell her what had happened to me. I didn't know the details, although I felt so violated. I had no idea what would happen inside me. I was even too frightened to tell her anything when I missed my period, but finally I thought I had better, so she took me right to the doctor, and he told her I was pregnant.

"She got hysterical. My father was so angry. They called the police and tried to keep it as secret as they could, but, like I said, my mother was so upset, she said she had to confide in someone, only she picked the wrong someone, and soon everyone knew about me, especially Penny Martin."

"But if you were drugged, how can they blame you and make it sound like you wanted it to happen?" I asked.

"They just do. They blame me for being so stupid and trusting. Penny and Wendi tell people I must have enjoyed it. I wish it would happen to them," she said, her eyes flaring. "Then we'll see how smart they are. We'll see how much they enjoy it."

She looked down at her wrists. Tears began to trickle down her cheeks.

"Autumn," I said softly. "You'll be all right."

"No, I won't!" she cried. "Even though my father knows how it happened, he blames me, too," she revealed. "My sister does. Everyone does!" she cried.

"That's not fair."

"Tell me about it," she said, taking deep breaths. "They make you feel so dirty. A hundred baths won't make you feel any cleaner. No one wants to be friends with me. My own family hates me. I know my father hopes he's transferred soon. He wants to go somewhere where no one will know about me. I'm an embarrassment for him, especially now after what I have done. I'm like an ugly stain on his uniform."

"No, you're not," I said, but not with any conviction. Many of the naval officers and personnel I had met in my life gave me the feeling they had to have every aspect of their lives polished and shiny. Any blemish on their reputations diminished them dramatically. How many times had I heard the lecture about how we represented the country?

All I knew was my daddy could never hate me or be ashamed of me. I was luckier than Autumn. We weren't just another naval family; we were a family.

"Thanks for saying that," Autumn told me, "but you're new here, and soon enough you won't want to come around. It's all right. I don't care anymore. You want to know something? I'm looking forward to going to a special school. I'm looking forward to going anyplace else."

"I hope you don't. As soon as you can, come visit me," I said. "I'll be your friend," I promised.

She looked at me skeptically but with some joy in her eyes.

"Just be careful," she said. "Don't trust anyone. You're better off." She closed her eyes. "I'm so tired," she said. "It's because of some medicine they are giving me."

"Okay. I'll come back to see you soon," I said.

She didn't reply. She slid down in her bed and kept her eyes closed. I looked at her for a moment. Most of what she said and felt unfortunately was true. In the world we lived in, if something bad happened to you, it had to be your fault. You didn't do something you should have done to prepare or to prevent it. You should have anticipated, expected, known, followed procedure. There was no such thing as a pure victim. We were all guilty always.

" 'Bye," I said softly. "I hope you feel better soon."

She barely acknowledged me with a slight nod, and I left her room.

As I started out of the house, I saw Mrs. Sullivan sitting in the living room, staring at the doorway.

"Oh, I'm sorry, Mrs. Sullivan," I said. "If you were sitting here when I came in, I didn't see you."

She looked up as if she had just that moment realized I had come to visit.

"I wish I really was that invisible," she said.

"Autumn will be all right," I told her. I don't know from what well of information and confidence I drew that, but it raised her eyebrows.

"You think so?"

"Yes, ma'am, I do," I said.

"You young people today . . . nothing important

seems to matter to you. All that's important is a good time."

"No, ma'am. That's not true for everyone."

"You all behave as if there are no consequences to your actions." She nodded. "We all learn pretty fast that we pay the piper," she said. "Just remember that."

"Yes, ma'am."

"Thanks for coming," she said, and sat back, taking on that far-off look in her eyes again.

" 'Bye," I said, and left the house.

I hurried home to tell Mommy everything. When Daddy came home, I told him about my visit, too. We talked about it at dinner, and I could see they were both afraid I would fall victim to such events.

"Autumn's mother isn't all wrong, honey," Mommy said. "You have to be a little paranoid in today's world, especially today's youthful world. Every new generation seems to inherit some additional dangers. Sometimes I wish we lived back in the eighteen hundreds."

"No you don't," Daddy said. "You'd be waiting half a year for me to return from a sea duty."

They laughed at that, but I had often mused about living at a different time. Movies and books could make it seem so much more romantic. Maybe people did spend more time with each other, but swirling about them freely and unchecked were devastating diseases, more opportunities for accidents, and terrible poverty. We pay a price for progress, Mommy told me, and for a moment she looked worried about what my share of that price might be.

Nightmares had a field day in my sleeping brain for a week after my visit to Autumn. I never heard anything from her, not a phone call, and then, one morning at breakfast, Mommy told me Autumn's parents had indeed decided to send her to a special school. In fact, she was already gone.

At school, her name fell through the floor of conversations to the basement reserved for the long forgotten. Wendi and Penny looked very satisfied with themselves. Penny, especially, made a point to tell me I should have listened to them.

"You have to know who you should be loyal to and who you shouldn't if you want to get anywhere in this world," she said. "We're deciding whether or not to give you another chance," she added, speaking down to me as if she sat on a high throne.

Many of the other daughters and even sons of naval personnel did seem to be frightened of them, always agreeing with anything they said and never challenging a word. At school they were like queen bees making little demands of the drones who swirled about them everywhere they went, hoping for a smile, a compliment, an invitation to a party. They threw me their condescending smiles, expecting me to join the pack, but I didn't. I wasn't afraid of being alone or having friends who weren't from naval families. However, they looked disgustingly confident that I would come around and soon practically beg for their friendship.

I didn't want to say anything negative about our new home and my life here, so I didn't tell Mommy about any of this. Daddy was so happy at work, and Mommy was making some new friends she truly enjoyed. In fact, I thought she was happier here than she had been anywhere. One night only a little more than a month after we had moved to the Norfolk base, she revealed why.

Daddy was on a night instruction, so Mommy and I had dinner ourselves, and then, after we had cleaned up the kitchen and I had done my homework, she surprised me by coming to my room. I heard the knock on my door and saw her standing there looking as if she could just burst with excitement. Without hearing a word from her, I smiled.

"What?" I asked.

"I want to talk to you," she said, and came in to sit on my bed. I was brushing out my hair. "Just do what you're doing," she said. "I like to watch you anyway, honey. You're getting to be a beautiful young woman."

"Oh, Mommy," I said, blushing. "I am not."

"Yes, you are, Grace, and why shouldn't you?" she teased. "Look how handsome your father is and how beautiful your mother is."

"That's true," I said, "but it doesn't always follow the children will be."

"Take my word for it, Grace. You're an attractive young lady and will only grow more so. Anyway, I'm not here to tease you about your looks. I'll leave that up to your father. You like it better when he teases you anyway," she said without any envy. Mommy truly enjoyed watching Daddy and me. I could see it in her eyes. "Soon I hope to have more on my mind," she added.

I stopped brushing and turned to her. "What do you mean?"

"Well, honey, your father and I have had a long discussion, and we've concluded that we should try again to have another child. While we have been here, I have seen an obstetrician, and I have taken tests. In fact, so has your father," she revealed.

"What sort of tests?"

"Tests to determine if we are capable of having

another child. We've tried at times in the past and failed, but we've never been as determined about it as we are now," she confessed.

I could see the resolve in her eyes. It took my breath away. Was it always just a matter of how much they really wanted a child?

"Anyway," she continued, "the tests have confirmed that we should have no problem. I know it might seem odd to you that we want another child with you already nearly fifteen, but I'm still of child-bearing age and knocking on the door of not being, so if we are ever going to do it, we have to do it now. Understand?"

I nodded, but it was not only strange to me to hear her speak so candidly about it. The prospect of her actually being pregnant and my having a baby brother or sister now was both fascinating and frightening. Surely such an event would change our lives radically. What if the new baby was another girl? Would she become Daddy's special Sailor Girl? Or what if the baby was the boy I knew he'd always wanted? Would both of them devote all their affections to him, and would I become more like a guest in my own home? I felt guilty even having these fears, but they were there, running under my thoughts, a stream full of selfish fish.

"We both felt that now that your father is truly settled into a position that has some stability, it would be a good time to try again. I haven't felt this relaxed and confident about our lives for some time. Besides your father earning more, this house is actually the first in which we could have a real nursery."

I nodded, not knowing what to say.

"Anyway," she said, smiling, "I wanted you to know

our plans so it doesn't come as a shocking surprise to you. I am so confident I'll get pregnant this time, Grace," she said with bright, happy eyes.

I realized that despite my introduction to sexual education in health classes and what I heard and knew from talking with other girls, I really didn't understand how someone just makes up her mind to get pregnant. Of course, I understood how birth control worked, but from the way Mommy talked about it, it seemed as though the man simply took better aim at those floating eggs, or all the times before they were both not fully committed to it happening, and that was why they had failed.

"I don't like the fact that there are going to be so many years between you and your little brother or sister, but that is just the way it has turned out for us. You will be more of a mother's helper. That's a good way to look at it, isn't it, Grace?"

"Yes, Mommy."

"It doesn't upset you or anything like that, does it, Grace?" she asked, her head tilted with some suspicion.

"No, Mommy. Why should it?"

"Good," she said, patting my hand. "I told your father I would talk to you about it. He's so old-fashioned when it comes to these sorts of discussions, and he refuses to admit to himself that you are practically a young adult and know more about it all than he wants to imagine.

"Daddies want to keep their daughters little girls more than they want to keep their sons little boys. It's just the opposite for mothers," she said.

How do you get to know all that? I wondered. It wasn't something taught in any classroom.

"We'll let him live in his illusion awhile longer, but

the first time you get serious about a young man, he's going to go into a nosedive. You haven't met anyone yet, have you?" she asked.

"No, Mommy," I said, laughing.

"What's so funny or incredible about it, Grace? Look at you," she said, forcing me to turn to gaze into my vanity mirror. "You're very attractive, and you already have a perky little figure. Don't tell me you don't notice boys looking your way," she said.

Of course I had, but I had avoided looking back at any of them. At my school in San Diego, I had developed a slight relationship, not worth describing when Autumn had asked. The most we had done was hold hands and kiss. The boy was actually shyer than I was, but I was comfortable with that and didn't mind.

Now, after what had happened here, I had a suspicion that Wendi and Penny were spreading stories about me. Lately I was growing more and more worried about some of the looks I was getting, the stares, the tiny giggles that followed. Not being privy to the so-called inner circle at school, I wasn't sure what sort of things were being said, but I had the feeling they weren't complimentary.

"Okay," she said, rising. "I just wanted you to be aware of what was going on. I'll let you know when the wonderful event happens."

I didn't realize I was holding my breath until after she had left and I let it out, freeing my chest from the band of tension around it. So often in our lives we were involved in new things, major changes, but the prospect of another child in our home was the biggest and most dramatic.

Daddy didn't come home until after I had gone to

my room to prepare for bed. He knocked on my door.

"Hey, Sailor Girl," he said when I told him to come in. I was already in my nightgown and had just crawled under my blanket. Even though he did it less and less these days, Daddy often stopped by to say good night to me. I knew most girls my age would think it immature, babyish, for me to like that, but I did.

"Hi," I said, and he approached the bed. He was still in his flight uniform, and I thought he looked as handsome and exciting as any movie star.

"So," he said, "Mommy tells me you guys had a good chat today."

"Yes," I said.

"We want you aboard on this, you know. It's a full family decision. I know that I got so used to being the only child in the house that the very thought of sharing even space at the kitchen table bothered me."

"I don't feel that way, Daddy."

"I didn't think you would." He gave me a side glance and then perused my shelf of books. "I hope your brother or sister will be as good a reader as you are, Grace. There is so much competition for everyone's attention these days, especially younger people, but reading is special. It's really a personal experience, isn't it?"

"Yes, Daddy."

"You can live a whole life through the books you read, not that it should be the only thing, of course."

"No, Daddy."

He seemed so much more nervous than he had ever been around me. He was working hard at making conversation.

"You know, our decision to have another child now doesn't guarantee it will happen," he warned.

"I know, but Mommy said you've gone through tests."

"She told you that, too, huh?"

"Yes, Daddy."

"Um," he said. "You understand all that, of course."

"Yes, Daddy," I said, smiling.

"I guess I'm going to have to face facts about you whether I like to or not, aren't I? One of these days you're going to come around with someone and tell me you're in love and planning a life of your own."

"That's a long way off, Daddy. I want to go to college."

"Right. You should. Women should be more independent these days. And you should be careful about in whom you think you want to place your confidence. Most of the men I know don't grow up until they're almost twice the age I was when I was on my own," he said sternly. "You ought to see who they are sending around to be in control of a multimillion-dollar piece of equipment these days. However, they grow up fast under my command," he assured me.

"I bet they do, Daddy."

"Right," he said, nodding.

I could just imagine what the man I brought around to meet my father would be feeling. He would probably be trembling at the door. The image brought a smile to my face.

"What?" he asked.

"Nothing," I said.

"C'mon," he urged.

"I was just thinking about the day I bring someone around to meet you."

"Is that so? Your mother says the same sort of thing. I'm no ogre, but I can tell you this: Whoever thinks he can take my Sailor Girl on a voyage of his own had better be fully equipped and obey every rule and regulation."

"Aye, aye, Daddy," I said, and he laughed.

Other girls my age often made me believe they were annoyed by their fathers' interest in their comings and goings. They wanted no advice, no supervision, and they resented questions and concern. All I could think of was how protected and secure my father made me feel. He was my personal radar screen, picking up and shooting down anything that was in any way a threat to my health and happiness. Why would I ever resent that? If anything, I would miss it if my husband wasn't as strong and as competent as he was.

I also wanted a man whom I could never stop loving and a man who could never stop loving me or he would die, absolutely die on the spot. Was that too romantic, too idealistic? Mommy always made me feel that was the love she had.

"Anyway," Daddy continued, "I wanted to reassure you that nothing will ever diminish my love for you, Grace. You'll always be my Sailor Girl," Daddy said.

"I know that, Daddy."

"Good." He looked at the door. "Well, if your mother asks, tell her we had a very mature conversation, will you? She's been driving me mad about it," he whispered.

I laughed. "Okay, Daddy."

" 'Night, baby," he said, and leaned over to kiss me. He shook his head. "You sure you're almost fifteen already? You were just four."

"I'm sure, Daddy, otherwise I would be very advanced for my age."

He laughed, saluted with his two fingers, and left.

I pulled my blanket up to my chin and closed my eyes. How happy I felt, how warm and secure.

And then I thought of poor Autumn Sullivan, sleeping in some strange place, never hearing her father or her mother say good night.

She was truly like someone lost at sea.

3

A Convenient Sprain

In the days and weeks to follow, I occasionally saw Autumn's father, but whenever I did he barely acknowledged me with a nod. Whatever I knew about Autumn now I found out through Mommy, who tried to develop a friendship with her mother. It wasn't easy because her mother had become quite withdrawn after Autumn's attempted suicide and avoided company and being with the other women at any social occasion. Caitlin wouldn't even look my way if we were close to each other, especially at school. I think she was afraid I would ask about her sister and she would have to say something that was embarrassing. It did seem to me as though Autumn's father and Caitlin especially would rather pretend she didn't exist. The Sullivans were all invited to a barbecue Daddy and Mommy had in honor of my fifteenth birthday, but none of them appeared.

The school year was coming to a rapid ending, and

with the work I had to make up and my new assignments, I was too busy to involve myself in much more. However, one afternoon as I was leaving history class, Trent Ralston came up beside me and started a conversation. I couldn't help looking at him from time to time and even listening to him talk to other students. Autumn's infatuation with him had drawn my interest. The truth was, she was right about him. He was one of the handsomest boys in school, if not the handsomest, and what interested me about him just from watching him at a distance was his apparent oblivious attitude about himself. It was as if he had never looked into a mirror or received a compliment. I wasn't sure if it was aloof arrogance or simple innocence.

"How do you remember all those kings and queens and what happened under each one's reign like that?" he asked as if we had known each other for ages. "Mr. Caswell never catches you with your notebook down," he added, his voice full of admiration. He widened his eyes and twisted his torso. "While I shiver in the back, afraid he'll remember I'm in his class, too."

I laughed. Out of the corner of my eyes, I could see Wendi and Penny looking our way. *They never miss a beat,* I thought, and turned to Trent almost as much to spite them as to please myself.

"I have a secret," I told him.

He raised one eyebrow. His good looks didn't sit only in his near-perfect facial features. He had a unique shade of blue-gray eyes. I had seen him in his physical education class and knew he had one of those sleek, muscular male bodies that models have in fashion magazines.

"I'll pay you," he said.

"How do you know what it will cost?"

"I don't care. I'll even give you one of my vintage Mickey Mantle bubble gum cards."

I laughed again. "Right, it will complete my own collection."

"So, what's your secret?"

"I study," I said. He started to grimace. "No, I mean it. I really study. I concentrate and don't let anything distract me. I don't listen to the radio, a CD, let a television blare on in the background, interrupt with phone calls. I just set down a period of time and make it sacrosanct."

"You make it what?" he asked, grimacing as if he had bitten into a rotten peach.

"It means untouchable, inviolate, holy."

He shook his head. "No wonder you can transfer from one school to another nine times a year and still get A's," he said.

"I don't transfer nine times a year."

"Yeah, well, you and some of the others from naval families move around quite a bit, don't you?"

"Our fathers get transferred often. It can't be helped, but after a while you get used to it."

"I guess some can take it and some can't. I heard about Autumn Sullivan," he said, lowering his voice. "Some people talk a little too loud on purpose, if you know what I mean," he added, gazing at Wendi and Penny.

I nodded. "I know exactly what you mean." They turned away from my glaring eyes.

"Maybe we could get together and study for the history final," he said. "I promise I won't turn on any music or television," he added when I didn't respond.

I had never thought much of studying with any of my classmates. It always turned into a gab session.

There were just too many opportunities to interrupt or take breaks that went on and on. In the end it was always what I did on my own that made a difference, but I was tempted to break my own rules for Trent.

A part of me was hesitant, however, for another reason. I remembered how much Autumn liked Trent, and I couldn't help feeling like someone who was getting too involved with her friend's boyfriend, even though he was far, far from that. She had barely spoken to him. It was ridiculous to feel that way. I knew it and put it aside.

"All right," I said.

"How about tonight?" he fired back at me before I could even think of taking another step. "We shouldn't waste any time!" he added with a look of exaggerated panic. "At least, I shouldn't."

I stopped myself from laughing again. I was beginning to feel like one of those girls who giggled after practically every word said to them, especially when they are standing in the glow of some good-looking boy.

"Okay," I said. "Come to my house at seven."

"Your house?"

"I'll leave your name at the gate. Here's my address." I tore a sheet of paper from my notebook. He spoke as I scribbled and made a little map of the street.

"I was thinking I could maybe come get you and take you to my house. It's going to be very quiet there. My parents are going to a charity event, and my sister is sleeping over at a friend's house."

I handed him the paper. "I don't go anywhere on a school night," I said with a finality that made his shoulders sag.

"Oh. Your father's like a general or something, isn't he?"

"No," I said, laughing with good justification this time. "The navy doesn't have generals. Admirals. My father is a lieutenant commander, an instructor in Heliops."

"Huh?"

"Helicopters."

"Oh."

"Don't look so worried. The last time he bit someone, there was no sign of rabies," I added.

"I just thought we would be more comfortable at my place."

"I'm very comfortable at home. I have my own room. No one will bother us. I promise," I said. "All we're going to do is study anyway, so why worry?"

"Right," he said. He glanced at the group of students hovering around Wendi and Penny and then smiled at me and said he would be there at seven.

Before the end of the day I saw him again. He gave me a big smile and waved on his way to baseball practice. I knew he was one of the school's star pitchers and there was one more big game to be played. I had yet to attend one and thought that I just might go to this game, scheduled for Friday at the home field.

Despite my determination not to let our study session be anything else but that, I couldn't help feeling excited about it. I tried to be as casual and nonchalant as I could when I informed Mommy that Trent was coming to study with me. Daddy was still at work, and then he called to say he wouldn't be home for dinner. He had a meeting with his command to plan an elaborate exercise. At dinner Mommy asked me about Trent, and I told her he was the boy Autumn had a big crush on. I explained how popular he was, a star on the baseball team, and very good-looking. I added that I had told him how seriously I took my studying for tests, practically growling about it.

She smiled to herself as if she knew something about me that I didn't know.

I went on and on about how helping someone study reinforces everything for yourself. She listened and nodded but kept that soft smile on her lips.

"What?" I finally cried. "I know you've been laughing at me, Mommy."

"I'm not laughing at you, Grace. I think you're cute justifying a study session with this boy. You let slip how good-looking and popular he is, not to mention what a hero he is on the baseball team. You like him, don't you?"

"I don't know him enough to like him, Mommy."

"Okay," she said, and then dropped the smile from her lips and looked hard at me. "Don't let what happened to Autumn Sullivan dominate your relationships with boys, honey. Keep it all in mind, be cautious, but don't be afraid of yourself. Do you know what I mean? I want you to have fun, too. There's a balance you have to find. If you make every boy you meet feel like he's a rapist, you won't ever have any good times, and before you know it, you'll have left all the opportunities behind and never have a real youth. With all the moving we've done, I'm always afraid you will miss out on the fun."

"How do you find the balance?" I asked.

"You'll find it. You've got a good head on your shoulders. Just listen to all the little voices and warnings and take your time before you place your trust in anyone. That's the best advice I can give."

"Didn't Autumn's mother give her any advice, Mommy?"

She shrugged. "Maybe not, honey. Some people are afraid of bringing any of this up. They have this faith that somehow, miraculously, everything will turn out all right. I don't think Autumn had too good a self-image, either, do you? She was too desperate for acceptance. At least, that's what I've concluded after listening to her mother talk about her."

"Yes," I said. I started to help her clean up.

"Go on. Prepare for your study session," she said. "There's not much to do here, and I know how you are about your room whenever anyone, not to mention a handsome young man, looks at it."

She winked and nudged me with her shoulder.

I smiled at her and then went to my room. Nervously, I set it up, placing two chairs at the desk, then thinking they were too close, then too far away. I adjusted the blinds, debated about how much light we needed, fixed my bed until it looked as snappy as a military bunk, cleaned the vanity mirror, dusted, set out my books and my notebook, started to plan a strategy for studying our history notes, checked myself in the mirror, brushed my hair, debated about putting on lipstick, thought about putting on some cologne, and then finally sat and stared at the clock. It was five minutes to seven. The guard at the gate would be calling any moment to let us know we had a visitor.

Wendi and Penny were sure to find out about this, I thought. I wondered if it would raise my status in their eyes or simply frustrate them more. They had done their best to isolate me from the other students who came from naval families, as well as many of the students in our class, portraying me as snobby. That was ironic. Who in the school was more conceited than those two? I knew that my shyness was often misinterpreted that way, however, so I realized they were having success. This would be their first big failure, and it hadn't come too soon with the school year's end just around the corner.

I began to get antsy at five after seven. I told myself not to get upset, civilians didn't have the same commitment to time and schedules as we did. When someone in the Navy was told to report at thirteen hours, he or she was there at the striking of the hour. Lateness was almost as sinful as disloyalty.

However, by seven-fifteen I was seriously concerned, even a bit angry. I opened my notebook and began to review the day's new material, trying not to look at the time or think about it. At twenty-five after seven, Mommy knocked on my door.

"Didn't you say he was coming at seven?" she asked.

"Yes. He was supposed to be here by then."

"Oh. Well, I told Lorraine Sanders I would stop by at seven-thirty to help her choose some new wallpaper for their kitchen."

"Don't wait around, Mommy. He's rude to be this late and not call me."

"Just don't get yourself upset over it, Grace."

"I'm not," I lied. "I'm doing the studying I have to do anyway."

She nodded. "I'll call you in an hour. You know where I am if you need me," she added.

I heard her leave the house, and then I sat back and folded my arms under my breasts. When I gazed at myself in the mirror, I thought I looked as if I was fuming enough to start a stream of smoke out of my ears. Wendi and Penny must have gotten to him, I thought. They must have found out, and they must have pulled him aside and told him ridiculous stories about me. My rage blurred my eyes when I went back to my notes, which only made me angrier.

Finally, at seven thirty-five, the phone rang. I made up my mind I would tell him the thirty-five minutes we lost couldn't be made up. We were stopping at nine no matter what. I had other things to do. People had to realize the consequences of their inconsideration.

To my surprise it wasn't the guard at the gate. It was Trent.

"I'm sorry," he said. "I sprained my ankle at baseball practice, and they took me to the hospital emergency room. I just got home, and I'm sitting here with ice on my ankle."

"Oh."

"I would have called you earlier, but with all the excitement and waiting for the X ray . . ."

"That's all right," I said. "Is it painful?"

"Not as much now, but I'm out of the game. I might even have to stay home tomorrow. I don't know. They gave me a crutch so I would stay off the foot, but maybe if I just rest it I won't need it.

"Anyway," he said before I could respond, "I'm really in deep trouble now studywise and need your help more than ever. Would it be all right if I send a cab to pick you up and pay for one to take you home?"

"What?" He was speaking so fast I couldn't absorb the idea.

"The taxi could be there in twenty minutes. I already found out. Actually, I've already sent him to your address, hoping you'll say yes. We could still get in a couple of hours. My notes are a mess."

"I . . ." I looked in my mirror and saw myself shaking my head. "A taxi? That's expensive, isn't it?"

"It's worth it. My parents will be proud that I spent money on a good thing for a change."

There was a beep on the phone.

"Hold on, someone's calling," I said, and pressed the button marked Flash.

"I have a taxi arriving for Grace Houston," the guard at the gate declared.

"What?" He really had done it.

"Sending him through," the guard declared.

"Wait," I started to say, but the line went dead. I flicked the button. "The cab is already here!"

"Great. See you soon. He knows my address," Trent said, and hung up.

When I looked at myself in the mirror again, I saw how my jaw had dropped.

Quickly I rose, went out to the kitchen to find the Sanders's number on our Rolodex. I heard the taxi driver beep his horn. As soon as I found the Sanders's number, I punched it out, but it rang and rang and rang, and no one picked up. Whoever was on the phone was not going to permit an interruption. The driver sounded his horn again.

I went to the front door and waved to him. "Just a minute, please," I called. He nodded.

I returned to my room and stood there for a moment, completely indecisive. Then I gathered up my books and notebook and went back out, stopping in the kitchen to call the Sanders's home again. It still rang and rang, so I gave up.

As quickly as I could, I wrote a note to Mommy, explaining what had happened, and left it beside the phone. Then I hurried out to the cab. The driver was standing and smoking. He flipped his cigarette at the street and opened the door for me. I got in, and he backed out of our driveway. My heart was thumping. *This is both exciting and crazy,* I thought, never recalling doing anything as impulsive.

Minutes later we were on the highway, and I was sitting rigid in the back, embracing my books as if they were a parachute and any time I wanted I could pull the cord and bail out. I replayed Mommy's advice to me as if it was a prayer. *I want you to have fun, too. There's a balance you have to find. If you make every boy you meet feel like he's a rapist, you won't ever have any good times, and before you know it, you'll have left all the opportunities behind and never have a real youth. With all the moving we've done, I'm always afraid you will miss out on the fun.*

Those words calmed me down, and I sat back until we pulled into the driveway of what was obviously a very expensive home in one of the upscale communities.

With his crutch under his right arm, Trent came to the front door. I saw he wasn't wearing a shoe on his right foot, and it was bandaged about the ankle. He grimaced.

"Sorry about all this," he said. "Thanks for coming."

"How did it happen?"

"Bad slide into third base. I tried to make a double into a triple and paid for my greed," he explained with a laugh. "Come on in."

His house was a beautiful ranch-style home with a large front lawn. The stonework on the outside looked very expensive, and when I entered I saw a chandelier, plush area rugs, and elegant furnishings. No home we had lived in was even half its size, I thought. I remarked about how beautiful his house was, and he flipped on some lights by a patio door to show me the patio and the swimming pool.

"C'mon," he said, turning the lights off. "I know how sacrosanct your study time is. See? I'm not only learning my history with you, I'm improving my vocabulary."

We both laughed.

He limped his way down the corridor and turned into his room, which was easily twice as big as mine. I was impressed with how neatly it was kept. He had school banners up on his walls, trophies on the shelves, and pictures of sports heroes. There was an expensive-looking computer station as well as a separate desk. He had a king-size bed with thick posts and a massive headboard, all in a dark cherry wood.

"I'm connected to the Internet in case there's something you want to look up," he said, nodding at the swirling heavenly bodies on the monitor screen. "I downloaded that screen saver from the Hubble telescope site."

I didn't have a computer. Now that we were somewhat settled in Norfolk, Daddy had mentioned he was going to buy one for me, but I didn't say anything and pretended to know exactly what Trent was talking about.

"You want anything to drink, juice, soda, anything?"

"No, thank you," I said. "I'm fine."

I put my books on the desk, and he hopped over to a chair and brought it closer.

"Then let's go at it," he said, flipping the cover of a notebook open. He looked up expectantly. I smiled.

Not every boy is a rapist.

This was nothing more than what it was intended to be, what he said it was. I was glad of that but also felt a strange contradiction. What if that was really all he wanted from me, history help? Maybe I wasn't as attractive as I hoped I was or as much as Mommy assured me I was. I didn't want to be invited under false pretenses, but my feminine ego was complaining.

Look, Grace Houston, I told myself, *make up your mind. Do you want to exchange historical facts or kisses?*

"Here is how I've organized it all," I began, and he leaned over to glance at my pages.

We studied hard for a good hour. Every once in a while I saw his eyes brighten with an understanding. He copied information quickly, rearranging his own notes.

"You've got an order to everything that makes this so much easier," he complimented. "I guess I never really learned how to take notes properly."

"I redo it all when I get home. It helps reinforce it in my mind, too."

"Yeah, I can see why. Does all this orderliness and structure come from military life? My father's always threatening to send me and even my sister to military school."

"Maybe it does," I said, wondering about it myself. "It's not something I'm aware of constantly, but I suppose when you are around it all day and all night . . ."

"Exactly." He glanced at the clock. "We haven't studied as long as you thought we would, but is sacrosanct over yet?"

I laughed. "I think we did pretty well."

"Good. Let me show you my card collection," he said excitedly, and got up and went to his closet. He took out an armful of albums and plopped them down on the desk beside me.

"This first album has my oldest cards. Most of them are reproductions, of course, but they are still rare or hard to get," he said. "These first cards were distributed in cigarette packs."

"Really?"

"Yeah. A lot of people don't know that."

"I didn't."

He nodded and smiled. "Here. This is Ty Cobb stealing third base for Detroit. This is Tris Speaker batting for Boston, and here's Cy Young. You've heard of the Cy Young award, of course."

"Of course," I said. I had heard of it, but I wasn't ready to tell him what it was.

"Baseball cards were first issued during the 1880s when tobacco companies wanted to promote sales. The cards depicted more than a thousand ballplayers from teams in thirteen different leagues and seventy-five cities!"

His enthusiasm brought a wide smile to my face.

"Look at this," he said, flipping to the rear of the first album. "Members of the All American Girls Professional Baseball League from 1943 to 1954. That's Alice 'Lefty' Hohlmayer. She had a record of forty-three scoreless innings in 1948. She once got a base hit off Satchel Paige in an All-Star game. And this is Lavonne 'Pepper' Paire, who led the league in the least strike-outs at bat. Six in 392 times at bat!"

He glanced at me and at the album and then at me again. "You think I'm nuts, huh?"

"No, Trent. I'm amazed and really impressed. You could make a wonderful talk in our history class about baseball history and use these as displays."

"Really?"

"Absolutely. I bet you would get extra credit."

"I could use some extra credit," he said, nodding thoughtfully.

"Ask Mr. Caswell. I bet it's not too late."

"Maybe I will," he said, nodding. "Thanks." He

smiled. "Most of the girls I show this stuff to are looking for ways to make a quick exit before I get to the second page, much less the second album."

"It's a wonderful collection, fascinating," I said sincerely.

He opened some of the other albums to show me the cards he cherished the most and explained why or how he had managed to acquire each.

"My father thinks it's okay that I do this, but he has no idea what it's all worth now. If he did, he would have it up for sale. He's a broker."

"Oh. I wouldn't sell it ever. It's something you'd want your own son to have someday, I'm sure," I said.

"Exactly!" he replied, his eyes full of excitement.

He sat back and stared at me a moment.

"What?" I said, smiling.

"Don't get mad at me," he said.

"Why would I?"

"I just thought you were like one of my cards, a valuable find," he said.

"Why would I get mad at that?"

He smirked. "Not too many girls would appreciate being compared to baseball cards, Grace."

"Oh." I laughed and then thought aloud, "It's not what you're being compared to so much as what the person doing the comparison thinks of it, how he values it."

"Smart and beautiful, too. I'm going to kick myself in the head later for taking so long to say hello to you," he said, and leaned forward to kiss me on the lips, a short but soft kiss I saw coming but still greeted with surprise.

He kept his face close to mine, searching my eyes to see how I had reacted, and then he kissed me again. We were in an awkward position, both on chairs, leaning toward each other, but we held on to each other until he tried to get me to my feet and put too much weight on his bad ankle. He groaned in pain, stumbled, and barely caught himself. I reached out and held on to his left arm, helping him get his balance. His face was twisted in agony.

"Sorry," he moaned. "Wow, that was like a shot of electricity, right to my heart, and unfortunately it didn't come from our kiss," he said.

"Get off your feet, Trent."

I helped him back to his bed. He sat and then lowered himself slowly and stared up at the ceiling.

"Are you all right? Do you want something?"

"I'm okay. It's easing up. I wouldn't take the painkillers. I knew you and I were going to study tonight," he said.

"Oh. Well, maybe you should now."

"Yeah. I guess. Let me call for your taxi first," he said, then struggled into a sitting position and lifted the phone receiver. "Maybe you can get me a glass of water in the meantime."

"Of course," I said, and hurried out to the kitchen. It was so long and wide, with beautiful cabinets and granite counters. I found the cabinet with the glasses and filled one with water.

"The cab will be here in ten minutes," he said when I returned. He was lying back on his pillow. I gave him the glass of water, and he took a pill out of the bottle on the nightstand and downed it quickly.

"Do you want me to put away your albums?"

"No, that's all right. Relax," he said, patting the space beside him. I sat, and he reached up to touch my shoulder. "Looking at you already takes the pain away."

"Sure it does," I said, smiling at him skeptically.

"Kissing you does for sure," he followed. He fixed his eyes on mine, and I smiled and leaned down to kiss him again. It was a longer kiss, his arms around me, holding me until I sprawled out beside him and he kissed me on the cheek, ran his fingers through my hair, and then turned my face to kiss me again. He lowered his chin to my breasts and moved over them, gently caressing them with his cheek. It clamped a surge of warmth over me that brought a small moan from my lips.

Most of the girls my age had done far more with boys and were far more experienced. Of course, I wondered if I had kissed him right, if I should let him touch me as he was touching me, but the excitement and the gentle way he caressed me kept panic and fear deeply buried under my own fascination with every new feeling.

"If I could keep you here beside me all night, my ankle would be all better in the morning," he whispered.

"Sure. I'm a miracle worker. I have the power in my hands and lips."

"To me you do," he said. He kissed me again, this time with his hands moving over my breasts. I started to pull away, but he fell back instead and smiled. "Wow, I'm feeling the pill already," he said. "Do me a favor. Take off the shoe on my left foot. And the sock."

I did so quickly. He sat up and raised his arms.

"My shirt," he said.

I helped him lift it off his body. He undid the buckle of his belt.

"I'll sleep in my underwear tonight," he said. "Tug away."

I had come over to study history, and I was about to help him take off his pants? My moment of hesitation made him laugh.

"It's just like looking at someone in a bathing suit," he said.

I shook my head but did it. Then I folded them and put them on a hanger for him. I did the same with his shirt.

"Thanks," he said, shifting under his blanket.

We heard the taxi driver sounding the horn.

"It's all paid for. You don't have to leave him a tip or anything."

"Are you all right?"

"Yes. I am now," he said, smiling with his eyes closed. "I'm just going to lie here and dream about you."

It brought a smile to my face. I thought for a moment, and then I leaned over and kissed him.

"Did I turn into a frog," he muttered, "or a prince?"

"A little boy," I replied, and he laughed. He kept his eyes closed.

"Put out the light, please," he said.

I gathered up my books, snapped off his lights, looked back at him, and said good night. He barely whispered a reply. I hurried out to the front door, feeling as if I was walking on a bed of marshmallows. Then I slipped out quietly and hurried to the waiting taxi. As we pulled away, I gazed back at the house, wishing I could have done just what he dreamed of me doing: slipping in beside him and lying with him all night.

Mommy and Daddy were sitting in the kitchen having tea when I arrived. They both looked up expectantly, neither looking upset but both looking curious, even a bit amused.

"A boy sent a taxi for you to help him study?" Daddy asked without saying hello.

"You read my note, didn't you, Mommy?"

"Yes, honey."

"Sprained his ankle," Daddy said. "I have heard of many different ways to get a young woman to your house. Men used to say, 'Come up and look at my paintings.'"

They both laughed.

"He really did sprain his ankle! He's a baseball player, and he slid into third trying to turn a double into a triple," I fired back at them.

"Oh," Daddy said. "That's different. So you got in some real studying, then?" he asked, still with a coy, impish smile around his lips.

"Yes, we did."

"No paintings?" Daddy asked, teasing.

The fury left my face and I smiled at him. "No, not paintings, but lots of old baseball cards."

"Baseball cards? Now that is really a new one. I can see bubble gum, but the cards?"

"They are very valuable cards, Daddy. He has a wonderful collection worth a lot of money, not that he would ever sell it. He even has cards of famous women baseball players."

"Is that right? I didn't know there was such a thing."

"And cards that were first put on cigarette packs, not bubble gum," I added.

"Very educational evening," Daddy said, nodding. Out of the corner of my eye, I could see that Mommy was battling to keep from laughing.

"For your information, it was," I said. "Make all the fun of me you want," I added, and shot off to my room. Mommy couldn't stop her laugh from following, but I slammed my door closed behind me and dropped myself to my bed facedown. About a minute later there was a soft knock on my door.

"What?" I cried.

The door opened slightly, and Daddy poked his head in.

"Has the minefield been cleared in here? I don't want to step on anything."

"Very funny." I turned and folded my arms under my breasts, my face in a pout.

Daddy stepped in and closed the door behind him. "Okay, okay, I'm sorry I teased you," he said. "You were just an easy target of opportunity I couldn't resist."

"I was not."

He tilted his head to see if I was serious. I turned away so he couldn't see me starting to smile.

"You have to admit that spraining his ankle and sending a taxi for you was a bit unusual. I bet you thought so yourself," he said, inching closer to the bed. "Come on, Sailor Girl, be honest."

I kept my face turned away, but my lips were crumbling like the walls of Jericho. I looked at him and laughed.

"That's my Sailor Girl."

"I was suspicious, yes, but Mommy told me not to be overly suspicious or I would never have any fun."

"Oh, she did, huh? She left that little detail out of her summary," he said.

"She only meant to help me, to keep me from being too frightened to enjoy life," I said.

"I know. It's good advice. There's nothing pleasant about paranoia. So, I gather it was a good all-around experience. You like this disabled ballplayer?"

"He's not disabled, Daddy. He just sprained his ankle."

"Yeah, that's no fun," he said. "Since we're being honest with each other, I'll confess I'm just being a jealous father. Every father has to realize there will come a day when he will no longer be the center of his daughter's world, when someone else will step in and capture her attention and interest. I'm just a sore loser. That's all."

"No one has captured all my interest," I said.

"Maybe not, but it's a start. It's all right. You don't have to defend yourself for doing what every healthy young woman should do. I just have to grow up."

"Grow up? You?"

"We all have to grow, change, adjust constantly, Grace. It's part of life, maturing. Some resist it more than others and suffer more."

I shook my head. I couldn't imagine my father having to change a bit.

"When you stop learning, stop being open-minded, you die or wilt on the branch. This is an ongoing process, this thing we call life, honey. We're on a journey, and we soon realize that's what's most important: the journey itself. If you reach a goal and stop traveling, what's the point? Understand?"

"I think so," I said.

"You will. I have a great deal of faith in you. So," he said, standing, "how's he going to take you to the end-of-the-year dance or prom if he can't stand?"

I laughed. "He didn't ask me to any dance, Daddy."

"Maybe he's not as smart as I thought. Maybe you need to put your picture on a baseball card and give it to him," he kidded.

"Daddy, stop it."

"If he's got any sense, any grit, he'll be calling and asking. If not, he's failed in his mission. Anyway, I didn't want you going to sleep angry at me."

"I wouldn't," I said. "I just wouldn't sleep."

He laughed. "Okay, Sailor Girl. Sweet dreams, no matter whom they are about."

He leaned down to kiss me on the cheek and then gave me a salute, which I returned.

I kept my smile until after he left. I felt very lucky, lucky to have him, to have a mother like the one I had. Maybe we lived like nomads and we were uprooted too often and suffered in ways other people didn't, but I didn't feel cheated. I would never feel that way as long as I had my parents and we continued to care more about each other than we did about ourselves.

I did dream that night.

I dreamed of Trent sliding into third only not hurting himself.

He stood up and then turned toward home because I was standing there at the plate, waiting for him.

4

Men and Their Toys

When I went to school the next day I felt more confident and self-assured than I had ever felt at this school or any other. I couldn't explain why. Trent and I hadn't done much more than a pair of junior high students might do these days, but somehow I could sense a new maturity in me. I felt older, experienced, more invulnerable, especially to whatever Wendi and Penny could throw my way. It was as if I had gained some ancient wisdom or woken it in my sleeping brain and now realized that the Grinchy twins, as I liked to think of them, weren't worth a minute of worry when it came to how they would affect my life and happiness. It was better and far easier to pretend they were invisible.

I told that to Trent when he and I sat together in the cafeteria while, at the next table down, Wendi and Penny squirmed like two termites into the brains of all their devotees. He laughed and nodded.

"I do the same thing sometimes, pretend people I don't like or people who just annoy me aren't there. I look right through them, block out whatever they say. My friends think I'm daydreaming, but it's easier that way."

We talked so much that day, every opportunity we had. He had come to school on his crutch, of course, and all of his buddies and many other girls hovered about him as though he had been wounded in a gallant battle, showing great courage. The crutch was a medal, an honor. Some actually wanted to touch it as if it had a magical quality.

As quickly and as gracefully as he could, he escaped from them to come to me every chance he had. The result was that more and more of the students who wouldn't give me the time of the day before were now interested in me. I knew a few of the girls had crushes on Trent as heavy as the one Autumn had carried secretly in her heart. I knew they thought that if they found reasons to be with me, they would be with him, and competition for his attention grew more intense. Before long we were struggling for opportunities to be alone, even if it was for a few moments in the hallway or the minutes we had together in the cafeteria before they descended on us like honey bees drawing whatever succor they could from Trent's smile or friendly words.

First thing in the afternoon after lunch was our history exam. Mr. Caswell offered to give Trent a makeup test if he felt his injury had made it impossible for him to study well. I thought that was generous, but Wendi nudged me to say, "If he wasn't a school sports hero, he'd be left to sink or swim." To her surprise and even a little to mine, Trent refused the offer and said he was better prepared than ever. Of course, he looked my way and smiled, which turned every other girl's spotlight eyes to me for a moment of envy so thick and green it made the air around me hot and hard to breathe.

Moments later the class was quiet and the test had begun. There was nothing on it that Trent and I had not covered. One of the essay questions looked as if it had been created out of my very notes, in fact. I saw Trent smile with confidence, glance back at me, and then go at it. Afterward he made a point of telling me how much studying with me had helped him. He said it loudly enough so that anyone who didn't know by now knew we had spent some of the previous evening together at his house.

Whatever new image I had developed simply because he was showing me attention in the halls and cafeteria of our school exploded into celebrity with this revelation. In an instant I was being thought of as Trent Ralston's new steady girlfriend. It was as if I had won the lottery.

When he asked to study English with me for our upcoming exam, I couldn't help but feel a little ball of excitement swirl up from the pit of my stomach to the center of my thumping heart.

"I'll even come to your house and take a chance that your father won't bite. The doctor said I can drive as long as I don't take any painkillers, and I want my mind clear when I'm with you. I mean studying with you," he said.

I felt it was all right for me to invite him without first asking my parents. I knew Daddy had a major training exercise all day and into the early evening hours. When I got home and told Mommy, she asked me why I didn't invite him to dinner as well. The thought had not occurred to me, but I felt as though I had missed an opportunity and perhaps disappointed him.

"You can still do it if you want," she said. "It's not that late in the day."

"Should I?"

"Sure," she said, making it sound like almost nothing when to me it was like running the two-minute mile or something, a major accomplishment. I had never invited a boy I liked to dinner with my parents.

"Just don't make it sound like we're having something special. I'm doing chicken burgers with home fries and string beans. Maybe I'll get something special for dessert," she concluded. "You'd better tell him just in case he doesn't like chicken burgers. Tell him I'll make him a peanut butter sandwich if he won't eat my chicken burgers."

"Mommy!"

"Just kidding. Your father loves my chicken burgers. I add a lot of secret ingredients." She studied me a moment. I saw the amusement in her eyes, amusement at my nervous hesitation. "Let me know if you work up enough courage to call him and if he accepts, so I can put out another plate and prepare a little more," she said.

I berated myself for being so silly and bashful and went right to the phone. The first question from Trent was, "Is your father going to be there, too?"

"Stop worrying about him, Trent. He's just a naval officer. He's not an ogre. And anyway, he will be late tonight. He's on a training exercise."

"Oh. Sure, well, that's very nice of your mother. I'll be there," he said.

Despite myself, when I told her, I couldn't contain the underlying flow of excitement in my voice. If only she knew how important I had felt all day and how happy I was, I thought, but then I wondered how I would tell her about all that without sounding like a lovesick puppy.

"Okay. Since we have a guest for dinner, I'll put out silverware so we don't eat everything with our fingers," she joked.

"Mommy!"

She went off laughing, and I retreated to my room, suddenly feeling as if everything in my life had become more vivid, more vibrant, whether colors, sounds, or even the scent of my colognes and shampoo. For me there was an electricity in the air. It was more charged than it had been for any birthday or any previous special occasion. Was I being foolish? He was just a boy I had become more friendly with, I told myself. But when I looked at my face in the mirror, I saw how futile it was to think I could lie to myself. The truth was there in my eyes, in the flush in my cheeks, whether I wanted it to be there or not.

A few minutes later the phone rang. My heart went on pause. Was it Trent now telling me something had come up and he couldn't come after all? Mommy spoke for a while, but her voice was muffled. Then she came to my room.

"That was your father. He wants us to go over to the airport to see the helicopters take off. It's an impressive sight, he says. I told him you had homework to do and I had to go get some things for dinner because we had a guest coming, but he sounded so disappointed. I told him you and I would stop by on my way to the supermarket. Okay?"

"Of course," I said, practically jumping out of my shoes, first because it wasn't Trent canceling and then because I knew it would be exciting to watch all those helicopters lift off with Daddy in command.

"Well, let's hurry," she said, and we went out to the car and drove over to the airport.

It was a beautiful, clear twilight with the sky turning into that navy blue with clouds smeared across it as if they had been spread with a butter knife. Daddy had left word we were arriving, so we were passed through security. Mommy parked the car, and we walked toward the helicopters. There were about two dozen, all resembling gigantic alien insects. I knew what kind of power they possessed and how deadly they could be.

Daddy was very busy with preparations and could barely look our way and wave.

"Men and their toys," Mommy muttered.

Yes, I thought, and then thought how impressed Trent would have been if I could have brought him along with us.

"I wish they'd hurry," Mommy said. "Don't they know I have things to do?"

I smiled at her and looked at Daddy again. By watching the way the other men reacted to what he said, I could see the respect and authority he commanded. It made me proud, and I knew from the look of admiration and love in Mommy's face that she felt the same way.

Finally he walked toward his waiting men. When he reached them he turned toward us and gave me our special salute, which I, of course, returned.

The engines on the helicopters were activated.

"How he stands that noise is beyond me," Mommy said. My eyes drifted to catch a sea gull. I watched it turn back to the sea, and then we saw the helicopters lifting in a massive roar, like an entire hive of hornets rising at once.

"C'mon," Mommy screamed over the noise. She

tugged me. I looked back as the helicopters made their turns in perfect formation

"Grace," Mommy urged, and we went to our car.

"I will admit it is impressive," Mommy said as we drove off. "And a big responsibility for him. He loves us seeing that sort of thing, especially you. He's just a big boy," she kidded lovingly.

I smiled to myself. *I'm lucky,* I thought. *Civilian kids don't think so because we move around so much, but I'm the luckiest girl in the world.*

Mommy and I flew through the supermarket, scooping up what she wanted, and then we hurried home. An hour and a half later the security guard at the main gate informed us that Trent was there. A few minutes later I was waiting at the front door.

I saw immediately that Trent was more nervous than I was, and the military presence at the gate only heightened it. Still on his crutch, of course, he limped through the entryway to meet Mommy.

"Welcome, Trent," she said. "I'm glad you like chicken burgers."

He glanced at me. He had confessed he had never had them, but he assured me he was eager to try them.

"Thank you, Mrs. Houston."

"Call me Jackie Lee," she said. "Mrs. Houston makes me sound like someone's grandmother."

Trent nodded, amazed. Clearly my calling his mother by her first name was something she would never ask me to do and never permit. I led him into our living room, and Mommy sat with us for a while. I was always impressed with how easily she met people. All my life, because of our traveling and moving, she confronted new people, different personalities, and seemed able to do it with little difficulty.

I once asked her about it, and she had paused, thought, and then said, "It's like trying on different styles of clothing for me. I can see or feel quickly whether or not we're going to fit. We have to meet too many different people to luxuriate in shyness. Our lives are far more obvious to the people we know and share experiences with. We can't put on any false pretenses. We're all sort of in the same boat, sometimes literally."

She had tweaked her nose and looked at me. "It's going to be different for you, Grace, unless you end up marrying a Navy boy or someone from another military branch."

Whom would I marry? I couldn't help wondering. Would I follow in my mother's footsteps, be part of some tradition? Or run off with a rock star?

I saw how Trent felt very comfortable because of Mommy's casual manner. He was more talkative with her, in fact, than he had been with me. In minutes she had him telling his life story, all about his family, and even his dream to become a professional baseball player.

"I've been going to a professionally run baseball camp every summer since I was nine," he revealed. He hadn't told me that.

"You're going to it again this summer?" she asked.

"Oh, sure," he said. "As long as my ankle heals well."

"Well, just follow your doctor's orders explicitly, and it will," she assured him. Then she excused herself to set out our dinner. I offered to help, but she insisted I stay with Trent.

"Start studying or something," she kidded.

"Boy, I like your mother," Trent said the moment she was gone. "My mother would have taken your blood and urine and had it off to the lab by now."

I laughed and accused him of exaggeration. I hadn't met his mother yet, but I couldn't imagine her to be as severe as he was portraying her. However, he didn't relent.

"She treats our family name, reputation, and status no less than she would if we were royalty. It gets embarrassing and difficult at times. My father is easier and not as taken with himself.

"But," he added, seeing the look of concern on my face, "I'm sure when she meets you she won't be able to do anything but melt."

"Not unless she's made of ice cream," I said.

"No, she would rather be thought of as rich butter," he replied, and we laughed.

"I didn't know you were going off to baseball camp this summer."

"Yeah, but it's not that far away. I'll be around to eat chicken burgers as many times as I can."

I laughed, but it felt good to hear how much he wanted to see me.

Before Mommy called us to dinner I showed him one of our family albums with Daddy on different ships, one an aircraft carrier, the USS *Enterprise.*

"There are more than twenty-eight hundred sailors on it, more than one hundred seventy chiefs, and more than two hundred officers. With the air wing there could be more than five thousand people on it. It's like a little city, Daddy says. I was very little when he was on it, so I don't remember ever seeing it, but I have seen it in harbor."

"I guess you're a real Navy girl," Trent said, smiling. "You know so much detail about the ships and all."

"Sailor Girl."

"What?"

"That's what my father calls me."

"Oh, right."

He laughed. We looked at some more pictures, and then we went in to dinner. Trent really loved Mommy's chicken burgers. I could see he wasn't simply being polite. When I started to help her clean up, she insisted I get right to studying. She gave me a look that told me she approved of Trent very much.

He thanked her, and we went to my room. The first thing he noticed was all the dolls and souvenirs Daddy had brought me over the years, each unique to the place he had been. I had set up my notebook and our textbook with bookmarks for our studying.

"We'd better get to it, huh?" he said. "First the sacrosanct."

"Time for a new word," I countered. "Stop being facetious."

He laughed. "Okay, okay," he said, holding up his hands while still leaning on his crutch. "Let's go at it."

As before, his problem was the disorganized manner in which he kept his notes. Organizing it all helped us to study. Mommy stopped by once to ask if we needed anything more before she settled into watching television and waiting for my father. She made watching television sound like a warm bath.

After she left us Trent leaned over to kiss me.

"I figured since she invaded the sacrosanct, I could. Just for a moment, of course."

"It's not the sacrosanct. It's an adjective, not a noun. We are studying English, and Madeo will have vocabulary on the test, Trent."

"Aye, aye, sir," he said, and saluted.

For a moment the salute gave me a strange chill. My father's face flashed before me. It threw me back to the moment of discomfort I had experienced at the helicopter liftoff. That nervousness surged through my body, rattling my bones. I glanced at the clock. Daddy was going to have a very late dinner tonight the way this was going.

"You all right?" Trent asked.

"What? Oh, yes. C'mon, let's review the quotes from *Julius Caesar,*" I said, and turned to those pages in my notebook. Involving myself in my work was the only way to keep the annoying finger of anxiety away from my heart. I had no idea why it was there, and that made me more jittery. Every once in a while I glanced at the clock and took note of the time. Trent caught me doing it and asked if I thought he should leave soon.

"No, we have more to do," I insisted, and we continued.

When the doorbell sounded about forty minutes later, it seemed to ring inside me as if my heart had become a gong to strike. Anyone at our door had to be someone living within the gated compound, since the security guard hadn't called to announce him or her, but Mommy had not mentioned any of her friends coming over to visit. Most anyone would call first to see if we were home or if it was a good time to come.

The logic of all this ran at supersonic speed through my mind in a computer-like process that brought me to my feet. Trent looked up from the notebook with surprise. I stood there, frozen, and then I heard what had begun deep inside me back at the heliport: a tiny yet persistent cry that ballooned into a scream, Mommy's scream, a scream I would hear for the rest of my life.

I turned and hurried out of my room toward the front door, my cry for my mother on my lips. What I saw put stone in my legs and stopped my heart. Mommy was unconscious and in a naval officer's arms. He and the officer with him were struggling to get her to the sofa in the living room.

"Mommy!" I cried.

Trent came hopping up behind me. We both watched in awe and then slowly followed them into the living room.

The older officer turned to the younger one. "Get me a cold damp cloth and a glass of cold water," he ordered.

"Yes, sir," the younger officer said, and snapped to it, rushing by me as if I wasn't there.

"What's happening?" I demanded. My tears were streaming down my face in anticipation.

"There's been a helicopter accident involving your father," he replied. "I'm sorry."

Within those two words were all the tragedy and pain I could ever feel in my life. He didn't have to explain any more or add any descriptive words.

I'm sorry? I'm sorry your father is gone forever? I'm sorry something mechanical went wrong and changed your life and your mother's life forever? I'm sorry someone as strong and wonderful as your father could be gone in seconds, just removed as if he had been swept off in a hurricane?

There are no words in our language adequate to explain or comfort anyone when something like this occurs, I thought. Despite the fact that my father was part of a military machine that could be and often was placed in harm's way, those fears were so hammered down and hidden from our consciousness that we refused to confront them. Every time we had seen Daddy go off or had watched him fly in a plane or a helicopter, there was a moment when our breath was seized and our hearts were on pause. It passed quickly, and we relaxed in the knowledge that he was one of our country's finest and our country had the best and the safest equipment in the world.

Military people, the families, have a second level of faith beyond religion. They believe in the structure, the procedures, the efficiency, and the power of the branch, whether it be the Navy or the Air Force. Daddy used to say flying military was ten times safer than commercial. Just consider all that security, all those men working around equipment, being supervised and observed by officers, taking pride in efficiency and success, standing straighter, beaming with their medals. These men wouldn't permit such things to happen.

But something had gone wrong with Daddy's helicopter. They couldn't recover. Mommy was told the details. There was that *we don't hide the facts from our Navy family* attitude in the face of the officer who sat with her and with me. It was as if knowing how it had happened brought some relief, when, in fact, it only added to the misery and horror as far as I was concerned.

What was Daddy thinking when that helicopter began to have trouble and all his training, all his knowledge, wasn't helping? Were his last thoughts about me, about Mommy? Was he terrified? Did he scream, or did he maintain his composure in front of his men as his superiors would have us believe?

Does any of it matter the next day when you open your eyes and realize, no, it wasn't a nightmare? *He isn't here. He will never be here again.*

I was at Mommy's side when she regained consciousness. She held me, and we rocked back and forth as if we were on our little rowboat already, cast out to sea with no safe harbors in sight, no Daddy to bring us back.

I forgot all about Trent, of course. He made a quick, quiet exit, probably shocked and terrified. I didn't even remember he had been there until hours and hours later. The senior officer who had come was a doctor and had brought sedatives. Mommy refused them, but he insisted she consider taking at least one pill. It would deaden the pain, disguise it, hide it a little or just enough to get her through the first terrible hours, he said.

I wanted to take the whole bottle. Later he pulled me aside and told me to remain as alert as I could so I could watch over her for the next twelve to twenty-four hours. He made it sound as if she might take her own life, and that put even more terror into my heart, as I remembered what Autumn had done to herself for something I now considered trivial in comparison.

I couldn't speak, but I nodded. I helped Mommy to bed. Other wives of naval officers began to arrive soon afterward. As if they had all had training in what to do when this happened, they took over our home, helped organize and manage our immediate needs. Of course, I appreciated it, but their stoic efficiency made me suspicious. It was as if they all always knew this was going to happen. That was ridiculous, of course, but it was part of my dark thinking, thinking I couldn't stop.

Daddy's naval funeral was elaborate and impressive, full of tradition. It was a terribly beautiful day, a day that should have been reserved for wonderful, happy events, with the sky so clear blue and the few tiny clouds like small puddles of milk, pure white.

The sea breeze was warm and as gentle as a mother's kiss.

Not only was Vice Admiral Martin in attendance, but the secretary of the Navy was flown down. Three other men had been killed in the accident. It was in the national news for a few days. Officer after officer came to us to tell us how much they had respected and admired Daddy: "He would want you to go on." "Hold yourself up." "Achieve in his name." The laying of responsibility and obligation on my shoulders was their way of helping me cope. Nothing seemed to terrify them more than the sight of my tears. Perhaps it reminded them all how vulnerable they and their families were, and that was something they couldn't tolerate and continue to do what they had to do. Salutes, handshakes, some hugs, everyone in proper uniform and attention, was the order of the day.

I'll never be able to tell anyone how I felt standing at that gravesite and staring at that flag-draped coffin. *My daddy can't be in there,* I thought. *This is all just another exercise, a rehearsal, a ceremony. Soon it will end, and Daddy will be back to tell us how well we performed and how proud of us he was.*

"I knew you could pull it off well, Sailor Girl," he would tell me.

There he would be, standing as proudly and looking as handsome and exciting as ever, my movie-star Daddy who sailed the sea and flew in the clouds and gave men confidence and hope, who made me cry when I sang the national anthem and said the pledge because I knew how important it was to him and to all the men around him that we feel what they were doing was so very important. It wasn't just my imagination when I saw how children of naval families looked more somber and serious when we had to do this at school. Disrespecting the flag or the anthem was the same as disrespecting your parents. Disrespect eventually put them in danger, which put us all in danger.

These were the thoughts that I had developed as a young girl, but somewhere out there in the dark, over the ocean, in a matter of seconds, Daddy had died tragically and made them all fall back. A great door would come crashing down on this world, the only world I had ever known. The mournful sound of Taps would lift us away, and we would say goodbye to "the life."

In the days that followed Mommy gathered her strength. She told me that at the moment she felt as if Daddy was just away on another sea duty.

"I keep telling myself he'll be back or we'll hear the phone ring or get a letter," she said. "I know it's silly, and I have to stop it."

I wasn't crying anymore. I had drained the well of tears dry. I tried to occupy myself with some of the schoolwork that had been sent home for me, but it was as if I had lost part of my mind or that place was now empty and hollow. Words and thoughts drifted aimlessly through it without any purpose.

Trent called, but even the sound of his voice didn't lift me enough to come out of the dark. He tried.

"I wish I had met him," he said.

Yes, I thought, *I wish you had. I wish Daddy would have been able to come to my room afterward and tease me about you and then take joy in my declaration of loyalty to him, that I could never love anyone more. He would smile and shake his head and say, "You'd better, Sailor Girl. I want grandchildren."*

Grandchildren.

If I had any, all they would be able to do would be to look at an old photograph. They'd have some curiosity for a moment, and then it would pass, and he would be like any other historical face.

One day about a week after the funeral Mommy came to my room to tell me we would be moving. Of course, I had expected it.

"I want you to take your exams as best you can, Grace. Finish the school year at least. It will be important for you when you start somewhere new."

"Where will we go, Mommy?"

She sat on my bed. "I have a good friend who lives in West Palm Beach, Florida," she began. "She was my best friend in high school. We've been talking. She was one of the first people I called. Her name is Dallas Tremont. She and her husband own a famous upscale restaurant called the Tremont Inn. I thought we would move to West Palm Beach and I would work in her restaurant."

"Work in a restaurant? Doing what?" I asked, surprised. "Cooking?"

"No," she said, smiling. "I'm not a gourmet cook by any means. No, I'll hostess and waitress."

"Waitress?" I couldn't imagine my mother doing that.

"What else can I do, Grace? I never went to college, honey. I was a Navy bride almost immediately out of high school, so I'm not qualified to do much more," she said. "Take a lesson from me, and be sure you go to college and develop some sort of career before you get married."

She saw the look of shock and fear on my face. We were leaving the sanctity and comfort of the naval community. We were going out there, beyond the gates. It was almost like going to another country, where my mother would work and not be a Navy wife.

"Don't look so worried, honey. After your exams, we'll pack the car and head south. It will be fun for us this time. We'll take our time, see some sights along the way. Dallas is finding us a nice apartment nearby, and she assures me there are excellent schools for you to attend, maybe even a magnet school. For once you will be somewhere with some real permanence."

I didn't say it, but I would be willing to move every week if I could have Daddy back. I didn't have to say it. She knew it.

"One other thing I want you to know," she said, looking away. My heart began to race in anticipation. "We told you our intentions, so I don't want you thinking about it and worrying. I am not pregnant. Maybe my body is smarter than I am," she added. "I don't think I could stand having your father's child without him being right there, and taking care of a little baby now seems like a monumental task."

I didn't know what to say. I wasn't happy or sad about it. I just nodded and let it go like something that just wasn't meant to remain with me.

There was much for Mommy to do before we left, and I did have to concentrate and do as well on my exams as I could. A few days later I returned to school. I hated it because I could see the pity and even the fear in the faces of many of the other students. Wendi and Penny did their best to be civil to me, but I wouldn't let them feel satisfied. I wanted it to lie heavily on their consciences, if they had any consciences.

Of course, Trent was as loving as he could be. I saw the deep disappointment in his face when I told him

Mommy and I were leaving Norfolk and going to live in West Palm Beach.

"I know of a two-week baseball camp held in Florida during the winter. Maybe I can get my parents to send me there," he said. He didn't know what else to say. We promised to write and call and e-mail each other as much as possible when I did get a computer, but these were promises that came from us like jet-propelled ideas. We knew they would lose their fizz and fall to earth like exhausted rockets.

Remarkably I did well on my tests. Trent said he did better than ever and again thanked me. I knew I hadn't helped him all that much, especially with the other subjects, but he was determined to make it seem as though I had been the reason for his improvement in everything. The day we were leaving, he came over to our house to help us pack the car. He was doing much better with his ankle now and just limping a bit, not using a crutch. Some of the other officers' wives came by, too. There was a lot of hugging and kissing and wishing of good luck.

Trent and I stood on the sidelines watching it all as if we were in a movie theater and it was happening to fictional characters. How I wished that were so. The minutes that ticked by were so heavy I could almost feel the movement of the clock's hands inside me. When we looked at each other, the truth was so evident in our faces we could have had it printed on our foreheads: *We'll never see each other again. We'll never really know each other, and maybe after a phone call or two, a letter or an e-mail, we'll fall away from each other, drift off, and find someone else.*

Trent, I thought, *you will be forever my first love. All men I meet I will measure against you, even though I*

*don't really know all about you. I'll invent the rest. You
will be my perfect beau.*

I imagined he thought the same about me.

At least we had given each other that much.

We went off to kiss goodbye, to hold each other and
make the suitable promises.

Then we walked hand in hand to the car where
Mommy was talking with Vice Admiral Martin's wife,
who was so nice I wondered how she could have a
daughter like Penny.

"You'll always be a Navy wife," she told Mommy.
"It gets into your blood."

"I know," Mommy said, but I could see she didn't
believe that or want to believe it. "Well," she said, turning to us. "Time to get on the road, Grace. Trent, I'm
sorry we didn't get to know you more."

She held out her hand to him, but when he reached
for it she gave him a hug instead.

"Me, too," he said practically in tears. "But I'll stay
in touch, Mrs. . . . Jackie Lee."

She smiled. "I hope so." She looked around as if she
wanted to cement everything in her memory forever,
and then she slipped into the car and started the engine.

I'm leaving, I thought. *I'm really leaving, and I'm
leaving Daddy behind.*

Trent looked at me so sadly it broke my heart. We
kissed again, and then I got into the car.

He stood there as we pulled away. I turned around
to look back at him. He lifted his hand, and then,
because I had told him about it, saluted the way
Daddy and I saluted each other. It made me smile and
froze a tear under my eye. I didn't want to cry, not
now. I didn't want to do anything to make it harder for
Mommy.

In a moment we turned a corner, and Trent was gone. I turned around and looked forward.

Our future was all on the road ahead now.

And anyone looking at both of us would see we were of one face: full of fear, full of hope, full of sadness. Both suddenly little girls again.

5

Two Girls Together

Mommy tried to keep me busy and keep my mind off sad things by making me our flight navigator for the trip south. Captain Morgan, the naval officer who had lived next door to us, was from Florida and had written out directions for the fastest route that would bring us to I-95 South. Many of the turns were only half a mile or so apart, so I did have to keep alert, although I had a suspicion Mommy had already committed the itinerary to memory. I know that during some of our other trips together without Daddy she gave me a similar responsibility just to keep me from becoming bored.

We had some kind of music playing almost all the time, whether it was a CD or the radio. Whenever we were quiet for long periods of time, I would see Mommy quickly flicking a fugitive tear from just under one of her eyelids. I pretended I didn't notice, because if I didn't pretend, my tears would soon be following

hers. Mommy tried to fill the gaps of silence by pointing out different sights along the way, whether it was a
beautiful or interesting house or just a patch of trees
whose leaves had captured the sun, making them look
as if they grew gems on their branches.

Before we reached I-95, Mommy decided we would
stop to have some lunch. Once we were on the highway
she wanted to make as much time as she could before
we stopped for the night. She estimated we had about
eight hundred miles to go, which she thought we could
easily do in two days.

The roadside diner was called Mother Dotty's
Kitchen. It looked like an old-fashioned diner with its
booths in imitation red leather and a counter with lots
of chrome that ran almost the entire length. A Shania
Twain song was playing over the sound system, and
its upbeat tempo helped lift our spirits. Everyone was
very friendly, and with the aroma of different meats
and potatoes being made our appetites were stimu-
lated. Neither of us had eaten very much during the
last few weeks. Each night, especially when we ate
alone, we pecked at our food like finicky chickens.
When she told me to eat, I told her to do the same, and
we both stopped trying to push food down each
other's throat.

Maybe the change that came over us now was a
result of simply getting off the base, leaving what for us
had become a world of sorrow with days that were forever overcast. I could see the differences in Mommy's
face. Her former brightness and glitter hadn't returned,
but she looked less weighed down by the pain. Her
forehead was smooth again, and there was more energy
in her voice and movements. I wondered if, not when,
that would be true for me.

"You never talked much about Dallas Tremont before, Mommy," I said after we had ordered.

"It's always been one of those friendships you don't lose but don't nurture much. We were inseparable in high school, but after I married your father and joined the Navy, so to speak, Dallas and I lost touch. We tried to maintain a close relationship, but with our moving around and all, it became impossible. Our phone calls were soon fewer and farther between. Our letter writing stopped almost entirely. Still, we never forgot each other's birthday, and we always managed to send each other something at Christmas, some small but intimate thing. I'd always let her know where we were, of course.

"I did attend her wedding. You wouldn't remember because you were only a year and a few months old, but I left you with my mother and returned to Raleigh where Dallas and I had grown up. Daddy was on sea duty. She was married in the church her family attended, and then she and Warren moved to Florida. He was always in the restaurant business and had an opportunity in West Palm Beach.

"Warren had been married before and had a little girl, who is now seventeen. His first wife was killed in a motorcycle accident. According to Dallas, she was like oil to Warren's water. They married mostly because she was pregnant with Phoebe." Mommy smirked. "According to Dallas, she named her daughter Phoebe because of the phoebe bird outside the window of the maternity ward. Lucky it wasn't a crow," she added, and I laughed.

It was the first time I had laughed since Daddy's death, I thought, and it felt as if I had taken off a jacket made of lead. Mommy smiled. "I've always loved your laugh, Grace. No matter how old you will be, when you laugh it will always sound innocent and true and make other people feel good about themselves."

I stared at her, at the warmth in her eyes, the love in her face. Would anyone ever see as much good in me and love me as much as she did?

"Anyway," she continued, "while Warren became involved in business and began to develop a nice little fortune for them, Petula, better known as Pet, continued her self-centered ways, leaving the baby with a sitter for hours and hours while she associated with her unmarried friends, a group of whom were into motorcycles. Warren refused to buy her one, so she went out and bought it herself. A year later she lost control going, they say, about eighty, and broke almost every major bone in her body. It was one of those accidents where you hope the victim died instantly. And she did.

"There he was, left with an infant. Dallas was working for an associate of his, and they began to see each other. She never said so, but I had the sense that they were seeing each other romantically before Pet's inevitable date with death.

"She gave me details slowly over the years. We had a few hours together four years ago when I was connecting flights. I had met your father for that weekend in San Juan. He had some shore leave, and we thought it was a good opportunity for a little holiday. Remember?"

"Yes."

Every time Mommy mentioned Daddy in a passing reference, her smile deepened and warmed. I was jealous of her cherished memories, even though I had so many of my own.

"Dallas met me at the airport in West Palm Beach,

and we had a nice time reminiscing, looking at each other's family photographs."

She paused when our food was served. She stared at her plate for a moment and then shook her head.

"Fate. I read once that we're all crossing paths, intersecting in ways we don't even realize. Here I am coming full circle and meeting up with Dallas again, something neither of us thought would ever be." She smiled quickly. "But you'll love her, honey. She's down-to-earth and always lots of fun."

I nodded. If Mommy said so, I was sure it would be.

"Eat up, and let's get on our way," she said with more enthusiasm. It was infectious. I felt a surge of interest and expectation. We were like two swimmers, pushed under the sea and held down in the dark cold until we almost drowned, and then permitted to come up for air, finding ourselves in an entirely new world.

I think Mommy and I were closer to each other than other mothers and daughters because Daddy had been gone so often and for such long periods, especially during the earlier years. However, even she and I, a mother and a daughter who couldn't be much closer, had much yet to learn about each other, mainly me learning about her. The reason became clearer to me as we traveled and she talked more and more about her own youth, her first boyfriend, her youthful adventures.

Mothers have to wait until their daughters are mature enough to appreciate and understand what they will tell them about themselves. She could have told me all she did now years ago, but I wouldn't have valued her revelations as much or understood as much. We really become different people, changing as we grow older, I thought. Mommy's confessions and descriptions of herself were far more frank and detailed than they would have been if she had told them to me even a year earlier.

Daddy's death had somehow plunged me into a stage of maturity perhaps years ahead of my time. It had certainly washed away much of my innocence. The world could be a very cruel and hard place, and the more you came to realize that, the more you cherished a true friend. What better or truer friend would I have than she was, I thought, and hoped she now felt the same about me. I was old enough now to hear her fears and concerns. She no longer had to be worried that I would suffer childish nightmares. I would address each problem alongside her, and together we would go on.

She had no hesitation about answering any question I asked about her younger days.

"Did you love anyone as much as you loved Daddy?" I wondered.

"Oh, I had some terrible crushes on boys and had my heart shattered like an eggshell when I learned they didn't feel anywhere near as much toward me as I did toward them. No," she concluded after a little more thought, "I know it's assumed or accepted that we all fall in love early and then try to find it again in someone who might resemble or remind us of that first love, but I can honestly say your father was very, very special."

She smiled that soft, deep smile to herself again as we drove on monotonously down the superhighway, cars whizzing by with other people mesmerized by their own speed and thoughts, all of them looking to me like entrapped creatures in moving metal cages.

"Your father had so many wonderful qualities, but what was truly wonderful was how balanced they were. He had a great sense of humor, but boy he could turn

serious on a dime. He was strong but so romantic and
gentle. You know what most women suffer when they
marry?" she said suddenly, turning to me.

I shook my head, having no idea but fascinated with
the topic.

"They suffer from gross expectation. They either
don't want to face their husbands' limitations and admit
them to themselves, or they honestly don't see them
and so they are continually frustrated and disappointed.
They marry and suddenly discover the men they have
married are not the men they thought they had married.
Sometimes it's not their fault, of course. They are
deceived by promises. But I think most of the time they
deceive themselves.

"Your father and I never lied to each other, Grace.
That was the secret. No matter what the consequences,
we told each other the truth, and that became the glue
that cemented us forever."

She swallowed hard. "Forever," she muttered. "That
was the only deception we permitted."

I turned and glared at the highway, which seemed
liquefied now, a flow of macadam, lines going on and
on. *When will the ache stop? Will it ever stop?*

"We'll be all right," Mommy chanted. She nodded at
the windshield as if we had an audience along the way.
"We'll be all right."

She dropped her right hand and reached for mine.
We held hands for miles and miles, and then we talked
about where we would stop and what we would have
for dinner. Thinking about tomorrow was the only
escape from today.

Finally we decided to pull in for the night. We
always tried to find a motel that looked well main-
tained. Mommy believed that usually if the owner cared

about how his property appeared to people passing by, he cared about how it appeared inside as well.

We had been in motels many times before, and when I was very young we would treat each like another magical adventure. One of our favorite games was trying to imagine who had been in our room before us.

We would lie awake for a while and make up stories about our room's invented former inhabitants. Almost by instinct, perhaps to protect ourselves from the darkness and the troubled thoughts it would bring, we did it this night.

"Two young women were just here. They're on an adventure before starting college," Mommy began. "They want to see as much of America as they can and hope to have many interesting experiences."

We had two double beds with a small television mounted on the wall in front of us, but we didn't bother turning it on. We created our own pictures, our own stories, after we were snug in our beds. We were able to leave the screened windows open to get some fresh air. It wasn't home, but it wasn't unpleasant.

"One of them is coming off a bad love affair. She's trying to cheer herself up," I said.

"No. It wasn't a bad love affair. It was a good love affair, but she and her boyfriend decided to break up and go out with other people."

"Just to see if they really loved each other?"

"Yes. Her friend had no boyfriend, and she . . ."

"Hates men."

"And tries to get her girlfriend to stop calling her old boyfriend all the time."

"But she went out and called him anyway."

"And they said they missed each other and they thought the whole thing was a bad idea."

"So she decided to turn around and forget about having adventures on the road. She doesn't want to waste another day without seeing the man she loves."

"But she doesn't reveal it until the morning, at breakfast."

"And her friend is so angry, but after a while . . ."

"After a while she confesses she was just jealous, and she wishes her good luck."

"And it all happened here," I concluded, and we both laughed.

It was just like old times.

Only we weren't rushing to meet Daddy. We were rushing to get to sleep and forget. More exhausted emotionally as well as physically than we thought, we were both soon asleep.

We were up early in the morning and back on the highway. Neither of us said it, but the miles we put between us and the naval base had the effect of a double-edged sword on our hearts and nerves. On one hand we were leaving everything we had loved behind, but on the other we were dreaming about what awaited us over the next horizon. When we crossed into Florida late in the day, we looked at each other. We didn't have to speak. It was as if we had crossed more than just the border of another state. We had crossed the border between the past and the future.

"We'll get into West Palm too late if we keep going, Grace," Mommy decided. "Let's just have a nice dinner somewhere and a good sleep and be fresh in the morning. The world is a different place when you're rested."

Of course, that sounded good to me. I was very nervous about meeting new people and leaving "the life." It would be the first time I would feel like a civilian, and I wasn't sure I would like it at all.

Somehow, even with all our moves and traveling, I had never been to Florida, so I was looking forward to that. The plush greenery, the palm trees, the sight of the ocean from time to time, made it all interesting the next day. We had an early breakfast again and started immediately. We took a more scenic route because Mommy said we had made good time. Neither of us was very interested in stopping to see any sights along the way. We had no appetite for it. We just wanted to get to where we would be and close the door behind us.

Now that we were in Florida, we both relaxed a bit. At one point we even pulled to the side of the road, where we had a beautiful view of the ocean, and just sat gazing out at the breakers.

"It's funny," Mommy said. "We were a naval family, but we didn't do all that much sailing or have that much contact with the water. Oh, we visited ships and were there at the docks to greet or to say goodbye, but as for being out there ourselves . . ." She laughed. "Your father once got very seasick. Did I ever tell you about that?"

"No," I said, wondering how something like that was not told to me.

"He had some exercise that involved being in a raft for a prolonged period, and the sea was rough that day. When I saw him, he was as white as the inside of a potato. 'I'm staying up there,' he said, pointing at the sky."

She sighed. "Maybe now that we're here, we'll learn how to sail or spend some time at the beach. Wouldn't that be fun, Grace?"

"Yes."

"Dallas and Warren have a motorboat, but they both work so hard they don't get to use it that often. Maybe with us here they will," she said, and started the car.

A little more than three hours later, I saw a sign indicating that we were entering Palm Beach County.

"We're going right to their restaurant first," Mommy explained. "Dallas is going to take us to the apartment. It's in an area known as Palm Beach Gardens. Sounds nice, doesn't it?"

I nodded. Now that we were really here, it was hard to keep my heart from pounding and my stomach from feeling empty. The only similar experience I had had in my life was when I was in a play for the first time at school and had to walk out onstage in front of hundreds of people. I thought my throat would close or I would freeze and have to be carried off like a log. Once out there, however, my lines came to me and I did okay. To Daddy, who had come, I had deserved the Academy Award.

There was so much traffic and so much to look at once we turned onto Dixie Highway. Both of us began to recite the street numbers until finally the Tremont Inn came into view. It certainly stuck out because it was a larger building than the ones beside it, but it was in so much better condition. It looked as if it had just been built, while some of the others looked seedy and windworn, their colors faded, their windows cloudy, and the grounds around them unkempt.

The Tremont Inn looked as if it had once been a house. Later we would learn that it had. There was even a small front porch. It had its own parking lot, which at the moment had only half a dozen or so cars in it. We pulled in and parked. After she shut off the engine Mommy just sat there, catching her breath. She gazed so long at the steering wheel I thought something was very wrong.

"Mommy?"

She lifted her hand and swallowed hard, nodding as she did so. "I'm all right," she said. "I'm all right." She closed her eyes and then took a breath and forced a smile. "Let's go, honey," she said, and opened the car door.

I stepped out, still concerned. She came around and looked at the building.

"It's open only for dinners," she said. "Isn't it nice?"

Cars whizzed by on the highway as we walked around to the front. We found the door locked. It was a decorative paneled oak door. The front of the restaurant had a rich-looking wood cladding with cream-colored shutters. Mommy tapped on the glass. There were some lights on within, but they were dim. She tapped again, and we could see a door in the rear open, the light from the kitchen spilling out and silhouetting the figure of a woman who paused a moment in the kitchen doorway and then hurried toward us. In fact, she looked propelled.

Seconds later the door was unlocked, and we faced a woman about Mommy's height with light brown hair styled in medium length, curling just under her chin. She wore a headband pulling her bangs back to reveal a smooth but very lightly freckled forehead. She had large hazel eyes that brightened with happiness at the sight of us. Her smile puffed out her cheeks around her cheekbones, but I thought she had a pretty face with very soft, feminine lips and a graceful jaw line. She was a little slimmer than Mommy and actually so many years younger I wondered if it was Dallas.

"Jackie!" she screamed, ending any doubt I might have had. They embraced. She held on to Mommy, her eyes closed, and they rocked in each other's arms. "Oh, honey, I'm so sorry, so sorry."

Tears filled her eyes and she blinked rapidly. They

looked as if neither would be the first to let go, so they would be holding on to each other for days. Finally Mommy pulled herself upright, and Dallas Tremont turned to me.

"This can't be Grace. It can't be. Look how beautiful you've become, and grown-up."

"I guess you know this is Dallas, honey."

I started to nod, but she surged forward and embraced me tightly, popping a kiss on my cheek.

"Welcome to Florida," she cried. "Come in, come in. Warren's in his office pounding the computer keyboard to get it to come up with more favorable numbers. How was your trip?"

"It was fine," Mommy said. "We're actually both too numb to remember anything about it," she added to bring that topic to a quick end.

Dallas paused in the entryway and nodded.

"I'll bet." Her moment of concern collapsed quickly into a wide, bright smile that centered around those big hazel eyes. It was the kind of smile that could put a prisoner on death row at ease. "But you're here now, and you'll take some time to rest and put Florida on like a new set of clothes. Come in, come," she urged.

We stepped forward. The entryway had a hostess desk on the right with a telephone on it. Behind it was a large painting of a green-tinted lake set in the lap of two heavily wooded mountains. Deer were at the rim of the lake, most drinking but two with their heads lifted as if they had just heard us enter the restaurant.

"You remember this," Dallas said. "Greenwood Lake, our magic mountain retreat in North Carolina. To this day Warren moans and groans about our selling that cabin. Like he would take the time off to spend a summer there anyway," she said, shaking her head.

After the entryway, there were two good-size dining areas, each with two large windows. The floor was a lighter oak, the tables darker, but all with tablecloths and vases of pretty artificial flowers. There were more paintings of mountains and lakes on the walls in each room.

"This isn't your typical Florida restaurant," Dallas explained quickly. "But that's the secret of our success, that and having the best chef on the southeastern coast. And the best service, of course," she added. "People, our regulars, whom you'll get to know quickly," she added, making the first reference to Mommy actually working there, "tell us the decor makes them feel cooler, as if they've left Florida for some mountain village. It's all smoke and mirrors when you get right down to it, isn't it? Image, decor, a show. The most successful restaurants, other than the chains, are little happenings. Warren always believed that going to a good restaurant was like going to the theater or stepping into a movie.

"He must be right. He's a successful restaurateur. Wait until you see the quaint uniforms the waitresses and waiters wear. The waiters have these great vests, and the waitresses have little aprons sewn onto their skirts and bodices with lace collars. We look as if we're situated in the Alps or something. You'll love it," Dallas added.

I looked at Mommy. She was holding her smile, but I knew her well enough to know that smile was becoming a little plastic by now. The thought of her taking orders from people, wearing a costume, rushing about this place, filled me with a deep, dark sense of dread. Daddy would be so upset, I thought. From the wife of a naval officer to this. It wasn't that the job was beneath us or wasn't probably a good job. It was just so abrupt and so dramatic a change in lifestyle.

"We have four small private dining rooms in the rear for special parties or clientele. We get some very important people here, celebrities, wealthy Palm Beach residents who cross the moat to mingle with the masses."

"The moat?" I said.

Dallas laughed. "That's what Warren calls the Flagler Bridge. You cross it to enter Palm Beach."

"I thought we were in Palm Beach," I said, looking at Mommy.

Dallas laughed again. "Oh, no, honey. Don't ever let a Palm Beach resident hear that. This is *West* Palm Beach. Palm Beach is a country unto itself, another planet. Some of the wealthiest people in the world live there. They think it's one level below heaven."

She smiled at Mommy and shrugged. "Who knows, maybe it is." She turned to me. "After you guys get settled in, you'll do some touring and go to Worth Avenue, and then you'll understand. Don't worry about it," she said. "In a matter of days you'll be like an old-timer here, and when you meet people with flies up their noses you'll laugh them off.

"Let's say hello to Warren, and then I'll show you to your condo in Palm Beach Gardens. It's only about twenty minutes away, which will make it really easy for you, Jackie. I was thinking Grace might enroll in the school Phoebe attends. Unless you were thinking of a private school for her. They are pretty expensive."

"No. Grace has always attended public schools," Mommy said.

"You're going to love it, honey," Dallas said, reaching out to touch my hand. "I'll make sure Phoebe shows you around and helps you get settled in when the school year starts. She's a senior, and you know that seniors are big deals."

"Where is she? I haven't seen her in so long I can't imagine what she looks like," Mommy said.

"She's at the beach with her friends. They went to Singer Island today. You'll love the beaches here, Grace. There is so much for a young person to do."

"She never lacked for that," Mommy said.

"I imagine not," Dallas said. "Living on naval bases among all those sailors and ships and planes. Come on," she said, seizing my hand and pulling me ahead of Mommy. "Let's disturb Warren."

I looked back at Mommy, who laughed and followed us to the door in the rear simply marked Office. Dallas knocked and then opened it before anyone inside could have time to say, "Come in."

Behind a desk that was far too big for the small room sat a man with curly dark hair and two black pearls for eyes. He was round-faced, cleanly shaven, with a nose a little long and a strong pair of lips that sliced sharply above his slightly protruding jaw. When he saw us and stood up, I saw he was stout, leaning toward pear-shaped. His smile settled in his face like a strawberry in cream, pulling his lips in and bringing out the glimmer in his ebony eyes.

"Jackie!" he cried, and came around his desk as quickly as he could. Mommy stepped forward, and he hugged her. "We're so sorry for your trouble. What a horror," he said.

Mommy just nodded. "It's nice to see you, Warren. It's been too long."

"Yes, but how I wish it was for different reasons," he replied.

"Not any more than I do." Mommy turned toward me. "This is my daughter, Grace."

"Hi," Warren said. "I only knew you from the pictures your mother sent us from time to time, but I can see you've got a lot of your daddy in you."

Hearing that brought tears of happiness and sadness to my eyes.

"Pretty girl," he told Mommy. "We're going to have to teach her the martial arts."

"Oh, she can take care of herself," Mommy said proudly.

"Sit down, sit down. There's so much to tell you," he said.

"I want to get them right to their place, Warren," Dallas said. "Get them settled in and let them get some days of rest before you start converting Jackie Lee to the restaurant business."

He laughed. "Hey, this is far from a walk in the park. You build up a clientele, and then some novelty restaurant starts down the street and you lose everyone for a while, or at least until they realize what quality means. Peaks and valleys, that's the business. The trick is how to smooth it all out."

"Wonderful," Dallas said dryly, and turned to Mommy. "Don't be shocked when he comes to you and complains about the rise in the price of butter."

"It's all the bottom line, Jackie. Someone has to watch it, and there's no one better than you, yourself, to watch your own affairs. Everyone I know who has a manager running his affairs is either out of business or well on his way to it."

"Oh, please," Dallas said. "Give the woman a chance to get a tan."

Warren laughed and retreated behind his desk.

"Okay, okay. I'm here if you need anything, anything whatsoever, Jackie."

"Thank you, Warren."

"You just let me know when you're ready."

"I will," Mommy said.

"Are we excused now?" Dallas asked him.

"See? See the abuse I take?"

We laughed again and followed Dallas out. She paused to introduce us to some of the kitchen help, including their chef, Christian Von De Stagen, who was from Belgium and had been a chef in Napa Valley in California before Warren enticed him to come to live and work in West Palm Beach. Dallas revealed that Warren had given him a piece of the business.

We got into our cars, and we followed her to Palm Beach Gardens. Our condo was in a small development off Holly Drive on a street called Fuchsia. There was a small pond in the center of the complex and, as Dallas pointed out, a nice walking path around the area. It was far enough off the major highway to be quiet. Both Mommy and I were pleasantly surprised by the condo, which was a ground-floor unit. It had two bedrooms, a nice-size kitchen and living room, and a small dining area that had a patio door facing the pond.

We had a garage and a small storage room as well. Dallas explained that we had no maintenance to worry about because it was taken care of by the home owners' association. We were subletting from the condo owner, so it was stocked with kitchenware, dishes, and silverware.

"I did some basic shopping for you," Dallas revealed. She had bought bedding for the two beds, stocked the kitchen cabinets with some basic foods, and had even bought us soap, detergents, sponges, and bathroom tissue. "I just tried to think of anything and everything I would want the day I moved into a place."

"This is so nice of you, Dallas," Mommy said. "It's lovely. Thank you so much for making these arrangements."

"It's the least I could do, Jackie. It's a nice little place," she said. "Until you find something bigger."

"Right now I can't imagine wanting anything bigger. The biggest home I've lived in was the house we had when I was a little girl. Quarters on a naval base were never that elaborate. The nicest home we ever had since we were married was the one we just left."

Dallas nodded, biting down on her lower lip. "Well, let me help you guys unload the car."

"Oh, you've done so much. You should probably get back to the restaurant."

"Are you kidding? Warren will have me working twice as hard back there. Please," she said, "let me take advantage of your arrival."

Mommy laughed, and we all seemed to relax. I was amused by them anyway, especially when they started to unload the car and talk about their early days. Every once in a while they would both stop and develop a reminiscence, wondering what had happened to this girlfriend or that boy. They took a break, opened a bottle of white wine, and continued chatting. Listening to them, hearing Mommy's laugh, was fun for me. I felt as if I was watching a movie replayed. It was all light and playful until their rendering of history brought them to Mommy's first meeting Daddy.

"I just can't believe he's not coming home, Dallas," Mommy said.

They hugged, and Mommy let herself cry, let those pent-up tears loose.

I left them because watching her being comforted by her old friend made my heart ache too much. Instead I slipped out the patio door and walked down to the pond. A pair of ducks were so still in the water I thought they were fake, until one ruffled its feathers and the two started across the pond toward me. It brought a smile to my face.

"They're expecting you to feed them something," I heard, and turned to see a tall, lanky boy with a shock of reddish brown hair, the long strands down over his eyes, coming slowly toward me. He wore a T-shirt with a cartoon on it. It showed a fish holding a fishing pole. A hairy, potbellied man looked as if he had taken the hook and was being pulled from the sea. Underneath it read, "How do you like it?"

"I throw them pieces of bread sometimes," he said as he continued toward me. When he swiped his hair to the side, I saw he had aqua blue eyes and a lean face with a very distinct jaw line. He wasn't handsome, but he had an interesting face. As he drew closer, his eyes were penetrating, his gaze so fixed I felt a little uncomfortable. I noticed he was barefoot.

"Here," he said, pulling his right hand out of his jeans pocket and opening it before me. There were bread crumbs in his palm. "It's their favorite," he added. "Rye bread. You give it to them, and they'll be your friends forever. Go on, take it," he practically ordered.

I plucked some from his hand and cast the pieces into the water. The ducks hurried to them and began to bob. When they were finished they looked to me again.

"Best friends already," the boy said. "Quackie and Queenie, meet . . . tell them your name. Go on, they understand more than you think."

I shook my head and smiled. "I'm Grace Houston," I

told the ducks. They looked as if they bobbed their heads.

"You might as well give them the rest," the boy said, taking my hand forcefully, turning it palm up, and depositing the remaining pieces of bread in it. "Go on, don't tease them," he urged when I looked at him, a bit annoyed. I didn't like being ordered about so much, especially by a stranger.

I turned and tossed the pieces, and the ducks went for them again.

"Great. You're now an official duck feeder."

"Who are you?" I asked.

"On a summer day not unlike this one," he said, gazing around, "my parents decided in their infinite wisdom to name me Augustus Brewster. Anyone who wants to be friends with me calls me Auggie. My mother hates that and never fails to correct anyone. Fortunately, few listen. Now here's the funniest part. My dad calls me Gusty unless he is angry at me, which is quite often. Then he calls me Augustus, even Augustus Brewster, as in 'Augustus Brewster, what were you thinking when you put a firecracker in Miss Wilson's garbage pail last night?'

"I was, of course, thinking it would make a large boom and scare the panties off her, which I believe it did. I didn't tell my dad that. I just don't answer when he asks me why I do things, and he eventually gives up trying to understand me, saying something like 'Talking to you is like talking to the wall.'

"So, hi," he said. "Visiting someone?"

It took me a moment to digest everything.

"Close your mouth," he whispered. "There are tiny bugs that will think it's a place to sleep and propagate."

"Huh? Oh. No, I'm not visiting anyone. We just

moved in," I said, still amazed at how he spoke about himself and his parents to someone he had never before met.

"Moved in?" His eyebrows were hoisted. He considered a moment and then asked, "Unit fourteen?"

"Yes."

He nodded. "I knew she was trying to rent it. About a month ago she moved in with her lover, a recently divorced accountant. My mother is very good friends with Mrs. Dorahush, who knows everyone else's business even before they do. So don't try to hide anything from me. I'll know it soon anyway."

"Is that all you have to do, poke into everyone else's life?"

"No. I feed the ducks, too. You already know that," he said.

The ducks, seeing we weren't going to give them any more, set out for the other side of the pond.

"You know a lot of people here?" he asked.

"No. Just my mother's friend and her husband."

"Two? Well, that's already more than I know. I know about people, but I don't know any," he confessed.

I turned and grimaced. "You're kidding, right?"

"It depends on your definition of kidding and of knowing. In my opinion, which I'm told will carry a great deal of weight someday, people don't really get to know each other at all. Or let's say it's rare when they do. Which is fine," he added quickly. "It makes it all more interesting. You know, surprises, disappointments, little betrayals, big betrayals. For me most people are predictable, and that makes them very boring. I can't hide it, and they don't like it, so I have no real friends. *Comprenez?* That's French for . . ."

"I know what it is."

"Oh, *parlez vous francais?*"

"No, but I know some words. Do you speak French?" I wanted to add *big shot.*

"*Mais oui, et allemand et italien et un peu chinois. Mandarine.*"

"You speak German, Italian, and a little Chinese?"

"*Tres bien.* You do understand a little. Yes, to answer your question. Permit me to fully introduce myself. Augustus Brewster, genius extraordinaire. I was discovered in the second grade reading Dickens's *Tale of Two Cities* and promptly sent to the school psychologist, who decided I belonged in some special educational environment. You are now looking at one of a select dozen students attending a special government school preparing me to become a research scientist. They hope I'll invent a better bomb or bomb shelter or something."

"How old are you?"

"Chronologically, sixteen. Mentally, off the board. Probably about thirty. We are taking what would be considered graduate studies and beyond," he added dryly.

I tilted my head.

"Skeptical, eh? Go on, ask me anything. I am forbidden to be on any quiz or game show, and I have to register with them when I enter the cities from which they transmit."

"Yeah, right."

"What, no questions?" he challenged, folding his arms across his chest and pulling his shoulders up.

I thought a moment. *What he needs is someone to wipe that egotistical smile off his lips. All right, he asked for it,* I thought. Daddy was always proud of my knowledge of U.S. naval history.

"When was the first submarine used in U.S. combat?"

He pulled his head back. "Interesting choice for a challenge. It was in 1776, actually. Invented by David Bushnell, a small, egg-shaped craft constructed of wood and operated by one man who turned a propeller. The science was quite innovative. They submerged by admitting water and then surfaced by forcing it out with a hand pump. Fulton picked up on it and applied some of the principles to his *Nautilus*," he recited.

I guess my jaw had dropped so low flies or bees could form a hive in my mouth.

"Grace," I heard Mommy call, and turned toward our patio.

"Yes?"

"Dallas has to go. Come say goodbye," she cried.

"Okay. I'll be right there." I turned back to Augustus Brewster.

"Are you a history major or something?" he asked.

I shook my head.

"That was a surprising question. Most people ask me what's the tallest building in the world or who invented the telephone. Something ordinary," he added. "See? You're interesting already. I'm better off not knowing you."

He turned and marched off, taking long, quick strides, his head bowed, strands of hair flying about his temples. I watched him for a moment and then hurried back to our new home.

"Who was that?" Mommy asked, looking in Augustus's direction.

"I don't know. He lives here, but he's a very strange boy," I said.

"Now you've got it," Dallas told me. "They're all

strange. Always assume that about men, and you'll be fine. Call me if you need anything else, Jackie. 'Bye, Grace. I'll have Phoebe call you."

"Thanks, Dallas," Mommy said. They hugged again, and Dallas left.

We were alone for the first time in our new home.

We both looked about the condo for a moment, and then Mommy nodded.

"It's going to be harder than I thought," she said.

6

Augustus and Phoebe

For me that was an understatement. I couldn't even conceive of how hard it actually would be. It hit me when I went to my room and started to unpack my cartons of dolls and souvenirs. Each one stung me harder than the previous. In the end I decided to leave them all in the cartons and keep them in the closet.

"Why aren't you putting your things out and dressing up your room, honey?" Mommy asked after she came to my doorway to see how I was doing.

"I can't," I told her. "Maybe later."

She just nodded and walked away.

We spent the next few days learning about the area, where to shop for this or that. Dallas was a great help, advising about the best stores and setting us up with a doctor and a dentist.

"They all claim they're not taking new patients, so someone they have has to recommend. It's another scam, if you ask me, making you grateful you're giving them your business," Dallas told us.

The more time I spent with her, the more I liked her. Phoebe hadn't called me yet, and she was annoyed about it.

"That girl is so absent-minded," she told us, but I suspected it was more than just a matter of forgetfulness. It was more that she didn't want to be bothered with a younger girl. I did finally overhear Dallas tell Mommy that "the girl is just selfish, and Warren puts up with it. He's simply blind when it comes to her and her faults. He carries some unreasonable guilt for Petula's motorcycle death."

Thinking about forgetfulness, I figured that was the reason I still had not heard from Trent. The day after we had moved in I called to let him know where I was and how to reach me. He was already off to his summer baseball camp. His mother answered the phone, and after I explained who I was and what I wanted, she said she would give him the message. Since I hadn't heard from him and it was nearly a week after I had called, I assumed she had forgotten to tell him. Of course, it also occurred to me that she didn't want to tell him. However, I thought he was sure to ask because I had told him I would call. I waited another day and called again, this time getting an answering machine. I left the same message.

Even with all the time Mommy and I spent together those first few days, I still had time to myself and wandered down to the pond occasionally, curious about whether or not I would meet Augustus Brewster again. Despite his weirdness, I couldn't help but be interested in him. I brought bread crumbs for Quackie and Queenie, but Augustus didn't appear. I began to wonder if he even really lived there.

And then finally one day when I looked out toward the pond, I saw him sitting with his legs crossed, his arms hanging limply at his sides, facing the water. Intrigued, I left the house and approached him. I heard what I thought was him sounding a deep, low note. It sounded like "Oooommmmm." I stepped up beside him and saw he was indeed making that sound. His eyes were open, but he looked as if he couldn't see anything, almost as if he was blind.

"Hi," I said.

He stopped making the sound, but he didn't turn to me for a long moment. Then he tightened his arms and turned slowly toward me. He didn't speak.

"What are you doing?" I asked.

"I was in meditation, plugging into the great unknown. The ducks tell me you've been feeding them often."

"The ducks speak to you?"

"Of course. Everything speaks to me when I'm plugged into the great unknown. We're all one, all in the same vast spiritual sea!" he declared with such emphasis the veins in his neck strained against his skin.

"Where have you been?" I asked, trying to change the subject.

"Here."

"I haven't seen you," I said.

"That's because you're blind. Don't worry. Most people, nearly all people, matter of fact, are blind."

"You're weird," I told him, and turned to walk away.

He jumped up and seized me by the elbow. "Why? Because I talk about things that are strange and new to you? If you're afraid of what you don't know, you'll remain ignorant."

"I'm not afraid of what I don't know. I just know you're very weird."

"Okay," he said, embracing himself. "Define *weird*."

"You said you talk to the ducks and they talk to you."

"They speak to me in their way. Everything speaks to everything else in its way. You just have to learn how to listen and understand. Don't the trees tell us when the weather will change? Don't birds tell us when it's going to get colder? Doesn't the sea tell us when it's going to be rough? Doesn't a house tell us when it's about to topple or food tell us when it's spoiled? Well?"

"I suppose, if you think of things that way, that's true," I admitted.

"How else can you think of them? Look at Quackie and Queenie. You can see their anticipation. They're speaking to us. Don't be like most people and ignore all the communications. If you can understand the basic language and you free yourself of the obstacles, you can hear more important or deeper things in the world around you. Didn't you ever feel that way?" he asked. He looked as if he was hoping for the right answer.

I thought about the day Daddy died and the sea gull that had acted so strangely and had given me an eerie, cold feeling.

"Yes," I admitted.

"So there you are, Grace Houston. You're weird, too."

We stared at each other for a moment, and then I laughed. "You're still weirder than I am," I insisted.

"If *weird* means better at communicating with the world around me, I agree. But if you will let me, I'll show you how to be better at it."

I looked away. "I'm not sure I want to communicate more with this world," I muttered.

"You lost your father in a terrible accident. I know

what happened and why you and your mother moved here," he revealed in a single breath.

I looked up quickly.

"Mrs. Dorahush knows all," he declared, deepening his voice to pretend some supernatural events had occurred. "I'm sorry for you. I know you're very despondent, but if you learn to listen and see, you will realize your father isn't gone. He's just another form of energy now. He still communicates with you."

I squinted skeptically.

"I know, you're thinking I'm talking about all that silliness with seances and all, but this is different," he said, turning and raising his arm as if he was some Old Testament prophet. "It's out there, and it's in here," he said, spinning and poking me just above my breast. "C'mon," he added, before I could complain, "I'll show you some magic."

He started away and paused. "Don't be afraid."

"Where are we going?"

"To my laboratory, where I have created Frankenstein," he said, imitating Boris Karloff in a scary old movie. It made me laugh. I glanced back at the patio. Inside the condo Mommy was watching television, diverting her mind, following her favorite soap opera again.

"Okay," I said, "but I can't be too long."

He took long strides, his hair bouncing about his face. He was still barefoot. Today he wore a T-shirt with a picture of an atomic bomb explosion. Underneath was written, "Let there be light."

"Where do you get your T-shirts?" I asked him.

"I make them myself," he said. "I can make you whatever you want, or I'll give you one I've made. I've got a closet full. One size fits all."

We stopped at one of the bigger units. He looked around as if he were contemplating a burglary.

"Anything wrong?" I asked, still quite nervous about following him.

"I don't want to spook you," he said, "but not everything in the world is good. There are dark forces, too. Occasionally I sense them. I just wanted to be sure, that's all. We're clear," he said, and walked up to the patio door. He opened it and turned to me.

Dark forces? Was he teasing me, or did he really mean it?

"This is it," he said, nodding at the patio door.

It occurred to me that my mother had no idea where I was, and there was no one around to see me go into this home.

"I'll leave the door open if it makes you feel better, although it will probably be more of an invitation to bugs," he said, reading my mind.

I was thinking up a good excuse to leave quickly when suddenly I heard a voice, and a tall gray-haired woman appeared. She had her hair down in a rather long ponytail for someone who looked to be well into her late sixties, maybe seventy. She wore a one-piece house dress with a flower pattern and a pair of light blue sandals.

"Augustus, why are you leaving the door open?" she asked him, and then she saw me. "Oh! Is this . . ."

"Grace Houston, yes, Grandma," he told her.

She smiled at me. "Welcome, dear. You should come in quickly. We've had trouble with mosquitoes lately."

I walked in, and Augustus closed the door.

"I hope you and your mother are settled in okay," she said.

"Thank you. We're doing okay."

"I'm showing her my laboratory," Augustus said.

She studied him a moment to see if he was serious and then smiled. "Oh, that's fine. If you would like something cold to drink, please come to the kitchen. I'm working on our dinner."

I thanked her again and followed Augustus to a room. There was a sign on the door that read, "Enter at your own peril."

"So far it's worked," he said, nodding at it. "No intruders." He opened the door and stepped back for me to enter.

The walls were covered with computer sheets on which were printed sayings in a large font.

"What is all this?" I asked.

"Every time I come across a statement I think makes sense, I print it out and put it up."

There were quotes by great philosophers, people in history, and even some politicians, as well as rock stars and lines I recognized from songs. On the floor of the room were piles and piles of books and magazines. There was so much around it that his unmade bed looked lost. A computer was on with a moving picture of bubbles rising out of water, each with a tiny pop. Papers were stacked and scattered over the two long tables and the desk.

One of the closet doors had a sign on it that read, "Government nuclear site. Restricted."

"What's in there?" I asked.

"My laboratory," he said, and opened the door. It was a walk-in closet once. Now there was photographic equipment as well as a narrow long table upon which were mathematical equations seemingly randomly running over pages and pages. I gazed down at it all and shook my head. It was much higher math than I had ever seen, and it looked like one big mess.

"What is this?"

"My project. I'm working on time travel, converting matter into energy and then restructuring it."

"Like that movie about the fly?"

He smirked. "Hardly," he said. "This is real."

"And you're into photography?"

"That's how I make the T-shirts, among other things."

"How do you know where anything is?" I asked, astounded at the books and notepads piled on the floor here, too.

"Everything is in its place," he said, gazing about as if I was the one who was too disorganized. "You want Freud, I have Freud," he said, spinning and lifting a book off the top of a small stack. It was titled *The Interpretation of Dreams.* "You want Thoreau, here's Thoreau," he continued, slipping a book out from under another. "Plato?" He reached under a table. "Here's Plato."

I shook my head in amazement. I supposed he was brilliant. Maybe he would be a world-renowned thinker someday.

"Now for the magic," he said. "This way."

He directed me to the far right corner of his room, where he had a small table. On it was a tiny metal marble suspended in midair between two metal squares that were humming.

"How did you do that?"

He smiled. "Years ago people would believe I had magical powers. Magic is simply science not yet understood. The ball is caught between two opposing magnetic fields of equal power. Here," he said, plucking it from the air and handing it to me. "Say some gibberish, and put it back in the spot where it was. Abracadabra. Go on. Do it."

I took it and put it where I thought it had been, and it seemed to slip out of my fingers on its own and remain suspended. I jumped back, and he laughed.

"You're a wizard too, and now," he said, "people will call you weird."

I shook my head and gazed around the cluttered room again. "What do your parents say about all this?"

"Nothing," he replied quickly. "They pretend I don't exist. It's all right," he added. "I do the same in regard to them. We have a mutual nonexistence pact."

I thought for a moment. This wasn't that much bigger a unit than ours. Where would his parents sleep if his grandmother lived here, too?

"How about something cold to drink, dear?" she asked, coming to the door of his room. "Or perhaps you would like to stay to dinner with us. I have a pot roast."

"No, thank you. My mother must be wondering where I am. I have to get home," I said, joining her in the hall.

"Oh, well, please don't be a stranger," she said.

"My grandmother was a famous poet," Augustus said quickly.

"Oh, stop," she told him.

"Her poems are still reprinted in many magazines, and she is often asked to do readings of her works. The groups that ask her to read don't understand the poems, but they think themselves intellectuals for asking her and listening and nodding their heads. Right Granny?"

"Don't listen to him," she said, a blush coming into her cheeks.

"She plays guitar, too, and writes songs. She was at Woodstock. Do you know what that was?"

"Yes," I said, looking at her more closely. She had a pretty face and wore no makeup at all, not even lipstick.

Now I saw the necklace of precious stones around her neck.

"My grandmother was a hippie. She still is. She refuses to accept her AARP card and never takes senior citizen discounts."

"I simply don't understand why merely getting older entitles people to anything extra. We should be giving the discounts to teachers and nurses and social workers."

"Celebrities care only about themselves. Heroes care about others," he recited. "Right, Granny?"

"Yes," she said.

There was a moment of silence.

"I've got to get back to work," Augustus said. "See you at the pond," he added. "Don't forget to listen."

He turned and went back into his room, closing the door.

His grandmother smiled at me as if there was absolutely nothing wrong with that.

"I'd better get home," I said, and walked to the patio door. She followed and opened it for me.

"It's very nice of you to be friends with Augustus," she told me. "He has no friends, really. He's a brilliant boy. He's already achieved his high school diploma and is in home study, so he doesn't meet many people his age."

"You mean he doesn't attend a school?"

"Not in the ordinary way. He's in a special program. Once a week he goes to see his mentor. They expect big things from him."

"Why does he say his parents act as if he doesn't exist?"

"Is that what he said?" she asked. I nodded. She sighed deeply. "His parents have been dead for more than five years. A horrible, horrible car accident. You of all people know how devastating that can be, so don't blame him for whatever he creates to contend with it." She smiled. "Please give your mother my regards and best wishes. Tell her if there is anything I can do to help you two, please don't hesitate to call. I'm in the telephone book. Clarissa Dorahush," she added, smiled, and closed the patio door.

Dorahush? But I thought Augustus said . . .

For a moment I stood there and looked at her standing in the patio door window, and then I hurried away, a little terrified by what the pain of deep sorrow could do, even to someone with Augustus's incredible mind.

Phoebe Tremont finally called. When the phone rang I was hoping it was Trent, hoping he had finally been given the message. I practically lunged for the receiver.

"Is this, uh, Tracy?" she asked.

"Who?"

"Wait a minute," she said in an annoyed tone of voice. "Oh, Gracey."

"It's Grace Houston, yes," I said.

"This is Phoebe Tremont. My stepmother wanted me to call you to see how you are doing and if you would like to get together with me and some of my friends," she recited as if she was reading it from a cue card.

"Oh."

"You're going to attend my school, I understand. I feel sorry for you," she added, and laughed. Someone, a male, laughed behind her. "Anyway, can you go to the beach with me and a few of my friends tomorrow?"

"The beach?"

"Yes, that's a place with a lot of sand near the water," she said, and the boy behind her laughed again. "We'll pick you up about one. No one gets up too early these days. Bring a towel and a change of clothes. We'll probably go out later. Bring some money," she added.

"Oh, well . . ."

"Don't worry, I know where you live. My stepmother has it tattooed to the inside of my eyelids."

There was more laughter, and then the phone went dead.

"Who was it, honey?" Mommy asked. I told her. "Oh, that's nice. You should be meeting young people, normal young people," she added with wide eyes. I had told her about Augustus and his grandmother.

"Phoebe sounds weirder than Augustus," I muttered, but I couldn't help being somewhat excited about meeting girls and boys about my age who were what everyone would consider normal. Like Mommy, I needed some diversion, too.

I waited near the front door at one o'clock the next day. They didn't show up until nearly one-thirty. Mommy had gone to lunch with Dallas. She was doing better than I was, actually, and was thinking she would begin working this coming weekend. She wished me a good time, and I promised to call her later to let her know what we were doing.

I was beginning to think Phoebe wasn't going to show up at all when suddenly I heard a horn blaring and saw a classic old Cadillac convertible whip around the turn to our condo. It was as long as a boat and bright red with high rear fins. A boy with blond hair cropped short on the sides was driving. He wore a white athletic shirt and looked lean and sinewy like a tennis player. I really didn't know what Phoebe looked like, but I imagined she was the dark-haired girl in the front seat, practically sitting on the driver's lap. Another boy sat beside her.

He, too, had a short haircut but darker brown hair with a blond streak running through the middle.

Phoebe was in her bathing suit, a rather abbreviated two-piece. I had my bathing suit under a pair of dark blue shorts and a white halter. I wasn't sure what clothes to bring, so I had put a pair of jeans and a blouse in my bag along with my towel.

There were two other girls and another, younger-looking boy in the rear of the convertible. He had curly black hair. I noticed that while the others were laughing he looked very uncomfortable. One of the two girls in the rear looked much younger as well.

The driver pressed on his horn before I could open the door and step out.

"Come on," Phoebe cried the moment I appeared. "We're wasting precious time."

I hurried to the car.

"Hey," the boy on her right said as I stepped up. "I thought you said she was a kid. She looks older than you, Phoebe."

"She *is* a kid," Phoebe declared. "But you wouldn't know the difference, Wally."

"Hey, Randy, you lucked out," Wally told the younger boy in the rear seat.

He gazed at me with interest but dropped his eyes quickly when I looked at him. He had small facial features and a slim body, almost birdlike with thin wrists.

"All right, idiots," Phoebe said. "Grassy, this is Roger Winston," she said, tapping the driver on the top of his head. "He thinks he's my boyfriend, and for my own amusement I let him think it."

They all laughed, even Roger.

"You just met Wally Peters, who's never met a girl he didn't like."

"Ha, ha, very funny," Wally said.

"That's Ashley Morris," she continued, gesturing at the taller, older-looking girl in the rear seat.

"Hi," Ashley said. She had dark red hair but was plain-looking except for her nearly Kelly-green eyes. She, too, was in her bathing suit, a one-piece that revealed her heavy legs and wide hips.

"Her sister Posy and Randy Walker who is in your grade."

Posy smiled at me. She looked about twelve with red hair a shade lighter than her sister's. She was prettier, with the same beautiful green eyes.

"Hi," I said. "My name isn't Grassy, though. It's Grace," I told them.

"We decided to call you Grassy," Phoebe declared, as if that was that and there was nothing more to be said about it. "Let her in, Wally, and keep your hands to yourself," she ordered.

He smiled, opened the door, and pulled back the seat. Ashley and Posy moved to their right to make a place for me next to Randy, who looked as if he was trying to push the other side of the car farther out. I squeezed in beside him, and the moment Wally closed the door, Roger gunned the engine and made the tires squeal. They all screamed. He spun the car around, backed up, and shot forward.

As we headed for the front entrance of our complex, I caught sight of Augustus standing by his home. He had his hands behind his head as if he was lying back on the grass and looking up at the sky. His face was expressionless.

"Where are we going?" I asked.

"We were planning on going to the beach," Phoebe shouted. The wind was whipping us all because of the speed we were traveling. It was hard to hear. "But lucky us, Roger's parents are off to Bermuda with some friends for a couple of days, so we have the house. There's no beach, but it's on Singer Island in Sugar Sands. We have the boat, and we can water-ski, and there is a pool."

"Do you water-ski?" Posy asked me.

"No. I've never really done much boating at all."

"I thought your father was in the Navy," Ashley said. "Didn't you go in boats all the time?"

"No. He was a pilot," I said.

"I didn't know the Navy had planes," she replied.

I smiled to myself, remembering how proud Daddy was of the naval air command.

"You're so dumb, Ashley. Didn't you see Tom Cruise in that movie?" Wally asked her.

"I did, but I didn't know they were in the Navy."

"The Navy air command goes back to the Second World War," I said.

"See, Ashley, you shouldn't have failed history last year," Phoebe teased.

"I didn't fail. I almost failed."

"Your teacher gave you two points just to get rid of you," Wally told her.

"So? At least I passed," Ashley retorted. "Which is more than some people in this car can say."

The three in the front seat laughed. Who had failed? I wondered. Had all three? How could they laugh about that?

"How do you like living in Florida?" Posy asked me. Randy turned quickly to listen to my response.

"I haven't lived here very long," I said. "It's hotter than I expected."

"You get used to it," Ashley said. "I did."

"Like you have a choice," Wally told her.

She twisted her mouth and shook her head at him.

"Be nice, or I won't let you lick my face later," he threatened.

"Ugh, how gross," Posy cried.

"Didn't you tell your sister about that?"

"Shut up, Wally. He's an idiot," Ashley told me.

For a group of people who were supposed to be friends, they sure acted nasty to one another, I thought. How did they treat people they didn't like?

The first time Randy spoke I understood why he was so shy. He had a bad stutter.

"Are . . . yo . . . yo . . . you taking any, any, elect . . . electives?" he asked me.

"I don't know. I haven't been to the school yet," I said. "I don't know what's available and how much time I have."

"She's taking sex education, Randy. Maybe you can give her some pointers," Wally teased.

"Leave him alone," Roger said.

"Just trying to help him get started."

"Worry about yourself," Roger followed more firmly. He glanced at him, too.

Wally immediately retreated, pulled out a pack of cigarettes, and offered one to Phoebe. She took it, and he lit his and hers. The smoke came spiraling back at us. Phoebe turned to talk to me.

"So, you going to work in my father's restaurant, too?"

"Me? No," I said. "I don't think so. I've never been a waitress."

"We always need dishwashers or busboys."

"She's a girl, or haven't you noticed?" Wally said.

"Busgirl, like big deal."

"If I can help, I'll help," I said nonchalantly. She looked as if she didn't appreciate the fact that I wasn't frightened by the idea.

"Like it wouldn't hurt you to help out once in a while," Roger told her.

"Shut up," she snapped. She looked at me again, her eyebrows turned downward and in toward each other as if she was struggling with a deep thought. I noticed how twisting herself had deepened her cleavage and revealed more of her breasts. Wally was glued to the view.

"Your eyes are drooling," she told him, and he laughed and turned away, gazing quickly at Roger first.

Phoebe stared at me a moment longer and turned around again. "Can't you go any faster?" she asked Roger.

"Like I can afford to get another speeding ticket."

"I feel like we're on our way to an early-bird special," she said. Wally laughed hard.

"Damn it," Roger said, and accelerated. "If I get stopped . . ."

We were going so much faster now, my hair was snapping at my cheeks. Ashley crouched to lower herself below the front seat.

"Put your arm around her, Randy," Wally told him. "So she don't blow out of the car."

Posy was turned into the rear of the seat. We were whizzing past cars. I leaned forward to get a view of the dashboard and saw we were going ninety miles an hour.

"We're going too fast!" I cried.

"I thought you were the daughter of a Navy pilot," Phoebe shouted back at me, and laughed.

Finally we reached an exit and Roger slowed down. He wove the car through some side streets, and a little while later we came to a gated community. The guard recognized him and triggered the main gate. He watched us suspiciously as we passed through.

"That's Gerson Weiner, retiree with the big mouth. He'll tell my parents I had a few dozen people over for a party," Roger muttered.

His home was a white and pink stucco house with a screened-in pool and a three-car garage. It was right on the water, with its own dock. The rear section of the house had two stories. When the garage door went up I saw a black, late-model Mercedes convertible.

As soon as he turned off the engine, Phoebe spun around to face me. "Just remember, Grassy, whatever we do is our business and nobody else's, get it?"

"As long as we don't murder anyone, it's fine with me," I said, and everyone but Phoebe laughed, even Randy. She poked Wally in the ribs.

"Open the door already," she ordered, visibly annoyed, and he jumped out.

She got out, and I saw she was taller than I thought, with a slim waist. The bottom of her two-piece was cut sharply, leaving less and less to the imagination.

We all got out and followed her and Roger into the house. It was a beautiful home. Everything in it looked new. There were many windows and patio doors providing natural light. The decor was Spanish, with tiled floors and expensive-looking artifacts, vases, statuary in the halls, and vibrantly painted scenes in gilded frames.

Phoebe moved through the house as if it were hers. She went directly through the den to the patio doors that faced the pool and the dock.

"C'mon," she urged the rest of us. "We wasted enough time diverting to pick up Grassy."

"My name's not Grassy," I muttered, mostly under my breath. Randy heard me and smiled.

"I won't, won't ca . . . call you that," he promised.

Roger led the way to the dock, where there was a good-size motorboat.

"It's a 2500 LSR Regal," Wally told me, as if he was the proud owner. "Powerful, 310 horse."

"Help me get ready instead of gabbing," Roger ordered. "You, too, Randy."

"Where's your bathing suit?" Ashley asked me.

"I have it on underneath."

"Leave your clothes in the cabana by the pool," Phoebe commanded. "Put on some sun screen. I don't want to have my stepmother on my back because you got sunburned."

"I brought it along," I said.

"Good for you," she said. "C'mon, Ashley. I want you to help me with something."

Posy followed me to the cabana. She had her bathing suit on under her shorts and blouse, too.

"Do you all go boating here often?" I asked her.

"I've been along only once before."

"How old are you, Posy?"

"I'm thirteen next month. Don't worry. I'm not a blabbermouth," she said with feigned sophistication.

"Blabbermouth about what?" I asked as I folded my clothes and put them in the bag.

"Anything," she replied, heading out.

"Who's going to be first today?" Wally cried from the boat when we walked onto the dock. Phoebe and Ashley were already on the boat. Ashley sat in the rear, but Phoebe was lying on the front, sunning herself.

"Why don't you show everyone how to do it first, Wally?" Roger said.

"Sure. No problem," he said. He wasn't as slim and muscular as Roger, and I thought his bathing suit was too tight and revealing.

"See something you like?" he asked me. I couldn't help blushing and moved quickly to a seat. Roger started the engine, and we moved away from the dock.

"Better get down here," he called to Phoebe.

She rose and made her way beside him. Roger gunned the engine, and we were bouncing over the waves. Ashley and Posy screamed with glee. Randy was smiling, and Wally was finding music on the CD unit. I couldn't help but be excited. The water, the sunshine, and the wind were all invigorating.

"Like Florida a little more now?" Ashley shouted at me.

I nodded, smiling. I saw Phoebe gaze at me and turn back to whisper something in Roger's ear. They both laughed, and he slowed down.

"Get in the water, Wally. We don't have all day. Stop fiddling with the music. Who the hell can hear it anyway?"

"Right, right," Wally said. "Prepare yourself for a real treat," he told me, and slipped on a life vest. Then he dropped the skis into the water and jumped in.

Phoebe attended to the line and handle and moments later signaled to Roger that Wally was ready. He began to accelerate the boat, and Wally rose out of the water. I was genuinely surprised at how agile he looked and how well he moved, bouncing on the waves, following the wake the boat created. Very soon he was showing off, lifting one leg and skiing with only one.

Phoebe said something to Roger, and he began to

speed up and turn the boat more sharply. Wally did his
best but finally took a flop, flipping over in the water,
the rope and handle flying ahead and bouncing over the
waves.

"Is he all right?" I cried.

"He's fine," Ashley said.

We circled until he was alongside the boat. Phoebe
reeled in the line and handle.

"You bastard, Winston!" he shouted.

Roger gunned the engine and pulled away from him,
leaving him bobbing in the water. We could hear him
screaming. Roger made a wider circle, leaving him
there longer. When we pulled up alongside him this
time, he was silent.

"Nice," he said, climbing aboard.

"You ready to try it?" Phoebe asked me. I looked at
the others. Randy looked worried.

"I don't think so," I said.

"What do you mean, you don't think so? We wasted
time and money picking you up. How many kids your
age get this kind of an opportunity?" Phoebe snapped at
me. "You want to be with us, you've got to be initiated.
Get in the water. Wally, get back in there with her, and
show her how to set up."

"Sure," he said eagerly.

"We're too far out in the ocean," I moaned.

"Oh, we are not. Like you really were a Navy person. Roger, tell her."

"We're very close to shore here, and these are relatively calm waters. Nothing is going to happen to you.
Once you're up, you'll love it," he said.

"Everyone here has done it," Phoebe insisted.

I looked at Randy. He looked down, which was
enough to tell me that it wasn't so. Nevertheless I could

see Phoebe wasn't going to be satisfied until I tried to water-ski.

"Okay," I said.

Randy handed me a life vest, and I slipped it on. My legs were trembling, but I sat on the edge of the boat and slowly dropped into the water. It was warmer than I had expected. Wally dove in and brought me the skis. He fit my feet into each one. My legs were going every which way on their own.

Phoebe threw the rope, nearly hitting me with the handle.

"All right," Wally said. "This is easy. Hold the handle here," he instructed. "Get the rope between your skis, points up. Come on."

"I'm trying."

"Get them up," he urged, and then he came around behind me and took hold of the handle, making me pull it closer to me. "I'll help you get those skis up," he said. He put his hands on my waist. "Come on, point them up."

I did it, and he dropped his hands to my rear end, cupping it and lifting me.

"Now isn't this nice?" he said.

"No!" I cried.

"As the rope tightens, tighten your legs and stand up. When you're up, relax your legs. Think of them as springs and go with the bounce. Don't fight it, and don't lean forward. Let the boat do the work.

"She's ready!" he cried.

My heart was pounding. Roger moved the boat forward, and I felt the pressure.

"Lean back!" Wally screamed.

I tried, but I went forward instead and fell on my face. The rope was ripped out of my fingers. I swallowed some salt water and coughed and choked. Wally was at my side.

"You've got to lean back and let the boat do the work, and you didn't tighten your legs and stand."

"It was going too fast."

"No," he said. "It has to move at least that fast."

They brought the boat around again.

"You get only three chances," Phoebe said. "If you don't stand after three, you're the gofer for the day."

"What's that?"

"You go for anything we ask you to get, and you do anything we ask you to do," she replied.

"Here we go again," Wally said, setting me up.

The boat started away. This time I held on a lot better and actually started to stand, but I leaned too far to the left and fell again. I held on to the rope too long and got dragged a little. However, I kept my mouth closed and didn't swallow any water.

I bobbed and waited until the boat came around.

"Three strikes and you're out," Phoebe warned.

"Oh, she nee . . . need, need, needs more of a chance," Randy said.

"You want to be next?" Phoebe snapped at him.

"No."

"So shut up. Get her ready, Wally."

"I'm on it," he said. His hands were on my rear end again, only this time they were sliding in between my legs. I tried to wiggle free of him. He laughed, and then the boat went forward. I held on tightly, stiffened my legs, and rose out of the water. I was standing and skiing. I know I didn't look too good because I was falling forward and then pulling back, but I was going, and it was exciting.

When Roger sped up, I felt my heart leap out of my

chest. It frightened me, and I let go of the handle. I sank slowly into the water, the rope and the handle bouncing on the waves, but I did feel successful.

They brought the boat around faster. Phoebe glared down at me. "Why did you let go?"

"You were going too fast. I couldn't keep up," I said.

"She's, she's ri . . . right," Randy said. "She needs to go slower fir . . . fir . . ."

"Oh shut up," Phoebe said. "We don't have all day to waste on her. Get in the boat," she ordered. "Wally."

He was right behind me, pushing up on my rear. It made me move faster and slip over the edge.

"That wasn't bad," Posy told me. "For the first time."

"It was pathetic," Phoebe said.

"Why don't you go next and show me how it's done?" I asked her.

Everyone waited to see what she would say.

"I'm not in the mood. I'm in the mood to mellow out instead," she announced.

Roger smiled. "Sounds like a plan. Wally, reel in the rope for now," he ordered.

"Let Ra . . . Ra . . . Randy do it," he said.

Roger turned on him. "I asked you to do it," he said firmly.

"All right, all right."

Whatever Roger's bad qualities were, I thought, he was at least protective of Randy.

While Wally gathered in the rope and the skis, Phoebe opened a cooler that had no ice in it. She brought out a plastic bag and unraveled the string around it. Then she dipped into it and plucked out what was clearly a joint.

"Go slowly," she ordered as she distributed one to each of us. "We're getting low on our stash."

"You can have mine," I said, handing it back to her.

She looked at me with disgust. "It makes me nervous to smoke in front of someone who doesn't," she said, and gestured at the others. "It makes us all nervous. You wanted to be with us. You had your mother beg Dallas to get me to call you."

"I didn't ask my mother to beg."

"Well, you're here, and you're with us, so be with us or get out."

"Get out?"

"Swim home," she said.

I looked shocked, I'm sure.

Then she laughed. "Forget it. I heard about the way you lived on naval bases, saluting everyone. You're about to get a real education now that you're in the real world," she said.

"I *was* in the real world."

"Anchors aweigh," she told the others, and lit her joint. They all lit theirs, too.

"What are you so uptight about, Grassy?" Roger asked me. "It's just a little pot. No big deal."

"It's illegal, and it leads to other things."

"What other things?" Wally asked. He leered at me. "You mean sex?"

"No. I mean other drugs."

"So what did you Navy kids do for fun?" Phoebe asked. She was leaning back against Roger. Wally was now in Ashley's lap. "Play spin the bottle?"

"I don't mind playing that if it's strip spin the bottle," Wally said.

"Is that what you did?" Phoebe asked me quickly, sounding like a prosecutor in a courtroom. Everyone looked at me in anticipation.

"No, of course not."

"So, what did you do for fun, or are you just too ashamed to say?"

"Sta, sta, stop pick . . . pickin' on her," Randy suddenly cried.

It turned everyone's attention to him.

"Well, look who's the knight in shining armor," Wally said.

"He's right. I'm tired of it," Roger declared.

Phoebe sat up and turned on him. "Is that so? Like what . . ."

"Hey," Ashley said, "what kind of boat is that coming toward us?"

Roger sat up to look. "Damn," he said. "Quick, throw it all overboard. Quick!" he screamed. "It's a Coast Guard boat!"

Everyone scrambled to the other side and threw their pot into the water. Roger dropped the plastic bag over the edge and went to the controls. He started the engine and turned the boat slowly toward the dock.

The Coast Guard patrol boat followed alongside, a cadet watching us through binoculars.

"Nobody do anything stupid," Roger ordered. "Look like we're just out here having fun."

"Aren't we?" I mumbled.

The Coast Guard boat veered away as we drew closer to the dock.

"That was close," Roger said.

"We just wasted everything, Roger! We didn't have to throw it all overboard!" Phoebe shouted at him.

They started to bicker louder. Everyone else tried to ignore them. Wally jumped onto the dock and tied the boat down.

"Thanks for bringing us good luck," Phoebe snapped at me as she stepped past me.

"What are you blaming her for?" Roger asked, smiling.

"We threw away a few hundred dollars' worth of dope," she reminded him with her hands on her hips and her head wagging. She turned to me. "I bet you're satisfied."

"Did you ever wonder why they call it that?" I asked her.

"What?"

"Dope," I said.

And Randy laughed so loud everyone but Phoebe did, too.

She just walked off in a huff.

7

A Game of Secrets

Phoebe was unforgiving. She was obviously used to lording it over her friends. She was pretty, sophisticated, and bubbling over with self-confidence. The new girl on the block, me, wasn't supposed to present any sort of challenge, especially a younger girl. Recognizing that, I tried not to say or do anything else that would annoy or challenge her. I was afraid of what she would tell Dallas about me, and I was afraid of how it would affect Mommy.

Now that their pot was gone, they turned to the bar. Posy and I went to the cabana and changed out of our bathing suits.

"I can see Randy really likes you," she said. "He's never had a girlfriend because of how he talks."

"That shouldn't matter so much. He's nice."

"Was it true about your father? He was shot down in his airplane?"

"Who told you that?"

"Wally said that's what Phoebe told him."

"No, it was a terrible helicopter accident. He was an instructor at the naval base."

"Oh. Were you close?"

"Yes, of course. Aren't you close to your parents?"

"Our parents are divorced. My father lives in Miami with his girlfriend. We don't see him that often. He even missed my birthday this year."

"I'm sorry," I said.

She shrugged. "My father was the one who named me Posy. My mother didn't want me to have that name. She's always trying to get me to change it to Paula or something."

"Why?"

"It was my father's first girlfriend's name. At least that's what she says."

"He named you after his first girlfriend? Why did your mother go along with that?"

"She says she didn't know at the time. Maybe it's not true. They're always saying nasty things about each other now. Anyway, I like my name. You have a nice name. I don't mean Grassy," she added.

"Thanks." I thought a moment. "My father used to call me Sailor Girl."

"Did you have a uniform and everything?"

"No," I said, laughing. "It was just a nickname."

"That's what my mother says about my name: It's just a nickname, not a real name."

"If you're happy with it, I guess it's all right," I said.

She looked happy about that.

When we entered the house they were all in the den listening to music. Roger, Wally, Ashley, and Phoebe were talking about the upcoming school year. It

sounded like mostly complaints about getting up earlier, having to study, the new teachers they disliked.
Was it school or prison?

Everyone had a drink in his or her hands, and no
one's looked like a soft drink.

"What's yours?" Roger asked me. He was behind the
bar.

It was a beautiful room with a white marble floor, a
pool table, leather furniture, and a large-screen television. I glanced at Phoebe and saw she was just waiting
to pounce on me if I said I didn't drink. The only time I
ever drank I had a little of my mother's vodka and
orange juice, a drink they called a screwdriver.

"Screwdriver," I said.

"All right, Grassy. Good choice," Roger declared,
and began to prepare it. He poured in nearly half a glass
of vodka before adding the orange juice and ice cubes.
He looked at Phoebe, who smirked and lay back on the
sofa. She was still in her bathing suit.

"I still can't believe you threw away all that pot,
Roger," she complained.

"Get over it," he said, handing me my drink.

"I will when you replace it," she shot back at him.

"No problem." He smiled at me. "I bet you could be
court-martialed or something for having drugs on a
Navy base, huh?" he asked.

"It would be very serious, yes, especially if it
involved officers who are in charge of many men and
expensive equipment. It has a serious, detrimental
effect on your judgment."

"Oh, spare me," Phoebe moaned. She sipped her
drink and narrowed her eyes.

I sipped mine and looked at some of the plaques on
the wall. They were mostly for winning golf tourna-

ments, and most of them looked as if they had been awarded to Roger's mother.

"This feels like a drag," Phoebe said. "Let's spice it up. Let's play secrets."

"Yeah," Wally said eagerly, rubbing his hands together. "Let's."

"What's that?" I asked, since everyone else seemed to know what it was.

"Get the cards," she ordered Roger without answering me.

He went behind the bar and brought out a deck.

"Gather 'round," Phoebe commanded.

"What are we doing?" I asked.

"You'll see," Ashley said, enjoying knowing something I did not.

Everyone moved to a tighter circle at Phoebe's feet. Roger handed Phoebe the deck, bowed his head, and said, "Your wish is my command, your majesty."

"Sit down," she ordered.

"I'd like to know what it is we're playing," I told Phoebe.

"Everyone gets a card, one card each round," she explained. "The one with the lowest in value has to reveal a secret, and if we don't think it's much of a secret, he or she takes off an article of clothing. As you can see, I'm at a big disadvantage since I'm the only one still in a bathing suit."

"Who can say if someone's secret isn't much?" I asked.

"Are you suggesting we would all be unfair? Besides, it has to be a unanimous rejection, so don't worry about it, Grassy."

"I don't like to be called that. It makes me sound like a pothead," I declared.

"You're far from that," Phoebe agreed. "Okay, I'll think of a new name for you."

"What's wrong with my name as it is?"

"It sounds too goody-goody. Grace," she spat disdainfully. "Don't worry about it. Let's begin." She dealt each of us a card. "One additional rule. If you don't think you have the lowest card, or even if you think you do, you can refuse to show it. Someone can challenge you. If yours isn't the lowest, you get a pass when you get the lowest. If it is, you have to reveal two secrets."

"What happens to the person who challenges?"

"No one ever asked that before," Wally said.

"She's smart," Ashley said. Phoebe glared at her, and she looked down.

"If you don't have the lowest, that person has to reveal his or her secret even though he or she doesn't have the lowest card. So there's risk on both ends."

"The person challenging should have to reveal two secrets, too," I said. "To make it logical and fair."

"All right, two. Satisfied? Damn. This isn't some school game."

"Forcing people to tell secrets can backfire on everyone," I advised them.

"Oh, please, stop being such a . . . a Grace," she said, and gave me those narrow eyes again, dark brown streaks of suspicion. "I bet you're still a virgin."

"Hey, that could be one of her secrets," Roger chimed in.

"Right. Only one look at her, and see it's not much of a secret," Phoebe quipped. "So don't try to use it," she warned me. "All right, check your cards and make your moves. Who is confident?"

"I am," Wally said, and put a king on the floor.

"Lucky creep," Roger said. He revealed a seven of spades.

Phoebe looked at me. "Tell you what, Grace," she said. "I'll challenge you and make the game exciting right away."

"But I haven't refused to show my card."

"That's all right. I threw a challenge anyway, and like I said, if I have a higher card than you have, you reveal a secret even if you don't have the lowest card in the group. If I don't, I have to reveal a secret."

"I don't remember being able to do that," Ashley said. "You always had to wait for someone to refuse."

"We can make up new rules as we go along. That's the fun of it," Phoebe snapped at her. "Well?" she asked, looking at me. "Accept or decline the challenge?"

"It doesn't make any sense," I said. "If I had the lowest card in the group, I'd lose. I would lose either way."

"Someone could have lower than you, unless you have an ace." I could see she was wondering if I did have an ace. "We value an ace as a one the first round and then every other round."

"Since when have we decided that?"

Phoebe turned on Ashley sharply again, and she bit her lower lip and looked away.

"Accept or decline?" Phoebe demanded of me.

I looked at the card in my hand. I could feel everyone's eyes on me. I thought back to when Daddy and I played cards. He taught me gin rummy and showed me how important it was to keep in mind what everyone picked up. He also taught me blackjack and how important it was to have a face that was unreadable. I gazed at Phoebe.

"I bid two secrets," I said.

"What?"

"If I lose I give two, and if I win you give two. Back to the original gamble. You said we could make rules as we went along," I added.

"You did say that, Phoebe," Roger reminded her with a smile.

"I know what I said." She looked at her card and at me.

"All right, two secrets," she said.

I stared at my card. "Let's make it two secrets and one article of clothing."

"You already made the bet," she complained.

"It's called seeing and raising."

"Hey, she's played cards before," Wally cried with glee. "That's what they did on the Navy base, I bet. What did you play, strip poker?"

"How much will you bet to find out?" I asked him, and Ashley and Roger laughed. Posy looked at me with surprise, and Randy smiled. Only Phoebe looked unhappy.

"Match her bet, Phoebe, or give up two secrets," Roger told her.

"Shut up, you idiot. Most of my secrets have to do with you."

"I'm not ashamed of anything," he said.

"Are you sure?" she asked, looking directly into his face.

He shrugged and sipped more of his drink, shifting his eyes in retreat from her penetrating gaze.

Phoebe was glaring at me again, deciding. I kept my face as bland as I could, remembering Daddy's advice to think of something entirely different when trying to hide your thoughts about your cards.

"It wouldn't be a fair bet," she concluded. "You're

wearing too many more articles of clothing than I am."

"You didn't complain about the risk before," Wally reminded her.

"Well, I am now. This is different. The rules are changed."

"You sa . . . sa . . . said we could change them," Randy piped up.

She narrowed her eyes and considered me again. I tried not to blink. "Okay, Grace face, I'll match your bet if you strip down to a bra and panties first," she said, smiling at her brilliant rejoinder.

"All right now," Wally cried, clapping his hands. "This is getting interesting."

"Do it. It's the same as a bathing suit," Roger told me.

Phoebe looked so self-satisfied. My reluctance was giving her the upper hand again. She was positive I would crumble.

"Remember," she sang, "two secrets if you fold."

"And an article of clothing anyway," Wally added.

Without speaking, I began to slip off my sneakers. No one uttered a sound. All eyes were on me again when I stood up and undid my skirt. Phoebe started to squirm.

"Wait a minute!" she cried, holding her hand out. "What the hell are we doing this for? It's only making these boys excited and at our expense."

Roger and Wally groaned.

"What do we do?" I asked her.

"We're changing the game. It will be the four of us girls against the three of them."

"Oh, no," Roger cried. "I want Grace on my team if we're having teams."

"Forget it then," Phoebe snapped, and rose to her feet. "I'm going swimming."

"Wait," Wally called as she started toward the patio door that opened to the pool. "Let's just see what would have happened."

He turned over her card. It was a ten of diamonds. Then he looked at me.

"C'mon," he said. "It doesn't matter now."

I looked at Phoebe. Then I handed him the card, and he bellowed.

"What?" Roger demanded.

He turned my card around to show them. It was a three of hearts.

Phoebe's face took on a shade of red that resembled a fresh strawberry. She spun on her heels and marched out of the room, diving right into the pool.

"I wouldn't turn my back on her if I were you," Roger said, but with a look of admiration in his eyes. "Maybe you'll teach me how to play cards like that," he added with a wink, and went to join her.

Wally and Ashley followed.

"I'm putting my suit on again," Posy said. "I don't care what anyone says. This is proving to be an exciting day." She rushed out.

Randy sat with me. I looked at him and then went to the bar and poured out the remainder of my drink. I replaced it with straight orange juice.

"There's far too much vodka in this. It will make me sick," I explained.

He just smiled. I gazed at the others through the patio door.

"You di . . . di . . . did good at se . . . secrets," he said.

"I didn't want to get into any arguments with her."

"Everybod . . . bod . . . body gets into ar . . . arguments with Phoebe. She doesn't care."

I shook my head. "I don't know why anyone would

like that," I said, and went to the bookcase. There were shelves of expensive-looking leatherbound classics, including Shakespeare.

Randy came up beside me.

"What does Roger's father do for a living?" I asked as I checked out all the titles and authors.

"He's a deve . . . deve . . ." He closed his eyes, struggling with the word. I could feel his frustration.

"Take your time," I said.

"Developer. He owns a mall in Boca Ra . . . Ra . . . Raton."

I plucked out a copy of *Romeo and Juliet* and flipped through the pages.

"My favorite," I said. "Did you read it in class?"

He shook his head. "Not yet."

"I have a quote for Phoebe. So she won't struggle so hard trying to come up with something to call me," I told him, and pointed to some lines. " 'What's in a name?' " I recited. " 'That which we call a rose by any other name would smell as sweet.' "

"Show her," he told me. "May . . . maybe she'll shut . . . shut up."

We both laughed.

"What's so funny?" Posy asked on her way through to the pool.

"None . . . none . . . none of your business," Randy told her. She grimaced and went out. "We can . . . can have our own se . . . secret without the cards," he said.

I smiled at him. "I won't tell if you won't," I said, and he beamed.

We sat on the sofa, and I described what it was like living on a naval base and being around ships and sailors, planes and helicopters.

"It sou . . . sounds like fun," he said.

"It was exciting," I said, remembering.

"I hate to break up this love fest, but we're going for pizza," Phoebe announced. She marched past us and down the hallway.

Roger, Wally, Ashley, and Posy came in behind her.

"Be careful, Randy. You're dealing with a card shark. She'll have your pants off before you know it," Wally said.

"He'd like that," Ashley quipped.

"So would you," Randy countered.

"Well, whaddya know, he didn't stutter that time," Roger said, smiling. "She must be doing something right."

He jabbed Wally in the ribs, and they all went to change.

It was as if Phoebe had decided to make me invisible. She asked me no questions, and she directed no remarks my way. Whenever anyone else spoke to me she immediately changed the subject. Actually I felt more comfortable with that. All her barbs and sarcastic arrows were shot at different targets. She enjoyed picking on Ashley. I assumed she wanted her around for that purpose only, and Ashley was so grateful for being permitted to be in the company of the prince and princess of the school, she took the punishment, practically thanking Phoebe for remembering she was there, even if it was only to belittle her.

A number of times I felt the urge to come to her defense but quickly realized that Ashley would appreciate it the least. If there was anything she didn't want it was to ally herself with someone Phoebe didn't favor.

I phoned Mommy right before we left for the restaurant, which was in Boca Raton in Roger's father's mall.

"Are you having fun, honey?" Mommy asked.

It was always hard for me to lie to her. My voice would betray me even if with all my heart I wanted to hide something from her.

"I'm all right," I replied.

"It's always hard making new friends," she said. I could hear the trembling in her voice and knew that despite the happy faces she was putting on she was still crying inside. I didn't have to add any of my little problems to her heavy burden.

"I know. I like this boy who is in my class. He's sweet," I told her.

"Oh, great. Have a good time," she said.

After we had pizza we wandered through the mall. Randy and I broke off from the others and went to the bookstore. He found a book about the U.S. Navy and decided to buy it.

"You'll know more about the Navy than I do," I said, laughing.

"Good," he said.

When we met up with the others Wally made Randy show him what he had bought and teased him about it all the way back to West Palm Beach.

"She'll make a sailor of you yet, Randy," he told him.

I noticed how Phoebe sat quietly, holding a small, icy smile on her lips. As it turned out, she was like a submarine slinking its way silently under the sea until it was in position to launch its deadly attack.

We had pulled into my condo development and up to my new home before she fired at me.

"I'll ca . . . ca . . . call you," Randy practically whispered.

I nodded with a smile and got out of the car.

"Maybe I'll see you at the restaurant," Phoebe said, sounding very pleasant.

"Okay."

"Until then, good night, Sailor Girl," she said, and followed it with a laugh that Wally and Ashley quickly joined in chorus. Roger smiled and shook his head.

It was truly as if I had been hit by a dart in the chest. I turned quickly to Posy, who was smiling but directing her eyes toward the stars. I could feel the tears burning under my eyelids, but I would die before I ever shed one because of something Phoebe did or said. That was a vow I quickly took.

"Gee, Posy," I said, "and you didn't even have the lowest card."

There was a moment of deep silence, and then Roger burst into laughter.

"Let's get out of here," Phoebe ordered. He began to accelerate but kept laughing and shaking his head. I watched them turn and then drive away, Randy looking back at me as they disappeared around the turn, the music from the car's CD first shattering the night and then drifting off with them.

"Those your new best friends?" I heard, and turned to see Augustus standing in the darkest shadows by our home.

"Hardly," I replied.

He stepped forward into the light spilling down from the front of the condo, his hands in his pockets. This time he wore a black T-shirt with a large eye at the center of his chest.

"Don't you ever wear shoes?" I asked him.

He looked down at his feet as if he hadn't realized he was barefoot. "Just forgot," he replied.

"Just forgot?"

"Once I almost went to school without shoes. My grandmother caught me getting into the car and sent me back for them."

I shook my head.

"Where did your not new friends take you?" he asked.

"To the driver's home. His family has a boat. We went water-skiing. Or I tried, I should say. Then we went to Boca Raton and had pizza and hung at a mall for a while."

"Sounds like you're going to fit right in after all," he said with some disdain.

"I'm not as sure as you are."

He raised his eyebrows with interest. "Disillusionment is the first step toward rebirth," he quoted.

"Right now I just want to get some sleep and leave my rebirth for tomorrow. How is your project coming along?"

"Today I finally figured out how to dissolve myself, metamorphose into pure energy, and disappear. What I haven't figured out is how to reappear.

"Maybe I won't bother," he added, and retreated again to the shadows. He was gone so quickly I wondered if he had just done what he claimed he could.

Mommy was waiting for me. She turned off the television as soon as I came into the condo.

"Hi," she sang, dressing her voice in bells. "Was it a nice mall? Was the pizza good? What's Phoebe like?" She fired her questions in machine-gun fashion, which was something she and I used to do to each other all the time. It made me laugh.

"She's a spoiled brat," I said, sitting across from her.

Mommy nodded. "Dallas as much as admitted that. Wasn't she nice to you at all?"

"She's too concerned with being the center of attraction. She's older than I am, so I don't see myself hanging around much with her anyway, Mommy."

"Well, you'll pick and choose your friends carefully. You always do. Daddy was always impressed with that."

I nodded, and we were both silent.

"Oh," Mommy said, "that nice boy back in Norfolk called for you."

"Trent?"

"Yes. He said he didn't find out you had called until today, and he apologized. He left a number. It's by the phone."

"Great," I said, jumping up. It was too late to call, but I took the slip of paper with his number to my room and kept it beside my bed. One of the first things I did the next morning was call.

"Hey," he said when he came to the phone. "How are you?"

"Okay," I said. Anyone could tell my okay was not okay, but he went right into a description of his baseball camp, the coach he had who had been a major league pitcher, and how much he was learning.

"I struck out twelve batters yesterday," he bragged. "And he says I hit better than most pitchers hit. I have a natural ability."

"That's wonderful, Trent."

"I wish you were coming back to our school," he finally said.

"Me, too."

"I'll try to keep in touch. I'll send you the sports pages from the school paper when the baseball season starts," he promised.

"Okay."

"Gee, I gotta go," he said. "Take care of yourself."

I could actually feel his hand slipping out of mine. Time and distance were too much to overcome. We were going in different directions.

"Goodbye," I said.

The click brought down a lead curtain between us.

Maybe Augustus wasn't all that weird after all, I thought. Maybe we disappear more often than we think.

As she had planned, Mommy began working on the weekend. For the first few weeks Dallas and Warren thought it would be best for her to serve alongside a seasoned waitress. Even so, she came home tired, mostly, I thought, from the emotional strain of worrying about whether she was doing things right. She would flop in our big easy chair and put her feet up on the hassock. I would take off her shoes and rub her feet for her while she moaned with pleasure.

"I've got to get the right shoes for this. There's so much walking involved. You don't sit from the moment you arrive till the moment you get into your car, but at least it isn't boring. They do have some very interesting customers, many, as Dallas said, from Palm Beach. Sometimes, the place is glittering with enough jewelry to light up a football stadium. They do tip well, though," she said with a smile.

I knew she didn't like leaving me at home alone, but Randy called me on that first weekend to invite me to a movie at the nearby theater. He gave me the bus schedule and the station as well, since neither he nor I was old enough to drive or had a car available anyway. I told Mommy, who thought it was wonderful I had a date already.

I saw Augustus that morning and asked him if he

ever went to the movies. He looked at me for a long moment and said, "Every night. In here." He pointed to his own head. I thought about inviting him along but decided to leave that for another time.

Randy was waiting for me at the bus stop near the mall. He was very eager to show off his knowledge of the U.S. Navy and talked about the different ships. I knew how much he wanted to impress me, and I was flattered, but after the movie, when he returned to talking about the Navy, I reached across the table in the restaurant where we were having some ice cream and put my hand over his to stop him.

"Thanks for learning all that, Randy," I told him. "But every time we talk about the Navy now, I think about my father, and it's painful for me."

I said it as simply and as softly as I could.

"Oh," he said, his eyes filling with some panic. "I . . . I . . ."

"It's okay. I love that you learned all that, but let's talk about you, too. And tell me all about the school and our teachers," I suggested.

We had a good time then, and he insisted on riding the bus back to my station and walking me to my door.

"But then you'll have to wait so long for another bus, and you won't get home until so late," I said.

He had told me he was the youngest of three boys and that his older brothers were now in college, both very athletic and both good students. His father worked in the city water department and had a managerial position. His mother was a grade-school teacher.

It wasn't difficult to see that he had always felt inferior to his brothers and always believed his parents loved him less because of his speech problem.

"That's why I . . . I like to work wi . . . with com . . .

com . . . puters," he said. "No one know . . . knows how I spe . . . speak."

I told him I had never had one and that my father was going to get one for me when we had settled into our new home in Norfolk.

"I'll hel . . . help you ge . . . get one," he offered. Despite my pleas, he accompanied me home and walked me to the condo. When we got there, we found Augustus lying on our front lawn, looking up at the sky.

"Who . . . who . . . who's that?" Randy asked with some concern.

"His name is Augustus Brewster. He lives in one of the units. He's a genius and goes to a special school," I explained quickly. "Don't worry. He does whatever he wants at the spur of the moment. Augustus?" I called, and he sat up.

"Oh, I was looking for you. I wanted to tell you about this movie I saw tonight," he said excitedly. He looked at Randy. "You're the boy in the backseat," he said, pointing his forefinger at him.

"Wha . . . what?"

"This is Randy, Augustus."

"Right. Do you want to hear about this movie or not?"

"Sure," Randy said. "Where . . . where did you . . . you see it?"

"Here," Augustus replied.

"Here?"

"Augustus, Randy has to catch a bus. It's late. Maybe some other night," I said.

"I won't remember it some other night," he angrily shot back at me.

"I . . . can . . . can stay a li . . . little longer."

"You have a pronounced speech defect, huh?"

"Augustus," I snapped, chastising.

"It's wrong to pretend it doesn't exist. Some people have thought that addressing the problem makes the stutterer or, as the English call it, the stammerer more aware of his problem and more sensitive and withdrawn. That's medieval," Augustus concluded.

Randy continued to look impressed.

"How long has it been since you had any treatment?"

Randy just shook his head.

"Your parents never had you in any therapy?"

"No."

"Typical. They bury their heads in the sand expecting him to outgrow it. He's too old. It would have happened already."

"He has a school therapy program. He told me so. Right, Randy?"

He looked at Augustus.

"He lied," Augustus said nonchalantly.

"Randy?"

"I . . . gotta . . . go."

"Don't worry about it," Augustus said. "We all don't have that much worthwhile to say to each other anyway."

"Stop it, Augustus."

"We'll all be communicating through computers soon. The phone will become an antique," Augustus continued.

"I'm . . . I'm on a com . . ."

"Computer? Me, too. I'm sending e-mail to God and getting back 'No longer at that address.' Let me know if you find him," Augustus said, and looked at me. "I forgot the movie." He turned and walked off.

"Don't listen to anything he says. He's brilliant but crazy," I told Randy.

"No . . . he . . . he's not," Randy said. "He's right about my . . . my par . . . parents. Good night." He turned to leave, his head lowered.

"Randy!" I called, and he stopped. I walked up to him. "Thanks for a nice evening," I said, and kissed him on the cheek.

He smiled and brought his hand to the spot as if my lips were still there. He walked off, his head high again.

Behind me, Augustus walked toward home, too.

Who was more unhappy, I wondered, Augustus, Randy, or me?

Maybe the secret was simply to keep moving, keep busy, don't think about it. It was only when we stopped and realized where we were that we felt any loneliness.

8

Counteroffensive

I saw Randy twice more before the summer ended and school began, once for a picnic at the park and once to go to a movie. I did a great deal of reading, catching up on any and all books Randy told me he had been assigned in his previous classes. As it was with most of the school changes, I had read most of the works my new teachers required or used in class, but there were also many differences.

Mommy began to enjoy the work at the restaurant and, because of her looks and warm personality, I think, was soon one of the highest-tipped waitresses or waiters there. Ironically Phoebe had made a good prediction. Eventually I did go to work at the restaurant. I assisted Dallas with the hostess responsibilities on weekends, and I was impressed with how quickly Mommy picked up on everything. When I remarked about it, she revealed for the first time that she had been a waitress often before and that was how she first met my father.

"It was always a good way to improve my income," she told me.

I could see that many of the men who came in flirted with her, even when they were with their wives or girlfriends. One night I overheard Dallas say, "Too bad you have a teenage daughter. You could pass for late twenties, and there are plenty of wealthy young bachelors to hunt in Palm Beach."

I hadn't considered that. Was I now a burden for my mother? Mommy never did anything to make me feel I was any sort of burden to her, and I couldn't imagine her hunting for a wealthy bachelor anyway. Sometimes I wished I had been in the helicopter with Daddy. I'd rather be wherever he was. At least working at the restaurant kept my mind occupied.

Phoebe, on the other hand, was unwilling to do anything that even appeared to be work at the inn, despite the fact that her father owned it. If anyone had the attitude that everything was coming to her it was Phoebe. I saw her occasionally when she stopped by to get her father to give her some money. She got him to buy her a car before the summer ended, too. She was just as happy avoiding me as I was avoiding her, and when Mommy asked about it I reminded her that Phoebe didn't want to spend time with someone younger. It was mostly true anyway.

I was more nervous about the start of this particular school year than any other I could remember, no matter how young I had been or how abruptly we had been withdrawn from one community and deposited in another. This time I was, after all, attending school as what Mommy described as a civilian. I didn't have that cadre of built-in children of military personnel there to make a transition easier.

Maybe it was my imagination, but when I attended schools where other children of military personnel attended I could easily see who they were, and we were quickly drawn to each other. I liked to think we were better behaved. We dressed a little more formally and peppered our conversations with "please" and "thank you" and always referred to our teachers with a higher degree of respect, even if we all agreed that a teacher wasn't very good or nice. It wasn't that none of us ever got into trouble. It was simply not as frequent and usually nowhere nearly as serious as with most of the other students we knew.

There was no other student like me in my Florida school in that respect, and I did have this strange sense of loneliness, despite Randy's great effort to help me feel at home. Every time another student or a teacher centered his or her attention on me, I wondered if he or she saw something very different in me as well.

Randy proved to be a great help, however. He came over to visit the day before school began and tried to ease my anxiety by describing everything from the quirks of some of the teachers to the worst table in the school cafeteria, worst because the sun was always beating down on it through the unshaded portion of window. He was that detailed. Mommy was terribly amused by Randy and called him a "little darlin'." She said it only once in his presence, and I saw him wince. He didn't mind being called "darlin'," but the "little" part underscored his slight build. Some of the crueler students teased him and called him Bird Bones.

He was there at the front entrance of the school waiting for me that first day, and he did introduce me to some of his friends who were like him, mild mannered, a little insecure. One of Mommy's favorite expressions, inherited from her own mother, was "Birds of a feather flock together." I thought of that often during the day, observing different personalities and the way they were drawn together to form the cliques in the school population. I didn't want to consider myself insecure. I really didn't think I was, despite my nervousness. Before the day ended I was talking with other students, more confident and upbeat than most of Randy's friends.

I saw Phoebe often in the hallways and cafeteria, but each time she acted as if she had never seen me before, barely looking at me for more than a second. I decided to consider that good luck.

Unfortunately, near the end of the week I discovered Phoebe hadn't been ignoring my existence as much as I had hoped she had. She had done a very good job of spreading "Sailor Girl" around the high school. Some of her male friends were saluting me in the halls. My first reaction was anger and indignation, but then I decided to go with the flow. Another one of Mommy's favorite expressions was "A branch that doesn't bend breaks." To fight them, to show them they were getting to me, would be defeating myself, I thought. Instead I started to salute back. At first they thought that was funny, but soon they became bored with it and then became annoyed if I did it to them first.

Roger was the first to break ranks and came to me in the cafeteria the last day of the first week to tell me I was the most frustrating person Phoebe had ever encountered.

"She as much as confessed it to me," he revealed. "You're confusing her. She doesn't know how to spoil things for you."

"Tell her to become my friend. That will ruin my day," I said, and he burst into laughter so loudly he drew the attention of most of the students around us.

"You're terrific," he said with what I thought was sincere admiration in his eyes.

Phoebe had just come in and was obviously annoyed that he was speaking to me, and I suddenly realized my own power and opportunity to launch a counteroffensive, as Daddy would put it.

"Thanks," I said. "Can I ask you a favor?" I smiled as coyly as I could.

"You can ask," he said, flirting back, "but that doesn't mean I'll grant it."

"I've got to get home as quickly as possible today. Could you possibly drive me home?"

He considered my request a moment and then glanced back at Phoebe, who was shooting poison arrows from her eyes in my direction.

"Okay," he said impulsively. "Just meet me in the parking lot. I have my mother's car today, the black Mercedes convertible. It's not hard to find. It's the only Mercedes there," he said.

"Thank you," I said demurely. "I'll be so grateful."

"Right. Okay." He looked nervous, but I thought his eyes also betrayed an explosion of excitement.

He returned to Phoebe and ignored me the remainder of the afternoon. How he got away from her after school I didn't know, but he was waiting nervously in his car when I approached.

"Get in," he said urgently as if we were making a getaway.

The moment I did, he backed up and shot out of the parking lot, sharply turning us onto the street. I hadn't even gotten my seat belt fastened.

"Do you always drive this fast?" I asked him.

He looked as if he wasn't going to talk to me at all but just deliver me to my home and take off. Finally, a good mile or so from the school, he relaxed and slowed down.

"I'm sorry. I didn't mean to inconvenience you in any way," I said.

He looked at me. "I'm not inconvenienced. No, I don't drive that fast all the time. I'd better not. One more speeding ticket, and my father will take away my license and not let me use any of the cars." He smiled. "I'm sort of on probation. I guess where you come from you would call it demoted or something, huh?"

"No. You're on report, but you're still a lieutenant junior grade."

He laughed. "Look," he said. "Let me give you a little advice. Don't go head to head with Phoebe. She has a real mean streak in her when she feels threatened."

"How could I possibly threaten her?"

"Anyone who continually confronts her is a threat to her. She hasn't forgotten how you beat her at that card game in my house. She has a lot of friends at school, friends a lot like her, if you get my meaning. I've seen them go after someone. It's not pleasant."

"Why do you go with her if you dislike her so much?" I asked him.

"I don't dislike her."

"You don't like her," I insisted. "You can't like someone who does things you don't like."

"Where did you get so much wisdom about people?" he asked, smiling.

"I listen, and I don't forget," I said.

"You've traveled about a lot, haven't you?" he asked, looking at me with a new interest.

"Yes. I wasn't happy about it, but we had to move when my father was transferred to a different base."

"I guess that is hard, making new friends all the time," he concluded. He looked sorry for me.

"I survived," I said, and he laughed.

"You more than survived. Despite all that chaos in your life, you're smart and," he added, glancing at me, "pretty as well as pretty sophisticated."

I didn't say anything. Once when Mommy and I were having a serious conversation about boys and romance, she told me the hardest thing to do is distinguish between a sincere compliment and one lavished on you for a selfish purpose. The school I was in at the time had a Great Books program as an extracurricular activity, and I had been admitted. One of our books was Chaucer's *Canterbury Tales,* and one of those tales was "The Nun's Priest's Tale," which told about the fox that trapped the rooster Chanticleer by flattering him and how Chanticleer turned the tables on the fox by flattering him back. I summarized the story for Mommy, and she nodded.

"My mother used to say, 'Flattery brings up one question only: What do you want?' You have to separate the baloney from the sincere compliment."

"But how can you tell the difference, Mommy? Especially when a man gives it?" I asked her.

She thought for a while and then said something I don't think I'll ever forget. "When it makes them happier than it makes you, it's sincere. Some people might call it pride, I guess. They are proud of you, proud you care for them."

Pride was an important word to a Navy man and a Navy wife. It didn't surprise me that Mommy chose it to help her explain what she meant. I saw how proudly

Daddy stood in his uniform at ceremonies, but I also saw how proud he was when we went to social affairs and he had Mommy at his side. I saw it in her eyes as well. Their pride in each other made their love that much stronger and more passionate. Whenever he returned home, even if he had been away for only a short period, he would take her in his arms, and they would kiss as if they hadn't seen each other for years.

"You busy tomorrow night?" Roger asked when we stopped at my condo.

"My mother doesn't like me going out on school nights," I said.

"She works every night at the restaurant, doesn't she?"

"Every night but Monday," I said.

"Well, how about I come around tomorrow night? That way you don't go out," he said.

"I like to get my homework done."

"So? I'll help you."

I thought a moment. His request excited a part of me but made another part of me nervous. Phoebe would go ballistic if she found out. Maybe I was playing with fire and I would lose the little control I had.

"Relax," he urged. "You've got to learn to have more fun. We're not going to be teenagers forever, you know. This is supposed to be the best time of our lives."

"All right," I said, and wished I could pull the words back into my mouth the moment I had uttered them, but another saying of Mommy's came roaring back to me: "You can't unring a bell."

"Thanks for the ride," I cried, getting out quickly. This was my own fault. Why had I asked him to take me home?

I heard him laugh, and he drove off as I rushed into

the house. Mommy was getting ready to leave for work. Twice this week, because of the time it took me to get home on the bus, I had missed her, and we didn't see each other until the following morning.

"Grace," she called from her bedroom.

"Hi," I said, stepping in. She was at her bathroom mirror, doing her makeup.

"How was school today?"

"Better," I said. "I found out I've already read half the new required assignments in English."

"I bet. Remember how Daddy used to tease you about leaving your nose in a book?"

"Yes."

Time had made it possible for me to smile at most of my good memories and not feel as if I was about to cry out my heart.

I watched her a moment, wondering if I should tell her about Roger. I didn't think she would be angry about it, and yet I couldn't help feeling guilty. I decided I wouldn't tell her, because I would find a way to cancel his coming, and why mention it if I not was going to have him come over?

Roger caught me completely by surprise the next day, however. He was with Wally and a group of boys when I spotted him in the hallway between classes. Phoebe wasn't too far off, with Ashley at her side listening to her hold court with some of her devoted followers. I approached Roger. There was only three minutes between classes, and we didn't have more than a minute or so left.

"Hi," I said.

He looked at me and then at the other boys as if he was surprised I would greet him so openly. They all smiled. Wally had no hesitation whatsoever when it came to recognizing and speaking to me. He gave me a big hello.

"Looking for a card game?" he asked.

"No. I wanted to speak to Roger."

"Me?" He looked to his right to see if Phoebe was watching. She was. "What for?"

"I wanted to tell you tonight was no good."

"For what?" he said, looking confused.

"For what? I mean about your coming over to my house."

"Who said I would do that? What, are you having delusions or something?" He looked at his friends, who looked at me and smiled.

Phoebe was starting toward us. I shook my head in disbelief and walked away quickly. If he wanted to be an idiot and a coward, let him, I thought. He got my message. I would have nothing to do with him.

Later, when I sat with Randy in the cafeteria, Phoebe, Ashley, and some of her other friends descended upon us, moving through the cafeteria like a flock of buzzards.

"I heard what you tried to pull," Phoebe accused even before she reached us. Everyone sitting at the tables nearby stopped his or her conversation and turned.

"I didn't try to pull anything," I said.

"What did you think, that by pretending Roger liked you, you would get him to like you? Is this some sort of sneaky technique you used when you lived on Navy bases, Sailor Girl?" she wailed, wagging her head and flitting her gaze from one side to the other to be sure her audience appreciated everything she was doing and saying.

"I didn't use any sneaky technique on anyone."

"No, of course not. He told me what you did. First you beg him to take you home, crying about some sort of an emergency, and then you try this. Did you have to get home that quickly? Well? What was the emergency? Care to explain?" she dared me, standing back with her arms folded under her breasts.

Despite myself, tears came into my eyes. "It's none of your business," I said.

"Oh, it's none of my business," she repeated, raising her voice to be sure the students at the farthest tables could hear our exchange. "You go after *my* boyfriend and it's none of my business?"

"I didn't go after your boyfriend. He came to speak to me," I cried.

I shouldn't be doing this, I kept telling myself. *I shouldn't let her bait me like this. She's getting me to fight her fight on her turf.* It was bad tactics for me, but I couldn't help it.

"Oh, Roger shows a little bit of compassion for a pathetic, whiny, spoiled Sailor Girl, and you make it out to be a love affair. Well, everyone here be warned, especially boys," she said, raising her voice. "You talk to Sailor Girl, and you're in her boat whether you like it or not. Right, Randy?" She turned to him.

"Sh . . . sh . . . shut up, Pheee . . . Phoebe."

"Ri . . . right, Ra . . . Randy. That's why she likes you. She can do all the talking, and you just li . . . li . . . listen."

The small crowd convulsed with laughter.

"That's cruel!" I screamed at her, and stood up. "You're a mean, egotistical person. If anyone is spoiled, it's you."

"Right, Sailor Girl," she retorted, and saluted with her shoulders back. "Aye, aye. Now back to swabbing the deck, and when you're done with that, clean the urinals." She pivoted and marched away, the trail of clones giggling and following like obedient rats.

When I gazed around, I saw dozens of students watching me in anticipation. My own face felt as if it was on fire. I had this great urge to leap over the table and tackle her. Randy, as if he could feel or hear my thoughts, reached up and touched my arm.

"Fo . . . forget her," he said, urging me to sit.

I gazed her way once more. Roger and Wally were at her table now, and they were all laughing.

"I can't let them get away with this," I said. I pulled free of Randy's slight grasp.

"Grace!" he cried, but I continued to march across the cafeteria. By now everyone had been given a blow-by-blow summary of my confrontation with Phoebe, and a few hundred eyes were on my every step.

Phoebe, Ashley, Roger, and Wally looked up, their faces full of surprise at my daring to approach them.

"How could you do this?" I asked Roger. "How could you pretend you didn't ask if you could come to my house tonight? Was this why you snuck out of the parking lot yesterday and drove like a maniac? Are you so afraid of her that you would slink about like a rodent and then lie?"

Roger couldn't hold my gaze. He smiled, shook his head, and looked down.

"I guess you're not as good at reading someone else's cards as you think you are, Sailor Girl," Phoebe said, her face overflowing with satisfaction.

"No, I'm good at it when I'm not playing with a bunch of cheats. And I'll tell you this, Phoebe," I added, fixing my gaze on her like a laser. "He might be afraid to tell you the truth to your face, but when he was with me he revealed just how little respect he has for you. Someday he might get up the nerve to tell you, and that," I said, turning, "is when he will become a man."

There was a great moan and then laughter. I glanced back and saw Roger's face was cherry red and Phoebe was so furious she was the one who now looked as if she had smoke pouring out of her ears.

I felt a little better, but I didn't stop trembling until I was in class again. I knew this was far from over, and I could just imagine what sort of trouble she would try to make for Mommy and me at the restaurant. I had to tell Mommy about it all as soon as I could, I thought, and regretted now that I had kept Roger's intention to visit me a secret.

I wanted to get home as soon as possible after school, but my intermediate algebra teacher had divided the class into groups of three and scheduled us for extra work three days a week. Today was my group's day, so I had to attend the session and remain at school an extra hour. By the time I got home Mommy was already off to work. She had left me a note about the food she had prepared and wanted me to warm for my dinner.

Despondent and frustrated, I hardly ate a thing. Randy called to see how I was doing. I told him fine and not to worry but thanked him for being concerned. He was a very sweet person, truly like a bird trapped in a cage constructed out of his own disability. Part of the reason I had fallen so quickly into the trap I now imagined Phoebe and Roger had set for me was my appreciation of how protective and compassionate Roger had been toward Randy, but that proved to be an exception and not the rule for his behavior. No one was what he or she seemed to be, I thought. Mommy had warned me of this. She had told me to take my time before placing my trust in anyone.

But how long did you have to wait, I wondered, and when did you know it was safe? Was it ever safe?

I phoned the restaurant, but Dallas told me they were very busy and Mommy would call me as soon as she had a free moment.

"It's one of those nights when everyone we booked comes on time. I could have used you, too," she shouted over the din.

I'd rather be there than here, I thought. I thanked her and went about preparing my dinner.

It had been a while since I had seen Augustus. While I sat at our dining table and gazed out the patio door toward the pond, I thought about him and wished I, too, could be in some sort of special home-study program. I was dreading returning to school the next day. Surely Phoebe would be setting some new trap or spreading some new story about me. How long would it go on? Why was it so important to her? I hoped that she would soon tire of it and aim her vicious guns at some other poor, unfortunate victim.

I was soon to learn that instead she was planning an even bigger assault.

Mommy didn't call me until nearly nine o'clock.

"I'm sorry, honey," she said. "This is the first real break I've had, and now there's a serious problem here, and I will be later than usual, I'm afraid."

"What kind of a problem, Mommy?"

She hesitated, and then in a voice barely audible, which told me she was trying not to be heard by anyone nearby, she said, "Money's missing. A lot of money."

"Money?"

"Warren is beside himself, and Dallas is practically in tears."

My heart skipped a beat and then began to thump. "No one thinks you took it, do they?" I asked.

"Of course not," she said. "Why would you even ask such a thing, Grace?"

"Was Phoebe there tonight?"

"Phoebe? Yes, why?"

"I'll tell you when you get home," I said.

"Oh, don't wait up for me, honey. You get your rest. We can talk in the morning."

"No," I said.

"I might not be home for some time," she warned.

"I don't care."

"What is it?" Before I could even begin, she said, "I have to go. Dallas is beckoning. Go to sleep," she ordered, and hung up.

Sleep? How could I ever fall asleep until I found out what was happening?

I sat staring down at the floor, trying to figure out what I should do next, when suddenly I felt I was being watched. When I looked up I nearly screamed. There was Augustus standing at our patio door looking in at me. His hair was as disheveled as ever, but for once he was wearing a plain black, short-sleeve shirt and sneakers. He didn't knock. He just stared in and stood there.

"What are you doing?" I asked, opening the door. "You frightened me."

He didn't look as if he had heard a word. His expression or lack of one didn't change. I wasn't even sure he was seeing me, his eyes were that glassy.

"Augustus?"

He turned slowly to me. "Mrs. Dorahush is in the hospital," he said.

"Your grandmother? Why? What happened?"

"Angina pectoris."

"What's that mean?"

"That is a disease marked by brief paroxysmal attacks of chest pain precipitated by deficient oxygenation of the heart muscles," he recited. He kept his gaze stoic, his eyes unmoving. "In layman's terms, she is on the threshold of a heart attack."

"Oh, Augustus, I'm so sorry. Will she be all right?"

"I don't know," he said.

How small and trivial my problems with Phoebe now seemed.

"Have you eaten? Do you want something to eat or to drink?"

He shrugged.

"Come on in. My mother left me too much lasagna. You like that? She makes it delicious."

He stepped into the condo and let me sit him at the table.

"Let me just throw it into the microwave," I told him.

I brought him a setting, silverware, and a napkin.

"You have to be brave for her, Augustus. I bet she's worried more about you right now than she is about herself."

He nodded. "I'm sure that's true. She was the only one who encouraged me," he said. "When I was little I frightened my parents."

"Frightened? Why?"

"They were unable to deal with a three-year-old who could read and write, and when I performed higher math at the age of seven they thought I was some sort of freak. Other children my age were afraid to be with me, and older children were embarrassed by the way I showed them up. It made it harder for my parents to keep their friends.

"In junior high the other students would pull as many pranks on me as they could. They stole my books and my notebooks in the hopes I would fail my tests, but I didn't need any of it, and that got them frustrated and even more angry. Finally, the guidance counselor told my parents I belonged in a special environment. That's a euphemistic way of telling them to get me out of there. They couldn't deal with me. Mrs. Dorahush found the program for me, you know."

"Why do you insist on calling her that? Just call her your grandmother."

"She's disappearing," he explained. "Like my parents. I'd rather she disappeared as Mrs. Dorahush."

I stared at him, understanding that this was his way of keeping himself emotionally protected. The formality was his cocoon.

The bell went off on the microwave, and I went for his food. Once he tasted it, he ate with enthusiasm.

"This is good." He paused and looked around as if just realizing we were alone. "Where's your mother?"

"At work." I explained where she worked and the how and why.

"Your mother is heroic," he declared.

"Why?" I asked, smiling. I liked to think that, but how did he come to such a conclusion?

"She has suffered a great tragedy, and she continues to move forward, to say yes to life and all the responsibilities. She doesn't wallow in her misfortune, and she doesn't let it shape or remake her.

"All life is suffering," he continued. "Everything that

lives, lives on something that dies. This food is full of things that were once alive: wheat used in the noodle, the meat, the vegetables. Orthodox vegetarians make me laugh . . . they won't eat anything that has a face or a mother. They don't realize that the earth is a mother. Everything is born, and everything dies."

I knew he was being dark and deeply philosophical because he was so despondent over his grandmother, but I thought, *How lonely he must be. He lives and thinks on a level so above the world I'm in. It's as if he's skipped over more than just a normal childhood.* He was more like a wise old man even though he was still a teenager. My problems with Phoebe couldn't begin to attract his attention, and yet I couldn't help wondering what such a genius as he could suggest.

"I have a problem at school," I began. "It's spreading like a disease, and I think it's infecting my mother as well."

He raised his eyebrows and sat back to listen.

"You've analyzed it correctly," he said after I concluded. "You shouldn't have gone after her and fought the same way. When you do that, you can't win, because you've become your enemy."

"I've become my enemy?"

"Yes, you've become just like her, using her tactics, living in her world. Soon you'll have your little faction, and she'll have hers, and that will please her because it will confirm that the way she sees you and the rest of the world is correct."

"What do I do?"

"Nothing," he said. "This is someone who is devastated if she is ignored. She'll do whatever she can to get a rise out of you, and the more you resist, the more frustrated she will become, and eventually anyone with half a brain who watches all this will become disgusted with her and tell her to get a life, get over it.

"It was the secret and still is the secret behind the nonviolent movement. The oppressors don't know what to do if the oppressed refuse to acknowledge them but yet will not fight them the way they expect. They are prepared for a battle, and when they don't get it they are confused and frustrated. So will she be."

"I wish you were attending my school," I said.

He smiled. "Sometimes I do, too."

"Can't you?"

"I'd only be bored in class, and my teachers would feel insecure and dislike me. It's happened too often."

"But there are other things beside studies. There are sports, activities, parties. Don't you miss any of that, Augustus?"

He shrugged. "I don't think about it."

"Then you're practicing the nonviolence on yourself," I said.

He smiled. "What do you mean?"

"You're avoiding the conflict, refusing to acknowledge feelings you have."

He looked at me a moment and nodded softly. "Maybe you're smarter than you think you are," he said.

"I wish I was smarter at math. I dread starting that homework."

"Oh? Let me look at it," he said.

We went to my room, and I showed him the text and the chapter. He began to talk about it and explain it in a way that was so much simpler than our teacher had. After he worked on a few of the problems with me, I understood and did the remaining ones in half the time.

"You could be a teacher already," I told him.

"No. I wouldn't be a good teacher. Normally I don't have the patience. It's like a runner who has to trot because the others can't keep up. It's too frustrating for me. I don't mean to sound egotistical. It's just how it is."

"I understand," I said.

"I think you do," he replied, and then he surprised me by leaning forward to kiss me. "Don't be mad," he said immediately.

"I'm not mad. I'm just surprised," I said.

"I wanted to do that the first time I saw you. Is that boy who stutters your new boyfriend?"

"No," I said. "He's just a very nice boy."

"Do you have a lot of experience with boys?"

"No, not really."

He looked happy with that answer. "I'd better get home," he said suddenly. "Thanks for the dinner."

"Thanks for helping me with this math."

"Thanks for letting me kiss you," he countered.

I laughed. "I didn't really let you."

"Oh. Well then," he said, leaning forward to bring his lips to mine, only very slowly, waiting for me to pull back. I didn't, and he kissed me again.

I looked into his eyes. They seemed to be blazing from the thoughts behind them.

"You're the first girl I've kissed like that," he admitted.

"How does it make you feel?" I asked, almost as curious about his reaction as I was about my own.

He thought a long moment. "Like not wanting to disappear," he said.

I smiled, and then he started out of my room. I followed him to the patio door.

"Let me know how your grandmother is doing," I told him. "Come by tomorrow, okay?"

"Okay," he said.

I watched him walk away. He paused, looked back at me, and continued through the deeper shadows until he was gone.

I fell asleep before Mommy came home, but when she entered I heard her and woke. I called to her. She seemed to take forever to come to my room.

"Why are you still awake?" she asked, silhouetted in the hall light.

"I fell asleep, but I heard you come in. What happened at the restaurant?"

I heard her release a deep sigh, and I leaned over to put on my lamp that was on the nightstand.

"They finally found the money," she said. "During the course of the evening Warren bundles what they've taken in up to that point and gets it ready for depositing the following day. He had left this sack of bills on his desk, and it wasn't there, so there was panic."

"Where was it found?"

Mommy looked up at the ceiling, tilting her head back as if she wanted to keep her tears from emerging.

"In the room where the waiters and waitresses keep our coats and purses and things. It was under mine," she said.

"Phoebe did that," I said immediately.

"Phoebe?" She thought a moment. "You were saying something about her on the phone before. Why would she do that?"

I summarized everything as quickly as I could. Mommy came into the room during my explanation and sat on my bed, listening.

"You're probably right then," she said, nodding.

"They don't think you tried to steal it, do they, Mommy?"

"No. Dallas was as upset about it as I was, and Warren was just so happy about finding it. They do suspect other employees, however, and that doesn't make for a pleasant working atmosphere. I'm going to tell Dallas everything you told me," she decided. "In the meantime, if I were you, honey, I would just . . ."

"Ignore her?"

"Yes."

"Someone else gave me that advice," I said, and told her about Augustus and his grandmother.

"That poor boy. He must be very frightened. I'll find out about her tomorrow," she said, "and see what we can do to help them. Now go to sleep, and don't worry."

She leaned over to kiss me and stood.

"Oh," she said, smiling. "With all the commotion and all, I forgot to tell you I met a very nice gentleman tonight. He came in and ate alone. He was very sweet. He lost his wife recently," she said. "We had a nice talk. It's funny, but when terrible things happen to you, you think they've happened to you and no one else, and you're surprised when you meet someone who understands because he's experienced something similar."

"It couldn't have been that similar," I insisted.

She widened her smile. "Well, it was close enough. I have a feeling he's going to be coming around again."

I said nothing. Finally she realized she was just standing there thinking about the man.

"Good night," she said, and left me in more of a state of confusion than I had been in before she came home.

Never in my wildest thoughts had I imagined Mommy with another man. It was still as if Daddy was just on sea duty.

How could she ever fall in love again?

How could she ever want to?

No one could ever take my daddy's place.

I would hate anyone who thought he could even try.

Life was so much less complicated when we were a naval family, I thought, and wondered how I could ever have longed for us not to be.

Try to sleep, I told myself.

Sleep?

It was like chasing a rainbow.

9

Mommy and
Mrs. Greenstein

The advice Augustus and Mommy gave me proved impossible to follow. If it was only me Phoebe was out to damage I might not have had such a difficult time of it. I went to school the next morning fully intending to do what Augustus and Mommy had suggested. I would even keep from looking in Phoebe's direction, I told myself. Actually I thought I was doing very well. Throughout the morning, passing from class to class, I avoided her. Randy was at my side constantly, and, as Augustus predicted, his friends also tried to be a buffer and were quickly becoming my little faction, mumbling about Phoebe and her friends, circling me as if I had become their queen bee in a separate hive. Phoebe's hive was well in place.

Just before lunch Ashley stopped me in the hallway. I felt my body tighten. *Whatever she says, I'll ignore,* I told myself. There was no doubt in my mind she was

Phoebe's little messenger, her human guided missile aimed at my heart.

"Are you all right?" she began, sounding so concerned and sympathetic.

"Why shouldn't I be?" I countered, full of suspicion. "I'm fine. Thanks." I smiled at her and started away.

"Because of your mother being arrested and all," she blurted after me.

It was as if someone had dropped an icicle down my back. For a moment I couldn't move, not even to turn on her. The other students walking nearby slowed down to listen. Randy, who was hurrying up the hallway from the bathroom, saw the look on my face and paused as if a small explosion had gone off in the corridor. He shot forward again, practically running in my direction.

"Who told you such a stupid thing?" I demanded, walking toward Ashley. She stood her ground, her smile set in her round face like a rock in whipped cream, cold and hard.

"Phoebe told everyone the story this morning. She said her father was so upset. Is your mother in jail? She said her father was seriously considering pressing charges because the stolen money was found in her coat."

"It's a filthy lie!" I screamed at her. "It wasn't in her coat. It was under it, and we all know Phoebe put the money there herself, hoping to blame my mother."

Ashley kept her smile, but I saw the way her eyes shifted to the right and looked back. Phoebe and her friends were watching from a classroom door.

"Phoebe says you need money badly because of your father's death, and her father might take pity on her and not insist she go to prison."

"Shut up!" I shouted.

Mr. Warner, our science teacher, had just stepped out

of his classroom. He turned to look our way, but I didn't care.

Randy came up behind me and tried to get me to walk away, but I shrugged off his hand.

"It will probably be in the newspapers anyway, so you can't pretend it didn't happen."

"I said shut up. You say anything more about that lie, and I'll rip out your tongue," I told Ashley.

"Your mother's a thief and a terrible one at that, stealing from the very people who tried to help her," she spat back at me, and all went so bright red I can't remember what happened next, especially how I had my hands entangled in Ashley's hair, pulling her down and dragging her along the corridor floor. Her screams brought more students. In seconds Mr. Warner had his hands around my waist and was trying to lift me away, but I wouldn't let go of Ashley's hair. Suddenly Mrs. Cohen, our math teacher, was there prying my fingers back and screaming at me to let go.

When I did, Mr. Warner literally lifted me off the floor and swung me around so forcefully I thought he had broken my ribs.

"To the office, young lady!" he ordered, pointing. "Now! Go on, march!"

Ashley was crying and folded up like a baby on the floor. The school nurse had been called and was hurrying down the hallway. I didn't look back. Mr. Warner had his hand on my back, pressing between my shoulder blades to be sure I kept walking.

"Move!" he kept shouting. By now everyone coming out of every classroom was watching.

"Sit," he commanded when we entered the principal's office. "And don't move a muscle, young lady."

He went to the secretary and told her what had happened in the hallway. She looked at me as he spoke, her face full of disbelief, her head wagging and her eyes widening. She buzzed the principal, Mrs. Greenstein, and Mr. Warner went into her office first. A few moments later he came to the door and told me to get myself in there immediately.

The red stain that had formed across my eyes diminished and was gone. For a moment I didn't know what I was doing in the principal's office. My rage had been that great. Then I sucked in my breath and entered the inner office. Mr. Warner closed the door behind me, and I looked at the principal. I had seen her only in the hallway and when she had spoken to the student body during the first-day assembly. She had set down the rules she considered "holy words," and I remember thinking she was as stern and hard looking as some of the naval officers I had met.

She wasn't much taller than I was, but she had shoulders that looked as if they were packed with football player's pads. She had a small bosom, wide hips, and hands that looked puffed up. Whenever I had seen her in the hallway her dark eyes were always in a scowl, and she pressed her lips together so hard tiny pockets of white formed at the corners.

"Is this true? Mr. Warner had to pull you off another student forcefully? And Mrs. Cohen had to assist?"

I nodded.

"That will be all, Mr. Warner. Thank you, and I'm sorry your lunch period was disturbed," she told him.

He glared at me and walked out.

"Sit," she said, pointing her sharp nose at the chair in front of her desk. Her mouth was small, but when she grimaced her lips stretched like rubber bands from one end of her jawbone to the other.

"I am going to see how Ashley is, and then I will return. If she is seriously hurt, I will do what I said I would do at our assembly. I will involve the police. Any assault on any of my students is as serious as it would be if it happened in the street," she said.

When she left the office she kept the door wide open so anyone walking past could look in and see me sitting there. I heard Phoebe's laugh and turned in time to see her go by with two of her friends.

How would I explain this to Mommy? I felt I had let her down and at precisely the wrong time. I lowered my head like a flag of defeat and waited, my body trembling in anticipation of what was to come.

First Mrs. Greenstein's secretary returned and placed a folder on her desk. Coming and going, she barely looked at me. Ten minutes later I heard Mrs. Greenstein's high-heeled shoes clicking down the hallway, her steps like tiny drumbeats to accompany my impending execution.

"Well," I heard a few moments later, and turned as she entered her office. "You are fortunate that she is not badly hurt."

"It wasn't all my fault," I whined.

She sat behind her desk and touched the tips of her fingers together in prayer fashion. Her eyes narrowed. She looked down at the folder her secretary had put on her desk, read, and looked up at me.

"So you are the girl who was brought up on Navy bases?"

"No, not always," I said. "When I was little we didn't live on a base. It wasn't until my father became an officer."

"An officer's daughter, and you behave like this? I thought the services ran a tight ship, especially the

Navy. Protocol, proper behavior, respect for authority are all essential, aren't they? Did you think that just because you were no longer living on a base you could behave like a wild animal in my school? Would your officer father be proud of you? How is he going to feel when I call him?"

I couldn't keep the tears from coming even if there was a way to plug up my eyes. They streaked down my cheeks.

"You can't call him," I said.

"Oh? And why can't I?"

"He's dead. He was killed in a helicopter accident, otherwise we would still be in Norfolk," I said, directing my anger against cruel fate.

"I see," she said, barely skipping a beat. "That is unfortunate. However, it is also more reason for you to behave yourself and not put another burden on your mother."

"You don't understand," I said, shaking my head.

"Oh, I don't understand? It's I who is at fault, is that it?"

"No, ma'am. I don't mean that."

She slapped the folder closed and sat back. "Well, what do you mean? Go on, explain your beastly behavior," she challenged.

I thought about how I would start. Everything seemed so silly and foolish, I was sure I would sound that way, but what choice did I have?

"We moved here because my mother's friend was giving her a job at her husband's and her restaurant, the Tremont Inn. Her friend's stepdaughter, Phoebe Tremont, doesn't like me and tried to make it look as if my mother stole money last night. Ashley screamed that my mother was a thief and was in jail. I told her to stop, but she wouldn't, and I lost my temper." I finished, gasping for a breath.

Mrs. Greenstein stared at me a long moment and then shook her head. "Did you invent this all yourself, or did you see it on some soap opera?"

"I wish it was all fiction," I muttered.

"What's that?"

"I said I wish it was invented, but unfortunately it's not," I told her firmly, too firmly because she snapped her back like a whip and brought those heavy shoulders up.

"I won't have violence in my school. We have a no tolerance policy for that, for knives or guns and especially any sort of drugs. The first violation is the last. You are suspended pending a full inquiry and possible expulsion from this institution. Get your things and leave the building immediately," she ordered. "I will call your mother and inform her you are on your way, so don't go somewhere else and try to lie to her about what's going on, as some of my students have tried."

"It's not fair!" I wailed.

"You knew the rules. You heard them along with the rest of the student body." She leaned forward. "I am someone who means what she says. You, who have lived in a military world, should appreciate that."

"But . . ."

"I think you should write a letter of apology to both Mr. Warner and Mrs. Cohen as well," she added. "That is all." She stood up to emphasize it.

I rose slowly. *What have I done? What will happen to us?*

The bell had already rung for the next class. The halls were empty.

The principal's secretary handed me my books.

194   V. C. ANDREWS

"Randy Walker brought them here," she explained. "They were scattered all over the corridor."

I took them, thanked her, and left the office, moving like someone under hypnosis. I just turned and walked out of the building through the nearest exit. I didn't remember the trip home. I was on a bus and then off, and I walked, and suddenly my eyes snapped with brightness and I was at my front door. My heart was pounding when I entered.

Mommy, who usually slept later because of her work schedule, was up and in her robe. She was standing at the counter in the kitchen, her hands cupping a mug of steaming black coffee. I knew she heard me come in, but she remained with her back to me until I said, "Mommy."

Then she turned slowly. Her face was pale, her eyes red, her hair as disheveled as it would be had she been scrubbing her scalp to stop the pain.

"How could you do such a thing, Grace? I don't understand," she said.

Through my sobs, I told her everything. "I couldn't help it. I just got so angry at her. Afterward I was frightened by my own actions. It was like I was two different people!"

"How horrible for you," Mommy said, slowly shaking her head. "What have I done? I should have stayed in Virginia and left you where you were going to the same school. You were making new friends, nice friends. I was just thinking of myself, how painful it was for me."

"No, Mommy. This is in no way your fault. It's that Phoebe Tremont. She's just so mean and hates me so much she would do anything to hurt me."

"How could anyone hate you and so quickly?" she

asked. She took a deep breath. "All right, we'll deal with it," she said. "If there was one thing your father taught me it was to stay calm in the midst of a crisis, take a breath, and not lose control of your thoughts and reason. Most of the time people defeat themselves. You shouldn't have resorted to violence, of course, but you were deliberately baited. We have a meeting with the principal tomorrow at eight."

"But you have to work and get up so early."

"It's nothing."

She sighed deeply, so deeply I sensed there was something else wrong.

"Are you sick, Mommy?"

"What? No. Well, maybe emotionally. I just saw Mr. Landers, the supervisor of the complex. He was giving the gardeners instructions. He told me about Mrs. Dorahush."

"What?" I asked, holding my breath.

"She passed away late last night."

"Oh, no. Where's Augustus?" I asked immediately.

"I don't know, honey."

"I'd better go see him. He has no one," I said.

Before she could say anything else, I charged through the condo to the patio door and ran across the lawn and the street to his unit. The windows were dark. I knocked on the patio door and waited. He didn't come. I peered in, but I didn't see him. I knocked again and called to him. When he didn't come I went around to the windows I knew to be the windows in his room and peered in.

"What are you doing?" I heard, and turned to see Mr. Landers. He was a short, stout man with thin gray hair. I had seen him from time to time. He barely acknowledged me with a nod, almost seeming distracted or per-

haps not interested in knowing any of the young people
who lived there.

"I'm looking for Augustus," I said. "I heard about his
grandmother."

"He's not there." He scratched his head. "They
brought him in a government car, and he went in to get
some papers and then left."

"Left? To go where?"

He shook his head. "All I know is someone will be
coming to organize what's in the house and move it
out."

"But . . . where will Augustus live?"

He shrugged. "I don't know, miss. That's all I know.
He was a weird kid anyway," he·said. "He made some
of the other residents nervous."

"That's because they don't understand him. He's a
genius!" I cried.

He grinned. "Right. A genius," he said, and walked
off to shout at one of the gardeners.

I walked home and told Mommy what he had said.

"How sad," she said. "Just when you think your life
is miserable, you meet someone worse off. Like my
grandmother used to say, 'A man complained all the
time because he had no shoes. Until he met a man who
had no feet.' "

"Can't we find out what happened to him,
Mommy?"

"Maybe. I'll try, honey," she promised.

I went to my room. All that had happened had
exhausted me. I closed my eyes as soon as I lay down,
and in seconds I was asleep. The ringing of the phone
woke me. It was Randy.

"I . . . I he . . . heard what ha . . . happened to you,"
he said.

"We have a meeting with the principal tomorrow morning."

"I . . . tr . . . tried to stop you."

"I know. It was my own fault. I let them bait me. I'm sure Phoebe is a very happy person." His silence assured me she was. "My mother says, 'What goes around comes around. Don't worry. She'll get hers someday.' "

"Good," he said.

"Don't you get into any trouble on my account," I warned. "I'll see you tomorrow."

"Okay," he said, his voice so tiny and thin.

Mommy left for work, and despite her brave face I could see the anxiety in her eyes. She called me from the restaurant and told me she and Dallas had a private conversation, and Dallas was going to speak to Warren about Phoebe. I tried to eat but pecked at my food and finally gave up on dinner.

When the phone rang again I was sure it was Randy, but it wasn't. It was Augustus.

"Where are you?" I practically screamed into the receiver, so happy to hear from him.

"It doesn't matter," he replied. "You heard about Mrs. Dorahush, I guess."

"I heard about your grandmother," I said.

He was silent a moment. "Yes, my grandmother."

"I'm so sorry, Augustus. I know how much she meant to you and how much you meant to her," I added.

"Yes. Well, she's returned to a pure state of energy. As you know, I am working on that. I expect to meet her again very soon."

"What do you mean? How?"

"Disappearing."

"You're not going to hurt yourself, are you?" I

asked, frightened by his tone of voice. He sounded so
far off, as if he had begun to disappear already.

"No, no, just the opposite. Don't worry. They're
sending me to New Mexico to a top-secret facility,
something known as pure research. I'll have whatever I
need, and I'll be with other people like me, but I'll miss
you," he said.

"Can't you write or call me?"

"No. I can't do anything to keep myself from disappearing. I can't hold on to this level of existence."

"I don't understand what you're saying, Augustus."

"It's all right. I just wanted to say goodbye and to
thank you again for being so nice to me. Take care of
Queenie and Quackie," he said, and hung up.

Of course, none of it made any sense to me. I had
known so many people for a short time, but somehow I
thought I might get to know Augustus better. I had
wanted that, and now that chance was gone. Would I
ever get to know anyone well? It made me afraid of
even trying. Mommy had told me love was an investment. It meant taking risks. Would I ever even get the
opportunity to take a risk?

I cleaned up the dishes and straightened up the
kitchen. Afterward I sat in my room and went through
all my dolls, recalling each and every one, where
Daddy had found them, and how excited I had been to
receive them. I fell asleep with a teddy bear from
England in my arms and this time didn't wake when
Mommy came home.

She was up before me the next morning and already
dressed. I kept apologizing for putting her through this
ordeal, but she had become steely-eyed and determined.

"We're not going to be victims all our lives, Grace. I

wasn't brought up that way or to accept it as inevitable. You come from a long line of resilient people," she assured me.

On the way to the school I told her about my short, strange conversation with Augustus.

"Every one of us has a destiny to fulfill, I guess," she said. "He was either blessed or cursed with his. We'll probably read about him someday after he invents something fantastic. Don't worry about him now, Grace. Your shoulders are too small to carry too many burdens. You have enough with your own."

Mrs. Greenstein made us wait in the outer office after we arrived, even though we arrived on time. Her secretary offered Mommy coffee, but she refused. Twenty minutes after our appointment time, Mommy went to the secretary's desk and told her in clear, firm language to inform Mrs. Greenstein that her time was just as important.

"If eight o'clock wasn't a good time to schedule this meeting, why was it scheduled for then?"

The secretary flitted about and went into Mrs. Greenstein's office. When she emerged she left the door open, and Mrs. Greenstein appeared.

"I'm sorry to have kept you waiting, but I had some rather important phone business to clear with a much higher priority than a student's misbehavior, and that took longer than I had anticipated. Come in," she said.

Mommy and I entered, and Mrs. Greenstein closed the door. There were two chairs in front of her desk now. She asked Mommy to sit and just nodded at me.

"I hope you understand the significance of all this," she began. "Violence has become all too common a thing in our schools today, and we have to be vigilant about preventing it."

"Of course," Mommy replied. "I applaud you for that. However, I want you to understand that Grace has never had an incident like this before. She has been, as you can readily see from her transcripts, an ideal student, always an A student."

"It takes only one incident to cause a bigger problem, Mrs. Houston. Someone's past history is important, of course, but violence is violence."

"Do you know the whole story?" Mommy countered, unflinching.

"I was told a story, yes," she admitted.

"They've been ganging up on her, baiting her. Grace shouldn't have fallen for it, but the others are not total innocents, Mrs. Greenstein, and in your dispensing of justice you should consider all of it."

"If I involved myself in the intrigues and soap operas of our students I wouldn't get anything accomplished. Maybe at the schools your daughter has attended the administrators had the time for all that nonsense, but we don't."

"Grace hasn't attended anything but regular public schools, Mrs. Greenstein, and judging someone or something with all the facts is not nonsense."

"Um. Well, here's what we'll do," she said, obviously either impatient with the argument or uncomfortable facing someone as strong as my mother. "She's suspended for the remainder of this week. She's on probation for the remainder of the year. Should she commit any other acts of violence, no matter how she is baited, she's out of here. I still expect letters of apology to the teachers who had to pull her off the other girl."

"And as far as the others go, no reprimands, nothing?" my mother asked.

"Let's be concerned only with your daughter, Mrs.

Houston. It would seem to me you have enough with just her. I'll look after the remaining students," she said with a cold smile.

"Grace will suffer her punishment because she did act in an improper manner, but if I hear another incident of her being baited or persecuted and nothing done about that, I will be back," Mommy said, and returned the cold smile. "There are all sorts of forms of violence, some even more painful than physical violence."

Mrs. Greenstein said nothing for a moment and then stood up. "Thank you for coming," she told Mommy. She looked at me. "Have those letters on my desk when you return on Monday," she said.

I nodded, and we left the office. Mommy said nothing, but I could feel the rage burning inside her as we marched out of the office and through the corridor to the nearest exit.

"That woman," she said through clenched teeth. "Your father would say, 'I wonder where she keeps her steel marbles.' Another Captain Queeg from *The Caine Mutiny*."

I was afraid to say a word. Before we got home, she shook her head. "I'm sorry you're in her school, Grace. I wish I could put you someplace else."

"I'll be all right, Mommy."

"Yes," she said, but not with her usual tone of confidence.

Since I wasn't attending school for the next three days, she suggested I come with her to the restaurant. Randy called and promised to get me all my homework. At least I would have that to do during the day.

I was glad to go to the restaurant and be with people. I was still feeling very sad for Augustus, as well as myself. Dallas was very sympathetic and nice to me. I put on one of my prettier dresses and helped her with the hostess work, as I had before. On the second night Phoebe showed up with Roger and saw me. She smiled and said, "Glad you found a job that suits you."

I didn't respond, but I glanced at Roger. He looked away guiltily. He followed her into Warren's office and then left with her.

All the next day I sensed that Mommy was excited about something. She spent more time on her hair, makeup, and fingernails before we left for the restaurant, and she was never as anxious about getting there. It puzzled me until a distinguished-looking older man arrived, and I noted he had a reservation for one under the name Winston Montgomery.

I had the feeling he knew who I was when he came into the restaurant. He approached the hostess desk and stood there for a moment smiling at me without speaking.

"Can I help you?" I asked.

"Winston Montgomery. I had a reservation for eight. Not for eight people," he quickly corrected. "For eight P.M."

I smiled and looked at the seating chart, realizing he was in Mommy's section.

"Right this way," I said, taking a menu. I led him to his table, the one in the far left corner.

"Thank you," he said when I pulled out the chair for him and handed him the menu. He spoke in sharp, crisp tones like someone who was conscious of every syllable, vowel, and consonant. His voice had the resonance of a radio personality's.

"Enjoy your dinner. The waitress will be with you right away."

"How well do you know my waitress?" he asked me before I could return to the desk. The impish glint in his bluish gray eyes assured me he already knew the answer.

"Fairly well, since she's my mother," I said.

"I had a feeling she might be. You look just like her."

"I wish," I said, and he laughed.

He was a tall man, about two inches or so taller than Daddy had been. His hair was thick but completely gray and cut stylishly. He had a narrow jaw but a strong, firm mouth and a nearly perfect nose. I saw he wore a beautiful gold pinky ring with a triangular diamond at the center. His Rolex watch had a band of gold that matched the gold of his ring.

"Like it?" he asked, seeing I was eyeing the watch. He held his wrist up so I could get a better look. "I just bought it this morning. I've never owned a Rolex before. I'm rarely extravagant when it comes to myself. I'd much rather spend my money on pretty ladies," he added with a demure smile.

"Oh, I see you have met my daughter," Mommy said, coming up behind me.

Winston Montgomery rose from his seat and gave a gentle bow. "I have indeed," he said. "I would have known her anywhere, Jackie Lee. She has inherited your best qualities."

"Thank you," Mommy said, blushing. I had never seen her like this. She was standing there with her eyes twinkling like a teenager's.

"I'd better get back to the front," I said sharply, and walked away.

When I looked back I saw Mommy standing beside him and looking down at him as if he was a movie star. Actually he was looking up at her the same way. It gave me a very funny feeling, a feeling of surprise but annoyance as well.

Winston Montgomery took hours to dine. He seemed content with simply sitting there watching Mommy move about the restaurant. I noticed that every chance she had she paused to speak with him at his table. Whenever I brought someone new into the dining area, he smiled and nodded at me.

Finally Dallas noticed how I was studying him and watching every move Mommy made around him.

"Do you know who that man is?" she asked.

"I know his name, Winston Montgomery," I said.

"He has an estate in Palm Beach. He's very, very wealthy, Grace. His family had major interests in pharmaceuticals. He's mostly retired now, I understand. Recently he lost his wife. They had no children," she added, raising her eyebrows. "There's no one immediate to inherit all that money."

I looked his way again. Mommy was serving a table nearby, but her eyes were catching his so often she nearly dropped a plate in someone's lap.

"How old is he?" I asked. He was good-looking, but the lines in his face and his gray hair made me think he was very old.

"Only in his sixties," Dallas said, laughing. "These days," she whispered, "older men are better catches, especially older men with money. Oh, hello," she said to a couple who had just entered the restaurant.

I digested what she had said and looked again at Mommy and Winston Montgomery. *She can't be thinking of him in a romantic way,* I thought, *not a man that much older.* She was just thirty-eight. *She's just being extra nice,* I told myself, *so she will get a bigger tip.*

When Winston Montgomery was finished with his dinner he didn't leave the restaurant. He went into the small bar. At about ten-thirty, things began to wind down. Mommy and Dallas were off whispering in a corner so often I thought I was at a high school dance. By just about eleven P.M. all her customers had paid their bills and left their tables.

When I looked for her I found her in the bar talking to Winston Montgomery. She saw me watching from the doorway and excused herself and came to me.

"We're going home," she said.

"You don't have to wait for everything to be proved as usual?" I asked.

"Dallas is covering for me. C'mon, honey. You did very well tonight. She has some tip money for you, too."

I glanced back at Winston Montgomery, who smiled my way and turned to the bartender. Mommy hurried me out of the restaurant and into our car.

"It was a good night," she said. "I did much better than I expected."

"I never ask you about money, Mommy. How are we doing?"

"We're okay, honey, but," she added, turning to me with her eyes bright and steely, "we're going to do better. Cruel fate has had its way with us, but I am determined not to let it enjoy its success too long." She spoke through clenched teeth.

"What do you mean?" I asked. I had never heard her speak with such vehemence. It was as if she truly knew cruel fate's address and would soon pay it a visit.

"I go to work in Dallas and Warren's beautiful upscale restaurant, and I see these women, some not much older than I am, bedecked in diamonds and gold, wearing the latest fashions, dresses that run in the thousands, and I think, why do they have so much happiness? What's their secret? What did they do to be so lucky?"

"What is the secret?" I asked her.

"Knowing what you want and going for it with resolution. Maybe even becoming obsessed," she said more to herself than to me now.

She didn't sound like herself. I couldn't help but wonder if what had happened to me at school was partly responsible for it.

"Don't worry," she added after a long silence. "We're going to do well. People like that principal of yours won't be so smug."

"I'm sorry, Mommy," I said. It was clear that was indeed part of the reason for her unhappiness and strange new mood.

"Don't you say that, Grace. Don't you ever apologize because of people like that. Damn," she said, pounding the steering wheel with the base of her palm. It made me flinch. "Your father would have chewed her up and spit her out."

I looked out the window.

We would never stop missing him, never stop needing him, never stop loving him.

When we entered the condo I went right to my room and started to prepare for bed. I heard Mommy moving about in her room: drawers opened and closed, water running. She was taking a shower, which in and of itself wasn't unusual, but she didn't sound as if she was winding down for the night. She had her portable CD player going, and she did that only when she was preparing for an evening out. Surely it was too late for that, I thought, especially after she had been on her feet all night.

After I put on my nightgown I went to her door and knocked.

"Mommy?"

"Just a minute," she said. When she opened the door I stepped back in surprise. She was wearing one of her most expensive dresses and had redone her makeup. The dress was an off-the-shoulder black chiffon with a sweetheart neckline. She hadn't looked this pretty and sexy since my daddy's death. She fiddled with her earrings a moment. "What, Grace?" she asked.

"Where are you going?" I replied. "It's after midnight."

"Things often don't start in Palm Beach until now."

"Palm Beach?"

"I'm going out with Winston. I'm tired of working and slaving and not doing anything that's in the slightest way fun. Don't look so upset."

"I'm not," I lied. "I'm just surprised. You never said anything."

"I don't have to say anything, Grace. I'm the adult here," she snapped back at me.

I bit my lower lip and felt my eyelids blinking quickly to keep the tears from forming.

"I'm sorry. I didn't mean to sound like that. I'm just . . . frustrated," she said. "I shouldn't take it out on you. It's certainly not your fault. Just go to sleep, and don't worry about anything, Grace. You're too intense. That's partly my fault, but we're going to start changing our lives for the better. We've got to lift ourselves out of the doldrums, or cruel fate will have its way with us."

She smiled. "Okay, honey?"

I nodded.

We both heard the sound of a car pulling up outside.

"I've got to go," she said, rushing to stand before the mirror once more. "How do I look?"

"Beautiful," I said. She did.

"Thank you."

She scooped up her purse and hurried to the front door. I followed slowly.

"Don't look so worried," she said, smiling. She opened the door, and I looked out, too.

There at the front of our unit was the longest, sleekest white stretch limousine I had ever seen. Mommy paused and sucked in her breath as if she was about to dive into an Olympic swimming pool to race. Then she stepped out and closed the door behind her.

I went to the front window quickly and watched as the chauffeur hurried around to open the limousine door. She stepped into the luxurious vehicle, and I just caught sight of Winston Montgomery's long legs and his hand reaching to help her. The chauffeur closed the door and slowly drove the limousine out of our complex.

Letting go of the curtain, I stepped back in confusion and awe. How could she go out with a man that much older than she was? A man who couldn't compare to my handsome, strong daddy, whom she had loved so much that the sun rose and set with his every smile, his every kiss?

What was happening to her? And to me?

I strolled slowly back to my room and paused in the doorway, looking at the teddy bear from London that I had placed against my pillow. It seemed to have a smile of confusion on its face as well. Hugging it to me, I crawled under my blanket and stared up at the dark ceiling.

People really do die more than once, I thought. *The second funeral takes place in your memory. You bury them under new events, new faces, new relationships, and when you do, you bury a little of yourself as well.*

What was it Augustus had told me? All life was suffering. Everything that lives, lives on something that dies? He was warning me, letting me know what to expect. As short as our friendship was, that was a significant gift.

"I don't care, Daddy," I whispered to the night. "I won't let go of you. Even if it means I'll never be happy again."

I fell asleep with that promise on my lips.

10

A Bridge to Cross

I never heard Mommy come home and attributed that to my having fallen into a very deep sleep. An earthquake probably wouldn't have stirred my eyelids. I was that exhausted, mostly from emotional strain. But after I rose and went out to the kitchen to start making coffee for us, I realized Mommy's door was wide open. She usually closed it before going to sleep. Curious, I went to her room and peered in. Her bed was unslept in, untouched. The realization that she had not come home yet hit me as sharply as a slap across the face. I actually heard myself say, "What?" as if I had to state the obvious to believe it. She wasn't home.

I stepped back, trembling. This could very well mean something terrible had happened to her. All sorts of wild ideas began to stampede across my imagination. Maybe this Winston Montgomery was some sort of wealthy serial killer. Maybe Mommy had decided to leave him and set out on her own and something happened to her. Or maybe they were in a bad accident and no one knew who she was yet. I started to get frantic. I debated calling Dallas but thought I might just get her upset and later Mommy might be very angry at me.

To keep my mind occupied I returned to the kitchen and started again to make some coffee. Just as I turned on the coffee maker, the front door opened and Mommy entered. She didn't look tired at all even though she had obviously been out all night. In fact, as she entered she was smiling, smiling until she saw me standing there.

"Oh, Grace. I was hoping to get home before you got up," she said.

"Where were you? It's morning. How could you stay out so late?" I asked, each question in a louder voice. "How could you do this without calling me?"

She looked as guilty as a teenager caught coming home after her curfew. All these events had ironically reversed our roles and responsibilities to each other.

"You're right. I'm sorry, Grace. It was just that I was having such a good time I didn't pay attention to the time. You know how that can be, I'm sure."

"No, Mommy, I don't," I shot back at her. "I've never done anything like this to you. How could you not realize it was becoming morning? How?" I cried, my arms up.

She nodded. "I know it seems fantastic, but . . ."

"Seems fantastic? It *is* fantastic! I thought something terrible must have happened to you."

"I'm sorry, Grace, but no matter how many times I say that, it won't change it," she said, losing her patience, "so let's drop it. It won't happen again." She marched down the short hallway to her bedroom.

I stood there in disbelief. Drop it? What would she

have said if the roles were reversed and it was I who had stayed out all night without calling? I followed and watched her get undressed.

"How could you not realize the time, Mommy?"

She paused. "We were having a good time listening to music at the club and meeting people. I haven't been out socially in so long I almost forgot what it was like. You should have seen the people there, the clothes, the jewelry. Do you know who just happened to be there? Philippe D'Anotelli. You know who he is, the famous Italian designer. All the movie stars wear his clothes. He stopped to say hello to Winston, and we were introduced."

"But you didn't stay there all night?"

"No, we went to Winston's home. Home," she said with a laugh. "Little castle would be more like it. It's walled in like most of the estates in Palm Beach. It's another world there, Grace. Dallas was right. When you cross over the Flagler Bridge and enter Palm Beach you think you've entered another country populated only by the rich and famous, with beautiful streets and shops and restaurants, everything looking new and fresh. People are so insulated there, Grace, so well protected. It's as if sickness and death can't come over the bridge. They don't even have a hospital or a cemetery!

"Anyway," she continued as if her excitement wouldn't permit her to pause, "the gates of Winston's home opened like the gates of heaven might, and we started up this beautiful mauve driveway which looked brand new. I think someone comes out and vacuums it every day."

"Vacuums a driveway?"

"I'm just kidding, but it looked like that. The driveway continued forever toward the Mediterranean-style pearl white mansion. With the elaborate lighting over the grounds I could see oleander bushes close to twenty feet high with salmon-pink, red, and white blossoms. There were fountains and small ponds and these great royal coconut palm trees lining the circular entry drive. Before we drove up I could see the ocean behind the house and another building down on the left toward the beach.

"Even at that time of the night we were greeted by a butler in a tuxedo jacket and a bowtie. I thought I had entered a museum. The artwork, the statues, and the rugs . . . he has a fortune in decoration and furniture. The moment we went to what he called the sitting room, but someone else might call a small ballroom, a maid appeared and asked him if he wanted anything. Can you imagine having so many servants who are always attentive, always available?"

"No, Mommy," I said, actually becoming a bit frightened by her exuberance. Why wasn't she absolutely exhausted? Could fun and excitement really give someone this much energy? I think I was a little jealous. Maybe I was very jealous.

"Well, we didn't order anything even though Winston made it sound as though I could order any-thing from apple pie to veal Marsala. We just had an after-dinner drink. He likes black sambuca. I had never had it before, but I must say I enjoyed it.

"We just sat and talked and talked. He told me all about his marriage, how his wife had died, why they never had children, and mostly what it was like for him to be alone after being married for nearly forty years. We had a lot in common, actually, even though your father and I were married barely half that long. He was a lot more sensitive man than I expected."

"Daddy?"

"No, Winston, silly."

"Then what did you do?"

"We both looked up when the sun was rising, both of us just as surprised. We laughed at how we had ignored and forgotten about time itself. Naturally he kept apologizing to me, and he quickly called for the limousine. He only travels by limousine. He said he hasn't driven a car for twenty years! Can you imagine that?"

"No," I said. "I don't think I'd want someone to be driving me about all the time."

"Of course you would, silly. You don't have any stress, and you can do other things. He was always a busy businessman, so he got a lot of work done while traveling. And he's been everywhere, Grace. Wait until you hear about the places he's been, the things he's seen."

"He couldn't have traveled more than Daddy," I said, now with an angry, sharp tone in my voice that made her wince.

"No, but it was a different sort of traveling from the traveling your father did, Grace. Your daddy was confined to his base or his ship, and he didn't visit grand hotels and wonderful restaurants and beachfronts. He didn't go into the mountains of Europe and places like Eze in southern France, Monte Carlo, the Côte d'Azur, playgrounds for the rich and famous. It wasn't the same thing."

"I'd rather have done what Daddy did," I insisted.

She smiled at me as if I was still a child. "Of course," she said.

"I would. I don't need chauffeurs and limousines and big houses!"

"Don't get yourself upset, Grace."

"I'm glad you had such a wonderful time," I practically spat and marched away to my own room. After I closed the door I realized I had the coffee machine on. What was there to do in my room now anyway except fume at the walls?

I went back to the kitchen and poured myself a cup of coffee. I considered having some breakfast, but my stomach was churning so much I thought I would just heave it all the moment I swallowed it. I looked up when Mommy appeared in her nightgown and robe.

"The coffee's made," I said.

"I think I'll just take a nap, Grace."

"A nap?"

"Well, it's starting to catch up to me," she said.

"How are you going to work tonight after staying out all night?" I said.

"I might take the night off. I'll call Dallas later and discuss it. Don't worry. I'll be fine if I just rest. Call me if you need me," she said, and went into her room, closing the door. I sat at the table, sipping my coffee and thinking about all she had told me. Maybe I was unfair. Maybe she deserved to enjoy herself a little. Maybe I was just a jealous child after all.

Just before noon there was someone at our door. Mommy was still fast asleep, so I hurried to it and faced a flower delivery man who had a box of long-stem roses.

"Jackie Lee Houston?" he asked me.

"No, that's my mother."

"Oh, well, this is for her," he said, and handed me the box.

I thanked him and took it and brought it to the table. There were three dozen mixed roses, white, red, and pink, and they looked as if they had just been cut. The stems and petals were still wet. I saw the card with it. Since the envelope wasn't sealed, I opened it and pulled out the card: "My apologies for forgetting time itself. Something not hard to do with you.—Winston."

I shoved it back into the envelope and dropped it onto the box as if it had turned to fire. Then I went out for a walk around the complex. I settled at the pond and threw some bread crumbs to Quackie and Queenie. After they gobbled them they remained there staring at me.

"You miss Augustus, I bet," I told them. It looked as if they were both nodding, and that made me smile. "Me, too. At least he was interesting. Without being rich!"

I saw a moving van pull up in front of Augustus's condo, and I wandered over to watch the two men taking some of the furniture out and loading it.

"Where are you taking all this?" I asked one, hoping to get an address.

"It's going into storage at one of our warehouses," he replied, barely pausing to look at me.

While carrying out one of the desks, the movers didn't notice a piece of paper that floated to the lawn. I picked it up after they returned to the condo and saw it was a sheet of Augustus's rambling mathematical verses, numbers, fractions, formulas that made no sense to me, of course, but nevertheless tied me to him. I decided to keep it. They would only throw it away anyway, I thought. I folded it and brought it back to our house, where I put it at the bottom of a jewelry box Daddy had brought me from India.

The house was still dead quiet, the roses undisturbed. I imagined that whenever Mommy did awake she would be hungry, so I went about preparing one of her favorite pasta meals, linguini in clam sauce. She liked it a little spicy. I was hoping the aroma of the sauce would snake its way through the condo and under her bedroom door. Eventually it did.

I turned when she stepped out, her hair disheveled, her eyes a little bloodshot. She scrubbed her face with her palms and smiled at me.

"What is that I smell?"

"I thought you might be hungry."

"Oh, that's so nice of you, Grace. Thank you, honey. I'll just take a shower and . . ."

"You had a delivery," I said sharply, and turned back to the pasta.

"Delivery?" She came into the kitchen and saw the flowers.

"Oh, how sweet," she said without even looking to see who had sent them.

I watched her face when she read the card. Her tired eyes regained their lively, happy glint instantly, and her cheeks flushed with glee.

"Hook and sinker," she muttered.

"What?" I asked.

"Nothing, honey. Isn't this nice? They're from Winston. I've got to put them in water quickly. How beautiful they are, and just enough to make a statement without being too ostentatious," she remarked as if she was an expert on social etiquette. "They know how to do everything properly."

"Who?"

"Palm Beach multimillionaires," she replied with a short laugh. "All of a sudden I am ravishingly hungry. I'll hurry." She rushed off to shower and fix her hair.

At the table while we ate our late lunch, Mommy continued her exuberant description of her late evening with Winston Montgomery, gushing over every detail as if she had to be sure I didn't miss a moment or a thing she had seen in that majestic house.

"There are at least ten bedrooms, I think, and there is a separate building for the help, a beach house. Can you imagine being a servant and living on the beach? Well, the reason for that is Joya del Mar has its own beach-front."

"Joya del Mar?"

"Oh, didn't I tell you the name of the estate?"

"The estate has a name?"

"Sure it does, silly. All those famous big homes have names. Joya del Mar, the jewel of the sea. Wait until you see it," she said.

"I don't want to see it," I replied petulantly.

"Why not?"

"It doesn't sound like that much fun for me."

"Oh, sure it is. The pool is enormous, with a Jacuzzi of course. He has a clay tennis court, a two-hole putting green, a small sailboat and a yacht and . . ."

The ringing of the phone brought her nauseating gushing to a halt. I expected it to be Randy. He hadn't called me for a while. I answered quickly, eager now to talk to anyone my age.

"Hello," I heard. "This is Winston Montgomery. Would your mother be available?"

"Just a minute," I said, my throat closing. I held out the receiver and looked away as if I was holding out a bloody knife or something equally horrid. "It's for you."

"Me? Thank you, Grace," she said. The moment she took the receiver in her hand, her tone of voice changed, and her pronunciation became so correct I didn't recognize it.

"This is Jackie Lee," she announced. She listened a

moment and then said, "They are so beautiful, Winston. Thank you so much for that kind gesture and those sweet words. I would have to admit it was as true for me. I lost track as well." She listened. "No, I'm fine. I had a good rest, thank you. Thank you for asking."

Oh brother, I thought. When did she ever talk to anyone like that?

"Of course," she continued. "When? Why, I don't see why not. I'm sure she would, too. Yes. That's very considerate of you. I look forward to it. Thank you." She listened and laughed. "Goodbye, and thank you again for the beautiful roses."

She cradled the receiver softly and stood there staring at it for a moment, a small smile on her lips. She turned to me as I was clearing the table.

"Well," she said. "Isn't that nice?"

I said nothing. I put the dishes into the sink and turned back to her.

"Winston has invited us to an afternoon on his yacht tomorrow. He'll send the limousine around about ten in the morning. Won't that be fun?"

"Not for me, for you," I said.

"Oh, no, Grace, you'll see. It's a yacht. We'll have lunch on it and . . ."

"He doesn't really want me along, Mommy," I insisted.

"Yes, he does. He made a big point of it. 'Be sure Grace comes,' he said. He was very taken with you last night."

"Why? All I did was show him to his table."

"He watched you. He's very observant, and he prides himself on his judgment of character. You'll like him, honey. He's really very down-to-earth for so wealthy a man."

"I'd better catch up on the schoolwork I've missed," I said, and finished clearing off the table. "Besides," I added in as phony and affected a voice as I could muster, "I don't have the proper attire for a day on a yacht."

"Oh, I know," Mommy said, taking that as a moment of weakness, my resistance dwindling. "That's one of the things we'll do with the rest of this afternoon: We'll go shopping for some adequate clothing and some new shoes, too."

"Isn't that a foolish expense?" I countered. "Just for a day on a yacht?"

"No, honey," she said, her face changing again, this time from adolescent excitement to cold calculation. "No, it's an investment."

"Investment? In what?"

"Our future," she said without a smile. Her tone was sterner, more determined. "Just do what I ask," she said. She put the roses into a vase and stepped back, admiring them. "Beautiful," she muttered, and then turned to me. "Aren't they?"

"Yes," I admitted.

She smiled again. "You'll see. You'll have a good time tomorrow, Grace, and you deserve that, honey. You deserve as much happiness as possible, and I'm going to be certain you will have it. I'll get ready to go out," she concluded before I could respond.

She returned to her bedroom. I looked at the flowers again, an explosion of color, opulent, overwhelming the modest condo. It was like putting a diamond ring on a homeless bag lady, I thought. Everything seemed so unreal to me, especially everything that had happened over the last week or so. My world was truly topsy-turvy, and to make sense out of any of it seemed impossible. I couldn't help but feel I was being swept along by some winds of fate.

Stop resisting. Just accept, a voice inside me was urging. *See to it that you restore laughter and smiles and do not make them painful or resent them. This is your heart giving you a direct order, Sailor Girl.*

Aye, aye, I wanted to say.

And, of course, I wanted to salute.

Mommy really enjoyed our shopping. Cost didn't seem to matter at all. I was shocked at the price tags for the sailing outfits she had chosen for us. The blouses, jackets, shorts, and shoes totaled nearly eight hundred dollars because of the designer name.

"This is too extravagant, Mommy," I protested. "How often will I be wearing these clothes?"

"More often than you think," she insisted.

"But you have to work so long and hard to earn this much money."

"Stop worrying so much, Grace. You'll get wrinkles in your forehead," she teased.

To me it seemed she was tossing caution and reason out the window. Was this all part of what happens to a grown woman after she has suffered so much tragedy and has had to change her life? Maybe she was having a different sort of nervous breakdown, I thought. The work, what happened at the restaurant, what happened with me at school, all of it was just too heavy for her fragile shoulders to bear on top of Daddy's tragic death.

After we had bought all the clothing, she decided she had to do something different with her hair. Unbeknownst to me she had already made an appointment with a beautician in Palm Beach. She insisted I go along so I could walk Worth Avenue and "get a taste of the better life." I thought I might call Randy and have him meet me there, but Mommy said what I thought was a very strange thing for her to say.

"Don't get too close with anyone at your school, Grace. You know how hard it gets to be when you have to leave."

"But why would I leave, Mommy? We don't have Daddy and the possibility of any transfer."

"Just take my advice," she said, sounding very cryptic. "Take a breath and step back. I don't want to see you have another minute of unhappiness."

"I don't understand," I said.

"Trust me," she insisted, and we headed for Palm Beach.

"I guess you're not going to work tonight then," I said.

"No. Dallas will cover for me. Besides, it's time I spent more time on myself." She looked at me and added, "For both our sakes."

Once again I felt there were forces and winds carrying me along, regardless of what I wanted.

I had never been to Palm Beach. All of our shopping and my school were in West Palm Beach. I didn't even understand that they were two separate entities, didn't understand until we crossed that bridge. My look of wonder began to rival Mommy's. It was as beautiful, as elegant, and as bright as she had described. I had never seen so many expensive automobiles and, when we were on Worth Avenue, so many ritzy-looking people, especially the women. Even the dogs on jewel-studded leashes looked spoiled rotten.

Mommy parked the car and walked to the beauty salon as if she had been there many times. There was a luxurious waiting lounge with television sets, racks of magazines, and a cappuccino machine. The air was fragrant, not only with the aromas of hair sprays but with flowers. To me it was a little nauseating, and I made up my mind quickly to leave and wander about outside while she had her hair done.

As soon as Mommy gave the receptionist her name we were greeted by the owner of the salon himself, a man named René who had curly hair as black as licorice and a complexion close to alabaster. I was positive he was wearing makeup, even a little lipstick. He had long eyebrows and a gold stud earring. Dressed in a black silk shirt and white pants with a pair of leather sandals, he swung himself around a chair and strutted up to meet Mommy. He was wide in the hips, so he looked more as if he waddled, reminding me of Quackie.

"Enchanté," he said, extending his hand as if he expected her to kiss it. He only offered his fingers to shake, which Mommy did. They were laden with rings, each a different precious stone. I was expecting her to laugh or to say something about his histrionics, but she simply stood there, glowing.

"Hello," Mommy said. "I'm sorry we called so late, but . . ."

"Oh, no, no, no, no," he replied, shaking his head so vigorously I thought he would rattle his brain. "I am so happy to be given the opportunity to do Mr. Montgomery a favor. Please," he added, stepping back so Mommy could enter the shop.

She turned to me. So Winston Montgomery had arranged this, I thought, a small detail she had forgotten to mention.

"Let me give you some money, Grace."

"I still have the twenty you gave me two days ago," I said.

"You might see something that costs a bit more here," she said, and René laughed. She handed me a fifty-dollar bill. I just stared at it. "Take it," she insisted, jerking it at me.

The receptionist watched with interest. I plucked the bill from Mommy's hand and shoved it into the pocket of my jeans.

Mommy smiled. "Explore," she said. "See for yourself how wonderful this place is."

"Oh, how I wish I was a young girl just arriving in Palm Beach," Reneé said, his eyes rolling like two green marbles in a dish.

You probably were, I wanted to say, but I left quickly instead. My nerves were so taut they were twanging like guitar strings. I just stood on the sidewalk, trying to calm myself. I wasn't looking at anything in particular. Cars floated by like magic carpets, glittering in the afternoon sunlight, a few driven by uniformed chauffeurs, their passengers poised like manikins in a store window.

"Excuse me," I heard, and turned to my right.

An elderly lady with tightly styled blue-gray hair wanted me to step back so she could have more room for her and her dog to pass. To me the dog resembled a miniature hippopotamus. It had loose skin in thick wrinkled folds, especially on its forehead. The dog looked just as arrogant and as impatient as its owner. All she had to do was tighten up a bit on the leash, and she would have plenty of room to go by.

"There's plenty of room for you to go by," I told her.

She pulled her head back and threw me a hard look. Her witchlike face screwed into a tiny wrinkled prune. I heard her "Humph" as she struggled to get the ugly dog closer. Finally she was able to walk around me. "Tourists," I heard her mutter disdainfully. The dog glanced back as if it understood and had the same disgust.

"You can get a ticket for that," I heard, and turned to see a handsome young man sitting comfortably in the driver's seat of a Mercedes convertible similar to the one Roger's mother owned. The man had a unique shade of gold-brown hair cut perfectly with a wave in the front. In the afternoon sunlight his cerulean eyes actually gleamed. He wore a light blue sports jacket with an open shirt collar. I could see his gold necklace.

"I didn't do anything illegal," I told him.

"You did here. You blocked the passage of a Chinese shar-pei. Grounds for arrest and imprisonment," he added with a small smile on his perfectly shaped lips.

"I thought it was a baby hippo," I said, and he laughed.

He turned away quickly as a woman came out of the beauty salon.

"What's so funny, Kirby?" she asked.

"Nothing, Muffy," he said. I thought she looked old enough to be his mother, but he looked at her flirtatiously. "You look ravishing."

"Think so?" she said, turning to catch her reflection in the window. "I let him darken my color and snip just a little more than usual."

"It's perfect," he said, and glanced at me. Something in his face told me he didn't mean a word of it. It was as if he and I shared a secret. He smiled and got out of the car quickly to open the door for her. As he came back around he looked at me again. "Remember, be careful," he teased.

When he got back into the car he leaned over to kiss the woman on the lips. Then he started the engine and drove off.

I continued down the sidewalk, looking in the windows of all the shops. Most of the clothing and shoes I saw on display had no price tags, but I could just smell how expensive everything was. I saw many different famous designer names. The people, mostly women, I saw emerging from these stores all seemed comfortable in their luxurious outfits, shoes, and jewelry, each one looking as if she was trying to out-glitter the next.

I did go into Saks and look at some clothing. After that I wandered around, looking at the ritzy hotels, garden restaurants, and designer shops, circling until I found my way back to the salon. Mommy wasn't finished yet, so I sat and thumbed through some magazines. Finally I heard her laugh and looked up. My breath caught, and for a moment I couldn't speak. She had permitted René to cut her hair shorter than I had ever seen it. I almost didn't recognize her.

Mommy's hair was always something Daddy loved. Because of that, I resisted cutting my own. He even enjoyed it when she tied it in a French knot or, for fun, wove two pigtails. He often told her that her hair was like woven silk. Many times I saw him run his fingers through it with such pleasure on his face.

"How do you like it?" she asked me, turning so I could see it from every angle. It was clipped to just above the nape of her neck, and the sides were drawn up sharply, curling. The style resembled some of the ones I had seen on other women in the shops and on the sidewalks of Worth Avenue.

I shook my head. "It's awful," I said.

Everyone around her stopped chatting. René raised his eyebrows.

"It's the latest style, honey," she explained. "I'm too old now to wear my hair the way I was wearing it. It's all right for a teenager, but . . ."

"You told Daddy you would never cut your hair," I reminded her. "I heard you."

"Daddy's gone, honey," she said softly.

"Not to me," I fired back at her, and charged out of the salon. I didn't know where I was going. I just walked quickly up the sidewalk, my arms folded under my breasts, my head down. I nearly walked into two women busily chatting and not watching where they were going. They gasped, and I shifted on my right foot in time to avoid slamming into them.

"My God!" one of them shouted after me. "Can't you watch where you're walking? Young people today," she muttered.

I paused at a fountain and caught my breath to stare at the half-moon-shaped tiled trough with a silver spigot that provided fresh water. A moment later an elderly man brought his poodle to it, and I watched the dog drink. The man smiled at me.

"Nothing too good for my baby," he said.

Expensive dogs were obviously very important to people in Palm Beach, I thought.

When the dog was satisfied, it tugged on the leash, and the man obediently continued his walk.

"What do you think you're doing, Grace?" I heard, and turned to see Mommy in our car. She had driven up and pulled to the curb. "Get in," she ordered.

I did, and she started away.

"I think I've been quite lenient and understanding when it has come to your moods, your emotional trauma, and your needs, Grace. I also think you are old enough and smart enough to treat me as fairly and as understandingly as I have treated you. What you did back there was very embarrassing for me. You behaved like a petulant child, a spoiled brat," she continued, her voice harder than ever.

"Yes," she went on, "I did wear my hair the way your father liked it. I did everything I could to please him. Many times when you were younger and I had to rip us up out of one home and go to another, I swallowed my own tears and anxiety. I did what I had to do to keep my marriage and to keep your father from having too much worry and burden. We loved each other more than most people who marry love each other, and I don't regret a moment, but I am in a different world now, a different state of existence, and I can't live in the past or in memories. I have our welfare to think about and our futures to consider.

"I'm not going to be the same person I was. That person died with your father, Grace. If I don't let go, I can't go on, and I have no right to wallow in self-pity. That was why I chose to move and to take the job and start in a completely different sort of environment in the first place.

"I need you to be just as grown-up and as realistic as I have to be." She looked at me. "There is just no more time to waste in mourning and feeling sorry for ourselves. I'm not going to permit it, but I can't do it without your full cooperation. Will I have it or won't I? Will you grow with me or not?"

She looked ahead at the bridge we were going to cross again, her eyes narrowing. "There are many bridges to cross in this life, and this just happens to be another, but it's a possible bridge to a better life for us."

Her lips trembled. She brought her hand to her eyes and wiped away tears. "I wish more than you know that this was all a nightmare and we would both wake up and your daddy would be coming home to us again, but he's not. He's not! Damn this world, he's not!" she cried, and pulled over and stopped the vehicle.

I was crying so hard I couldn't breathe. I barely got out the words. "I'm sorry, Mommy."

She reached for me, and we hugged and held each other. We were like that so long a police patrol car came up behind us, and a policeman approached.

"Are you all right, miss?" he asked. "Is there something wrong with your car?"

Mommy pulled back and looked out at him and then at me. "No, the car's fine, and yes," she said, "we're all right. We're always going to be all right."

He tilted back his cap, a smile of confusion written across his young face. "Okay, but you can't stay here."

"I'm sorry, officer. We'll move." She smiled at him through her tears. "But we'll be back."

He smiled and shook his head, and we drove on, both of us staring ahead, both of us somehow stronger.

11

The Myth of Icarus

I guess I didn't realize how tired I was and how much we did today," Mommy said a short time after we arrived home. We were going to have a simple dinner, just some scrambled eggs. She was almost too tired to eat that and drifted off every once in a while even while we ate. "I'd better get to sleep," she decided. "I want to be fresh and energetic tomorrow."

Randy finally reached me early in the evening. I could tell he was reluctant to reveal just how gleeful Phoebe and her friends were about the outcome of my altercation with Ashley, but I drew it out of him, his stuttering even more pronounced, especially when he revealed how he had spoken in my defense and made some enemies.

"Which was the one thing I asked you not to do, Randy," I chastised.

"I don . . . don't care," he said. "You're mo . . . more impor . . . portant to me than they are."

"Well, thank you, but please don't do anything else. Promise me," I said. "Promise me, or I will avoid you as much as I will avoid them."

"Okay," he said. "They're ha . . . having a par . . . party at Wally's house to . . . tonight," he added.

"You don't have to say it. I'm sure it's a celebration. Good riddance to them all."

"Can . . . can . . . can I see . . . see you tomorrow? Maybe we can go to a movie."

"No, I'm going someplace with my mother, and I'll be gone most of the day. We'll see each other during the week," I promised.

"Okay," he said, dripping with disappointment.

Afterward I tried to finish the homework Randy had given me the day before, but my mind kept wandering. I couldn't help thinking about Daddy, wishing he was here to give me advice in his confident manner, filling me with my own self-confidence and dissolving the ghosts of indecision, fear, and anxiety. I tried to imagine what he would say about all of this.

He would certainly tell me to have confidence in my mother, and he would absolutely insist that I stop moping about and let Mommy enjoy herself and enjoy myself as well. He loved that expression, "snatching victory from the jaws of defeat," especially when it came to famous naval battles.

Are you your father's daughter, or aren't you? I asked my image in the mirror.

I answered by putting on the outfit Mommy had bought me, looking in the mirror, and thinking about the day we were about to enjoy. I wasn't being honest with her earlier. I really was looking forward to seeing that estate, riding in the limousine, going out on a real yacht. What harm could come of it? I even liked how I looked in this expensive outfit.

Mommy was up early the next morning, tinkering about the condo and then working on herself, her makeup, making sure her hairdo was perfect. She seemed to be preparing for opening night in some great theatrical event. She was that nervous. I noticed how many times she looked at the clock.

"Winston is always on time," she said when I asked why she kept doing that. "I don't want to keep him waiting."

"How do you know that? You met him only once, not counting the restaurant, where everyone comes relatively on time or they'll lose their reservation."

"I doubt he would ever lose his, Grace. I can tell what he's like from the way he speaks about himself," she said quickly. "He hates it when someone is late for an appointment or someone keeps him waiting when he's on time. That's why I was so angry at your principal when she kept us waiting. I kept thinking Winston wouldn't stand for it."

Winston wouldn't stand for it? How much time had she spent with Winston Montgomery? And why base her life on what Winston Montgomery would or wouldn't do? Was last night their first and only date so far? I didn't want her to feel I was cross-examining her, so I dropped the subject and got myself ready. As she had predicted, Winston's limousine pulled up in front of our condo just as the clock struck ten.

"He's here!" she cried. "How do I look?" She pirouetted like a ballerina.

"Great," I said. "Relax, Mommy. We're only going for a picnic on a boat," I added, and she laughed so hard I didn't think she would have the strength to open the door.

"What's so funny?"

"Picnic on a boat. That's good. Picnic on a boat."

The first chance she had, she told Winston what I had said.

"Well," he replied, looking at me and nodding after we had gotten into the limousine, "Grace is right. That's exactly what it is. You both look fantastic," he said. "I'm sorry now that I arranged for a picnic on the boat. I should have taken you both to Miami's South Beach for lunch and shown you off: the mother and daughter who look more like two sisters. Perhaps another time," he added quickly.

I had to admit he looked pretty dapper himself. He wore a light blue windbreaker, white pants, and blue boat shoes. In the daylight I saw how tan he was and how that brought out the blue in his eyes. His snow white hair highlighted his complexion. He noticed the way I was studying him and smiled, so I looked away, but his attention was on me for most of the trip to his estate.

"What is your favorite subject in school?" he asked.

"I guess I like English the most, especially literature. I like to read."

"Well, I'm not the best speller," he kidded, "so I won't have you looking over my shoulder when I write anything, but I like to read, too. Lately I've enjoyed reading the old classics and plays, like *Romeo and Juliet*," he said, and I looked immediately at Mommy, who knew that was my favorite play. I confessed to fantasizing about myself playing Juliet in some lavish production. She quickly glanced out the window. She had primed him for me, I thought. How artificial.

What else had she told him about me? My favorite colors, foods, movie stars, and singers? Is he going to claim he likes them all as well?

"Really," I said dryly. "You recently read *Romeo and Juliet?*" I was considering asking him something detailed just to expose him and Mommy.

"Yes. I've even seen the ballet a few times. Have you ever seen it?"

"No."

"Of course you know *West Side Story* is based on *Romeo and Juliet?*"

I nodded, a little more impressed. Was he telling the truth? He did read a great deal and also liked *Romeo and Juliet?*

"If a production of either the ballet or the musical comes to Florida, I'll be sure to take you," he said. "Do you want to be an actress or a model?"

"Neither."

"You're certainly pretty enough. What would you like to be? Any ideas yet?"

"Maybe a teacher," I said. "A college teacher. A professor."

"I bet you can be anything you want to be," he said.

"Why?" I challenged.

He smiled and looked at Mommy. "You have a certain *je ne sais quoi.*"

"What?"

"A quality not easy to describe but nevertheless there, Grace. A real sense of yourself, a focus. I can see it, and my money is on you."

"I'm not a race horse."

"Oh, but you are, Grace. We all are, but don't worry about that. Competition is healthy. Don't be afraid of it. You're a winner," he said with a confident nod and a smile.

Mommy gazed at me. I could see the pleasure in her eyes. She looked so satisfied with herself. We weren't just with any man. We were with a very successful man who, like my daddy, had leadership qualities and could teach me something.

"I don't feel like a winner," I said almost under my breath.

"You will," he assured me. I looked at him. His eyes were full of kindness. Maybe I was being unfair. Maybe he really did like me. And just like that my body began to relax. When the walls and the gate of Joya del Mar came into view, I felt like a little girl about to be taken to Disneyland.

It was everything Mommy had described and more, because she had seen it in the evening and hadn't seen the flower beds, the hedges, all of the ponds and fountains. It was incredible to think that one man lived alone in a house this large. It looked more like a hotel.

Everywhere we looked people were working, pruning bushes and trees, planting new flowers, blowing away debris, whitewashing. I understood now why she said it wasn't so much of an exaggeration to imagine someone vacuuming the driveway. All the stone looked new, every window glistened.

Closer to the house the royal coconut palm trees stood like sentinels lining the circular entry drive. The house itself contained four pavilion-like structures punctuated by graceful arches with a tree-shaded main facade. The entrance was under a loggia or an arcade made of cast stone. Just as Mommy had claimed, we could see the ocean behind the house and another building down to the left toward the beach.

"Where's the yacht?" I asked, and Winston laughed.

"Down at the dock," he said.

"It's not the sort of boat you can hook to the back of your car," Mommy said, and they both laughed like conspirators. I blushed at my own stupidity.

"Don't sulk," Mommy urged when I turned away. "It's hard to imagine everything, I know. I told Winston his home is so big he might have some guests left over from a holiday party and not know it."

Winston grunted in agreement. "That actually once happened," he said. "I thought a guest of ours had left along with three others, and she hadn't. It was quite embarrassing when I stepped out in my birthday suit."

We walked through the house to the rear loggia. I couldn't help ogling everything. How could someone own so much art and not be considered a museum? The sitting rooms were large, but the dining room looked like a dining room I once saw at the naval officers school. The table went on and on as it would if it had a king at the head of it. How rich was Winston Montgomery? Did he own most of the country?

We paused at a huge portrait of him and his wife. She was almost as tall as he was, elegant looking with soft eyes and a gentle, Mona Lisa smile. Winston looked much younger in the portrait, and all of his good qualities had been highlighted by the artist.

"She was very beautiful, Winston," Mommy said.

He nodded. I wondered if this was the first time she had seen the picture.

He snapped out of his reverie quickly and smiled at Mommy. "I like to surround myself with beautiful things," he said.

"We can see that, can't we, Grace?"

"Yes," I said, noticing how he fixed his gaze on Mommy and she looked coyly back.

"We'll show you the rest of the house later, Grace," he said. "Let's get to the yacht now so we can go to one of my favorite places on the coast where we'll have our lunch. If you're good," he kidded, "I'll have the captain let you steer."

"Really?"

Mommy laughed and put her arm around my shoulders as we stepped out onto the loggia and I panned the rear of the estate. The pool was as big and as beautiful as she had described. There was a cabana behind it. I saw the private beach, the umbrellas and tables. Here there were also more gardens with people attending to the flowers. Off to the left was the so-called beach house, which to me looked like a small apartment building.

And then there was the dock and the yacht. I had imagined a boat like Roger's, but this was so big it took my breath away. It looked more like a small cruise ship. How could one man own all this?

"Now you see why I was laughing when you said 'picnic on a boat,' " Mommy told me, observing my big eyes.

"Our picnic boat is ninety-four feet long," Winston began as we started toward the dock. "It has three decks. At the top we have the wet bar, the flybridge, and the aft deck. You know what that means?"

"Yes," I said.

"That's right. I keep forgetting you were a naval family," he said, smiling.

We still are, I thought. Daddy used to say it was in his blood, so it was in mine.

"On the second level we have the dining room and the main salon, and on the third level we have the three bedrooms, the master stateroom, a VIP stateroom, which you can consider yours today, if you like, and a double stateroom for guests. That cockpit you see contains the pilot house, and that's Captain Gene. He's been with me ever since I bought the yacht."

"Are you sailing all the time?" I asked, and he laughed.

"No, no. When I'm not using it, I lease it out to a very select list of clients. It doesn't come close to paying for it, I'm afraid," he said, smiling at Mommy.

Besides the captain, a tall, lean man with a face leathered by years at sea, there were two other crewmen. Everyone was introduced, and we took a tour of the yacht.

"All the rooms, with the exception of the pilot house, of course, were designed and decorated for me by Giovanni Marcello," Winston said.

Mommy widened her eyes and nodded, but I could see she didn't know any more about this Giovanni Marcello than I did.

"He's done everyone's yachts down here and in Monte Carlo," Winston continued. He spoke nonchalantly about it, not sounding like someone putting on airs, I thought. "I was too busy to go interviewing and comparing designers. I left that up to my wife. It was one of the last big things she did," he said, not hiding his sadness. I liked that because it told me he wasn't ashamed to express in front of another woman just how much he had cared for her and how much he still missed her.

"She made an excellent choice," Mommy said.

He smiled. "Yes, we've always been complimented."

When we stepped into the galley, there were two women preparing our lunch. Now I really felt foolish calling it a picnic.

"This is Louisa, my chef, captain of the kitchen," he cried, and a short woman with black hair invaded by gray strands turned to beam a smile at us. She had a very soft, friendly face with eyes as black as her hair.

Her cheeks were rosy and plump, and she had a slight cleft in her chin.

"I'm no captain, Mr. Montgomery, just a cook," she gently chastised.

"And this is her daughter Angelina," Winston said.

Angelina nodded at us. I thought she wasn't all that much older than I was. She lowered her dark eyes shyly. She had her mother's hair but was much slimmer, with a narrow, almost bony face. Her hands were thin, too, the fingers spidery as she kneaded dough I imagined would be turned into fresh bread.

"What's today's picnic lunch?" Winston asked, smiling at me.

Mommy grinned from ear to ear.

"Calamari frittata and mushrooms stuffed with crab meat," Louisa began, "mozzarella and tomato salad, lobster bisque, poached salmon, fettuccine with fresh tomatoes and shrimp Alfredo. We are preparing the garlic bread," she said, nodding at her daughter.

"And dessert? We're all interested in dessert," he said, smiling at me.

"We have chocolate truffle tarts and crème brûlée and some Italian cookies," she said as if they had it every day.

"Crème brûlée! I love crème brûlée!" Mommy exclaimed.

Winston laughed. "As you can see, I stole Louisa from a restaurant in Capri one summer, and I have never returned her, although she threatens every now and then to go back," he said, raising his eyebrows and glaring at her with feigned anger.

"Some-a-day I will," Louisa said, meeting his challenge. Winston laughed. She glanced at her daughter, who just worked as we talked.

"I'll throw myself overboard when she leaves," Winston threatened, and Louisa gave him another repri- manding look that had us all laughing.

We went to the pilot house and watched Captain Gene get Winston's yacht under way. Then Mommy and I went down to the bridge and sat on some lounges while Winston and his captain discussed the itinerary.

The warm breeze blew through our hair. We could feel the spray of the sea as the yacht sliced through the waves. How bright and beautiful it all looked from this perspective. Even the clouds were whiter. I couldn't help feeling like someone special.

"Do you believe all this, Grace? Can you imagine what it must be like living like this all the time, doing whatever you want whenever you want to do it?"

"No," I said. "Doesn't he still have to work?"

"He has his affairs handled by a business manager. He oversees everything, but he's not involved in the day-to-day nitty-gritty anymore. He took a giant step back from all that after his wife's death."

"How did she die?"

"She had what they call an aneurism, cerebral. Fortunately, she didn't linger in a coma."

"Why didn't they ever have any children?" I asked.

"They tried. She had two miscarriages, and they gave up. They talked about adopting but never got around to doing it and finally decided they were both too old to be good parents. That's what he says. He had a nephew he was fond of and helped him financially. He says he can't help wondering if he bears any responsi- bility for his nephew's self-destructive ways, ways that eventually led to his death. He got heavily into drugs and died a horrible death in some flophouse in New Orleans. It broke his parents' hearts, and in their search for someone or something to blame they blamed Winston for being too generous. They became estranged. His brother died last year, and his sister-in-law kept it from him until it was too late for him to attend the funeral."

"I guess no matter how rich you are you can't escape from family tragedy," I said.

"Not if you're not responsible and up to being rich. Some people can't handle success, just as some can't handle failure. That's what Winston says."

"You and he did talk about a lot the other night, in just one night," I remarked.

She smiled like someone who knew a lot more than she was telling.

"Everyone wearing sun screen?" Winston asked as he approached.

"Oh, no!" Mommy said in a panic.

"Don't worry." He handed lotion to us. "Can't let my two beauties spoil their skin," he said. "Come along, Grace," he told me after I had put some on my face. "Let Captain Gene show you how this big toy works."

He reached for my hand and led me back to the pilot house, where Captain Gene gave me a beginner's course in yachting, while below Mommy and Winston sat talking or standing and looking out at the sea, Mommy looking more radiant than ever, as if she already owned it all.

When we reached the bay Winston loved, Captain Gene set anchor and we began our feast, everything brought out slowly to the dining area. Winston offered me some wine, and I looked at Mommy to see what I should do.

"It's okay, honey. Food like this almost requires good wine."

"Spoken like a true Palm Beach resident," Winston remarked.

"We don't live in Palm Beach," I said.

"Palm Beach," Winston said, sitting back and looking serious and philosophical, "is really a state of mind, a style. Some abuse it, overdo it, just as you can overdo your appreciation of any of the finer things in life, drinking too much of this excellent French wine, for example, eating too much of Louisa's wonderful food. The secret is reaching a level of enjoyment and holding it for a while and then retreating or knowing when to retreat."

He paused and looked at Mommy, who did seem to hang on his every word, and then he looked at me. "Oh, I'm sorry. I can get that way sometimes: heavy and philosophical. It's the old man in me."

"That's wonderful, Winston. It's nice to know someone who is willing to share his wisdom with others. And you're far from an old man," Mommy said.

He smiled at her, but he glanced worriedly at me. "I didn't mean to get too serious and spoil our day of fun," he said.

"It's all right. I think I understand what you're saying." I looked at Mommy and then back at him. "Do you know the myth of Icarus?" I asked him, glancing at Mommy, too.

He thought a moment and shook his head.

"Daedalus, an inventor in Athens, was exiled to the island of Crete with his son Icarus. He invented an escape using feathers and wings so they could fly off, but he told Icarus not to fly too high, or the sun would melt his wax and his wings would fall off. Icarus was so excited to be flying that he disregarded the warning and flew too high. He fell to the sea."

I glanced at Mommy again. She looked pensive, even worried. Was I telling her all this was simply too high a reach for us?

Winston was silent. Then he smiled. "I see we have a real student among us. I'm one who believes you're never too old to learn something new. I have a few business associates I'd like to tell that story to, Grace. I suppose having too much ambition is bad, but not having enough is just as bad, wouldn't you say?"

"Yes."

"The trick is finding the shoe that fits, huh?"

"Yes," I said.

"Well, back to having fun," he said, clapping his hands as if he could control the weather and the rise and fall of the sun itself. "Let's get the yacht under way again."

"Don't you have to get home to get ready for work, Mommy?" I asked.

"Not tonight. I've already taken care of that."

"Another day off?"

"It's all right, Grace. Don't worry," she said firmly.

Winston held his smile. "It's nice to see a young adult who can be serious and responsible," he said.

I knew he meant it, but I was feeling more like Icarus, letting the compliments, the opulence, the overwhelming world of Winston Montgomery carry me too close to the sun. What I feared most was that Mommy was closer than I was already. Her wings were melting fast.

How can I say we didn't enjoy this day? It was so much fun steering the yacht, making it go faster and slower. How different the world looked from this viewpoint. It all made me feel free and important. Mommy surprised me when

Winston suggested we all go for a swim in his pool. She had brought my bathing suit in her bag.

We ended up staying well into the evening. Louisa prepared a light supper of tasty salads, and we ate on the rear loggia, watching the sunset.

"It's so beautiful here, so peaceful," Mommy said. "You can feel you've escaped everything unpleasant."

"Yes. That is why I think the original owners named it Joya del Mar. The sea's gift is this sense of contentment.

"Well, Jackie," he said, turning to Mommy, "you've done it again." He pretended to be angry.

"Done what?"

"Caused me to lose all track of time."

"I did . . ."

"So I've come up with a solution," he said, and reached into his pocket to produce a slim cream-colored box. "This might help."

She looked at me astonished and then slowly opened the box. Before she took what was in it out, she screamed. "Winston! It isn't a real one, is it?"

"I don't know how to buy anything that isn't," he said, winking at me. "I refuse to have anything do to with anything or anyone who isn't authentic."

She held it up. It was a Rolex watch. "I can't accept . . ."

"Here," he said, interrupting and reaching over to take the watch. "Let me help you put it on." He fastened it around her wrist, and she stared for a moment with her mouth still wide open. Then she held it out for me to see.

"It's beautiful," I said.

"And keeps good time," Winston added. He laughed and signaled the maid to bring out their coffee. Mommy was glowing so brightly I thought she would rival the moon that was brightening into a quarter of itself every passing moment.

Afterward I wandered down to the shore and walked along, feeling the cool sand in my toes. The value of the gift Winston had given my mother was not lost on me. This was long past just a friendship, and that made me feel shaky and numb. Mommy and Winston went inside, and when I returned I did, too, but I didn't find them immediately. I sat and watched some television in his entertainment center, and about an hour later Mommy appeared.

"We'd better get home, Grace. It's been a big day."

"Where's Winston?"

"He had to make some phone calls. The limousine is waiting for us."

"But shouldn't I thank him?"

"You can do that tomorrow," she said.

"Tomorrow?"

"He's taking us to dinner, someplace very special," she said. There was an impish twinkle in her eyes.

"You're skipping another night of work then?" I asked as we started out.

"Yes. Dallas is fine with it."

She dozed as we were driven home. Her beautiful new Rolex twinkled in whatever light invaded the limousine. I sat looking out the window at the brightly lit streets of Palm Beach and then the bridge and the restaurants, nightclubs and gas stations we passed as we traveled through West Palm Beach, back to our condo development. Our apartment never looked as small to me.

"This is like a closet in Joya del Mar," I remarked after we had entered.

Mommy laughed. "Exactly," she said. "We're not staying here forever. That's for sure."

I hadn't meant it to sound as if I was suffering or ashamed of our home, but that was how she had taken it. Anyway, she was right about the day. Even though it was a day of total enjoyment, it was tiring. I wasn't in bed five minutes before I drifted asleep and slept contentedly, maybe for the first time in a long time, until the sunlight exploded in my room and opened my eyes.

I was surprised to see Mommy in my room. She was looking in my closet.

"What are you doing?" I asked.

"Just thinking about what you should wear to dinner tonight," she said. "I don't think you have the right sort of dress."

I sat up.

"What? What time is it?" I glanced at the clock. "It's only seven-thirty in the morning!"

"I know, silly. I was worried about it, and I'm right. We're going shopping."

"Today?"

"The store I want to go to opens at nine-thirty today," she said. "You're going to need some new shoes, too." She turned to me. "I might get myself something new as well," she said. "Get up soon so we can have breakfast."

I watched her leave, wondering if I was still asleep and dreaming the whole thing.

After we ate and dressed we headed out to the shop. Mommy knew exactly where she wanted to take us. It was back in Palm Beach and just reeked expensive. What was she thinking of? We were looking at clothing in the high hundreds and thousands, designer dresses and shoes. I wondered if the saleswomen who rushed about finding garments to show us had any idea what sort of income level we were on. None of that seemed to matter.

"Mommy," I whispered when she insisted I try on a Coco Chanel black dress. It had a dozen gold Chanel logo buttons on the bodice and two on each cuff and a gleaming gold belt with a buckle etched with Chanel, tuxedo lapels, and two slash hip pockets. "It's too expensive."

"But it's so practical," Mommy insisted. "You can wear it to most anything."

"Practical?"

Maybe it was less expensive in other stores, but here they wanted $995! She was already looking for the shoes to match the outfit. I half hoped it would look terrible on me, but when I stepped out of the fitting room and gazed at myself in the mirror there was no hope of that. Even some other customers stopped to compliment me.

Mommy beamed. "Perfect," she said.

The shoes she found were almost as much as the dress. I couldn't speak. Had she gone totally mad?

It took nearly another two hours for her to find a dress she wanted. I was very surprised at her choice. She had nothing like it in her own wardrobe. It just wasn't her style, at least before today.

The saleswoman told her the dress was based on a design especially made for a countess. It was a ballerina-length strapless dress of midnight blue with a dropped waistline. The bodice was draped with vertical pleats. The saleswoman explained that the bodice was embroidered with randomly placed diamante brilliants and the top layer of the tulle skirt was embroidered with diamante stars.

The price tag read $2,500. I stared in disbelief when Mommy decided it was perfect.

The shoes she chose sold for $1,100.

For a moment I couldn't swallow. I said nothing as the clothing and the shoes were packaged for us. At the desk Mommy did not present her credit card. The saleswoman smiled and had a young man carry everything out to our car.

When I asked Mommy why she didn't present her credit card, she said, "We have an account there. Don't worry about it, Grace. You look beautiful in your dress."

An account there? What did that mean, we were on some sort of ritzy lay-away plan? I truly began to believe my mother had gone crazy. I was unable to concentrate on anything for the rest of the day. We were going to leave rather early for dinner, I thought, five o'clock. When I asked her why, she said that was part of Winston's surprise, and if she said any more she would spoil it for me.

Mommy rested with cucumber slices on her eyes for an hour and then showed me some of the new skin creams and lotions she had recently bought. While I listened and watched her go on and on about herself, her skin, her hair, the things she had learned about putting on makeup, I wondered if grief could cause schizophrenia. Who was this new woman in my mother's body?

Once she had started on herself, she turned to me and sat me in front of the vanity table mirror in her room to supervise my makeup and hair. We were both dressed and ready by four forty-five, but Mommy kept returning to her room and her mirror for one final touch. Then she sat with that small smile playing on her lips and kept her anticipation focused on the street in front of our condo. Winston proved to be right on time again, the limousine gliding up to the curb exactly at five.

Winston himself wore an elegant, stylish tuxedo. I thought he looked like a governor or a president.

"Look at you two!" he cried the moment we stepped out of the condo. "I'm going to have rolls and rolls of pictures taken tonight."

"Where are we going?" I asked, bursting.

"You'll see," he said, his eyes twinkling with an impish glint.

I couldn't help but feel the excitement as we glided onto the highway. I looked out the window, watching and waiting for some hint. When we turned toward the West Palm Beach airport, I looked at Mommy, who seemed as if she was about to explode with excitement herself.

"What is this?" I asked. "We're going to the airport?"

"It's the best way to get there," Winston said.

"Get where?" I asked.

"My favorite restaurant in the Bahamas. On Paradise Island," he said.

I looked at them both. Was this some big joke?

We were ushered through the airport to a private hangar and a private jet. Moments later we were seated.

"Whose plane is this?" I asked.

"I lease it along with a few other people," Winston explained.

"Now you see why we had to have something special to wear tonight, Grace," Mommy said. She looked as if she was high on some powerful drug. Her eyes were shifting back and forth as she visually digested every little detail. We were offered something to drink.

Mommy and Winston had champagne cocktails. Mommy said I could have one, too, but I chose a soft drink. My stomach was doing flip-flops as it was, and I knew what one alcoholic beverage could do to me.

Minutes later we were off, and I gazed out the window at the lights below. I thought I should pinch myself to see if this was all really happening. Less than an hour later we were being driven to a beautiful hotel and a restaurant where there was a huge aquarium right in the dining room. We had the table that provided the best view. The staff fawned over us. The moment we lifted our eyes someone was there to ask if we needed anything. Surely kings and queens, princes and princesses, aren't treated any more regally, I thought.

I could see that Winston truly enjoyed seeing the excitement, surprise, and pleasure in Mommy's and my faces. Despite his wealth and position, he spoke to everyone respectfully, no matter how low his or her rung on the ladder of service. It was also obvious that he was well known here and everyone truly liked him.

There was music at the restaurant, and during a lull in our dinner Winston asked Mommy to dance. She glanced at me nervously for a second and then smiled and went with him to the dance floor. As I watched them I thought about the way Daddy and she looked whenever I saw them dancing together. It would take them only a few moments to glide harmoniously into each other's movements, so that they soon looked like professionals. I was always taken with how other people were drawn to them and smiled softly to themselves.

Mommy and Winston looked quite formal, but he was a graceful dancer who never lost his sophisticated elegance. They chatted as they danced. I wondered how they would be if I wasn't there watching them so closely.

Just before dessert was served, Winston surprised me again, this time by asking me to dance with him. The music was quite a bit more upbeat. I started to shake my head.

"Oh, go on, Grace. Have fun. You can do this sort of dance better than I can. Go on."

Winston was up, holding his hand out to me. "Mademoiselle, may I?"

It wasn't just that I was shy. Daddy always made sure to ask me to dance whenever I was with them at any occasion where we could dance.

"Hey, Sailor Girl," he would say, "let's you and I show them how it's done."

I stared at Winston Montgomery's hand, and then I swallowed away my tightened throat and took his fingers. They closed so quickly on mine it was as if I had stuck them into a trap. He escorted me to the floor, looking prim and proper, and then, without any warning, began to dance like a teenager. I couldn't help but laugh and get into it myself. When I looked at Mommy she was laughing so hard I could see tears of happiness streaking down her cheeks.

"How did we do?" Winston asked her when the song ended.

"You blew everyone else off the floor," she said, then reached for me and kissed my cheek. "You look so beautiful, Grace. I just want to cry."

She sat beside me on the plane afterward, and I rested my head against her shoulder. Everything about the evening still seemed unreal, magical. The limousine was there waiting for us on arrival, and moments later we were heading for home.

"Go on ahead," Mommy said when we pulled up and the driver opened the door.

I left her speaking softly to Winston and went into our condo. The light on our answering machine was blinking. I had just turned on the playback when Mommy entered behind me.

There was a beep and then Dallas's voice. She was almost impossible to understand because she was speaking through tears and sobs.

"Jackie . . . Phoebe was in a terrible car accident. She's alive, but a boy in the car was killed . . . the police told Warren she was high on pot. They found it in the car . . . she's in intensive care . . . Warren is beside himself."

Mommy held her hands between her breasts and looked at me.

"I know the boy, too, Mommy. I'm sure it was Roger Winston, the boy you saw with her at the restaurant. Oh, Mommy . . ."

She hugged me, and we held on to each other for a few moments.

"I'd better call Dallas," she said.

I nodded and went to my room. All the fun, the excitement, the wonder of the evening leaked out of my body like air from a punctured balloon. I sat on my bed and stared at the floor. No matter how mean Phoebe was to me and to Mommy, I couldn't hate her enough to take any pleasure in this, and Roger, so handsome, with so much ahead of him . . .

Nearly ten minutes later Mommy came to my door. I was still sitting on the bed, dazed.

She looked even more terrible than she had before.

"Is Phoebe dead, too?" I asked quickly.

"No," she said. "But the boy who was killed . . . it

wasn't Roger Winston, honey. I'm sorry. It was Randy Walker. He was in the rear seat, but he was thrown forward and into the windshield."

It was as if the air had gone out of the room and my lungs had filled with steam.

I saw her face. I could see her lips moving, and then all went dark.

12

Twenty Dozen Roses

Of course I wondered what Randy had been doing in Phoebe's car. I thought they were mad at him for defending me, and I thought he would have nothing more to do with them. I couldn't imagine what had they promised him to get him to go along. I was sure they had amused themselves with his defense of me and his feelings for me.

The accident was on everyone's mind and lips at school. As the details emerged I learned that Phoebe hadn't put on her seat belt, and even though her air bag had gone off, she had been thrown from the vehicle. Roger had his seat belt on, and the air bag saved his life and kept him from anything but some minor abrasions. Ashley had been in the car, too, but she had been thrown into the front seat which cushioned her impact. Even so, she had a broken arm. Fortunately, her sister wasn't along.

The events laid a cloud of gloom over the student body, and the dark depression was heaviest and most noticeable at lunch. The ordinarily loud, cacophonous cafeteria was quite subdued, the clang of dishes, silverware, and pots and pans heard over every conversation. If someone laughed others stopped talking and looked his or her way, and the laugh was cut short.

Of course we all knew that none of us was invulnerable. Death could come knocking on our doors any time it wished. The natural order of things—birth, youth and strength, maturity and accomplishment, retirement and wisdom, age and death—had been dramatically changed, however, and for a while at least each of us saw his or her own mortality reflected in poor Randy's passing. It was almost as if death had cheated and won unfairly, broken rules. It shook up our world, made the ground tremble beneath our feet, took the wind out of our sails, and left us drifting. The moment of silence the principal asked for over the PA system in the morning set the tone for the remainder of the day.

I sensed that if it had been Phoebe who had died instantly instead of Randy, her friends surely would have turned their grief and anger in my direction, expecting that I would be pleased. After all, she had in a true sense declared war on me in this school, and it was to be assumed I would feel some kind of victory.

However, they were all just as aware of how close Randy and I had become. Whatever condition Phoebe was in, she was still alive, and my closest ally was gone, an innocent, gentle person was gone. So instead of searching my face for glee, they fixed their eyes on me in anticipation of tears and gloom. For the most part they got it. Every time I looked at Randy's empty desk or turned in expectation of his coming up beside me, my eyes glossed over and I eventually had to wipe a fugitive tear from my cheeks.

By the end of the day Wally worked up the courage to speak to me. He caught up with me in the hallway after the final bell.

"Hey," he said, touching my arm.

I turned to him. For most of the day I felt as if I was just making the motions, moving in a semiconscious state, drifting, staring at nothing, rarely hearing the teachers' voices.

"I just can't believe it," he said when I just looked at him. "I was almost in that car myself. I couldn't get away. My father had been doing stuff at the house."

"Lucky you," I said.

He nodded and shifted his eyes guiltily toward the floor.

"How's Roger?"

"He'll be back in school tomorrow. He's just shaken up badly. I spoke to him at lunchtime. He asked about you."

"Why?"

"He just thought . . . with what happened to Randy . . ."

"Why did he go with them, Wally? I thought Phoebe was mad at him!"

"I don't know," he said quickly, keeping his eyes down.

"I don't believe you. I had just spoken with him, and he had told me she was upset at the way he was defending me."

"I don't know," he said, waving his head. Then he looked at me. "I think she told him they were trying to find a way to make friends, that it had all gone wrong and she wanted it to be right. Maybe she was teasing him. I don't know. You know how she can be."

"Right, I know, and it didn't take me long. Look how long it's taking you."

"No one wanted him to die, Grace. Man oh man, everyone's sick about it, especially Roger. He often tried to protect him. You saw that. He hated when I teased him."

I softened a bit. That was true, I thought.

"How did this accident really happen, Wally?"

"Hey," he said, holding up his hands, "I don't know. I wasn't there."

"Right," I said, "hear no evil, see no evil." I turned to continue out of the building.

"I don't know," he insisted, coming up beside me. "Roger said that she was just driving way too fast."

"And that was all that was wrong with her?" I cross-examined, my eyes like steel.

"He said she had some pot before they started out, but he thought it had worn off."

I stopped walking. "You know what people do with situations like this, Wally?"

He shook his head.

"They go into self-denial. They actually lie to themselves so they won't feel bad. Or they look for someone else to blame. Randy's death is too heavy, even for someone as self-centered as Phoebe. If Roger asks about me again, you can tell him I'm fine. I didn't give Phoebe her way, and I'm not just as much at fault. Think you could remember all that?"

He looked as if he was going to cry. He nodded.

"Months from now when she's back behind the wheel of the new car she talked her father into buying for her and you're in the backseat, remember that," I said, and pivoted quickly to leave him behind. Fury gave wings to my feet. I walked and walked until I decided to catch a bus and go home.

Mommy was there. She had just returned from the hospital where she had been keeping Dallas and Warren company. "Phoebe's going to be all right," she told me. "It will be a long recuperation after which they will have to consider some cosmetic surgery. Warren's going to open the restaurant tomorrow. It's best that everyone get back to being normal and occupied. How were things at school?"

"Dreary," I said.

"Here I was hoping I had taken us from all the sadness and depression into a bright new world . . ." She shook her head.

"Maybe we can't get away from it," I said bitterly. "Maybe it will be with us for the rest of our lives, or at least with me."

"What kind of talk is that, Grace?"

"Realistic," I said, and went to my bedroom. I threw myself on the bed and buried my face in the pillow. Was it my imagination, or was it true that everyone with whom I had come into some close contact suffered soon afterward, from Autumn to Augustus to Randy? Somewhere deep in the back of my mind I could see that sea gull twisting in the air, turning as if in distress and pain, flying off just before Daddy left on his training mission, the mission that would end with his death. Could someone have a curse on him or her? Was I a Jonah, always bringing bad vibes to people I cared for or became close friends with?

Maybe I should become friends only with the people I don't like, I thought.

Mommy knocked on my door. "Grace?"

I turned and looked at her.

"I don't like you talking like that, honey. I know you're hurting for your friend, but you can't beat up on yourself. That won't help. It just makes it all harder for everyone."

"I can't help how I feel, Mommy."

"I know. I just spoke with Winston. He feels terrible for us, and he's coming over in an hour to take us both out to dinner."

"I don't want to go," I said sullenly.

"Please, Grace. I won't have a good time knowing you're home pouting and sulking. We have to go on and try to find some enjoyment in life, too. I'm not going to let this continue," she said firmly.

I looked up at her. "What continue?"

"This downward spiral, this streak of bad luck and gloom. We don't deserve it."

"Randy didn't deserve to die."

"Of course not, but we can't change what happened, and it does him no good for us, for you, to let it bring you further and further down. Fate will not have its way with us," she vowed. "Now put on something bright and joyful, and let's bring some sunshine back into our lives."

"I can't," I wailed.

"Grace." She stood there, her arms at her sides, her hands clenched in fists. "How do you think I do it? How do you think I woke up the morning after your father was killed and continued? I felt as if my insides had been kicked out. I wanted to jump into that grave with him. It would have been so much easier to pull the blanket over my head and deny, deny, deny. But life won't let you do that, Grace. And we're not going to be losers and sufferers forever," she declared.

"Now you get up and join me and Winston, and you look at the world again, and you learn to take advantage of every opportunity, every blessing, every little stroke of luck that comes your way. Our days of sacrifice and pain are coming to an end," she predicted.

I stared at her. I had been holding my breath the whole time she spoke. She looked so different I was sure if my father came back he would think he had entered the wrong house.

"Something bright and joyful," she reminded me. She turned and left my room with such power in her footsteps I thought she had sucked out the air behind her.

I went into the bathroom and looked at my glum face in the mirror. Of course I didn't want to wallow in sadness and defeat. I didn't want to wear the cloak of dark depression. I just didn't think I had Mommy's strength and ability to cast it off.

I began with a hot shower. I fixed my hair. I chose a bright blue blouse and matching skirt and put on some lipstick. When I gazed at myself in the mirror, I still saw the shadows in my eyes. I tried to smile, but my face felt so brittle I thought it might shatter if I tried too hard.

Mommy knocked on my door. "Winston is here, honey."

"Coming," I called back. I glanced at myself once more and then joined her. She looked as beautiful as ever, and she was wearing something else new, an off-the-shoulder red silk dress with a high slit. She had a new pair of gold earrings and a pearl necklace I couldn't recall.

"Where did you get that?" I asked.

"Our Palm Beach boutique," she replied.

Our Palm Beach boutique?

Winston was at the door. "Ladies," he said, holding out his arms. Mommy moved quickly to his right, and they both looked to me. After a slight hesitation I took his left, and he escorted us to the limousine. I really felt silly.

"Where are we going tonight?" I asked. "Not Bermuda or something, are we?"

Winston laughed. "No. Just a place on the water. Twenty or so minutes' driving. No big surprises." Then he turned serious. "I know what it's like for you, Grace. To lose a young friend like this," he said, shaking his head.

"I was hoping we wouldn't talk about it," Mommy interjected.

"No, no," Winston said. "We can't run from our disappointments and hide. We must find ways to grow stronger because of them instead."

I liked that. I liked that he was confident enough in himself to do what he wanted, what he thought he should, even if it displeased someone he wanted to please very much.

"When I was in college I lost my best friend in a similar way, automobile accident. He and I were runners."

"Runners?" Mommy asked.

"Yes, you know, track and field. I happen to have been a four-letter man, too. I was on the school's championship relay team, and I came in second at the allstate conference in the three-thousand-meter steeplechase. I looked like a gazelle in those days, all legs, lanky. My mother used to say I was so thin she could see my breakfast."

I laughed.

"Anyway, my roommate, Paul Thoreau, was a runner, too. He was actually the fastest in the two-hundred-meter and might have gone on to be in the Olympics. You couldn't meet a nicer guy, sensitive, considerate, very family oriented, and religious. In all the time I knew him I never heard him say a bad thing about anyone else. He would say nothing rather than do that, and he rarely cursed. We used to make fun of him for that," he said, remembering with a smile. "He would say things like 'Holy cow!' or 'Jeepers!' He was killed on his way back to college. A drunken truck driver hit him head-on. He never had a chance. The truck just veered into his lane.

"I like to think he's running in heaven, winning trophies. Anyway, I wanted to quit the team, give up running myself afterward, and my coach . . . I'll never forget him, Rolly Allen, pulled me aside and said, 'Don't you know, Paul will be running alongside you for the rest of your life, Winston. You can't outrun him.'

"I smiled at that, and you won't believe this, but I ran my best race soon afterward, and when I stepped off the track Mr. Allen was there, and I said, 'You were right. He was with me step for step.'

"If you're close with someone, Grace, you take them with you forever. Just think of that. It won't stop the pain and the sadness completely, but you can go on and run your races and do your work, and after all that's what is most important."

I didn't realize I was crying until he leaned forward with his handkerchief and wiped the tears from my cheeks. Then he touched my hand, and I seized his. We held on to each other for a long moment. I saw Mommy watching, a smile on her face, and then I sat back and listened to them talk about an upcoming charity event Winston insisted we attend with him.

*   *   *

Life was meant to go on, and go on it would at an even faster pace than before. Mommy returned to work at the restaurant, but as the weeks and months went by it soon became more and more of a part-time job. Every time Winston had a place to take her or take us both, she would call Dallas and get off that evening. Of course, I wondered how she could be buying all the new clothes, the new shoes, and the jewelry for herself and me as well, and then one morning she revealed that Winston paid our bill at the boutique.

"How could you let him do that?" I asked, astounded.

"It was his idea from the start, Grace. I didn't know anyone in Palm Beach and certainly didn't know my way around boutiques and beauty salons."

"You mean he even arranged for that, your hairdo?"

"It's something he enjoys doing. It means nothing to him financially, and . . ."

"But that's like . . . like taking advantage of someone," I blurted.

"Hardly," she said. "I can't imagine anyone taking advantage of Winston Montgomery. It's probably the other way around." She sounded almost critical. By now I had come to like Winston very much. I didn't see how he could be nasty to anyone. "I didn't ask him to buy these things for us, Grace. He offered."

"But . . ."

"No buts about it. He's on top of the world, and if he wants to rain down some of that gold upon us, I'm not going to throw up any umbrellas. I told you, I'm tired of being the victim, the suffering casualty of an unforgiving, relentless, and cruel fate. We'll beat it back until it leaves us alone and goes looking for weaker prey.

"Besides," she continued, "Winston wants me to go with him to the finest places, fly us places, take us to extravagant charity events. I told him we couldn't go because we didn't have the wardrobe for all that, and he said he wouldn't permit us to miss anything because of something so trivial as clothing and shoes. Those were his words. I told him we couldn't accept any charity, especially for expensive things we wouldn't use much, and he said we would be doing him a favor. He likes us, Grace!" she cried, throwing up her hands. "How can we be blamed for that?"

She waited for my response. I didn't know what to say. Winston never made me feel like a charity case or as if he was doing us any favors. Mommy was right. He was the one who always acted grateful and looked sad if we were even a bit unhappy or if there was any possibility we wouldn't accompany him to something. His favorite expression was "You two make me look good."

"I just . . . feel funny about it," I said.

"Well don't," she insisted. "If he doesn't want to do it, Winston Montgomery will tell us. He is not a man who does anything he doesn't want to do."

Was Mommy falling in love with him or just admiring him and enjoying his company? I wondered. Sometimes she sounded as if she thought he was so wonderful, and sometimes she sounded as if he was just someone she was occupying herself with until something better or more important came along. I guessed the biggest danger to being rich was being used, taken advantage of, but if you didn't mind, if what you received in return was satisfying, what difference did it make? Especially for someone as wealthy as Winston Montgomery.

"Okay," I said. I wasn't going to argue or make Mommy feel bad about anything.

The list of events Winston wanted us to attend seemed to grow longer with every passing week. Most of the time I was unable to attend. I had to study for an exam or complete a major homework assignment. I became accustomed to preparing dinner for myself. Mommy was always suggesting I invite a friend over to eat with me, but after the tragic accident and Randy's death I retreated to my own corner of the world. Time seemed to have little meaning. One week was like the next.

I was friendly with other students, talked about school and homework, but I resisted every invitation to every party. Two boys asked me out, but I made up so many excuses they soon gave up. Despite the lectures Mommy gave me I couldn't get over the dreaded feeling that somehow, some way, I brought others bad luck.

When Phoebe finally returned to school she was treated like some sort of heroine. Expensive cosmetic surgery had corrected almost all of her scars. What few could be seen were treated as if they were badges of honor. She had survived, but the accident and the ordeal that followed didn't change who she was inside. If anything, it reinforced her arrogance and her conceit. Now she was even more of a center of attention.

The one thing that did change was her focus on me. I stayed away from her, and she finally decided to really ignore me. Perhaps I was a constant reminder of Randy and his death, and she wanted to avoid that more than anything. Ironically I thought that was Randy's gift to me. He wanted Phoebe off my back, and he got her off. Only the price was far too high. I hated her for that, but I didn't dwell on it.

Winston became more of a confidant for me than Mommy was during those weeks. She had reached a place where she did not want to think about, hear about, or discuss anything unpleasant or sad.

"You permit one teardrop to slip under your door, and a flood of sadness comes pouring your way," she told me. "Think of only happy things, fun things, beautiful things."

She even stopped watching her favorite soap opera because it had too many sad events occurring in it. She would rather watch mindless sitcoms if she watched any television at all. Most of the time she was too busy planning her wardrobe or working on her appearance.

She turned her attention to fashion magazines, read the Palm Beach newspaper and magazine religiously to the point where she knew all the social gossip. Winston was at first amused by that and then occasionally looked at me with a troubling eye.

"Oh, Jackie," he said once after she was rattling off what this heiress had done and that trust baby had bought, "you don't want to dote on those people. And you certainly don't want to be anything like they are. Why, when they die, their souls will just go up in a puff of smoke." He and I laughed, but Mommy looked upset.

Later she told me, "Winston might make fun of those people with us, but believe me, they are the citizens of his country, and he pays more than just lip service to them."

I wanted to argue about that, but I didn't. *Let it go,* I thought. *Maybe all this will soon end, and who knows, maybe we'll move.* That was something we were accustomed to doing anyway. I would certainly not put up any fight if she suggested that. Winter slipped almost unnoticed into spring, and very often in the spring talk of our leaving for another base, another community, began.

However, what was to be now was quite the contrary, even though for a short time it looked as if it was not to be. One night in late May Mommy came home unusually early from a charity ball in Palm Beach. I was studying for my final in social studies, and I was still at my desk reviewing notes when I heard the front door open and then slam shut with such force the condo shook.

"Mommy?" I called from my door.

She went into her room without responding. I couldn't imagine what was happening, but I was so used to the sound of one shoe dropping I was trembling in anticipation of the next. I went to her room and peered in. She was throwing her jewelry and her clothes off in a fury.

"What is it? Why are you back so soon?" I asked. I didn't think she would respond, but suddenly she stopped undressing and turned to me.

"I don't mind a man who gets jealous and upset when you spend too much time with another man or other men. That I actually expect and enjoy. But a man who criticizes me for spending too much time with other women and agreeing to go to their lunches at the finer clubs is . . . is . . . infuriating!" she cried, and looked as if she would pull out her own hair.

"Maybe he just wants you to stay away from women he knows are not really nice," I offered.

"Why is it that all the men I've met in my life think they know everything, even what's best for me more than I do? Can't I tell who is and who isn't nice, who is and who isn't sincere? Do I have to depend on them for that?"

This was the first hint I had ever gotten that there was even an iota of dissatisfaction with Daddy. Unless, of course, she didn't include him.

"Daddy wasn't like that, was he?"

"Wasn't? Your father was a naval officer, Grace. He was in command. That wasn't something easily left outside the door when he came home to me."

She saw the expression on my face and relaxed. "It wasn't unpleasant. We didn't fight over things like most husbands and wives fight, but men in general feel superior. Don't you see that for yourself?"

I wanted to say no, but I was afraid.

"Most of the power in this world is in the hands of men, not women, Grace. They decide the important things, and every time a woman tries to take a piece of that away from them they cry that she's not a woman or she's too ambitious. The truth is, they're afraid of us, afraid we're smarter and we will take over everything," she said, nodding. She flopped onto the chair by the vanity table.

"So you had a bad fight with Winston?"

"No, not a bad fight. I just told him to take me home immediately. That put some hesitation in his steps. I told him if he had anything critical to say to me about me he should do it in total private and he should think ten times before saying it then. He got the point," she said.

She thought a moment. "If the phone rings, answer it and say I'm asleep or I'm in the bathroom if it's Winston."

"Okay," I said, retreating.

She was psychic. The phone rang an hour later, and it was Winston. I told him she was asleep.

"Oh. Well, tell her I'll call her tomorrow. How are you doing, Grace?"

"Studying for finals."

"That time already, huh? Time just flies. Before you know it, you'll be as old as me," he said with a light laugh. "Enjoy your youth while you have it."

"You're not so old, Winston," I said.

He liked that. "I hope I'll see you soon," he said. I felt sorry for him after we hung up.

Mommy came to her door. "Was that Winston?"

"Yes. I told him you were asleep."

"What did he say?"

"He said to tell you he'll call you tomorrow."

"I won't be home," she said. "Not until I feel like it."

She closed her door and then opened it quickly and looked out at me. "You'd better pay attention to this, Grace. Men have to be trained just like . . . like pets. We're always at a disadvantage, so we have to use everything we have, every emotion, every gesture, every word we say. And especially sex," she added. "Don't look so shocked. It's just another weapon in the arsenal. Women who don't take advantage of it will be taken advantage of. There are enough examples of that out there. Don't become another." She closed her door again.

I didn't know whether to laugh or cry. I was too shocked to do either. And my social studies notes provided no answers and no relief.

Winston might have called while I was in school. If he did, Mommy was true to her word and did not answer the phone. When I came home, however, I was greeted by the pungent aroma of roses, and when I looked in the kitchen I was nailed to the floor by the sight of what was there: not just two or three dozen roses but at least twenty dozen. The whole kitchen was covered, every available counter space, the table, the chairs, and some of the floor.

"Now this," Mommy said proudly, her hands on her hips as she nodded at the flood of roses, "is what I would call a decent apology."

I was soon to find out that it wasn't just an apology. It was groundwork for a marriage proposal.

It came two days later. Mommy had relented and gone out to dinner with Winston the night the roses arrived. She didn't return until very late, well after I had gone to sleep. I vaguely heard her come in. The following morning, she wasn't up to have breakfast with me as usual. I peeked in and saw she was dead asleep. Her dress wasn't even hung up. I did that on tiptoe for her, and then I went to school.

When I returned she was in a wonderful up mood. She was leaving shortly for work, but I had never seen her as happy about it.

"I prepared one of your favorite dinners for you, Grace, shrimp Parmesan. It's all in the dish in the fridge. You just have to heat it up. I'll be home late," she added, "so don't worry."

"Where are you going?"

"Someplace," she sang, laughed, and left.

Once again she didn't come home until long after I had gone to bed, but this time, when I woke in the morning, she was up as well, although still in her bed. She called to me when I went out to the kitchen.

She was sitting up, a smile on her lips, her blue eyes gleaming.

"Good morning," I said. "Where were you last night?"

"I was in a chariot," she said, laughing. "Made of gold and sparkling with diamonds. If you had looked out, you would have seen me crossing the night sky."

"What?" I held my confused smile.

"I have a surprise for you," she said, and extended her hand. At first I actually didn't see it. Maybe I didn't want to see it. She was obviously waiting for some big reaction on my part, but I just stared.

"What?" I said.

"Look, silly!" she cried, and held up her hand. Now, in the morning light, the large diamond twinkled so brightly even a blind person would see it. I stepped closer.

"What is it?" I asked, full knowing what it was.

"This is an engagement ring," she said. "He had it especially designed for me. It is a six-carat clear marquis. With the work that went into it, the quality, the color," she continued, turning her hand every which way to look at her ring, "it wouldn't surprise me to know this is worth a quarter of a million dollars."

"You're engaged to Winston?"

"Yes. Sit and let me tell you all about it," she said.

I backed away. "I've got to get to school."

"Forget school for a moment."

"I can't do that. I have a math final today."

"Well, you have time. I'll call you a cab and get you there faster," she added with annoyance. "This is important, Grace. C'mon," she urged. "Stop wrinkling your forehead and sit."

I did as she asked. A loud humming started at the base of my stomach and moved up to my chest. It was so loud I almost didn't hear her begin.

"From the first moment I met Winston I had the sense that he was sent to us."

"Sent to us? By whom?"

"By our good angel, of course. I could see it in the way he looked at me, spoke to me, smiled at me from across the restaurant. I knew who he was beforehand. Dallas had filled me in. She was doing that from the moment I arrived. 'It's not that I don't think a woman and her teenage daughter can't make it alone in this world,' she said, 'but why try?' "

Mommy laughed. "Dallas was always like that, looking for the easier way out. I never blamed her, now especially. Anyway, I didn't really expect anything would come of my conversations with Winston, but he was obviously determined to get to know me, and I let him," she said.

What does that mean? I wondered.

"As we became closer I realized he was a very nice man as well as being very rich. They don't go hand in hand all the time, you know. Not that I ever knew anyone as wealthy as Winston," she footnoted.

She looked at me, and I guess I was smirking. "I'm no gold-digger, Grace. I don't like using people or taking advantage of people, and we're not exactly destitute," she said. "We have what we need to live as we're living."

"So why did you accept the ring?" I countered quickly.

"I said to live as we're living. I have decided we deserve better. As I said, I didn't go after Winston like some gold-digger. You saw how I even told him off one night and made him take me home."

"But you said that was to train him."

"Whatever. I was willing to lose him when it came to my self-respect, and gold-diggers have no self-respect. He courted me, lavished gifts upon me and you, and I never felt I owed him anything for that, nor did I offer anything, and, to his credit, he never asked for anything. As I have told you many times, he truly enjoys giving to those he cares about."

"Are you in love with him, Mommy?"

"He is a nice man, Grace, a kind man, and he needs me almost as much as we need him."

"You mean his money."

"Let's not look down on it and what it will bring us." She gazed at the ring and then looked away a moment, blinking back a tear. "I'll never find anyone as wonderful as your father was anyway, and I don't like being out there like so much meat on display. The one great thing Winston has given me is taking me off the market. I could see it in the faces and the lusty looks of the young men who came to the Tremont Inn bar. After they learned whom I was seeing, they looked right through me, and that suited me real fine.

"It gave me some class," she said, raising her head. "I felt like somebody and not just a Navy widow everyone expects is dying for another man.

"Then, when he began to take us to the charity events and I met these . . . these rich-beyond-your-imagination people, I thought to myself that they are no better than we are. Why did fate give them so much and do so dirty a deed to us? Why should I let it stand?

"When I saw how beautiful you looked in those expensive clothes, how you glowed on the yacht and how you glowed when he took us to Paradise Island for dinner and you danced with him, I knew what I had to do for us, and I've done it. I'm not ashamed, and I feel no guilt."

"But . . . but you're not in love with him, Mommy. You're going to marry a man you don't love."

"I like him enough, Grace, and he loves me enough to compensate for what I lack. We'll be fine together, just fine," she insisted.

"He's so much older than you are," I whined. "He could be your father."

"Your father used to say he was my father, too. He used to say he had two little girls, two young women to take care of, and that's fine. I like a man to take care of me. I'm not one of these women who is out to prove she is as strong or as capable as any man. I don't have to prove it. I know it, but if I have the choice, I choose to be pampered, spoiled, protected, and made a citizen of the privileged class.

"Didn't you enjoy the way the stylist in the beauty parlor leaped to please me and the way the saleswomen in the boutique nearly broke their necks trying to make us happy? I did, and I will from now on.

"I can thumb my nose at fate now. I can tell it to bury its tail between its legs and go off. And as far as unhappiness goes, that's over for you, too, Grace. Next year you'll be attending a private school, and you won't have to battle any Phoebes or any other girl who thinks she's superior to you. You'll be able to buy and sell the whole lot of them, and they'll know it.

"No," she practically screamed at me, "I am not in love, but I'm in comfort and security. I've had love. It was ripped out of my heart, but I won't wilt like some flower without water or sunshine. I'll have my own sunshine whenever I want it, and we'll water our flowers with champagne.

"Be happy for me, Grace. Be happy for us both. Winston is so fond of you, at times I think he's fonder of you than he is of me. You're the daughter he never had but so wanted, and you like him, too. I know you do."

"I'm not saying I don't."

"Good," she snapped as if she was closing the lid on

any further mix of thought. "We're getting married in two months, and the wedding will be at Joya del Mar, and it will be a wedding fit for a queen.

"Your father and I didn't have a big wedding, just a simple ceremony with a few of our relatives. We had a two-day honeymoon at Atlantic City. We used to talk about getting married again and having a really big wedding and a real honeymoon."

"Does Winston know all this?" I asked her. "Does he believe you love him very much?"

"I'll just tell you what he told me last night before he gave me this ring. He said the day I was angry at him was the saddest and hardest day he's had since his wife's death, and that told him that he needed me to make his life worth living. He asked me if I would do that, and I said yes, yes I would, and I will. I'll be a good wife for him, Grace, and you'll be a good daughter. We'll give him happiness, and that is more than most men have in their marriages, believe me.

"Be happy for us, Grace, please," she begged, taking my hand into hers.

I looked down at our joined hands and nodded. "Okay, Mommy. If this is what you want."

"It is, yes, very much."

"I have to get to school," I said.

"I'll call for the taxi."

"I can still make the bus."

"But you haven't had your breakfast, and you have a final exam. Go on, eat something, and I'll call," she insisted. "We're not going to worry about the expense," she added, smiling.

I looked at her. *No, we won't,* I thought. "Okay," I said, and made myself some toast and jam and had some coffee.

When the taxi came I called out to her, and she called back, "Good luck, honey. That's all we're going to have now."

I hurried to the cab and told the driver where to take me. We pulled away, and I looked back at the condo which was truly only one of our many way stations. We were still on a long journey. I wanted to be happy for my mother. I really did, and I understood how much marrying Winston Montgomery meant to her and how it gave her a sense of security and purpose when all that seemed to have been stolen away with a tragic helicopter accident.

She was going to put it all behind us, and I supposed that was good.

But when she married Winston, I thought, on that day, my daddy would truly be gone. Her name would change. She would become another man's wife.

It was like closing a book and putting it on the shelf, burying it in a cemetery of emotions and memories. No more laughter and smiles because of something Daddy had said. No more waves and salutes.

All of that drifted away on the wings of a sea gull and left me standing alone on a beach in a strange new place, looking out at the water and waiting for a sign of what was now to come.

13

Happy Forever

I did remarkably well on my finals considering all that had occurred around me and to me during the final days of school. Mommy quit working almost a minute after Winston gave her the engagement ring. We wouldn't be needing the added income, of course, and she now had a great deal to do in planning the wedding itself. Winston gave her carte blanche on every aspect and told her to spare no expense.

"I know you think I've become obsessed with all this, Grace," Mommy told me when I muttered one morning that the event had taken over our lives.

She wasn't up a minute in the morning before she was on the telephone, and as soon as she gobbled down some breakfast she was out and about meeting with every person and every business that was involved in the affair. Winston provided her with the chauffeur and limousine to do all this. Sometimes I accompanied her, but most of the time I remained at home. She didn't seem to notice whether I was with her or not anyway. I couldn't believe how much time and energy she spent on the colors, designs, and fonts of her wedding invitation. I was sure the president-elect of the United States didn't spend as much time on the invitations to his inaugural balls.

"But you have to understand that we are getting married sooner than most people do in a proper Palm Beach wedding," she continued as a justification.

"Proper?"

"Well, the ideal duration for an engagement is from three to five months. Ours is barely two. If it weren't for Winston's influence with people we would have a very hard time booking caterers, decorators . . .

"Our engagement was announced the morning I showed you the ring, so people know about us. Normally we would have had an engagement party, but there is no time for that. Even so, engagement gifts have begun to arrive at Joya del Mar, and I have to get out thank-you notes ASAP. I'm working on the design and paper style for that now. Winston is having his personal secretary assist me. You met Virginia Wilson. She's very good at this sort of thing.

"We should be getting the wedding invitations out ASAP so people will have at least a month's advance notice. The people we're inviting have very busy and full calendars. Many will cancel their trips just to be there," she said proudly.

"You don't know anyone," I said, which was a big mistake.

She hoisted her shoulders like a hen and looked down at me. "I happen to have met many of Winston's business associates over the last month or so, Grace. I know many more people than you think. I've been to luncheons and charity events and have become acquainted with some of the richest people in town."

"The only real friend you have is Dallas," I persisted.

She softened her demeanor. "I know that. That's not something I would forget. Dallas is going to be my matron of honor. She's very excited about it."

"I guess that means Phoebe's coming," I muttered.

Mommy smiled. "I want her to come to see where you will be living. It will take the air out of her ballooned ego so fast she'll shrink right in front of you," Mommy replied. She looked happier about that than anything, certainly caring more than I did. "Naturally you'll be sitting at the dais with the immediate wedding party. She'll sit somewhere out there with a table of strangers."

"I'd rather she wasn't there at all," I said, but Mommy didn't hear or didn't want to hear. She was riding so high my voice could no longer reach her.

"You'll be my maid of honor. I'll be giving you a description of your responsibilities," she said. "The first important thing is our dresses. This will be a formal wedding. I'll be wearing a long white gown with a train, and I've decided to wear a veil, too. Normally that's optional, but I sort of like the idea, don't you?"

I shrugged. *I couldn't care less,* I thought. I certainly wouldn't lose a moment of sleep over it.

The pursuit of the proper wedding gown began the week after her engagement announcement. I thought to myself that the FBI didn't go after its most wanted criminals with any more intensity. Mommy met with wedding planners, experts who gave her a history of weddings in Palm Beach. She actually took notes! Later she pondered every possible choice and then spent nights tossing and turning, agonizing in fear that she might have made a wrong decision.

"This isn't a naval battle, Mommy," I made the mistake of saying at breakfast one morning. "It's just a wedding."

"Just a wedding! Are you mad? This isn't *just* a wedding. It's a way of introducing me to Palm Beach. I'm to be Winston Montgomery's wife, Grace. That means a great deal to people here. You had better get used to it, understand it. Afterward we'll be featured in the society columns, have our pictures taken often, be invited to practically every significant party or event. Why, the only comparison I can make is I will be like an admiral's wife," she said.

It was precisely the wrong thing to say as far as I was concerned. Being an admiral's wife was the fantasy she had enjoyed with Daddy. That was their fun dream, their pretend, and I was a part of it as soon as I was old enough to appreciate and understand it.

"Well, you're not an admiral's wife," I snapped back at her too sharply. It made her wince. "And you'll never be."

I marched out of the kitchen before she could respond. Ordinarily she would have come to see me, to soothe my bruised heart, but she was back on the telephone moments later jabbering with some decorator, and soon afterward the limousine arrived and she was off again.

"Be happy for us, Grace," she pleaded on the day we went for our gown fittings. "People here gossip like crazy. Don't let anyone think you're in the slightest way upset. Please."

I did what she wanted and wore a mask over my true feelings whenever we were in public. She tried to include me in every decision, running different ideas, gifts for the wedding party, favors, decorations, and styles past me. All I did was agree with every decision she made, but that was enough to satisfy her. I was at least paying lip service in front of the wedding planners. Not that they cared, but no one had any idea about my true feelings.

A week before the ceremony we moved out of our condo. When I say we moved out I really mean we picked up our most precious possessions, only what we could personally carry, and walked out. Winston had arranged for movers to do everything else. It was truly as if we were whisked away on a magic carpet. I had been given the choice of a half dozen rooms at Joya del Mar and picked one just down from what would be Mommy and Winston's suite. That week Mommy, like some virgin bride-to-be, stayed in one of the guest suites. While Mommy occupied herself with the wedding dinner arrangements I became more acquainted with the maids and the butler, as well as Winston's chef. I even met the head groundskeeper.

For a while I felt as if I was staying at a very expensive resort. I didn't think of it as my new home. Our breakfast was prepared whenever we wanted it. We had about as much choice as anyone would have in a hotel, and we could easily have it brought to our rooms on silver trays. I had no household chores anymore. I could spend my time reading, swimming, learning how to sail, being chauffeured to shopping or anywhere else I chose. It was truly as if one day I was a scullery maid and the next I was a princess.

Mommy had little or no time to spend with me. When she did finally settle down for an hour or so she was always complaining about how exhausted she was.

"I might need a vacation before our honeymoon," she quipped.

Winston was keeping their honeymoon destination a surprise until their wedding day.

"I love the way he does that," she told me. "He enjoys overwhelming me with unexpected things, like he did the night he took us both to Paradise Island for dinner. That's sweet, isn't it?" She held her eyebrows up, waiting for my reaction.

"Yes," I admitted. I really had nothing bad to say about Winston. He was always very sensitive to my needs and feelings and even spent more time with me that week than Mommy did.

He described many of his wedding guests to me, explaining that his best man was a long-trusted business associate. He was very concerned with what I would do the week he and Mommy were on their honeymoon.

"Maybe you should come along," he suggested.

I shook my head quickly. It was one thing to see Mommy on his arm at balls, dinners, and charity events or to see them kiss on the cheeks occasionally, but to be there when they were spending what to me was always the most romantic time of married life was surely too much to bear. Their kisses would have to be more passionate, their time together closer and far more intimate.

"I'll be fine," I said.

"Soon you'll be making new friends," Winston assured me.

He and Mommy had chosen a new school for me to attend. It was called the Edith Johnson Wood School, named for its principal benefactor. It was only twenty years old. A group of very wealthy Palm Beach residents had created it, and it was like no school I had ever attended, and I had attended quite a few.

It was located in North Palm Beach on a 250-acre tract of land with a waterway, bridges, fountains, and palm trees, everything beautifully designed. The buildings looked brand new. It had a very modern small theater that could hold eight hundred people, an up-to-date computer laboratory, a beautiful gymnasium, and classrooms designed for only ten, possibly fifteen students at the most. The school's population was kept to an exclusive 750 students from kindergarten to grade twelve. My entire class would have fewer than fifty students.

Ordinarily any prospective new student would have to go through an admission procedure not unlike that of an Ivy League college, but Winston's contributions to the school fund put me at the top of the list. I could have been a mass-murdering drug addict, and I would have been admitted. Everyone I met was overly solicitous. I wasn't used to or comfortable with teachers and administrators who were so concerned about how I felt and how happy I was.

No one could not be impressed with what was offered to every student, however. There was an elaborate music program, a program in theater arts, an art department, and a language program. Every student practically had a personal trainer when it came to physical education.

Mommy squealed and clapped at the sight of everything. "I wish I was your age and attending this school," she told me. "Aren't you excited about it, Grace?"

"Yes," I said, but overwhelmed was more like the truth. The school year at Edith Johnson Wood began in late August, so I would be back in class faster than I had expected. I was happy about that, though. I needed desperately to occupy myself with things other than the recreation available to me at Joya del Mar.

The night before their wedding, Winston stayed away, supposedly having dinner with close friends. He told Mommy he wanted to give her some space. We dined on the rear loggia overlooking the setup for the wedding: the tables, the dais, the dance floor, and the various kiosks to serve the great variety of food and drink. The altar had been created out of flowers.

"All this for me," she said, shaking her head. "I have to pinch myself every five minutes."

She smiled at me and reached for my hand. "We've beaten fate, honey. We've driven it out. We'll never have a sad day from now on. If anything displeases us, we'll get rid of it or buy something else. When we have some dark moments we'll call up and make reservations for dinner at the best places in the world, and whenever we're bored we'll get on the private jet and see something new. No one at school will ever look down on you again, and you can be or do anything you want."

She waited for me to smile back. I knew how important that had become for her. "Okay, Mommy," I said, giving her that smile. "We'll be happy forever."

"That's my girl," she said. "That's my Sail . . ." She stopped herself, bit down on her lower lip.

"You can say it, Mommy. None of this ever changes that," I told her with firm, steely eyes.

She nodded. "I know, honey. I know." She quickly wiped off any semblance of sadness and smiled, practically jumping in her seat. "Oh, I'm so nervous I can't eat anything. I think I'll go up and soak in a hot bath and try desperately to relax. Come see me before you go to sleep, okay?"

"Okay," I said.

I watched her go inside, and then I sat and looked out

at the ocean, watching the sun sink below the horizon and waiting for the first star. I waited so long that by the time I went up to see Mommy I found her asleep in her bed, a smile of pure happiness on her lips.

"Good night," I whispered, and went to my room where the silence and the solitude finally brought home to me what was going to happen tomorrow.

The wedding was everything Mommy had dreamed it would be and far more than I had imagined. I thought she looked beautiful in her wedding gown, and I could see from the faces of the guests that many of them did as well, especially the men who looked enviously at Winston. As he moved through the line of well-wishers his more contemporary friends either gave him lusty smiles or leaned in like roosters to peck at his ear with something similar to "You lucky dog," I'm sure.

For her part Mommy surprised me by not looking half as nervous as I had anticipated. In fact, she looked as if she had been brought up here among these very wealthy people. She knew so many by first name. It was apparent to me that she had taken detailed mental notes at every single social event to which Winston had taken her. Most of the guests she spoke with looked as if they had expected no less. How could you forget that this one was called Brownie or that one Muffy or Bunny, even though they were married to men with names like Chester Lloyd Marlborough and Stratton Newton Polk, Jr.?

When they were introduced to me I could see their thoughts in their eyes: Winston was old enough to be my grandfather, not my stepfather.

My legs trembled as I walked down the aisle of flowers to the altar with Mommy. The sheer opulence and grand scale of this wedding made it seem all the more unreal to me. Looking around at the army of servants, the decorated tables, the ice sculptures, the wonderful displays of every imaginable food, the dance floor, and the twenty-six-piece orchestra, I thought I was surely in some fantasy. I had wandered into another woman's dream, and soon I'd wake up in bed, blink, and realize none of this was happening.

When the ceremony began, the minister's voice assured me it was real. Mommy avoided looking at me through most of it. I think she was afraid of what my face would say and how that would affect her. She focused entirely on Winston, and together they repeated the vows until the minister declared them husband and wife. Winston gave her a quick, almost fatherly kiss, and the guests cheered.

Everything went as it had been orchestrated, down to the very toasts of good wishes, Winston's friends rising to speak for exactly forty-five seconds, almost to the man jokingly warning him not to be "too vigorous a husband." Many of the couples I met resembled Mommy and Winston, however, the women looking years younger than their husbands, mostly, I thought, as a result of thousands and thousands of dollars' worth of cosmetic surgery.

Both Dallas and Warren were very happy for Mommy and me. At one point I overheard Mommy tell Dallas she owed it all to her. They swore they would never stop being friends, and they cried and hugged. I had to look away, and that's when I was forced to confront Phoebe, who was sitting and glaring at me, scowling. If ever a face was a glass window it was hers. She was probably not even aware of how it was betraying her jealous, hateful thoughts.

"Lucky you," she spat when I approached her. She was so angry and envious it brought tears to her eyes. She threw back her head and brushed her hair from her cheek, turning back into her old defiant self again quickly. "I'll marry someone this rich someday and have just as much."

"You probably will, Phoebe," I said.

"You think you're better than me now, don't you?"

"Not because of having money or living in this grand estate," I said.

"Right," she muttered. "I didn't want to come here, but my father said if I didn't I couldn't get my car replaced."

"Well, I'm glad you didn't come because you wanted to come. I would have worried more."

She squinted and pursed her lips when she looked back at me. "Don't think you can now invite all my friends over here or invite Roger and Wally and have them hate me," she warned.

"I won't. You're welcome to them."

"Oh, so you're going to make better friends and go to a ritzy private school now, huh?"

I stared out at the boisterous crowd of guests, some of the women dripping with diamonds, glittering like alabaster statues, their laughter tinkling with its thinness, its artificiality. All around me women were air-kissing one another, commenting on gowns, comparing designers, and then conspiring to say something unpleasant about someone they had just greeted with gushing joy. I felt I was at a costume party more than at my mother's wedding. Why couldn't she and Winston just have had a simple, authentic, and sincere ceremony with just a few really close and dear friends? Why was all this required? Would it make their marriage any more substantial or guarantee their happiness any more? At least they would have albums, wedding pictures, and other mementos to give the day a false sense of immortality, I thought.

"You know what, Phoebe," I said, continuing to look out at the wedding party. "If some angel appeared at this very moment and asked if I would trade all this, give it all up, and become poverty stricken to bring Randy back . . ." I looked at her. "I would do it in a heartbeat."

Her stern mask of defiance shattered like brittle china. Her lips trembled.

"Have a good life," I told her, and walked off. I spent as much time alone as I could, sitting off to the side of the dais, watching the festivities. Despite the variety of delicious foods, I had little appetite and ate almost nothing.

Winston finally realized I was off by myself and quickly came to ask me to dance. I started to shake my head.

"Oh, you have to," he said. "We've got to show these stuffy Palm Beach people how to have a good time, Grace. Please," he begged.

I couldn't help but smile and give him my hand. He led me out to the dance floor, and just as he had predicted, almost all eyes were on us. I saw Mommy sitting and looking proudly at us. Winston held me firmly. I thought to myself that he must have been a really good athlete in his youth. He had a wonderful sense of timing and rhythm.

"Think we made your mother happy?" he asked me.

"Yes," I said.

"I hope so. She deserves to be happy, and so do you, Grace. Making you guys happy will make me happier, too. Let me do that, okay?" he asked with a twinkle in his eyes. "Don't resent me for wanting to give you too much."

He was so sincere. His hand lightly brushed over my hair, and I felt myself crumbling under the weight of so much sadness mixed with so much joy. I wanted to let myself fall into his arms and let him hold me and protect me and keep out all the demons. Maybe Mommy was right. Maybe it could be only within this castle.

"Okay," I said in a small voice, and he smiled and kissed me on the forehead. "Welcome to Joya del Mar forever and ever, Grace," he whispered.

The tempo of the music picked up.

"Oh, no," he cried with feigned panic, but he didn't let go of me.

We started to dance just the way we had on Paradise Island and some of the guests actually cheered. Some looked absolutely shocked right down to their Gucci undergarments. Before we finished I glanced to the right and saw Phoebe, who had been talking with some younger people, turn and shoot off, her hair bouncing on her neck, her hands clenched in fists. When I had first met her I was for a short while actually envious. I wanted to be like her: beautiful, popular, powerful. That seemed ages ago. I felt as if I had grown up overnight. I was no longer a child. I would no longer think like a child. I would put all that away forever.

Mommy and Winston had decided to leave on their honeymoon in the morning. The wedding ran late. I actually went to bed before the last guests left. I understood that for many of these people an all-night event was not that unusual. After all, what did they have to do the following day besides sleep if they wanted?

I was still asleep myself when Mommy stopped by

nearly at noon to say goodbye. She was dressed and ready to leave. I tried to grind the sleep from my eyes, but it was still like looking at her through some gray veil.

"Did you have a good time, honey?" she asked.

"Yes," I said. I had actually eaten late and enjoyed the wonderful wedding cake. Other men had asked me to dance after I danced with Winston, younger men. I had, but I didn't remember all their names. I had drunk some champagne, too, and my thoughts became foggy, my memories merging.

"It was a wedding they will talk about around here for a long time. It's sure to make the front page of the Shiny Sheet." I knew that was the Palm Beach newspaper's nickname. "And be featured in the magazines. I'll call you from the yacht," she promised.

"Yacht?"

"Winston's surprise was hiring a yacht to take us to some wonderful places in the Mediterranean. We're flying to Nice where it is waiting for us. There is someplace on the coast of southern France he especially wants me to see. He's thinking of taking a villa there for us next summer. Won't that be wonderful?"

I nodded. Actually I had a small headache, and nothing she was saying made sense to me.

"You look like you need to sleep, Grace. Don't rush to get up. Invite anyone you want over, if you like."

"I don't know anyone I want to invite," I said quickly.

She looked unhappy about that. "Well, after you start your new school you'll make new friends. You'll see," she assured me, kissed me, and started out. "We've done it," she said from the doorway. "We've given nasty fate the old heave-ho."

Then she was gone, and I let my head full of lead

drop back to the pillow. I slept well into the afternoon, and when I woke up I realized it was all true. We were really here, and I was a modern American princess.

But I was alone.

Mommy called the following day. She was very excited.

"I'm calling you from the yacht, Grace. I'm looking at the port of Nice. We're on our way to Monte Carlo and then to ports in Italy. Winston promised Louisa we would stop in Capri and visit with her brother and sister-in-law. The scenery everywhere is beyond words. I'll take lots of pictures. Are you all right?"

"Yes, Mommy, I'm fine," I said, almost laughing. It hadn't been quite twenty-four hours. "I'm getting started on the reading list for my new school."

"Try to do something that's fun, too, Grace."

"I will," I said, a promise as hollow as an empty peanut shell.

"You can reach us anytime you want. Jakks has the numbers," she said, referring to our butler.

She called me every other day and gave me a quick summary of what they had done, always asking me what was new. She even called the day before they were returning, but that was for more special information.

"Winston and I have chosen a villa for next summer," she declared. In the few days that had gone by it was now "Winston and I." "We're bringing a video so you can get a good idea of it all. How are things back there?"

"Nothing's changed since you called day before yesterday, Mommy," I said. She told me how much she looked forward to seeing me and how I would love the gifts she and Winston had bought for me.

The following day I fell asleep on a lounge by the pool while reading and woke to the sound of her calling my name from the rear loggia. For a moment I didn't know who it was. She had done her hair again, this time in an even shorter style, but she had colored it as well.

"Grace, we're back," she announced, and spun on her heels to model her new self. She was wearing a pretty two-piece pants set and new shoes.

"What happened to your hair?" I asked.

"Don't you like it? I had it done over in Monte Carlo. The stylist thought I might look striking in black hair. Winston likes it."

I shook my head. "You look . . . different," was all I could manage.

"That's the idea, silly. Now come into the house to see what we brought back for you. I had it all brought up to your suite," she said, and gave me a quick hug. "I have so much to tell you and pictures to show you. Stop staring at me like that and come along."

I rose and followed. Inside Winston was giving the servants instructions. The moment he saw me he stopped and rushed over to hug me as well.

"How do you like your new mother?" he asked with a wry smile.

"I'm not sure," I replied honestly. "It's too shocking a change."

"Oh, you'll get used to it," she assured me. "C'mon," she said, grabbing my hand and leading me up to my room.

I stopped in the doorway. The bed was covered with boxes. There were even some piled beside it.

"What is all this?"

"Clothes and jewelry and shoes and some pictures for your walls and perfume. Oh, and this wonderful

French facial cream that will keep your skin soft forever. I bought a lot in Saint-Tropez. There were wonderful artists and handicraft makers in Eze and Saint-Paul-de-Vence."

I began to look at the gifts. It was truly overwhelming.

"There's so much," I couldn't help saying, and she laughed.

"Get used to it," she told me, and proceeded to go through each and every present, explaining where she had been, how Winston had helped negotiate prices, and what she had bought for herself as well.

I couldn't deny that Mommy was happy. Sometimes in the days and weeks that followed I felt she was forcing herself to be happy, but that might have been what I was doing. One of the first things she did in the house was take over one of the dens and create her own office, just to handle the social schedule. Winston's personal secretary soon was working with her as well, at times more than she worked with Winston, I thought. An oversized calendar was put up on the office wall. Every weekend for months was filled with one event or another, and soon the weekdays followed. It wasn't that she wanted to attend everything. In fact, she gave me a short lecture about the differences between the A-list parties and events and the others. The ones that were considered A actually had an *A* inscribed alongside them.

One of the first publications Mommy acquired was something Winston's secretary called the black book. It was *The Social Index* directory, a Who's Who of the most important people, their addresses, and other important data. These were the people she said she would invite to any affairs at Joya del Mar. Any affairs any of these people invited her to she would be sure to attend. When I said it reeked of snobbery, she actually flamed up and turned her temper on me.

"That goes both ways, Grace. You can't dislike people just because they have money and influence. There's nothing wrong with associating with people who are in your class."

"In our class? We're not blue-bloods, Mommy. We're simple people."

"Of course we're not simple people. My forefathers and your father's were important people," she declared.

I smiled incredulously at her, and she looked away quickly. What fictions was she creating in her own mind? Later Winston found me sulking down by the beach.

"Hey," he said, "you've been a stranger all day today. Anything wrong?"

"No," I shot back, practically taking his head off with my reply.

"Oh boy," he moaned, and sat on the sand beside me. "I used to do this a lot," he began. "You get so busy and so wrapped up with things you forget to stop to smell the roses. An hour or so out here is good spiritual medicine. I could stare at the sea for hours and hours."

I felt my body relax and snuck a glance at him. He was looking intently at the breakers. Off to the right, sliding against the horizon, we could see a cargo ship.

"Your mother thinks we should have a party just for you, invite the young people who belong to some of the families we know. What do you think?"

"I won't come," I said.

"To your own party?"

"I don't need to be put on display and practically beg for new friends, Winston."

He smiled. "That's good," he said, surprising me. "I didn't like the idea, either."

I turned to him. He was being truthful.

"My parents always did things like that, tried to get me involved with this one or that one because it would be a good social contact. They even tried to arrange my marriage once."

"Really?"

"Yes, with the daughter of an oil executive who had an estate here, in Palm Springs, in the Hamptons, and in Monte Carlo. I felt just as sorry for their daughter. She knew she was being manipulated, too. In the end we were both honest with each other and ended it before it could get started.

"Meaningful relationships are like anything else. They'll find their own depths and levels if you leave them be."

"That's right," I said.

He smiled. "I know it's hard to change your whole life like this, Grace. It takes time to make so many adjustments, but I hope you'll be as happy as your mother seems to be. I'd like it if you would come to me with any problems you have."

"Okay," I said.

He leaned over and kissed me on the cheek and then stood up.

"You know, I was wondering, Grace. I'm sorry I don't know. But do you have your driver's license?"

"No," I said. "My father was going to give me driving lessons this year, but . . ."

"I'd like to do that," he said. "You should know how to drive, even though we have a chauffeured limousine always at your disposal. You shouldn't have any fewer skills than any other girl your age. Okay?"

"Sure," I said.

"We'll start tomorrow," he promised. "Watch that sunshine now. The sea breeze can fool you."

"I know," I said. "Thanks."

He smiled and walked off.

He did what he promised. We began my driving lessons on the property first, and then, to put the finishing touches on my lessons, he hired a private driving school instructor who helped me get my license.

To celebrate Winston decided we should take the yacht to Key West for the weekend. Actually he and Mommy would find the flimsiest excuses to do something expensive, whether it was to fly up to New York to see a show and shop or to rush off to Bermuda for a few days.

We did have a fun weekend in Key West. Winston, either at Mommy's request or after his own decision to cheer me up, spent more time with me and doted on me more than he did Mommy. He was eager to show me everything in Key West. Mommy went on another buying spree.

"I can't wear everything you've bought me as it is," I complained.

"Of course you can, and that doesn't matter. What matters is you'll have choices to make. Clothes accommodate and enhance your moods," she explained.

"Who told you that?"

"This designer we met in Monte Carlo. He's right. Some mornings you wake up feeling today is a turquoise day or a light green day, and if you have the outfit to wear you'll be happy you do.

"And then there is the style as well."

She could go on and on with these lectures if I let her, I thought. What I would do was agree and go do something else. Winston sat in the background or off to the side with that small smile on his lips. He and I began to exchange conspiratorial glances. Mommy didn't notice. I could just imagine how angry she would become if she had, but I couldn't help enjoying it.

In fact, Winston and I grew closer and closer before the summer ended and I had to begin school. Some days we just sat and talked at the pool, discussing books, news. Sometimes he would tell me stories about his youth. Mommy was often off with one or two of her new acquaintances, going to lunch or to some lecture on art. She stopped trying to get me to go along, but she wasn't happy about that.

"There are daughters of people I would like you to meet, girls with whom you can share things in common now, Grace, but to do that you have to come along with me occasionally."

"I'll make new friends in school," I promised. For the present it was enough to get her to relent.

"I hope so. At least you know the other girls and boys there come from good families."

"Why, because they're rich?"

"Yes," she said without hesitation, "that and the fact that they have important names and reputations to protect. When you don't care about your family name you don't care what you do and who knows it."

I shook my head. "Who is telling you these things?"

"No one has to tell me," she said, pulling herself up sharply. "It's obvious to anyone who looks and listens."

I clamped my lips together and stopped arguing. It was far easier to nod and retreat. Soon she didn't notice that, either. It upset me, but at least we weren't arguing.

Two days before school began Winston came to my room and knocked softly on the door. I was finishing up

The Scarlet Letter, one of the required books for my American literature class.

"Hi," he said. "I need your help with something if you have a minute."

"What?" I sat up, surprised that he would need me for anything.

"We've had a delivery, and it makes no sense to me. Maybe if you look it over you can figure it out."

"A delivery of what?"

"You'll see," he said cryptically. "Can you come?" he asked when I didn't move.

"Sure," I said, and slipped on my sandals. I followed him down the corridor and the stairs. "Where is this mysterious thing?"

"It's just outside," he said.

We headed for the front door. I caught sight of one of the maids watching us with a silly smile on her face. It piqued my curiosity. Winston opened the front door and stepped aside. I went out and looked down at a red BMW convertible. There was nothing else out there.

"What?" I asked him.

"That car," he said. "It was brought here and left here."

"Don't you know whose it is?"

"It makes no sense to me," he said. "This envelope came with it."

He handed me a small manilla envelope. My name was on the front. I took it slowly and looked at him.

"What is this?"

"I didn't open it," he said. "It's addressed to you, so I thought I'd get you and you could tell me."

I pulled back with a grin of confusion and opened the envelope. Two sets of keys were in it and a copy of a car's registration. I looked at the document. My name was listed as the owner.

I looked at the car and then at Winston. I suppose I had the funniest expression of shock on my face. He finally smiled, and then, coming out from where she was hiding below behind a bush, Mommy cried, "Surprise!"

"This car is mine?"

"You've got to get back and forth to school, and I thought it was too expensive to hire another limousine and chauffeur. And now you have your driver's license anyway," Winston said, laughing.

"This is less expensive?"

"Absolutely. Why don't you try it out?" he said. "I'll come along and help you learn all about the car."

I was speechless for a moment. Mommy stood smiling up at me.

"Enjoy it, Grace," Winston said softly.

I couldn't help it. Even though I had a vague fear of being bribed into this new life, my own car, a beautiful red convertible, was too overpowering. I threw my arms around him.

He and Mommy laughed as they exchanged looks of pleasure, and for a small moment, only a small, slight moment, I wondered with whom Winston was being the conspirator, me or her?

As soon as I sat behind the steering wheel of my beautiful new car it suddenly didn't matter who it was.

14

Welcome to Palm Beach

For me attending a private school was different from attending a public school in so many ways, but when I stripped away the polish and the shine, the expensive equipment, and the smaller classes, there were similarities that went to the heart of school life anywhere, public or private. Just as in any of the schools I had attended, there was the in crowd and those longing to become part of it. Almost all of the senior high students at EJW had known one another for years and socialized with one another. They were a very tight bunch, but what struck me as really different about the girls I met at the Edith Johnson Wood School was how like their mothers they were. To call them clones was not an exaggeration. Their conversations were centered around designer clothing they had bought or were going to buy, cosmetic surgery on their noses, and collagen injections in their lips. There was even a junior girl who had already had a breast enhancement. And then there was the endless talk about the world-class resorts they had been to during the summer months, some of them comparing itineraries to show they had been in more places. They reminded me of those motorhomes with stickers from every place visited splattered all over their rear ends.

I was sure the old adage "An apple doesn't fall far from its tree" was true for the boys and their fathers as well. They spent most of their free time comparing their luxury automobiles, their expensive clothes, and their very expensive toys, like jet skis, speed boats, motorcycles, and sound systems. One boy I met even talked about the single-engine plane his father had bought for him. It was truly a game of "I can top that," and it was very important to get it all out in the conversation as quickly as possible that first week back, especially in front of me. Both the boys and the girls did it, I think, to let me know just how low I was on the totem pole, even though I was living at Joya del Mar.

I was surprised by how much they all knew about me even before I set foot in the building. From the icy welcome most of them gave me I could tell immediately that they had been told Mommy and I had married into money, and we didn't come from any of the so-called core Palm Beach families. Often I felt they believed I carried contamination just because I wasn't brought up in their privileged world. Crossing that Flagler Bridge was slumming to some of them.

"You sound like you're the one who's being a snob, Grace," Mommy told me when I described my first day and the girls and boys to whom I had been introduced.

Marjorie Meriweather, a girl in my class, had been assigned to serve as my so-called big sister and show

me around. She made me feel as if I was a pimple on
her face. "This is Grace Montgomery," she mumbled
quickly to anyone who cared to listen. "New student,"
she added, making it sound more like a warning than an
introduction.

"Why don't you give them a chance, get to know
them before you condemn them?" Mommy continued.

"Give them a chance? Get to know them? How do
you do that when the girl you meet blinks a phony
smile and then turns her back on you before you can
finish a sentence?"

"I'm sure you're exaggerating. It's just your own
insecurity speaking, Grace. Once they get to know you,
they'll all want to be your friends. As soon as you find
two or three girls or even boys you like, invite them to
Joya del Mar for lunch and swimming. Once you do
that you'll see how quickly you'll make friends with so
many of the others."

"I don't want those kinds of friends, Mommy. I don't
want to have to bribe anyone to be my friend."

"It's not a bribe. It's what's expected. You'll see once
you get accustomed to living here. It will all work itself
out," she assured me.

*Get accustomed to living here? I'll never get accus-
tomed to living here,* I thought, but I gave up arguing
about it. She simply didn't understand, or maybe she
didn't want to understand. The one thing that helped me
go forward was that I liked my teachers, every single
one, and I could see after the first week that they liked
me too, or appreciated me. As far as I could tell, none of
the other students in my English class, for example, had
read all of the summer's required reading. In fact, many
hadn't read a single title. Most of the time I was the
only one raising my hand when Mr. Stieglitz asked a

question about one of the books. He had a very dry, witty sense of humor, too.

"Are you sure you're in the right school?" he kept asking me that first week. "This is the Edith Johnson Wood School. The students here don't read or write. They just sigh, moan, and complain."

Of course I laughed, but the others glared at me with pinched faces full of indignation and annoyance. Similar things happened in my other classes. So many students didn't do their homework or did it poorly. It was as if the sole purpose of school to many of them was social, a place to gather and gossip, plan parties, and court romances.

"School, college, any sort of professional training or education isn't as important to these students as it might be elsewhere," a boy named Basil Furness told me one afternoon in the cafeteria, if I could call it a cafeteria. It looked more like a fancy buffet restaurant with a selection of food every day that rivaled the best dining places in the Palm Beaches. There were more people working there than at any school I had attended, too, despite the school's small size. The students didn't have to pick up after themselves. Two older women bused the tables. In fact, that was how I met Basil. I had started to clear off my tray when he stopped me.

"You want to put these poor women out of work?" he asked, half facetiously.

"Excuse me?" I said. Everyone else wasn't exactly breaking his or her neck to start a conversation with me. For a moment I thought he was speaking to someone else.

"If you start a trend here you could put people whose job it is to look after us out of work. Leave the tray," he ordered. He actually looked angry.

He was a very thin, light-brown-haired boy with a bad complexion he was trying to hide under an unfortunate and pathetic attempt at a beard. His facial hair was almost transparent, and the combination did more to draw attention to his skin problems than if he didn't have the beard at all.

His eyes were a bit too beady, his nose too lean and long, and he had a lower lip that was so much thicker than the upper it looked swollen. It wasn't simply his unattractive physical qualities that separated him from the others, however. I quickly learned he was far too sarcastic and belligerent for them.

"Oh," I said, and took my hands off my tray quickly. Just at that moment one of the girls in my math class, Enid Emery, stopped to ask me if I had done the homework.

"Of course," I said.

"Oh, good. Could I borrow it to copy it quickly? I didn't have a chance to do it last night."

"No," I said.

"What?"

"I don't give my homework out to be copied."

"Well, that's pretty selfish," she said, pulling her head back like a cobra about to strike. "It's not like it's so valuable, you know."

"Then why worry about it?" I countered, and Basil laughed. She gave him a furious look and stormed off to complain about me. That was when Basil told me school wasn't important to these kids.

"They know their parents will carpet their futures with gold," he muttered, and then sauntered off before I could agree or disagree.

In the weeks that followed I was practically the only one he spoke to or who spoke to him. We didn't have long conversations, nor did he show any signs of interest in me, and I certainly did nothing to give the impression I was in any way romantically interested in him, which was why I was so shocked when one Friday afternoon Mommy asked me about him.

"I understand you've made one friend at the school, Grace," she said. "A boy named Basil?"

"What? Who told you that?"

"I'm often at lunch with the mothers of three of the girls at your school, Faye Wilhelm, Barbara Johnson, and Marjorie Meriweather. Why did you become so friendly with that boy? They tell me he's been in and out of therapy and would be in some special institution if it wasn't for the donations to the school that his parents make."

"I'm not so friendly with him. We just chat occasionally," I said. "And besides, what do all these women do, spy on their children and find out whom they speak with in school?"

"Of course not. They are just concerned. When you have position and significant wealth you have to take a lot more interest in your children. There's nothing wrong with that."

I stared at my mother for a moment. This wasn't her talking. Someone else had crawled into my mother's body. She could see my eyes narrow with anger. I saw how she braced herself.

"Are you more interested in me and my welfare than you were before, now that we have money, too, Mommy?"

"Of course not. That's not what I'm saying."

"What are you saying, Mommy?"

She looked at me and then shook her head. "Oh, let's stop this bickering over nonsense. If you don't make an effort to become friends with decent people I'll have to help you."

"What? What do you mean, help me? How are you going to help me?"

"We'll have a party and invite some of them and their parents. I've already discussed it with Winston, and I have convinced him it's a good idea."

"No you didn't. You forced him to agree it's a good idea. You'd better not do it," I warned.

"Stop it, Grace. You're going to appreciate it and thank me later on," she said, and left before I could protest any further.

As soon as I could, I complained to Winston. He had just returned from a game of golf and was heading up to their suite when I called to him from my doorway.

"Hey. What's up, m'dear?" he asked, pretending to be Cary Grant. "Someone forget to put out your deck lounge?"

I didn't laugh. I wanted him to understand this was serious right from the start. His smile quickly faded.

"Uh-oh," he moaned. I could see he knew what I was about to say.

"Mommy is threatening to stage a get-to-know-me-or-else party," I said. "She said you said it was all right."

"I see." He stepped into my room and sat on the settee.

"It's embarrassing, Winston. And besides, the one thing I don't want these girls to think is that I'm really dying to become their friend."

He nodded.

"I thought you agreed it wasn't the right thing to do."

"I did."

"So?"

"Well," he said, wrapping his hands around his knee as he crossed his leg, "there are friends and there are friends. For example, Grace, I know a lot of people, and whenever I've had parties I've invited almost all of them. We've had parties here with nearly three hundred people.

"But," he continued, "if you asked me how many friends I have, people I would really call my friends, I would have a hard time coming up with more than a handful. It takes a great deal of time and a significant emotional investment in someone to make him or her your true friend. I understand how you've been moved about so much in your young life that it was difficult for you to develop any close relationships. I hope that's ended for you, Grace. Your mother makes sense when she points that out. Things weren't exactly the same for you as they were for me."

"But a party!" I protested. "For people I really don't know?"

"It's just another opportunity to get to know someone," he said with shrug. "It's better to see them in a different environment, under different circumstances, sometimes. Maybe there'll be no one you want for a real friend. Maybe there'll be one or two. Explore at least. Give yourself the opportunity, or," he said, smiling, "give your mother the opportunity to do it for you."

I looked away, disappointed in his logic and how he had changed his mind just to please Mommy.

"I promise," he said, "I won't permit this to be a weekly or even monthly thing. She's just so anxious to show you off."

"She's never done this before," I said. "And like you said, I've been a stranger in lots of places."

"I bet there'll be plenty of things you won't have

done before, too," he countered with a smile. "For example," he said, rising, "I was thinking the other day that you don't know how to sail. What good is that sail-boat of ours if you don't know how to use it? Starting this weekend I could begin to teach you, if you'd like."

"Really? Yes," I said, "I would."

"Good. Just let this other thing happen. It won't be half as terrible as you imagine, and besides, it's time we had some jovial activity around here. Okay?"

"Okay," I reluctantly agreed. "Thank you, Winston," I said as he started out.

He turned and gave me a kiss on the cheek. "It was only after I had met you, you know, that I considered proposing to your mother. I knew I was getting a ready-made perfect daughter."

I felt the blood rush into my face after hearing such a compliment.

"Let that be our little secret, though," he added with a wink.

After he left I thought, *he'll never be as much to me as my daddy was*, but at least I had someone who cared. I should be more grateful, and I told myself I shouldn't condemn him for trying so hard to please Mommy.

Mommy planned the party for the weekend after the coming one. I did nothing more to oppose it. Her new Palm Beach friends, two of whom were sisters married to brothers, the Carriage sisters, became her chief advisors on how to plan and conduct a party in Palm Beach. Their names were Thelma and Brenda, and I found the three of them with their heads together almost every afternoon before the party. They went through the guest list as if they were screening for possible terrorists. I couldn't help but listen in. The Carriage sisters seemed to know everyone's personal life, who wasn't getting along with whom, who was about to get divorced, whose husband or wife was having an affair and with whom. Mommy seemed to enjoy this part more than anything.

Meanwhile Winston was true to his promise and planned our first sailing lesson on Saturday.

"This is a perfect little boat to learn on," he began after we walked down to the dock. "It's a twelve-foot, gaff-rigged wooden sailboat. You've got to learn the jargon if you want to be a sea-farin' lass," he added in a Scottish accent. "So when you're at the club havin' a bloody Mary, you can gab with the best of 'em. Gaff-rigged is a cutter with one mast," he continued, back in his own voice. "The mainsail has a spar below the sail called a boom and above the sail called the gaff. Well, let's go." He laughed at my serious expression. "Don't just stand on the dock thinking so hard about it. Get in the boat."

I did quickly.

"Sailing is almost like flying, Grace. I prefer it to motorboats, actually. You feel more like a magician, transferring the power of the wind into power for the boat."

I loved his enthusiasm. It made me even more excited about learning.

"Okay, to continue. We can have more than one sail going. The jib is the headsail."

He explained the riggings and showed me the running rigging which was used to manipulate the sails. The hoisting lines he called the halyards.

"I think I should have brought a notebook," I said. He was rattling it all off so quickly.

"Don't worry. You'll remember it all. It will become second nature to you, Grace. There's nothing like becoming one with the wind."

Winston explained how it was impossible to sail directly into the wind and because of that we had to compromise by zigzagging the boat windward. He called it making a series of tacks. On each tack we steered the boat into the wind as much as possible without flapping the sails. When we had that going, he called it being close-hauled.

"Changing tack is called coming about. As you can see we're doing it often before we find our way windward."

He made a sweeping turn to start us in the opposite direction.

"Sailing before the wind is called running," he said, "and now we'll let the sails out as far as possible. You'll see that the most fun is what we call reaching or sailing across the wind. If you have anyone in the boat with you, Grace, you have to warn him or her by calling 'Ready about' before tacking. Then push the tiller leeward, which is away from the wind, which will cause the bow to go in the opposite direction into the wind and keep your boat turning like this until the wind is on the other side. See!" he cried as the sail swung across the boat and the wind filled it again.

The sea spray spattered my face. I screamed with pleasure, and he laughed.

"Okay, when the wind is blowing over us starboard, the right side, we are on the starboard tack. When the wind blows over the port, the left side, we're on the port tack. Got it?"

"I think so," I said.

"As you perform everything I've explained I want you to talk it aloud, tell me what I told you."

He lowered the sail and brought us to a stop.

Fortunately, the ocean was calm. Even so, I knew now what sea legs were as he and I changed position.

"Hoist your sail, mate," he cried, and I began, doing exactly as he had instructed.

I almost turned us over a few times, but I couldn't remember having a day of more fun. Winston was patient with me, too. He never yelled. Whenever I made a mistake he took his time explaining why and showing me how to avoid it.

I had no idea how long we were out until he looked at his watch and told me.

"Aren't you hungry?" he asked.

I was, but I hated the idea of stopping.

"I'll tell you what," he said. "Let's keep going south. I know a good little restaurant where we can dock."

And that was just what we did. I couldn't stop talking about my lessons. I didn't even remember what I had eaten, and all the time Winston sat there smiling at me and laughing.

"You make me feel like I'm twenty again," he said.

He let me do most of the sailing all the way back to Joya del Mar.

"When can we do it again?" I asked the moment we docked.

"We can do it every weekend I'm here, as long as the weather permits. It's very important to learn about weather if you really want to be a sailor, Grace, and the tides. That will be lesson two, okay?"

"Yes," I said.

"Where have you two been?" Mommy asked as soon as we entered the main house.

"Grace's sailing lesson. I told you about it yesterday," he replied.

"But I thought that would be no more than an hour or

so. It's almost five, Winston. You missed the Hobsons. I told you they were stopping by for cocktails this afternoon."

"Oh, I must have forgotten," he said.

Mommy looked at me, at my windblown hair, and at the wild joy in my eyes, but she didn't seem to be happy about it. "You know you've gotten too much sun on your face. Go look at yourself. You're going to need some medicated creams for sure."

"It was wonderful. I don't care."

"Fine. Suffer. I'm going up to prepare for dinner, Winston. I hope you didn't forget we're going to the Breakers tonight."

"No, no," he said, but when he looked at me I could see he had forgotten. "I'll be right along."

Mommy shook her head and charged toward the stairway.

"I think I created a monster," Winston muttered, and then quickly smiled. He wanted me to think he was kidding, but I didn't, not for a second.

The following Saturday Mommy absolutely forbid Winston and me to go sailing. She said there were just too many things left to do for the party and I needed to rest and be a good hostess. Instead I went up to my room and sulked. We couldn't go sailing the day after, either, because Winston and Mommy had to attend a charity luncheon. She was insisting I go with them, too.

"You have to mix more with people and let more people get to know you, Grace. Whether you like it or not, we are now important people in this community," she told me.

I didn't want us to be important people in any community. If it weren't for how wonderful Winston was to me, I would have wished she and he had never met and we were still living in the small condo. It got so I couldn't wait to see him after school, to talk to him, to do things with him, to learn from him. Mommy was right about one thing: Winston was a man of the world, sophisticated, and very self-confident.

One afternoon just before dinner I referred to him as Daddy Winston, and Mommy's mouth gaped. I didn't plan to say it; it just came out in reference.

"Daddy Winston? You make him sound like Daddy Warbucks," she finally commented.

"Maybe he is," I replied. I certainly felt like Orphan Annie a good deal of the time.

She grimaced every time I said it, but after a while she stopped and even referred to him as Daddy Winston herself on occasion.

There was never any doubt in my mind that he was her Daddy Warbucks.

Whether she had said anything to him about it or not I wasn't sure, but one night at dinner he put down his knife and fork and looked at me with a smile on his face.

"What?" I asked.

"I have a request to make of you," he said. "I have my lawyer working on it so it will be fast."

"What?" I asked again, looking at Mommy, who did seem confused herself, and then back at him.

"I'd like to adopt you officially, Grace. I'd like you to be Grace Montgomery," he said.

Mommy gasped and then, almost immediately, started to cry softly. I looked at him, my breath catching. I would be giving up Daddy's name, I thought.

Winston anticipated. "Just call yourself Grace Houston Montgomery from now on," he said, shrugging as if it was nothing. "It would make me a happy man, Grace," he added.

Mommy stared at me. I could see it in her eyes. This was very important to her as well.

"Okay," I said in a small voice, and that was that. I had put a piece of my heart away forever.

The day before my party those who were invited did go out of their way to speak to me at school, but I didn't feel any of them was sincere about it. What they did want to know was exactly who besides them was invited and what sort of music we would have. A few asked about the food, wanting to know who was catering it. I wanted to shock them and say, "No one. My mother's making everything." The truth was, I didn't know whom Mommy had as a caterer. I didn't even know what the menu was, and the only reason I knew we had a four-piece band was they had come over one day to see about how they would set up out at the pool and I had met them. I did remember they were called the Renners after their lead singer and his English wife, Bill and Diane Renner. Denise Hovington said she had them at her Sweet Sixteen party and they were great because they got everyone up and dancing. It seemed to raise my popularity quotient a few centimeters, but I sensed it might last only until the party.

I was half tempted to invite Basil. He knew about the party because for that week at least, it was one of the topics of conversation flowing through the high school. Actually I felt sorry for him, but when I brought it up with Mommy, she almost burst a blood vessel.

"If the other mothers even heard you were considering such a thing, they wouldn't let their daughters and sons come. Don't you dare," she warned. I had to promise I wouldn't, but that didn't mean she would believe me.

Naturally she took me to buy a new dress just for the party. Someone, I suspected Thelma Carriage, had told her about a new designer who was becoming the rage in Palm Beach as well as in Europe, and she looked for one of his creations. The dress had a price tag close to three thousand dollars. I almost couldn't move when she ordered me to try it on.

"Stop giving me those big eyes of yours, Grace. This is similar to a coming-out party for a debutante, and those sorts of occasions are very big and important here. It's not unusual to be a little extravagant."

"A little?"

"Just try on the dress," she snapped.

Mommy was determined to belong, determined to become accepted and part of this world, and if she had to she would drag me into it crying and screaming. I did what she asked. The boutique had a tailor there instantly to discuss the adjustments.

From there we went to the beauty salon, and Dawn Meadows, who had become Mommy's personal beautician, set out to give me a striking new hairstyle. I complained she was cutting my hair too short, but Mommy stood right beside her agreeing with every snip and disregarding my protests as if I was nothing more than a manikin. What I thought at the end was that I had been made to look like most of the other girls in our new world. Slowly, inch by inch, I was losing myself. My identity was sinking into the mirror, and what replaced it could be found on almost every page of the Edith Johnson Wood School yearbook.

As soon as we were finished at the beauty parlor, Mommy insisted I go with her to her cosmetic shop. All these boutiques, shops, and stores had suddenly become "hers." It was the way all the women she now had as acquaintances spoke about places in Palm Beach and elsewhere. Their patronage and the special attention it brought them qualified a place to be "theirs." It gave the impression everyone else who frequented it was simply tolerated or being done a favor.

At the cosmetic shop I was taken through a series of lessons about makeup, what shades complemented my complexion the best, and what creams I just had to have to prepare my skin before and after. Once again, whatever objections I had were totally disregarded. I was even unsure I had spoken. *Maybe I am a manikin now,* I thought, and while they discussed my face I daydreamed about Palm Beach. Going over the Flagler Bridge was like passing through some magic door. On the other side, like some of the characters in *The Wizard of Oz,* I turned into a life-size doll. I moved like a doll, had this habitual happy smile on my face, and when squeezed said things like, "How ticky-tacky."

If Mommy noticed even an iota of displeasure in my face afterward she quickly put it out of mind or buried it in her catalogue of "things left to do." Back at Joya del Mar she behaved like a little general, whipping orders at our house servants, rearranging furniture, calling every purveyor and supplier of our party things to repeat her demands and confirm her orders.

I tried to withdraw from it all, but the day before the party Mommy called me to the sitting room where she and the Carriage sisters held their strategy meetings. I was to be given my orders and responsibilities, told how to behave at my party and what guests would expect of me.

"You have to greet each and every one of them personally as soon as they've entered," Mommy began, obviously parroting what she had been told.

"You should remain in one place during the early hours of your party so you can easily be located," Thelma added. "Extend your hand, and say something like, 'Welcome to my home. Please enjoy yourself.' "

"I have to ask them to enjoy themselves?"

"It's just a manner of speaking," Thelma replied dryly. "No one takes it literally."

"Then why say it? Why not say things people *will* take literally?"

She looked at Mommy.

"It's etiquette, Grace. Just do it."

"Mingle after the party is under way. One of the most discourteous things a host can do is single out one or two of her guests and ignore all the others," Thelma continued.

"I was told some people here throw parties and don't even show up themselves," I said.

"Who told you such a thing?" Brenda asked, looking more curious than upset.

"Someone at school."

"Well, that has happened, but it's certainly not the rule of behavior for a young girl to follow," Thelma said.

"She's probably referring to Pokey Astor's yacht party last month," Brenda said.

Thelma gave her a very hard look, and she recoiled.

"Be sure you are also around to bid your guests good night and thank them for attending your party," Thelma added.

"It sounds like I should plant myself at the door and remain there all night."

"Of course not. You don't stand by the door. That's for your butler."

"Thelma and Brenda are just trying to help make your party a success, Grace. You should be more grateful," Mommy lightly chastised.

I smiled. "Thank you, Mrs. Carriage and Mrs. Carriage," I said, turning to Brenda. "I will write everything down and memorize it." I gave them a small curtsey and left.

Afterward Mommy told me I had been rude.

"I'm warning you, Grace," she said. "If you don't help me make this a successful event . . ."

"You'll stop buying me expensive clothes and won't take me to your personal beautician anymore?"

Her eyes filled with tears, and I immediately regretted my tone.

"I'm sorry," I said. "I'm just . . ."

"You're just nervous, I know. I am, too, but I'm covering it up by being busy. Don't worry, honey, we'll show them," she said.

That was it, I thought. She felt obligated to prove herself here, and I was just a handy device for the moment. I sighed to myself and thought maybe I should consider her feelings more. She was the one who was under pressure, and she had as much as confessed she had taken this path for our benefit, making whatever personal sacrifices were necessary.

"Okay, Mommy," I said. "We'll show them."

"That's my Sailor Girl," she cried, and hugged me.

Afterward I cried softly and then went to bed and pursued sleep as an escape.

Winston's surprise touch for the party was having spotlights. When he brought Mommy and me out to see them slicing the darkness Mommy nearly jumped out of her shoes with delight. My heart thumped with embarrassment. Who was I supposed to be? What was this supposed to be? A movie premiere?

Winston saw the worry in my face and quickly whispered, "I did it for your mother. It's nothing. Don't give it a second thought. It's not that uncommon at galas here."

The parade of Rolls-Royces, Mercedes-Benzes, Jaguars, and Lexuses followed soon afterward. I watched the first dozen or so glide up our driveway, a number of them chauffeur-driven. The Carriage sisters and their husbands had arrived earlier and accompanied Mommy on her inspection of the tables, the food, and the decorations. At the center table was a nearly six-foot ice sculpture of a swan. The band began to play, and the party atmosphere was thrown over the property like a bright, sparkling tablecloth. Champagne bottles were popped open, and, like windup toys, the waiters and waitresses spread out over the grounds, carrying their trays of hors d'oeuvres and glasses of what Palm Beach socialites called shampoo. What champagne had to do with washing one's hair escaped me. Maybe some of these people did use it in the shower.

The girls from my school were dressed as formally as I was, if not more. Mother and daughter wore almost as much jewelry. That was something Mommy immediately moaned about.

"I should have given you more of my jewelry to wear," she practically wailed. "You look underdressed."

"I don't feel underdressed," I said, holding my plastic smile. I did as the Carriage sisters prompted, greeted each of my guests and repeated the same inane hope that they would enjoy themselves.

Later I felt I was back at school. The girls gathered as if they had magnets in their dresses and behaved as if

I wasn't even present. The music continued, but no one stepped onto the dance floor. Winston hurried over to me and asked me to dance.

"Come along," he said, taking my hand, "we'll show them a step or two."

Mommy intercepted before we reached the dance floor. "Stop it, Winston," she commanded, her tone taking me by surprise almost as much as it did Winston. "If you dance with her, none of the boys will."

"I just thought we'd get it started. I didn't mean . . ."

"Grace, mingle," she ordered.

I looked at Winston. He winked and moved off with Mommy. I felt as if I had been cast into the sea and told to sink or swim.

"Are all your guests here?" Marjorie Meriweather asked as soon as I approached one of the tables where some of the girls and boys from the school were seated.

"I think so, yes," I said. "Why? Is someone missing?"

Since I didn't have all that much to do with the guest list, I really didn't know.

Marjorie looked at Sonya Wilhelm and smiled.

"Maybe," she said, and the whole table laughed.

What was so funny? "I don't get it," I said.

Just at that moment, Sandy Marko, a boy in my math class, asked if I'd like to dance. He looked as if he had been threatened with being boiled in oil if he didn't. My moment of hesitation filled his eyes with hope I would say no. Was I so undesirable?

"Yes, I would," I said, and he walked toward the dance floor like someone going to his own execution.

His eyes were everywhere but on me. He looked nervous and afraid. The other students soon joined us, however, and we were all going at it, especially after the Renners upped the tempo. I saw Mommy looking very satisfied and sighed. *Just do it, and try to look like you enjoy it, Grace,* I told myself. For a few minutes I actually did. Even Sandy looked more relaxed. Maybe this would be a great party. After all, like Winston said, I didn't have to fall in love with anyone tonight, but that didn't mean I couldn't at least have some fun.

People were at the food tables. Wine was pouring like water. Mommy did look very beautiful and, I could see, was attracting the interest of a number of husbands. She was getting what she wanted, I thought. She was finding acceptance. Even Winston looked happier than I had seen him at any affair we had all attended previously. I started to sigh with relief when I noticed the kids around me had stopped dancing, even though the music continued. They were all turning toward the stairway down from the rear loggia, and none of them was speaking.

Sandy stopped dancing, too, and turned. I stepped around Bronson Simmons and looked.

There was Basil Furness wearing a bright blue blazer and a pair of white pants.

"He doesn't even know what season it is," Vanessa Waterman said, and others laughed.

The pause in activity drew the attention of more and more of the adults. Slowly, like a ripple across a lake, the pregnant silence traveled to be born in an audible gasp from Mommy's throat. She turned and looked at me. I shook my head. I had no idea why he was here.

He stepped down and immediately helped himself to a barbecued prawn. Slowly the silence was filled with chatter again.

"I knew all your guests hadn't arrived," Marjorie

said, and those around her laughed. "Aren't you going to ask him to dance?"

I looked from her to Basil and then at Mommy, who was walking toward me.

"What did you do?" I asked Marjorie.

"Moi? What could I have done?" she retorted, and they all went back to dancing while they kept an eye on Mommy and me.

"You went and invited that boy after what I told you," she began.

"I didn't, Mommy."

"Well, why would he be here? You'd better go find out immediately, Grace. Go," she ordered sharply. I winced and hurried toward Basil.

"Quite a little house party," he said before I could utter a word. "I wasn't going to come and decided at the last minute that I was hungry."

"You weren't invited," I said, amazed.

He raised his eyebrows and wiped his mouth with a napkin. "Really? What, did your social secretary make a mistake?" he asked, and drew an invitation out of his jacket pocket. He handed it to me, and I looked at it.

It was obviously a reproduction.

I turned and looked back at the girls around Marjorie. They were all watching us and smiling.

"It was someone's idea of a big joke, Basil," I said. "I'm sorry."

"Oh," he said. "I get it."

"You don't have to leave," I said.

"No," he said. "You've got it wrong. I don't have to stay."

He turned and walked back up the steps and through the rear loggia.

And I felt my heart had become a yo-yo on a string that had just broken.

No matter how well the party went afterward, Mommy was deflated. I could see her growing more and more paranoid over every group that gathered and spoke quietly. In her mind, those who might have had a legitimate reason to leave early were leaving because of the Basil incident, and nothing I or Winston could have said would change that interpretation.

After what they had done I couldn't make myself available to say good night to the students invited and thank them for coming. There were those who did look ashamed and embarrassed at what Marjorie and the others had concocted, but it was all too little and too late. Someone could have had the decency to warn me, I thought, but no one had. *I'll always be an outsider here.*

I went up to my room before the last of the guests left. I could hear the band packing up, and soon the noise and the voices died away. By the time Mommy and Winston retired for the evening, I was already in bed, dozing off. I heard her walk down the corridor and waited to see if she was going to stop by. A few moments later the door was opened slowly, and she peeked in. I kept my eyes closed. It was painful for me to ignore her, but I didn't want to talk about the party and its purpose any more this night.

She closed the door softly, and all was dark and quiet.

"Welcome to Palm Beach, Mommy," I whispered.

15

A Man Like
Winston Montgomery

"**I** guess what those kids did was as cruel to that boy
as it was to us," Mommy admitted the following morning at brunch. After so late a night none of us rose early
enough to have breakfast. I had given Mommy the
obviously duplicated party invitation Basil had
received, and now there wasn't going to be much of an
excited party review, despite the high marks the
Carriage sisters gave Mommy on her arrangements,
most of which they had had a hand in.

What the incident with Basil did do was put an end
to Mommy's trying to get me accepted into the so-
called Palm Beach in crowd represented by the privileged students at EJW. She now agreed with Winston
that I should be left to find my own way at the school,
find my own friends, my own relationships. I had
even less interest in doing that at EJW than I previously had. Instead I bore down on my schoolwork,

became a confirmed loner, and spent my weekends doing more and more with Winston or with Winston and Mommy.

Winston did try to get me into a younger social scene, making sure I attended whatever charity events or affairs were sponsored or frequented by a younger crowd. He even went so far as to arrange for me to go yachting with the son of a friend of his who was visiting from Germany, Joachim Walter. He was a nice enough young man, soft-spoken and good-looking, but there was no spark between us, and after a pleasant day we parted company forever. Both of us knew it would be that way, and neither of us showed any regret.

Winston and I continued our sailing lessons every possible weekend until he declared I was capable of taking the boat out myself any time I wished. I knew both he and Mommy were hoping I would invite someone, preferably a nice young man, to join me. I did sail as often as I could but never with anyone else along. I truly began to enjoy my solitude. It was comfortable and safe, even though I knew it wasn't something Mommy enjoyed seeing. One evening after dinner I overheard her complaining to Winston about me. Maybe she wanted me to overhear.

"She's becoming so introverted," she told him. "It frightens me."

Winston tried to make it seem like nothing. "When she's ready she'll indulge in everything young people her age indulge in, Jackie. You'll see," he promised. "Give her time. There have been so many dramatic changes in her life."

Nevertheless a pall crept in and over our otherwise perfect existence at Joya del Mar. I could see it in

Mommy's worried frown when I returned from school and went directly up to my room or out to the beach to walk alone. On the other hand, she continued to socialize as much as she could or, more accurately, to participate in as much as she was invited to participate in. The novelty of being Winston Montgomery's new wife began to show tarnish. Every once in a while she would discover she had been left out of some event or another, and even if it was just a so-called power lunch during which a group of Palm Beach women would plan some major event, she was emotionally wounded. She would moan and complain about how hard it was to make friends with some of these people in Palm Beach, how unfair the other women could be.

Poor Winston bore the brunt of it all on his narrow shoulders. He was always trying to find things for me to do, places for me to go, and he was continually providing excuses or explanations for one social snub or another to soothe Mommy's often bruised new ego. When summer came and we were going off to spend time abroad at the villa he and Mommy had discovered during their honeymoon, I felt as if we were truly in retreat.

The villa was as beautiful as the pictures and descriptions had suggested. We had a pool almost as big as the one in Palm Beach. Mommy, Winston, and I spent a great deal of time visiting famous coastal places like Cannes, Nice, and Saint-Tropez, as well as inland villages like Saint-Paul-de-Vence and even took a week in Paris so Mommy could see the newest fashions. We ate at the top of the Eiffel Tower and looked out over Paris at night, fully understanding why it was called the City of Lights. While Mommy slept late Winston took me to the Louvre Museum and then on to Notre Dame.

In the afternoon we took Mommy to a Left Bank café for lunch, and at night we went to Montmartre for dinner, and both Mommy and I had our portraits done by street artists. Before we left Paris to return to our villa we went to see the palace at Versailles.

The summer seemed to fly by because of all our traveling and activity. I was actually unhappy about returning home. On the airplane Winston and I talked about my future, and he agreed with my idea to seek early graduation and perhaps start at one of the nearby junior colleges this year. He told Mommy I might just be too mature for the students at EJW, and it was probably a good idea to jump-start my higher education. She didn't object to anything. She had settled comfortably in an attitude of *que sera, sera*.

"Whatever's best for her," was her standard reply to anything Winston and I discussed and decided about my activities or my future these days. Having a new and what I thought smarter objective to my education helped me return with a better attitude to EJW for my senior year, which I expected would be an abbreviated one. I was more relaxed, and as a result I even didn't mind sitting and listening to the others brag about their wonderful summers. Now I could interject stories of my own if I liked. I didn't really. I quickly settled into my separate world again, did my work and my additional home study, and took my high school diploma examinations when I had planned.

Mommy, Winston, and I celebrated my excellent results by taking a weekend in Bermuda, where Winston and I did some sailing and even talked Mommy into coming along for an hour or so. Winston and I had been visiting some area junior colleges, and we had settled on one in Jupiter Beach. I registered for

the spring semester and, just like that, found myself
studying and associating with older students, most of
whom were not from super-wealthy Palm Beach families.

I liked my philosophy professor the most and even
recognized that I was developing a heavy crush on him.
His name was Dr. Berger. He was married and had two
young children, whose pictures were on his desk. His
son had his flaxen gold hair and his perfect nose and
strong mouth. His daughter, two years younger, looked
more like his wife, who I had to admit was very attractive. I took advantage of every opportunity I had to be
alone with Dr. Berger, even if it was merely to discuss
some philosopher. I even went so far as to pretend not
to understand things just to justify a tutorial. He wasn't
mechanical or cold, but he was very careful about how
personal he was with his students. Rarely did he inquire
about anything in my private life and always kept his
greetings in the corridors or in class to a quick, soft
smile or a nod and a simple "Hello."

It was almost as if he recognized his own vulnerabil-
ity around so many attractive and flirtatious female students, not that I was ever obvious about how I felt. At
least not that I knew of. I had to admit to myself that I
wasn't looking into any mirror or seeing myself as others might, and I could very well be coming off as a
lovesick teenager.

I knew that Mommy, despite her apparent aloofness,
expected I would soon announce a date or some social
relationship. She looked for it almost every day I
returned from college and even began asking me in not
so subtle terms about the boys at the school. Maybe my
fixation on Dr. Berger kept me from returning interested looks coming my way or encouraging conversa-

tions with the male students. Most of them seemed so
immature to me. I guess I had an impatient and steely
manner about me that put them off, but I didn't seem to
care, and that began to build as a sour note in Mommy's
increasingly strident tone whenever she talked to me
about my school life and how I was missing out on all
the fun.

Winston desperately tried to keep the static out of
our lives, finding something new for him and me to do
every weekend. Except for my fantasizing about Dr.
Berger, I didn't enjoy being with anyone more than
I enjoyed being with Winston. One night, when Winston revealed he had tickets to an upcoming concert at
the West Palm Beach Auditorium, Mommy finally exploded.

"You've got to stop being her social director,
Winston!" she cried.

"Excuse me?"

During all the time they had been married I had
never witnessed truly hard words between them.
Winston seemed incapable of losing his temper with
her, no matter what she did or said. He would just shake
his head and move aside or bend with the hard, heavy
winds of potential conflict.

"You're part of the reason she doesn't socialize with
people her own age, Winston. Every weekend practically you have something for her to do with you or with
me. How is any young man expected to compete or
attract her interest? What does he have to do, book her
two months in advance?"

He looked at me, and I looked down at the dish in
front of me.

"I was just trying . . ."

"I know you're trying, but stop trying!" she cried,

and reached out to seize the tickets from his hand. I looked up as she tore them into pieces. "No more. If she doesn't find things to do, young people with whom to socialize, let her sit at home. We don't do half the things we should be doing on weekends because you're so worried she'll be bored going to them or she won't have anything to do."

"I would expect that to be your concern as well, Jackie, even more so," he shot back, his face finally turning somewhat crimson.

Mommy sighed so deeply I thought her heart would shatter in her chest. "It has been, Winston, but I'm tired of it. I don't sleep at night thinking about her . . . her damn retreat from what should be the most exciting time in her life. It was for me and for just about any other woman I know."

I looked up at her, my eyes so glassed over with tears I could barely see the tightness in her lips and the frustration in her eyes.

"I'm a freak, Mommy," I cried. "I'm just a freak, is that it?"

"Of course not, but Daddy Winston," she said out of the right corner of her mouth, "isn't helping you doing the things he's doing. I don't know what will help you anymore," she added before Winston could offer a defense. "I buy you everything to make you attractive and keep you up with the latest styles. I arranged for you to have the best hairdressers, the best cosmeticians. We've bought you a beautiful new car. You have all this to share with anyone you like: a private beach, a magnificent swimming pool, a sailboat," she said, waving at the house and the grounds. "And what do you do, you sit in your room and read or take long walks alone on the beach or go sailing for hours and hours by yourself!

"How can you enjoy being by yourself so much, Grace?" she asked with a pinched, pained expression.

"Maybe I'm a multiple personality," I cried through my tears, "and I'm not alone."

"What?"

I jumped up and ran out of the dining room and up to my suite where I buried my face in my pillow to smother my tears and sobs. Although their voices were quite muffled, I could hear Winston and Mommy having their first hard, loud argument below. Soon afterward I heard Mommy crying and her footsteps on the stairway. A door slammed, and then all was quiet.

I turned over and looked up at the ceiling. Was I a freak? Was there something wrong with me? Shouldn't I want a boyfriend, someone to be with, more than I did? Did I place too much emphasis on school and not enough on a social life? Maybe I should have been more like the girls at EJW after all or been more like Phoebe Tremont. I should learn how to giggle more, roll my eyes, turn my shoulders, and stop showing up the boys in my classes. Maybe I should stop fighting what I had come to think of as the Love Game.

Winston didn't come to my room afterward, and neither did Mommy. All of us withdrew to our own private cocoons and the next day tried to pretend none of it had happened. Winston retreated from me somewhat over the next few months and didn't suggest any social activity. He and Mommy returned to a more normal Palm Beach social life, relying mostly on his contacts now. I went sailing only once and then, almost like someone agreeing to take castor oil, encouraged and accepted an invitation to go to dinner with a boy at the junior college, Charlie Packard.

In her eyes I could see that Mommy couldn't have designed a better first college date for me. Charlie had light brown hair and Wedgwood blue eyes and was a firm, six-foot-two-inch young man who happened to be one of the school's basketball stars. I had helped him with a research paper in English. I really didn't think he had any other interest in me even though I was warm and maybe somewhat overly friendly. Even so, I was surprised when he asked me on a date. Just from casual observance of the social scene on campus, I knew he had dated a few other girls. I assumed his failure to develop a long-term relationship with any of them meant he was looking for someone more substantial. As it turned out my assumption was drawn from my well of innocence, inexperience, and expectations that were far too high.

Mommy practically fell over herself welcoming him when he came to pick me up. He wasn't from a family anywhere nearly as wealthy as we were. I could see the look of surprise and astonishment in his eyes. Confronted with such affluence, he looked at me through different eyes. I could practically hear his questions forming and anticipated each one.

"How come you're going to this junior college and not one of those fancy ones up north or something?"

"I chose it because it had the programs I wanted and it was close to my home," I told him.

He shook his head. "How old are you really?"

He was happy to know I was over eighteen, but why, he wondered, wasn't I off studying in Paris or something? Why wasn't I going out with a prince or the son of a corporate giant? How come I was so modest at school?

"I'm just me, Charlie," I told him. "I don't think I'm some sort of royalty."

I could see he was actually embarrassed by the choice of restaurant he had made for our dinner. "I guess this is like slumming for you, huh?"

"It's fine," I kept telling him. I even said I was tired of eating in stuffy places where you see the same people all the time. I could see he thought I was just trying to be nice. Finally I said, "Really, I'm no princess, Charlie. I'm actually a Navy brat." He didn't understand, so I gave him a quick summary of our lives, which seemed to relax him. After dinner he suggested we drop in on a house party one of the players on the school's team was having.

A number of students from school were there. I could see some surprised faces when I walked in with Charlie. It was a nice house with a good-size living room, but Charlie muttered that the whole house could fit in my living room. Before the night was over he would be telling everyone about me, I thought, and whatever anonymity I had enjoyed at school would soon be blown away.

Apparently there was an understanding between Charlie and his teammate that the upstairs guest bedroom was reserved for him and his date. I even heard his friend say, "Your room awaits." Everyone was drinking. In the kitchen some were snorting coke. Charlie used the scene as a reason for us to get somewhere private, "away from all this immature behavior." I couldn't have agreed more, but I wasn't so sure about fleeing to a strange bedroom.

I kept thinking about how disappointed Mommy was going to be if my date was a failure, so I went up with Charlie, and he sprawled out on the bed and began to talk about all the jerks downstairs and all the girls he knew who didn't have "the long-term view of things." I wasn't sure what he meant, but he kept assuring me I had it.

"You're not only very pretty," he said, "but you're very smart and a lot more mature." *Mature* seemed to be his catchall word for everyone and everything. "I would have sworn you were at least twenty."

"I don't think there's all that much difference between eighteen, nineteen, and twenty, do you, Charlie?" I asked.

He shrugged. Then without any warning he leaned forward and kissed me on the lips, quickly moving his lips down over my chin to my neck, while his hands began to grope my breasts. He moved so fast I thought he had developed a second set of arms and hands. It was like feeling a hundred spiders crawling all over you. I tried to pull back, but he held me firmly and used his nose and his mouth to pull at my blouse buttons, getting the top two undone with remarkable dexterity and burrowing his mouth and his tongue into my cleavage so fast I gasped.

"You know, you're one of the few girls I know who wear a bra," he said. He said it with a tone of annoyance. "I'm sure you don't need it."

He had most of the remaining buttons of my blouse undone and slipped his hands in and under the bra, lifting it off my breasts with one swift motion. His thumbs stroked my nipples, and he kissed me hard on the lips, forcing me back on the bed.

"I knew you didn't need that bra," he quipped.

I heard him unzip his pants.

"Wait," I said.

"It's all right. I practice safe sex," he said, and, like a magician, snapped his fingers to show me a contraceptive. He held it up as if it were some sort of a ticket admitting him to my body.

"I can't," I said.

"Why not?" he asked, grimacing.

"I'm sold out."

"What? What's that, some sort of joke?"

"No. What I mean is making love has something to do with love. All we have done so far is share some food, Charlie. We've barely gotten to know each other, much less fall in love."

I sat up, pulled my bra back over my breasts, and began to button my blouse.

"What is this? I thought you wanted to be with me."

"We don't have the same definition of *being with*, Charlie."

He shook his head. "Why is it all you smart girls are so . . ."

"Smart?"

"No, frigid," he countered. "Don't say it," he added with his hand up before I could respond. "I know. We don't have the same definition of *frigid*."

I smiled. "And I thought you were just another jock."

"Very funny," he said. He stood up. "Let's go downstairs unless you want to go home."

"I think I'd rather go home," I said.

He nodded. "Figured," he said.

The ride home was mostly in silence, but before we reached the gate he looked at me and said, "I suppose you're saving it for a guy with a fat bank book, huh?"

"I don't judge people on the basis of their net worth, Charlie. You shouldn't, either," I told him.

How ironic, I thought as we drove up to the main house. Our new great wealth was not always an advantage after all.

Mommy was actually waiting up to see how my date had gone. I anticipated it.

"Did you have fun?" she asked immediately. Winston was already in bed upstairs.

I shook my head. "No, Mommy. We just weren't right for each other."

"Why not?" she snapped, her face filling with impatience and intolerance.

"Well," I said, fixing my eyes on hers, "when he didn't order any dessert at dinner I thought that was his athletic self-control, watching his diet and such."

"So?"

"But what he expected was that I would be his dessert," I said, and she blinked her eyes quickly and pulled her head back.

After a moment she said, "He seemed like a very nice, polite young man, Grace. You can't be afraid of a little intimacy, honey."

"We don't have the same definition of *intimacy*," I told her, and started away.

"What?" she called. I didn't look back, but I heard her mutter, "Damn."

Rejecting a popular boy at school can do a girl lots of damage, I discovered. Charlie Packard's ego wouldn't permit him to accept any sort of rebuke. It had to be the fault of the girl, and unfortunately for me I was that girl.

Invitations to go out on dates never materialized much after that. I had made applications to four-year colleges almost on entering the junior college anyway and didn't care if other students there, especially the boys, liked me or not. At the end of the school year what was important was that I had achieved a full semester's worth of credits and would have that advantage when I began my full college education.

We returned to France for the summer, only Mommy was interested in doing more traveling. I decided to take up the study of the French language and enrolled in a language school in Villefranche while Mommy and Winston did a series of trips, including a week's cruise to Venice. At the language school I became friends with an English girl, Kaye Underwood. She was interested in working in the hotel and travel industry and felt she had to learn French. She did better than I because she took room and board with a French family, which was the best she could afford, but she soon lived by the rule that no English could be spoken in the house, only French.

Kaye wasn't a very attractive girl. She had a round face that looked as if it had never shed its baby fat, and she was at least twenty-five pounds overweight. She wore her hair too short and was not very sophisticated about makeup and clothes, practically wearing the same things every day: a Grateful Dead T-shirt, brown Bermuda shorts, and a pair of well-worn walking shoes. When Mommy finally met her she was, I thought, a little too snobby and cold. She actually wondered aloud what drew me to be friends with such a person.

"You have so little in common with her, Grace. Winston has introduced you to so many girls from substantial families over here, and you haven't so much as exchanged phone numbers with most of them."

"I'd rather be with a substantial person than a substantial family," I replied. I suppose it wasn't so much that Kaye was substantial as she was safe. She never demanded much of me, never talked about boys or our lack of romantic adventures, and was in no way competitive.

Mommy grimaced in pain at my response and shook her head. "I don't know why we even bother anymore," she said.

She didn't need to worry. When the summer session at the language school ended, Kaye and I rarely saw each other. She took a job in a small hotel in Beaulieu-sur-Mer, a beautiful coastal village. Mommy and Winston had too many places for us to go and things for us to do for me to find time to visit Kaye, and then we returned to Palm Beach.

Kaye and I had exchanged addresses and had promised we would stay in touch, but after she wrote two letters and I didn't respond she never wrote again. I was occupied with starting college and used that as a rationalization for why I didn't continue our friendship. Mommy was right, I also told myself. Kaye and I came from worlds so different we might as well be from different planets.

I was accepted to every college I applied to but decided to attend the University of South Florida in Saint Petersburg. I suppose when it came right down to it, despite my bravado, I wanted to be somewhat close to Mommy and Winston. The day I was to go to the school and settle into the dormitory just happened to be the day of a major off-season charity event, an excursion to the Bahamas. Mommy had her heart set on going. I think she believed if she attended every possible social function right from the start she would somehow reclaim the place she had temporarily held in the social scene after she and Winston had married. The compromise was that she would go, but Winston would accompany me. I told them I didn't need either of them, but he was persistent, and Mommy agreed.

When I look back at all the things Winston did for me and with me, I have to put this at the top of the list. I recalled how Daddy used to fantasize about taking me to college.

"Leaving home for the first time is one of the most dramatic and emotional things you'll do, Sailor Girl," he told me, and then described what it had been like for him.

Winston had the private jet he leased fly us over to St. Petersburg. He had planned to have a car and driver waiting for us, but I thought the sight of me being brought to the school in a chauffeur-driven limousine might be too much. He laughed but agreed, and instead we had a rental car and arrived just like most of the other students, their parents visiting the campus with them and delivering them to their dormitory rooms.

My roommate was a Cuban girl from Miami, Celia Caballero, a diminutive five-foot-one-inch girl with ebony eyes like beautiful black stones. She was bubbly and outgoing and probably the sort of personality I needed. I know Winston was delighted with her.

"Well," he said when it was time for him to leave, "I know you will make us proud, Grace. You've already done it in so many ways."

"Not according to Mommy," I muttered.

"Oh, she's just too intense, too worried. She'll come around and learn how to relax. I'm dedicating myself to it," he promised. He gazed around. "You know what, Grace. I would trade everything I have to be your age and starting over like this. Now I know why Shaw said 'Youth is wasted on the young.' "

I laughed, and he hugged me and started for the car.

I had been on my own much more than most girls my age, and in foreign countries, too. We were an independent bunch when I was one of the naval brats. Yet somehow seeing Winston drive off, thinking about Mommy involved with socialites instead of being involved with me at this moment, I had never felt as alone.

"Come on," Celia cried, seizing my hand before I could refuse. She practically tugged me off my feet. "Let's go to the student activity center and join the other freshmen."

I wanted to remain and unpack, but I went along. I was happy I did because I discovered I could sign up for the sailing team. I also joined the student educational association. After all, my goal was still to go into teaching. Celia, who was already in the college band, having qualified in an audition with her clarinet, also joined the glee club. Our interests were quite different, but I didn't think that would present any obstacles to our rooming together.

Mommy was happy to hear I was doing something else beside studying and going to classes. I knew again what she expected would come of it. Celia got into the dating game much faster than I did, practically the next day, in fact, and soon was dragging me along to meet the friends of friends. I dated three different boys during the first half of the year, but I didn't get seriously involved with any of them. Maybe I was being too picky. I knew I had developed a reputation of being too virginal. Some of the boys nicknamed me Grace the Virgin Queen, referring to Queen Elizabeth I, who had kept a variety of suitors at bay for political reasons.

In time Celia stopped trying to fix me up with one of her current boyfriend's friends, and I was left to my own resources. I did begin to develop a relationship

with one of the boys on the sailing team, Walker
Thomas. He was one of the most, if not the most, dedi-
cated team members. In the beginning almost all of our
conversation centered around sailing. He came from
Marco Island on the west coast of Florida and had a
boat like Winston's. A number of times we went sailing
together and had a wonderful time.

I liked him a lot because he didn't seem driven to be
as intimate as possible as quickly as possible. He
wasn't shy, but he was easygoing, moving in small
ways toward a more intense relationship. Maybe I was
old-fashioned or something, but I actually set a date in
my mind when he and I would make love. I had slowly
permitted myself to feel more affectionately toward
him than any other boy in my life, and I believed I was
ready.

He was coming over to the dorm. Celia was going on
a date that she made clear would keep her out all night.
Walker and I were going to have a light dinner, go to a
movie, and then return to the dorm. About five-thirty,
however, he called to tell me he wasn't coming. In fact,
he was on his way home. His mother had suffered what
looked like a stroke.

He called a few days later to tell me she had indeed
suffered a stroke. It was massive, and she was in a
coma. I was in the middle of finals, but I offered to go
to him. He refused to hear of it. Two days later his
mother passed away. I had taken my last exam and was
packing to return to Joya del Mar.

Walker and I had planned to spend a good deal of
our summer together. I had already informed Mommy
and Winston that I wasn't going to Europe with them. I
was, after all, nearly twenty now. There was no reason I
couldn't spend my summers as I saw fit. I called Walker

with the intention of flying to Naples and then driving to Marco Island. When he was hesitant about it I took a deep breath and finally asked him why.

Sometimes you can hear everything in a small silence. Your heart has already heard it before the other person begins to speak. It was that way for me. I kept my eyes closed and listened.

"There's someone here, someone I was kind of serious with before I started college, Grace. She's been at my side the whole time, and we've sort of gotten back together. I'm sorry," he said.

"That's okay. As long as you're doing fine," I said quickly. "See you on deck," I added.

"Grace . . ." he called, but I was already hanging up the phone.

"Jonah," I spat at my image in the mirror and crawled under my blanket, wishing I could sink into the mattress and disappear altogether.

In the morning I informed Winston and Mommy that I had changed my plans and would be going with them to Europe after all. Winston was delighted, but, ironically, Mommy, who at first was worried about my staying home alone most of the summer, looked disappointed.

"What happened with that boy?" she asked. "Walker?"

"Nothing," I said. "Nothing was supposed to happen." I refused to talk about it anymore.

Winston bought a sailboat for me in Cannes, and I was back at it again—the wind, the water, the sea gulls, and me. I did a great deal of reading, went with them on most of their excursions, and took tennis lessons. Before the summer ended Winston and I were playing doubles against other couples or just playing with each other. Mommy wasn't into it and after one or two lessons gave up trying. She said she preferred golf, and soon it became a strange competition for Winston's time. He would have to play golf with her or tennis with me. Sometimes he tried to do both.

"Keeping two vigorous women happy is proving to be challenging," he confessed. He also confessed sotto voce that he preferred tennis. Golf, especially with Mommy, was like watching paint dry, he said, but never once showed it in front of her. He was a jewel of a man, I thought.

Once I had believed I shouldn't settle down until I found a man exactly like Daddy. Now I was looking for one exactly like Winston Montgomery.

Walker did not return to college in the fall. When I inquired about him I learned he had transferred to the University of West Florida in Pensacola. I found out from one of our sailing teammates that he was going there because his girlfriend from Marco Island was going there. Somehow it all took the spirit out of my sailing activity, too, and eventually I left the team, using the pressure of my studies as an excuse. The truth was, my interest in school itself was dwindling, shrinking and diminishing like some star fading into the night. Solitude became my best friend again, and before the semester ended Celia asked to be transferred from our room in the dormitory, claiming I was too dark and depressing a roommate, never talking, never listening to music, never wanting to do anything socially with her. I didn't blame her or argue about it. After she moved out I anticipated someone new, but word about me seemed to spread like a virus, and no one asked to be transferred into my room, even any of the girls who were tripled.

When I returned home for the holidays I seriously debated continuing with college. Maybe I needed a year off. I didn't bring it up with Mommy, but I did with Winston, and I could see he was very troubled by the suggestion. He was silent for a long moment and then nodded slowly.

"Perhaps I have really been the one with my head in the sand when it comes to you, Grace," he said. "Maybe I have been ignoring your difficulties or trying too hard to distract you. Wrapping Joya del Mar around you and withdrawing from the world isn't going to solve anything," he said. "Give it all a second and a third thought. Please," he pleaded.

As it turned out, I didn't have to give it any more thought. Fate, that creature Mommy had been so confident about defeating, had only been waiting in the shadows, waiting and watching for it's opportunity. When it arose, it slipped out quietly and tiptoed up the stairs of our elegant home. It did so sometime during the night, glancing once perhaps my way and smiling and then continuing down the hallway, past all the magnificent and beautiful art, until it reached Mommy and Winston's door.

There it paused and glanced over its shoulder, gesturing toward another shadow that is always ready and waiting to be beckoned like an obedient servant. They entered together and left together.

Mommy's screams rode on the wave of morning sunlight that lifted the night off of Joya del Mar and replaced it with a different sort of darkness, a blanket of gloom woven with the mournful cries, shrouds, and dust of centuries. My eyes snapped open, and my heart stopped and started. I was trembling so hard I could barely move one foot ahead of the other. When I stepped into the hallway the servants were rushing up the stairs, coming from every direction.

Mommy saw me standing there, my hands clutched between my breasts.

"I keep shaking him and shaking him, but he won't wake up!" she cried. "He won't wake up!"

Somewhere outside another sea gull turned and went screaming out to sea on its wings of panic.

In my mind I heard the roar of helicopters.

16

None So Blind

I didn't want to wallow in self-pity after Winston's death. It seemed to me a selfish way to be, but I was more convinced than ever that everyone I cared for or who cared for me suffered some cruel fate. Surely this proved it was some sort of curse I brought along into every relationship. I was a Typhoid Mary. I carried the disease, but I didn't get it.

There was still my mother, of course, but that didn't mean she was exempt. In time I couldn't help believing that something terrible would happen to her, too, and all because of me. I didn't tell anyone about these thoughts. They came to me again and again, especially during Winston's funeral. In church, when I looked around at the people in attendance, I was sure I saw the accusations in their granite faces. They were staring at me too hard and too angrily, whispering and nodding at me. I imagined a wave of long, sharp forefingers pointed in my direction. Maybe they believed I had taken up too much of his time, had given him too much to worry about, or had exhausted him. Why else would a man who had been so fit and such a great athlete have a fatal heart attack when men fifteen, twenty years older were still active and alive and not half as healthy-looking?

The mourners looked at Mommy in a different way, too. Almost no one but Dallas and Warren gazed at her with any sympathy. Most had wry smiles writhing over their lips. Everyone knew that as Winston's wife Mommy had inherited a considerable fortune. She was just another jeweled fruit ripe for plucking. I overheard comments to that effect at Joya del Mar after the funeral when most of these people came to pay their respects. Some unmarried men and widowers even stood around adding up the value of everything as if they were deciding whether she was worth the trouble. They were nothing more than a different form of buzzard disguised as eagles with gilded wings, especially the lawyers and financial managers who descended with their plastic smiles and air kisses, clicking their lips around her face and around each other so much it sounded like an invasion of crickets.

I was glad when it all ended. Like some very young girl I harbored the hope that it had all been a dream, that I would walk out onto the rear loggia the next morning and find Winston sitting there, comfortably reading his *Wall Street Journal.* He would look up at me and smile warmly, and we'd have coffee and talk about the condition of the sea and the winds while the sailboat bobbed invitingly at the dock.

Now I felt I could never sail again. The very thought of doing it and then returning to a house without

Winston to share in my excitement and enjoyment sickened me. The deep emptiness in my stomach was much like the emptiness I had felt after Daddy's death, and just as I avoided looking at anything even remotely connected to or reminiscent of the Navy, I wanted to ignore and be blind to all those things Winston and I had shared and loved so much together. Without him they were simply reminders of the pain. I hated even living here in a palace that had become a prison of memories and sadness.

I realized I wasn't thinking enough about Mommy. After all, she had lost deeply twice, too. I always knew she didn't love Winston with the same sort of passion she had loved my daddy, but she had become quite fond of him and certainly very dependent on him over these last five years. She was well aware of the fact that the new world, the new life she had so wanted for us was now seriously compromised. I could see she trembled with insecurity even though she tried to put on a brave face for me the very next day at breakfast.

"Well, Grace," she began after we both had gazed sadly at Winston's empty chair, "we're back to just each other again. It seems cruel fate has not retreated as far into the background as I had hoped.

"However," she said, nodding at her own thoughts, "we are not going to hunker down like frightened rabbits. We're going to continue to enjoy and to appreciate each and every opportunity. For starters, I don't like this idea of you not returning to school."

"I'm not sure what I want to do with myself," I replied.

"But isn't college the best place to explore all that?"

"No," I said firmly. "There's too much distraction. I will take some time off and . . ."

"And do what, Grace? Hide in your room? Walk on the beach? Go sailing by yourself for hours and hours, not go to any parties with young people your age? What? What will you do with this time off?"

"I'm not sure, Mommy. Let me be," I said. I said it with such authority I surprised even myself.

"Well, I'm telling you this, Grace. I'm not going to become some pathetic widow draped in black and in retreat. I want to be just as vibrant and alive as I was. Otherwise fate has had its way with me," she said with defiance. "If you don't do the same, you're victimizing yourself. I promise you this as well," she continued. "I won't spend the rest of my life lecturing you and trying to get you to do the right things for yourself. You're old enough to make the right decisions for yourself now."

I said nothing. We ate quietly, me nibbling at my food like a small mouse and she deliberately attacking hers with a vigorous vengeance. The grandfather clock bonged, the servants scurried about doing their chores as usual, and Joya del Mar, like a ship set on a course that couldn't be changed, continued.

However, it wasn't long before Mommy discovered her plans and expectations were built with an optimism that had no substance. It was all as airy as dreams. Even the artificial friends she had developed over the past few years drifted away. Invitations became less and less frequent. It wasn't long before it became crystal clear that the only reason she had been included in anything the so-called core families and A-level society conducted was Winston. He and his family had been old Palm Beach with something akin to royalty rights. Mommy was just another usurper, an accessory. What good were earrings without ears, necklaces without a neck, bracelets without a wrist? Winston had been the body, and he was gone. She was as unimportant as last month's gossip on the pages of the Palm Beach Shiny.

And so those first six months or so after Winston's death were very difficult. Almost immediately a nightmare began to shadow our days. More often than not Mommy would walk about with a worried frown drawing her eyebrows together. She resembled someone with a constant headache. I often heard her mumbling angrily to herself about this one or that. Even the Carriage sisters stopped coming around and taking her phone calls. Hardly anyone she called returned a call, and every time she learned about an event from which she had been excluded she went into a new rage. It got so I tried to avoid her. Fortunately the house and the property were so large it wasn't all that difficult to spend most of the day without confronting each other.

I did as I had planned, dropped out of college for what I thought would be about six months. I kept up my reading but rarely went anywhere except to the bookstore or to shop for necessities and, on rare occasions, to see a movie by myself. I knew I was becoming an old maid, even though I wasn't even in my mid-twenties. Whenever I stepped out to do anything I felt myself close up like a clam and begin to tremble inside. I thought I could even be diagnosed with agoraphobia and placed in therapy.

Every once in a while Mommy succeeded in getting a handful of guests to come to dinner at Joya del Mar. I realized before she did that they were really coming not to be friendly again, but just to see how she was doing, how the property was doing, so they could have some new gossip to spread. There was nothing like being at the forefront of a new story or rumor in Palm Beach. It gave the reporter some momentary popularity, and that was the coin with which they bought one another's company and friendship: popularity.

Mommy's only real friend, Dallas, came by as often as she could or as often as Mommy invited her. They had drifted apart somewhat over the years because Mommy and Winston were in an entirely different social world. Whenever Dallas and Warren came to any affairs at Joya del Mar they seemed to spend most of their time talking to me and just watching Mommy move from guest to guest, both of them looking at her as if they were looking at some stranger.

Phoebe had started college but soon had met someone and was engaged almost before the first semester ended. Winston, Mommy, and I had attended the wedding and learned she was pregnant. Less than two years later, she was separated and working at the restaurant, something she had always disdained. She had an au pair taking care of her child, which in my mind was better for the child. Not wanting ever to be friendly with Phoebe, I lost track of everyone else I had known at the school. It truly seemed as if every tie Mommy and I had to our past had either been cut or was about to tear. I had contact with no one. I was like some small planet lost in space, passing closely by some face, some acquaintance, for only a moment and then continuing on into the dark beyond.

Whenever anyone who came to our infrequent dinners at Joya del Mar asked about me, Mommy would chime in before I could respond and claim I was on a sabbatical, doing independent study, and I was soon to be going to school in Switzerland or France or Italy, depending on the people at the dinner. She got the idea to use that response when she saw me perusing some old school brochures Winston had brought me during those times when he was trying to get me to be more outgoing.

I didn't deny anything she said because that was the easiest way to get the spotlight off me. Of course, Mommy tried to get me actually to do any one of those things. She used every argument she could, including claiming she needed me to be more educated to handle the complexities of our financial life.

"I don't know what I'm doing or saying yes to when the broker calls or our manager calls or the lawyer calls. Winston took care of everything when he was alive. Now we've lost some money, too," she revealed in an attempt to get me to become more concerned. "Some bad things happened in the market, and some real estate partnerships have gone sour. I've been advised to end the jet plane lease."

"We don't use it anyway, Mommy."

"That's not the point!" she cried.

I returned to what I was reading, and she stormed away.

Finally one night she didn't come down to dinner. Instead she stood in the dining-room doorway and announced she was going out.

"Where?" I asked. She was wearing a lot more makeup than usual and a very tight-fitting dress with a low neckline. It looked like something she might have ordered out of a Frederick's of Hollywood catalogue and was quite unlike the expensive, elegant, stylish designer outfits she had been buying and wearing all these years.

"Out," she said. "With you drooping about all day

and night and with the servants standing and waiting for constant instructions and the financial people driving me crazy, I've decided I need to get out."

Before I could ask another question she was gone. I had no idea what time she returned at night because I was long asleep. Soon she was going out two and then three and four nights a week. The phone began ringing again. She had developed some new friends. Of course, I was curious about it, but every time I started to ask a question she jumped down my throat and made a speech about how young and attractive she still was and how she was wasting her opportunities. According to her it was a lesson I should learn.

And then, one morning when I was down at breakfast, not expecting her to join me, as was usually the case these days, I heard her descending the stairs, but I heard a man's voice as well. It made my heart beat faster and faster as their footsteps grew louder and closer. She came through the doorway and smiled at me.

A man with thick golden brown hair and beautiful cerulean eyes accompanied her. He was wearing one of Winston's morning robes, and although he wasn't quite Winston's height, filled it out well. The first thing that struck me about him was that he was years younger than Mommy. There was also something vaguely familiar about his very handsome face, and for a few moments I actually wondered if he was an actor.

"Kirby," she said, "this is my daughter, Grace. Grace, this is Kirby Scott."

"Hi," he said. "She has your best features, Jackie," he told Mommy, and she smiled.

"I'm absolutely ravenous," she announced, and called for the maid.

Kirby Scott sat across from me. "Your mother tells me you're quite the sailor," he said.

"I haven't done it for a while," I replied, still a bit taken aback by his presence and the fact that they had obviously spent the night together right down the corridor from me.

"That's a shame. I've done quite a bit of sailing myself, although I was never on a sailing team or anything. I bet that was fun."

I looked at Mommy. How much had she told this stranger about me? I wondered. She had an expression of self-satisfaction on her face as if bringing this young, handsome man to breakfast was a major accomplishment.

"Maybe we could take the boat out today," he continued. "Jackie Lee wants to go, don't you, Jackie?"

Mommy smiled at him. "Yes," she said. "Yes, I do."

"But you hate sailing," I reminded her.

"I don't hate it," she said. "I just like to feel safe, like to feel like I'm with someone who really knows what he's doing." She turned an ingratiating smile on Kirby Scott.

Something turned and twisted under my breasts. "Winston was an excellent sailor. He obviously knew what he was doing, too. He taught me enough to qualify me immediately for the college team," I shot back at her.

She held her smile although it looked as if her whole face might shatter like thin china any second.

"So then, why not go out with us today?" Kirby interjected.

I turned to him with as hard and cold a look as I could manage, but he didn't flinch. His eyes met my eyes, and he widened his smile.

"I don't want to," I said slowly, pronouncing each vowel and consonant hard and sharply.

He shrugged. "If you change your mind, we'll be glad to have you join us. Say about noon. We were thinking of taking a lunch."

I looked at Mommy. Who was this man? *We were thinking of taking a lunch?*

"I thought you said eating on the sailboat was uncomfortable. The ocean rocked too much. You weren't even fond of eating on the yacht anymore," I reminded her.

"We'll find calm waters," Kirby said. It was as if he had become her mouth, answering everything for her, speaking for her.

"I hope you do," I said. "Otherwise she might throw up."

"Grace!" Mommy cried. "We're having breakfast."

"I'm not. I'm finished," I said. I rose.

"See you later," Kirby said, still holding that handsome smile.

"Whatever," I said, and left them. Almost before I reached the stairs I could hear them laughing. I went up to my room and debated getting dressed and taking a ride to the bookstore in the mall. After I showered and fixed my hair I paused at the window and looked out. I saw Kirby and Mommy moving toward the dock. He had a towel around his shoulders and wore only an abbreviated bathing suit and sandals. She was in one of her expensive sailing outfits she had rarely worn. Even from this distance I could see how trim he was. Mommy leaned on his arm, and when he said something, she laughed, and they hurried like two teenagers down to the dock and the sailboat.

I got dressed as quickly as I could, suddenly eager to be anywhere else.

After that, Kirby Scott became Mommy's constant escort. If he didn't stay overnight he was there by noon the following day, and they were off to do things together. Whenever I asked her about him, and especially asked about his age, she told me not to be so concerned. He was just a distraction.

"But what does he do?" I pursued. "He seems available to do anything you want anytime you want, and he doesn't look old enough to be retired."

"He's between things," was all she would say and leave it as cryptic as that.

I couldn't deny he was one of the best-looking men I had seen, and when he put on his tuxedo to take her to some extravagant Palm Beach charity event he looked strikingly handsome. Whether Mommy had been invited to something or not, she now made it her business to find out what was happening, where it was being held, and then, if it was a charity event, bought tickets for both of them, no matter what the cost. It was apparent to me that what she wanted was to be seen with him. Maybe it was her way of getting back at the stuffy social crowd, I thought, but I could actually feel Mommy slipping away, sinking into him. I had nightmares in which he was made of quicksand and she could not pull herself out, and I could not pull her out, either.

One day while I was shopping for some things I needed, the Carriage sisters approached me as I was leaving the mall. They were together so much I was beginning to wonder if they were joined at the hip.

"Oh, Grace, dear, how have you been?" Thelma

asked in a syrupy sweet voice. "Brenda and I were just talking about you and your mother. We were worried."

"And we were worried about you, Mrs. Carriage. Not hearing from you for so long, I mean," I said in a voice a pound of sugar sweeter than hers.

"Yes, well, we've been so busy with it being the season and all. What I meant was, we were worried about your mother," she corrected, her voice sharper now.

"My mother?"

"We heard she was being escorted by that Kirby Scott just about everywhere she goes these days," Brenda said.

"Oh, you know Mr. Scott?" I asked her.

"We know *of* him, dear," Thelma replied, pursing her lips which were so overladen with lipstick she looked as if she possessed a second set overlapping the first. "We do not *know* him. He's escorted many wealthy women in Palm Beach. I hope she's not thinking of him in any sort of serious light," she added. "He is a man of little means and, I'm afraid, little character. Any woman with means should be cautioned."

"I'll let her know your advice," I said, still holding the smiling mask over my face.

"I wish you would," Thelma said, not retreating. She pulled her shoulders back and shook them like a hen.

"And what about you, dear?" Brenda asked. "What have you been doing with yourself? Are you in college again?"

"Not yet. I have so much to do these days, it being the season and all," I said. "Nice to see you both and how little you both have changed and how much you know about everyone else's business. Goodbye," I said, and walked off, leaving them looking after me, their mouths moving to bring up the words choking their throats.

I had put on a good performance, but I was literally shaking so hard it took me a few moments to get hold of myself so I could drive my car home. If the Carriage sisters had the nerve to say all those things right to me, it was obvious people were talking about Mommy. What was Mommy doing? Why had she gotten so involved with such a man? It was one thing to have a lover but another thing to have one with whom you were proud to be seen. How did she think this was going to raise her status in the snobby social world?

I went home prepared to argue with her about it. She had been seeing Kirby for months and months now. He was certainly not, as she had told me, a distraction anymore. She had even forced me to go out with them on my birthday, a day I had hoped would be special for just the two of us. The truth was, he was there now for every unique occasion in our lives these days. Sometimes I felt he was paying more attention to me and resting his gaze on my face more than he was on Mommy's. Twice at events I had let Mommy talk me into attending with her and Kirby, he had asked me to dance and held me so tightly I was embarrassed. One time I was sure he was sexually aroused, and it made me very nervous. He was always touching me, taking an opportunity to kiss me, and too often, if not on the lips, close to them. Mommy seemed oblivious to it all. I had tried to ignore it and buried my head in the sand. I had to bring her to her senses.

Unfortunately, when I arrived home I could hear from their laughing voices that he was with her. I would have to wait for a better opportunity. Intending to ignore them and go up to my suite, I headed directly for the stairway, but one of the maids came hurrying out to tell me my mother wanted me to come to the den immediately. Reluctantly I did. They were both at the bar. They had music playing and were clinking glasses of champagne when I entered.

"Grace, honey, we've been waiting for you. We swore we wouldn't open another bottle of champagne until you got home, didn't we, Kirby?"

"Absolutely, but that was two bottles ago," he said, and they both laughed, pressed their foreheads together, and kissed.

I thought I was going to heave up the light lunch I had just eaten.

"I'm tired, Mommy. I'm going upstairs," I said.

"Wait, wait!" she cried. She poured another glass of champagne and held it out toward me. "Join us in a toast, honey."

"A toast? For what?" I asked, not moving any closer. Little bells of warning tinkled around my heart.

She held out her hand, palm down, as a way of replying. The new diamond ring picked up the light coming through the patio doors and glittered.

"Kirby and I are engaged," she said. "But don't worry," she added quickly. "We're not going to have one of those extravagant Palm Beach weddings and put you through all of that. No, we're going off to get married. Probably to the U.S. Virgin Islands."

I stared for a moment. When I didn't respond immediately, she pulled her hand back as if I had slapped it.

"Well, you could say something nice, like good luck or something, Grace, instead of just standing there and staring at us."

"Good luck," I said, turned, and ran out of the room. I pounded up the stairs as quickly as I could, their silly laughter full of champagne bubbles resounding behind me.

A good hour or so later I heard both of them coming up the stairs, giggling and laughing so loudly it was impossible not to hear them. I peeked out my door and saw Kirby scoop her into his arms and carry her the remainder of the way.

"Just like Clark Gable in *Gone with the Wind!*" he cried, and she laughed again.

A short while later it was very quiet in the house. I lay in my bed, sulking and thinking until I finally dozed off, but not so long afterward awoke when I heard someone knocking on my door.

"Who is it?" I called, annoyed.

"It's me," Kirby said. "May I speak to you for just a minute?"

"No."

"Please," he pleaded. "Just a minute."

There hadn't been all that many times he and I were alone, and despite his good looks I was grateful for that, but I didn't see how I could avoid it forever, especially now.

"What do you want?" I asked.

He opened the door slowly and peeked in. "Hey, how are you doing?"

"Just peachy keen," I said.

He nodded. He was in his shirt and pants, barefoot. His shirt was opened at the collar, and his hair was tousled. Usually his hair was perfect. He was an immaculate dresser, never appearing unkempt, even if it was just to be an appearance in front of me.

"I know you're upset," he said.

"Oh, do you?"

"Yes. Your mother has brought a new man into your life and so soon."

"You're not in my life. You're in hers," I told him.

"Now don't be like that, Grace. Once your mother and I are married you'll be just as much a part of my life as your mother will be."

I wanted to say, "I hope not," but something made me hesitant. Perhaps it was better not to banter with him, I thought. I turned my face away, hoping he would take that as a signal and leave, but he didn't. He came farther into the room and sat at the foot of my bed.

That took me by surprise and even made my heart pound.

"I wish you would leave," I said. "I'm tired, and I want to get some sleep."

"In a minute. I just want to assure you that I have your and your mother's best interests at heart. I know she has suffered some terrible disappointments in her life, and she feels very alone, very lost now. I want to end that and do my best to bring back happiness. She's a wonderful person and deserves it, and so do you."

"You make us sound like refugees," I said.

He laughed and then looked serious again. "We're all refugees from some emotional crisis or another in our lives, Grace. I'm no exception, and in time I hope you and I can grow closer and develop enough trust to tell each other about things we really feel and really think. I know from what your mother has told me that you're going through a tough time. You're not sure what you want to do with yourself, and I want to do all I can to help you decide. You're too talented, too intelligent, and far too beautiful to waste away, even in a place as beautiful and luxurious as Joya del Mar." He had such a steely-eyed, sincere look in his eyes I had to look at him without doubt and sarcasm.

He stood up. "That's all I wanted to say, Grace. Basically what I'm asking you to do is give me a chance. Don't base your opinion on anything but what I do and say. Okay?"

I nodded.

"Thanks," he said, smiling. He hesitated a moment, and I thought in that moment he was deciding whether or not to come to me to kiss me or something. He decided against it and just nodded and retreated. "I hope the day will come when you will call me Daddy, too. Sweet dreams," he said, and closed the door softly.

Call him Daddy? I felt as if some creature had crawled into my heart and was tearing it away.

Kirby Scott was in our lives. The question was for how long and how deeply.

There was a short article in the Palm Beach Shiny about Mommy's engagement and, as the journalist wrote, "Fast on its heels, elopement. The bride and groom were said to have pronounced their vows in a chapel on the U.S. Virgin Islands. Specifics are hard to come by."

There was then a reference to Mommy being the widow of "the recently deceased Winston Montgomery."

Most of the article was then about Winston, and toward the end there was a small mention of Kirby Scott having been married three times previously. Mommy never mentioned that to me, and I wondered if she even knew.

Even though the article was far from flattering, Mommy had it cut out and placed in a scrapbook containing any and all other times she had been mentioned in the paper. I was astounded by how she ignored the sarcasm and the criticism and saw only something wonderful in such gossip. It was on the tip of my tongue to tell her, "There are none so blind as those who will not see," something she had often said to me, but I knew she would just laugh it off or wave her hand at me and tell me I was being too serious or too silly. To her they meant the same thing now.

The week Mommy went away to elope was strange for me, especially every time I thought about why she had gone off. I suppose in the back of my mind I always believed she would marry again. After all, she was far from being an elderly widow. But I envisioned her marrying a man like Winston, someone substantial, mature. Maybe I was looking for another father figure. Maybe I had no right to decide whom she would marry again, just as I didn't want her to decide whom I would marry. And then there was the question of why it should be all right for a man to marry a woman so much younger than he was but not right for a woman to marry a man so much younger than she was. If anyone should hate double standards, it was we women.

Anyway, there was no question she was enjoying her holiday with Kirby. She called only once, right after they performed whatever ceremony they had planned.

"I'm now Mrs. Kirby Scott," she announced over the phone.

"Don't expect me to become Grace Scott," I said before she could even suggest it.

"I don't expect that, Grace. I expect you to become Grace Somebody someday, but not Scott, unless you happen to meet a man as exciting as Kirby who happens to be a Scott, too. Are you all right? Anything new?"

"Nothing's new, Mom. I'm fine. Have a good time," I said, and we hung up. I didn't hear another word from her until the day they returned, which wasn't like her.

She loved calling me from hotels and from yachts whenever she and Winston were away. She knew I was surprised about not hearing from her.

"We had such a wonderful time I lost track of time," she began when they arrived, the servants carrying their dozens and dozens of purchases up to their suite. I was sitting on the rear loggia, reading. She hurried out to me.

"I wasn't sure you were coming home today," I said. "You never told me when to expect you."

"I was going to call you every day, but Kirby said I baby you too much and that's why you're not trying to move on with your life."

"Really," I said dryly. "It's nice to have someone with so much wisdom come into our family."

"He could be right, Grace. He is a man of some worldly experience."

"More than Winston had?"

"No, but Kirby has a different sort of wisdom," she insisted.

On cue he appeared, tanned and rested, those blue eyes even bluer.

"Grace," he said, and kissed me on the cheek before I could pull myself back. "How's our little girl?"

"Our little girl is just fine," I said.

"Do any sailing?" he asked with an impish twinkle in his eyes.

"No," I said.

"We did," he said, putting his arm around Mommy. "And we enjoyed it, didn't we, Jackie Lee?"

"Every moment," she agreed. They kissed, and then Mommy declared she had to get upstairs and unpack.

"I bought you three new outfits and a new bathing

suit, Grace. Actually Kirby picked out the bathing suit. Come up to see everything," she urged.

"Soon. You get started, Mommy," I told her. "I want to finish something I'm reading."

"Okay, I will," she declared, and after kissing Kirby again, she shot into the house.

"She's a new woman," Kirby declared, looking after her. "Wait until you see. She's years younger. I can't keep up with her. You can see it in her face, can't you?"

"Yes," I admitted reluctantly, and looked away.

"Having someone else to care about is important, Grace. You need to develop relationships again, get yourself back into the world. Nothing will make your mother happier than to see you happy, and if she's happy, I'm happy. So you see, everything is up to you," he concluded.

I glanced at him and looked away again, tears burning under my eyelids. I hated Mommy for bringing someone like him into our lives, opening up our most intimate selves to him.

"I don't think her happiness is going to depend on mine," I muttered.

"Oh, but you're wrong about that, Grace. It didn't take me long to see how big of a heart your mother has."

"I'll bet."

"I mean for compassion and love for other people, not just me. How about we start anew? Let's get to know each other a little, spend more time together," he pleaded.

I started to shake my head.

"If you don't like me, if you're absolutely sure you can't ever get close to me, I'll leave you be, I promise," he said, raising his right hand. "All I ask is a chance to present myself as I truly am. I've knocked about a great deal, I know, but a woman like your mother doesn't come along that often. She makes me feel . . . substantial. She makes me want to be responsible, to care about things, and especially not be so self-centered," he continued.

I took a deep breath. There was a time when I would have said similar things about her, I thought. How I wished it was all true now, too.

"I'll bet there were occasions in your life when you wanted people to look at you one more time, to give you a chance to show them your best. Am I right?"

"Maybe," I said.

"Sure, it just stands to reason. Look, I know I can't be the man Winston was to you. He was much older than I am and had many, many more experiences."

"And successes," I added.

"Yes, and successes. But I'm not totally without success, especially in the social arena, and to be honest, Grace, you could benefit from some of that, couldn't you? Be honest," he urged.

"Maybe," I said again.

"That's okay. Nothing to be ashamed of."

"I'm not ashamed of anything," I said quickly.

"Nor should you be. Exactly. Hey," he said, looking out at the sea, "you ever do any wind surfing?"

"No." I almost smiled at the way he jumped from one subject to another. In some ways he was like a little boy, and when he was like that it wasn't easy to dislike him.

"Someone with sailing experience would have an easier time of it, I think. I did a lot of it on Maui last summer. It's a lot of fun and exciting."

"We don't have sail boards," I said.

"Didn't."

"What?"

He nodded in the direction he was looking. I stood up and gazed, too. Two men were bringing brand-new sail boards down to the beach.

"I had them ordered," he explained. "What do you say first thing tomorrow after breakfast I give you some lessons and you see if you like it. Okay?"

He had them ordered? When did he do that? How did he know I would be at all interested in doing this? He was moving so fast, coming in and taking over our lives. It all took my breath away, but when I looked at him and I looked down at the new sail boards I couldn't help but feel some excitement.

"Your mother will never do it, but we can show her. In a matter of hours you'll be sailing with the wind in your hair, and it's good exercise, too. How's ten A.M. sound?"

"I don't know," I said. "I'm not sure I want to do that."

"Well, we'll play it by ear. When you're ready we'll try it if you like. Once you start letting yourself enjoy yourself again, Grace, it will all follow. Everything you want will follow. You'll see," he said.

He looked up toward his and Mommy's suite.

"You should go up and see what she bought you. She was always looking for something nice for you. Even on our honeymoon you were never out of her thoughts."

I thought a moment, feeling guilty. I started into the house.

"And I hope you like the bathing suit," he cried, smiling. "It's hot."

The breeze lifted his bangs. He stood back with his hands on the railing, looking like a male model ready to be photographed. He was as seductive as the devil, I thought. I really couldn't blame Mommy. In a very dark time in her life he came soaring through like a comet and brightened her skies, and yes, her face, rejuvenating her heart.

What would he do to mine?

17

A Taste of
What's to Come

Everything Mommy bought me was beautiful, and it all fit perfectly. She made me model it all, parade before her, and although she didn't come right out and say it the implication was clear: These are clothes to be worn on dates or at parties. They are not clothes to be left hanging like unpicked fruit left to rot from neglect. I did not deny I was pleased with it all. No matter how deeply I had withdrawn into my own little world, I still enjoyed looking nice, even if it was only for the sea gulls.

The bathing suit Kirby had chosen for me, however, was far more revealing than anything I had bought for myself or Mommy had bought for me. It was practically a thong, the cut was so sharp, and the top, although it wasn't exactly a bikini top, was shaped in such a way as to leave most of my breasts exposed. I started to complain.

"In the Virgin Islands all the young women who had figures that could be flattered were wearing suits like that, Grace. It's the latest style."

"Not for me," I said, taking it off.

"How did I bring up such a prude?" she quipped. "You look beautiful in it, Grace. You should be proud of your figure, not ashamed of it. Believe me, there are thousands of women who wish they looked like you and wish they could wear that suit."

"Tell them to come and get it," I said.

She groaned. "Please don't tell Kirby you hate it," she said. "He was so excited about buying something for you."

"Really?" I raised my eyebrows. "He truly bought it?"

"Yes."

"With his own money?" I followed.

She shifted her eyes away guiltily. "We don't think in those terms anymore, Grace. When a man and a woman marry, they should be as one. What's his is mine, and what's mine is his."

"I don't mind that, but was there anything that was his?" I pursued.

"Grace, you're being unnecessarily unpleasant," she snapped back at me. "We're both trying our best to please you. Can't you see that? Have I been such a horrible mother to you? Do I deserve this?"

"I'm not saying anything like that," I told her, but she held the painful look on her face. "I just don't want you to be unhappy."

"Me?" She laughed. "I couldn't be much happier. I was very depressed, but don't you see how he's brought a new vibrancy into our lives? We'll show these Palm Beach core families that they can't get us down."

"All right, Mommy," I said. I was tired of arguing about all that. She was fixated on it, and that was that.

"Just try to be a little more . . . pleasant. That's all I ask," she said softly, and brushed some hair off my face with her hand. Then she kissed me on the forehead. "You're so beautiful and intelligent, Grace. It breaks my heart to see you depressed and unhappy and especially insecure about yourself. That's why you threw off that bathing suit, you know. You just don't have a good self-image, and there's no reason for you not to." She held the suit up against her own body and wiggled. "If you have it, flaunt it, I say."

I couldn't help but laugh.

She smiled. "Go on, take it, wear it," she said, holding it out toward me. "Would I advise you to do something that wasn't good for you to do? Can't you just try, Grace?"

She waited. I shook my head, but I took the suit. "Okay, Mommy, I'll try," I promised, and she clapped her hands.

"That's wonderful, Grace. That's all I hope for," she said, and hugged me.

Later that evening the three of us did have a nice dinner together. She and Kirby were like a comedy team, reviewing their honeymoon, relating some of the funnier things that they did or that happened to them. Mommy's laugh was free and innocent, and her eyes sparkled with such pleasure she looked as if she had shed years, certainly years of sadness.

Afterward the three of us walked on the beach. There was a full moon, and the light streaming down from the night sky made the water gleam as if it had been sprayed with glitter. First Kirby had her arm in his, and then he reached out for me, and the three of us were joined with him in the center.

"My two beautiful women," he declared. "We'll turn this place into a palace of happiness. You hear that, Palm Beach? This will be a palace of joy!" he screamed, and waved his fist in the direction of Worth Avenue.

Mommy's laughter was lifted by the breeze and carried out to sea. I took a deep breath and secretly prayed that all she expected would happen and once again she would feel she had defeated cruel fate.

Taking a cue from Kirby's enthusiasm, she launched an entirely new campaign to defeat those in the Palm Beach social world who had dared to snub her. She and Kirby began to stage party after party, each gala affair more extravagant than the previous. If we had a five-piece band for one event, we had a twenty-six-piece orchestra for the next. Whoever was the rage in catering at the moment was hired and told to spare no expense in creating dishes that were unique and, especially, "not at anyone else's party."

For one party they hired two dozen performers: magicians, singing groups, fortune tellers and psychics, dancers who went through the crowd of guests, staging mini shows. Of course, we had spotlights and hired one party designer after another to create a different theme for each event.

Soon Joya del Mar did become known as the party capital. The gala events were so lavish people wanted to be invited if for no other reason than just to have said they had experienced one of Jackie and Kirby's extravaganzas. To get themselves invited, some invited Mommy and Kirby to their affairs, but there wasn't the sort of quid pro quo Mommy had anticipated. She was still not on the A-list, and she couldn't throw off the sense that she was still being treated like an outsider, almost freakishly, as a curiosity, a subject for lunch gossip.

I had no idea how much money Mommy was spending on her own parties until I happened to overhear her having a conversation with her business manger. It was obvious he was warning her about depleting the principal of some of the best investments Winston had made.

"These parties are a different sort of investment," she told him. "To my way of thinking what they will bring in return is worth it."

I tried to talk to her about the money issues, but she always waved me off.

"Kirby is better at that sort of thing than I am anyway," she said. "He thinks our financial advisors are from the old school and are far too conservative, old-fashioned."

"Why didn't Winston think that?" I asked.

"Winston was ninety percent retired, honey. Kirby has his ear to the wall and knows what's really happening out there," she assured me.

I didn't like the sound of that. If he was so good at this, why wasn't he a wealthy man himself? I wondered, but I didn't ask her any more questions. She was floating in such a big, pink bubble I hated to be the one to cause it to burst.

Bubbles were something else I thought had become too much in her life as well. Never a big drinker, Mommy was suddenly very much into expensive champagnes. She and Kirby went to wine auctions and bid on rare vintages for our wine cooler. They included bottles of champagne that cost as much as two thousand dollars each.

"This will take the smirks off the faces of the Carriage sisters!" she cried. "We'll pop one open right in front of them next party."

Almost every night she and Kirby had some affair planned or someplace to go, all of them involving champagne, wine, and a new drink Kirby introduced her to. He called it a New York Cosmopolitan, and it involved vodka. Mommy wasn't good with hard liquor. If she drank too much she would get maudlin and then sometimes belligerent. I hated to see her drinking at all. Over time it was beginning to take its toll on her looks, too. She would sleep later and later into the morning and drag herself about, shoving pills down her throat to drive away headaches. Whenever I tried to point out this slow but consistent degeneration, she turned on me and moaned about my prudishness or my failure to enjoy my youth.

"I never had a chance to be young and foolish," she declared, as if that was something everyone should be. "I had to be the perfect naval wife, and then I was given all these new burdens. Just when I thought we were fine, fate comes and takes Winston. What difference does it make to be good? In the end we all find ourselves staring into the same dark space. At least Kirby makes me feel alive and young and beautiful, and everything we're doing is fun, Grace. Fun, do you hear me? Do you?" she cried, her eyes wide with near hysteria.

"Okay," I said softly, and retreated. There wasn't anything more I could do about it. She would have to come to her own conclusions about everything, I thought, and I hoped and prayed she would before it was too late.

As it turned out, I should have thought more about myself in the midst of all this anyway.

From the very beginning Kirby led Mommy and me to believe that he had decided to make me a priority, his new cause.

"If I bring anything to this marriage and family," he said one night at dinner when the three of us were alone, "I hope it will be doing things that make Grace a happier and more confident young woman."

Mommy looked at him adoringly as he made this pronouncement and then raised his wine glass to toast me. I wanted to say that when he talked about me like that he made me feel like a disabled person, but I could also see how much Mommy believed in him and appreciated what he was saying and trying to do.

I was always skeptical of Kirby or at least tried to be. If I was to be honest with myself I would have to blame myself as well as him for anything that happened. Maybe I'm too hard on myself, but I can't help believing in the old admonition, "buyer beware." I would just change it to "believer beware."

After Mommy had returned from their elopement and practically begged me to give Kirby a chance and have more confidence in myself, I did wonder if I wasn't being unfair to him and to her, for that matter. A part of me wanted to believe in him and wanted it so much it drowned out warnings from the other part of me.

Where Winston had been fatherly, loving, as supportive as a father should be, Kirby was more like an older brother, closer to acting and thinking like someone my age.

"You don't want to do only the things people your mother's and my age do," I remember him urging that morning after their return. "Wind surfing is for people your age."

"But you said you were just doing it a great deal on Maui," I reminded him.

He laughed. "Well, Grace," he said, nodding and looking so coy, "I can see I can't be dishonest with you. I've always tried to be younger in spirit, sometimes, I'm afraid, too young."

Mommy laughed to indicate they shared some intimacy about that. Whatever it was had something to do with their sex life. It nearly made me blush.

"But," he said, holding up his right forefinger, "a wise old man once told me, youth is a matter of mind over matter. Think young, and you'll be young. Doing things with you will keep me young," he declared, and then looked at Mommy and said, "and that is the way you want me to be. Right?"

"Absolutely," she said, laughing. "I have too many senior citizens in my life as it is."

With this emphasis on youth waving like some new flag over our lives, I found it more and more difficult, if not downright impossible, to withdraw to my safe solitude. Reluctantly, with Mommy cheering me on, I finally succumbed and got into the new bathing suit Kirby had chosen for me. Then he and I went down to our private beach where he began to give me lessons in wind surfing. The ocean wasn't as calm as it could be that day I first tried it, but Kirby thought it made for more exciting rides.

"You've got to take some chances, Grace. It makes everything more exciting and more worthwhile."

He had so much passion in his voice my heart skipped beats.

Kirby demonstrated all the instructions first while Mommy and I stood and watched him glide and jump with the waves.

"Look how graceful he is," she declared, "how athletic, those muscles gleaming."

Her lack of restraint in revealing her admiration for Kirby's body and, at times, his animal sexuality embarrassed me. While we had never sat and had a frank conversation about sex and men, time and our experiences had carried me from that almost asexual world young girls exist in to a world of sophistication and awareness, especially awareness of your own body and the feelings that flow through it with an almost radioactive frequency, stirring your imagination and your most secret fantasies. I don't remember when exactly Mommy stopped looking at me as her young daughter, her child, but sometime after Daddy's death and her dating Winston I found our conversations and the references she made far more revealing about her own sexuality. She had come to accept me as her sexual equal, and truthfully I wasn't as comfortable about that as she assumed. Even years later I still wasn't, and, for some reason, especially when it was in reference to Kirby.

He came back ashore with the board and guided me out on mine to practice the techniques he had just taught me. Soon I gained confidence, and I was out there doing it. He joined me, and we rode the waves together. Just as he had said, it was exciting, and I had a wonderful time. Mommy waved and screamed encouragement. She soon became bored with just watching us and retreated to the pool. On the way back to shore I took a bad spill. Kirby was by my side almost instantly, leaping into the water to be sure I was all right. He held me at the waist so I could catch my breath. It took a moment or two, but I did, and then I also realized that the abbreviated bathing suit top had been pushed off by the water. I was topless and turned away as quickly as I could.

He said nothing about it, which I appreciated. He let me think he might not have seen what had happened, although I couldn't see how that was possible.

After that, whenever I did go wind surfing, I wore a one-piece. Eventually I gave in and went sailing with him as well. He was good at it and, unlike Winston, wanted us to go faster, take more chances. In fact, everything I did with Kirby was on the edge in some form or fashion, even riding in my convertible. If he drove, he drove like a race car driver, usually getting me to scream caution and then laughing at me. It was difficult to deny that it was exciting and fun to be with him.

However, there were quieter times, too, like the nights they had nothing special to do and we would all play cards. He was always funny and charming. To my surprise he was even a good pasta cook and made us dinner occasionally. Whenever he did anything, he insisted I help and learn something.

During this very hectic and active first year and a half Mommy and Kirby took a number of holidays between their parties and events, each time trying to get me to go along. I refused no matter how Mommy pleaded.

"I'll only feel like a third wheel," I told her, which was a reason she at least understood and appreciated.

"You've got to get out of the rut," Kirby would say, but he didn't push and try to get me to go to events where I would meet young men. He even advised Mommy to do the same: Back off. "She'll find herself," he would say.

"Winston used to say that," she would reply softly.

"Well, he was right," Kirby insisted.

In the end I began to feel I had misjudged him. He

had been right to plead for a fair appraisal. Mommy and he were far too extravagant, but I couldn't blame that entirely on him, and he did always seem cognizant and concerned about my feelings, no matter what they did or what was suggested.

Maybe, I thought, we were becoming something of a family again after all. Was that too much to hope?

Almost two years after Mommy and Kirby eloped I began to reconsider my decision about not continuing my college education. I sent away for university brochures and perused them and the different programs each school offered. I was still considering a career in teaching.

Kirby often came by and looked in whenever I left my door open. He would stop to talk about almost anything, just, it seemed to me, to make conversation. He never stepped into the room without asking or saying, "Hey, how you doing? Can I come in a minute?"

Twice I had left the door open when I was half dressed and caught sight of him standing there. He moved on quickly without saying a word or knocking on the opened door to pretend he hadn't noticed.

"Hey, what are you reading now?" he asked this time. "Can I see?"

"Just some college brochures," I said, holding them up. He came into the room and looked at them.

"USC? You'd go to college as far away as Los Angeles?"

"We did a great deal of traveling, Kirby. Going to California isn't so overwhelming to me. For a while we lived in San Diego."

"Right, I know, but that's clear across the country. We'd miss you," he said. He had a different sort of look in his eye, almost a look of true sadness.

"Right."

"No, I mean it," he insisted. "We've become quite a threesome, and even though I know I'm dominating your time, I enjoy it. I hope you do, too."

"I do," I said, "otherwise I wouldn't be doing anything with you."

He smiled. "Why do you have to be so literal, so serious, Grace? I think that's part of your problem."

"What problem?"

"Making new friends, socializing. Can I be honest with you?" he asked, sitting beside me on the bed.

"That's all I ever want you to be with me, Kirby," I countered.

He smiled and shook his head. "You know, you make me feel we're batting a tennis ball back and forth whenever we talk these days. I suspect you're like that with most of the guys who try to get to know you. You're too defensive."

I turned away quickly, and he put his hand on my arm. "I don't mean to hurt you, Grace, but I hope we've gotten so we can talk to each other from the heart. Have we?"

I looked at him and nodded.

"Well, you give off this air of superiority."

I started to protest, but he put his hand up. "I watch you whenever we have guests here, especially guests who bring young sons along. You're always condescending, speaking to them like you're sitting atop a mountain." He thought a moment, his eyes darkening. "Can I ask you something very personal?"

"You can ask, but I don't know if you'll get an answer," I said.

"See? Okay. You've never been with anyone, have you?"

I looked back at him sharply. "What do you mean?"

"You know what I mean, Grace. You're nearly twenty-two, and I suspect you're far more intelligent than I am, so I know you understand the question."

"What difference does it make whether I've been with someone or not?"

"A lot of difference. I really don't think you are a snob, Grace. I think you're just frightened."

"Frightened?" I started to laugh.

"Of life, of experiencing it fully."

My smile flew away. "What are you doing, taking courses in psychology?"

"No, my school has been real life, no formal courses in anything. Well?"

"I don't think it's necessary for you to know the answer to that question, Kirby."

"Okay," he said with a shrug. "All I wanted to do is assure you that there is nothing to be afraid of when you give something of yourself to someone."

The tears that burned at my eyes were coming up too fast for me to stop. "You don't know what you're talking about," I said. "You don't know whom I gave myself to and what I gave and what happened afterward. Just leave me alone," I moaned.

"All right. Don't get upset. I'm just trying to be like a father to you, concerned, helpful."

"I don't need your help right now."

"Okay. When you're ready, I'll be there for you. That's all I want you to know."

I wiped the tears from my cheeks and took a deep breath.

"I'm sorry I made you cry, Grace. That really pains me."

"It's all right."

"I'm sorry," he said again, and leaned over to kiss me on the cheek. He held his lips there just a second longer than I had anticipated, then pulled back slowly and smiled, keeping his face very close to mine. "Forgive me?"

"It's okay," I said, finding it hard to breathe. His lips were inches from mine.

"Great."

He kissed me again, this time smack on my lips, which really took me by surprise.

"Your problem is just your inexperience, Grace. A beautiful woman is like a beautiful race horse. You only have to find your stride. I can help you do that," he whispered.

"What? What do you mean?"

"Just a little thing like how to kiss. I bet you never kissed a man like this," he said, and brought his lips to mine while he held me tightly at the shoulders and pressed his tongue into my mouth. I tried to pull loose, but he held on as if his lips were glued to mine.

"There," he said. "That was like no other kiss you've had, wasn't it?"

I just stared at him, breathless, still spinning. He smiled, taking that for his love powers, I'm sure.

"That day you lost your bathing suit top, I said to myself, 'This is a beautiful young woman who, like a beautiful flower, just has to be brought to blossom.' Why not let me help you do that? You can trust me."

I kept shaking my head. What was he saying? What was he offering to do?

"Don't think I haven't noticed how you flirt with me, Grace. That's all right. It's only natural, natural instinct. You have needs you haven't even begun to satisfy."

"I don't flirt with you."

"You don't? Well, maybe you're not consciously aware of what you do, but you do it," he insisted. He smiled and brought his hands up to my breasts. "How perfect you are, Grace." He leaned toward me. "You're more beautiful than Jackie and will always be," he said. "I know what you want. Let me give it to you."

"Stop," I said, putting my hands on his chest. I pushed, but he resisted, his face still close.

"Go on," he said. "Push me away. Go on," he whispered, his lips closing on mine.

I started, but my arms seemed to weaken. He kissed me again and then stood up.

"That's just a taste of what's to come. It's better if you are left in anticipation. It will make it all the more delicious and wonderful."

He stood there a moment longer and then slowly started away. "See you later," he said from the door.

I was unable to find the breath to speak. In a moment he was gone, and I felt the need to embrace myself. Why hadn't I pushed him away harder? Why hadn't I screamed? Why was he so sure I wouldn't tell my mother?

Had I been flirting with him?

I hated myself for what he had awakened inside me.

If I appeared introverted and withdrawn to people before, I imagine I came off looking practically comatose during the next few weeks. I couldn't shake off the veil of guilt that had been thrown over me. I was afraid it was clearly written on my face, and so I avoided Mommy, getting up much earlier than she and Kirby and having breakfast by myself. They were usually off somewhere for lunch and dinner anyway. When they weren't, I made some excuses and had my dinner brought to my suite. I went to sleep earlier and earlier and slept or dozed for hours at a time in the shade by the pool. I felt like a clam slowly closing its shell. Even the brightest days were cloudy to me, and when it rained I enjoyed the wind and the darkness just as someone with a morbid view of life might.

Mommy was unusually distracted with social activities during this time, even for her. Somehow she had wormed her way onto a committee for a major charity event to be held at the Breakers hotel, and that led to another and another event. The truth was, most of the women who went to the meetings, went to socialize and not really to do work. Mommy, on the other hand, was eager to get her hands on real activities. She accepted as many of the real responsibilities as she was given. She would be glad to research and visit with different providers, write letters, do mailings. It became quite clear to me they were merely taking advantage of her, but like someone absorbed by one of those cult religions, she became a devotee of the charity events. Her name would be included on the list of organizers printed on the invitations, and for her that was an accomplishment.

Every time I saw Kirby he smiled, but in a way so different from the smile he used to have. It was as though he and I shared a very intimate secret we kept from Mommy. I had no reason to feel this way, I told myself, but it didn't stop me from feeling it, and I was terrified that Mommy would see the exchange between us one day and wonder why. For now, however, she was as absent from my life as I had been from hers.

Eventually she even began to neglect Kirby. By month's end I saw they were doing more and more things separately. He was off on trips supposedly to find out about this investment or that. I noticed that a number of things took him to Las Vegas, too. A part of me was happy about this. Whatever activities he was involved in kept him from approaching me. It had been nearly two months since we had last gone sailing together, for example, not that I would have gone if he asked now.

Actually I was rarely in the mood to do anything physical, whether it was with him or not. My reading suffered as well because my eyes would drift from the page, and I would focus on something off in the distance and fall into a kind of trance, not realizing I was doing so until I blinked, looked at my watch, and saw I had let nearly twenty minutes drift away.

And then a strange thing happened. I began to have great difficulty falling asleep at night. Some nights I would lie there and stare at the ceiling waiting for my eyes to close and stay closed. I didn't sleep, but often, as in a dream, the faces of the people I had known since Daddy's death appeared like pictures projected on the wall. There was Autumn Sullivan, her face writhing with anxiety because of what the girls had revealed about her abortion. There was Augustus Brewster almost struck dumb by his grandmother's passing, and there was poor Randy struggling to get out his words. Winston seemed forever in a dark corner, watching me, smiling softly. Suddenly there was the light of morning sweeping him away with the shadows, and I hadn't bought a single hour of sleep.

It made me lethargic most of the day. Vaguely I understood that something very serious was happening to me. It was as if my identity, my self-awareness, was dissipating, thinning out until I was translucent. People would soon see right through me, and I would totally disappear just the way Augustus Brewster used to predict he would, and no one would even notice. I blamed it all on my insomnia.

One night when Mommy was out at one of her meetings and Kirby was off doing whatever things he was into those days, I snuck into their suite and rifled through Mommy's medicine cabinet to find her sleeping pills. I knew she often relied on them. I hated taking any pills at all, but I was at a point of near madness from the many sleepless nights and decided I had no choice.

I took one and went to bed. It made me doze and even drift off for a few hours, but I woke in the middle of the night and remained awake again, the same faces parading on the walls of darkness around me until the sun's rays burned through and around the curtains.

Encouraged by the few hours I had achieved, however, I took two pills the following night and slept longer. After that I began to rely on the pills more and more and eventually sent one of our servants to the pharmacy. The prescription permitted one more refill. I didn't tell Mommy about it, of course. Now I had my own.

Sleep became an avenue of delightful escape. I loved wrapping my blanket around myself and drifting into the haze. There were no struggles, no hard memories to confront, no decisions to make. In sleep I was truly free and undisturbed. I felt no guilt, no insecurity. I needed no defenses.

Vaguely I knew my appearance was changing. I woke and didn't bother to brush my hair. Sometimes I didn't shower, either. I never put on makeup, not even a little lipstick anymore. I wore the same dress for days. Mommy noticed my hair and remarked about it, but she

was so absorbed in her charity and social events she
didn't see much more, which confirmed my mad suspicion that I was truly slowly disappearing.

I wasn't sure whether Kirby noticed or not or, to be
even more accurate, cared or not. Something was occupying his mind and his time, too, these days. He was in
and out without so much as saying hello to me. I
thought perhaps he was disgusted with me or with what
I had let him do and had chosen to ignore me.

Then one night, the time being so blurred in my
memory, he came to my suite. I was already in bed,
captured within the powers of the pills, slumbering like
someone in hibernation. What was real and what was
part of my dream world were indistinguishable. I heard
a knock, but in my mind the knock was within a dream.
It was Daddy. He had come to my bedroom in Norfolk.

"Are you awake?" I heard.

"Yes," I said eagerly. I could feel the deep, happy
smile carving its way into my face.

In my memory there was a full moon, and I had forgotten to close the curtains. The room was so bright
with its illumination it looked as if it was on fire.

"Hey," he said. "How are you doing?"

"I'm fine. I'm glad you're here," I said.

I felt him sit on the bed, and then I felt his hand wipe
the strands of hair from my cheeks.

"I've been thinking about you a lot. I'm sorry I
haven't been around much these days, but that didn't
mean you weren't in my thoughts. I wanted to give
more time to you. I feel terrible about filling your heart
with expectation and then not fulfilling my promise."

"I know you do, but it's all right," I said, still smiling, my eyes still closed.

"I don't want you to feel alone or lost, Grace."

Grace? Why doesn't he call me Sailor Girl?

"You're missing a lot in your life. You're wasting the best years. You can't continue to live this way, shut up inside. As I tried to show you before, you've got to learn to let yourself feel, experience, grow. Whoever has tried to be with you was just wrong or didn't know what he was doing or, even worse, was simply too selfish. The best lover is one who gives as much as he or she gets."

I felt the blanket sliding down my shoulder until it was at my waist.

"Sleeping in the nude these days? Or did you just forget to put on a nightie?" he asked, and laughed.

"I must have forgotten," I said.

His fingers traced down from the back of my neck, down over my spine, moving the blanket farther until it was around the middle of my legs, just under the inside of my knees. His hand moved as softly as a breeze over my tush, as he used to call it.

"How's that feel?" he asked.

"Nice."

"Yes, it is nice," he said, and then surprised me by kissing me there.

"You're so soft," he said, "so special."

I smiled. Any minute he was going to say "Sailor Girl." I was sure of it. It was coming.

His hands moved down my legs to my feet. He massaged them gently, and I moaned with pleasure.

"Like that? I learned that in the Orient," he said.

Yes, I thought, *he's been all over the world.*

"There are places on your feet that affect places on the rest of your body. Nice, huh?"

"Yes," I said.

His fingers traveled back up between my legs and surprised me by touching me in my most private place.

I jumped, and he said, "Easy, relax. You've got to learn to relax, otherwise you'll never enjoy. There now, easy." I felt myself soften, and then an electric sensation of pleasure shot up through the small of my stomach to my breasts.

His lips were moving over me again. Gently but firmly he turned me on my side and cupped my breast, his thumb sliding over my nipple. His mouth was soon there, and his tongue, and I moaned again and let myself fall backward.

Feeling him naked and then his firm sex was the most shocking thing. This wasn't Daddy. I wasn't Sailor Girl. I struggled to open my eyes, but the lids seemed to be sewn shut. Just as I started to protest, his mouth was over mine, his tongue pressing onto mine.

"You're as sweet as I imagined you would be," he said. His hands went under my thighs, and he lifted me to fit himself into me. I gasped and shook my head and started to claw my way up out of the pit of darkness, but he was pressing harder and harder, driving me back. I started to sob. At least I thought I did. I heard what sounded like sobs, but no tears emerged from my heavy eyelids. Soon I was as helpless as a rag doll, moving as he wanted me to move, my meager resistance dwindling. I moaned and then heard him cry out with pleasure as he spurted inside me. For a long moment we were frozen together, paused as if on some video picture. Then he retreated, his heavy breathing at my ear because he was right beside me.

I sank into my bed and waited for the storm of mixed emotions and feelings to subside. That took me down deeper and deeper into the dark well again, and I had no idea how much time went by.

Before morning I felt him at me again, his lips everywhere on my body, gently nibbling around my breasts and then moving to the small of my stomach. My arms were like lead, my fingers stiff. He was in me a second time, turning and twisting me to make himself comfortable. I felt the heat, the wetness, and then the retreat.

I don't think I uttered a sound. When the morning light finally woke me I was alone. For a long moment I lay there wondering if I had dreamed it all. I quickly realized I hadn't. Panic kept me from moving a muscle. It was as if I expected to see him standing there beside the bed any moment.

Instead I heard the muffled sounds of the servants. I heard a phone ring. I heard footsteps, and then all was relatively quiet. I finally rose and went into the shower. I made it as hot as I could stand and washed myself so vigorously my skin was as red as it would be had I developed an allergic rash. I found something different to wear, and then I went out and down to the dining room. I could hear Mommy on the telephone in the den and paused to look in at her. She glanced at me.

"Oh, Grace, you're up. I have to take a ride to Boca Raton to meet a new caterer. Would you like to come along? Kirby hates these things, and he's off somewhere anyway."

I just stared at her for a moment and then walked on to the dining room.

"Grace!" she screamed. She came after me and pulled at my arm to turn me around. "What's wrong with you? You look at me, but you don't reply?"

"Breakfast," I said. "It's time for breakfast."

"Time for breakfast? It's nearly two in the afternoon. You mean to say you didn't have breakfast yet? You've slept in this long? Even I get up before this for breakfast, Grace."

She continued to stare at me. "Aren't you feeling well?"

I smiled at her. *That's an interesting question,* I thought. *Am I feeling well? I'll think about it.*

I continued to the dining room and took my usual seat at the table. Mommy came to the door and looked in at me for a moment, and then she shook her head and returned to her office and her phone.

The maid came and began to bring me my breakfast. I ate quietly, slowly, desperately trying to remember something. There was something I had to remember. What was it? Something that had happened, I told myself. *Think, think.*

Nothing came to mind, and finally I gave up and went outside. I lay on a lounge and looked up at the sky, watching the slow movement of the clouds from south to north. Occasionally a sea gull flew into my line of vision. I followed its glide until it disappeared, and then I gazed out at the ocean and watched the ships slide along the horizon. They looked so tiny and toylike. Maybe this was a makebelieve world after all. *Maybe I'm asleep now when I think I'm awake.*

An old Japanese poem came to my mind: "A man sat under a tree and dreamed he was a butterfly. Or was it a butterfly who dreamed he was a man?"

When are we really awake? When are we really asleep?

"Grace," I heard off in the distance. "Grace, look who's home. Come on, honey."

I sat up and gazed around.

"Grace."

I turned. Mommy was beckoning to me from the rear patio. "Come here," she was calling.

I stood up. Someone was coming up behind her.

"Daddy?" I muttered.

I saw him step alongside her. He took off his hat, and then he saluted. Two fingers.

Daddy?

"Daddy!" I cried, and I ran as hard and as fast as I could back to the rear loggia.

Only when I got there no one was there.

Not even Mommy.

My legs seemed to sail out from under me.

18

Subterfuge

When I opened my eyes I was looking up at Mommy, and I was in my room lying in my bed. Jakks, our butler, was standing at the foot of the bed, looking very concerned through his gray eyes and bushy eyebrows.

"Thanks for your help, Jakks," Mommy said. "She'll be fine, I'm sure." She put her hand over my forehead and handed me a glass of water. "Go on, drink some water, Grace."

"If you need me, I'll be right downstairs, Mrs. Scott," Jakks said.

"Thank you. Go on, Grace, take the glass and drink some water. C'mon, sit up. I don't understand this emotional hysteria. What's wrong with you? You don't seem to have any fever, and your color is good."

I took the glass from her and sipped some water. "Am I awake?" I asked her.

"No, you're in Never-never Land. What is going on

with you, Grace? You're worse than ever, and just when I have so many things to do. Well, talk," she urged.

I simply sipped some water.

"Apparently, from what the maid told me, you ate a good breakfast, and you've been eating good lunches and dinners, so there's nothing wrong with your appetite. What do I have to do, put you in some mental clinic or something? Because I will if you don't snap out of this. I mean it, Grace. You've had way more than enough time to get your act together. You can't go on like this."

I drank some more water and handed her the glass, which annoyed her.

"I can't be a wet nurse to a girl in her twenties. Do you have any pains anywhere? I'll take you right to the hospital," she, said making it sound more like a threat than an offer. "Well?"

"No," I said.

She stared at me a moment and shook her head. "This is all emotional, silly emotionalism. We all have disappointments in life, but we all have to go on, Grace. You've got to get hold of yourself and stop wallowing about in self-pity. It's unbecoming in a young woman. I'm leaving for a few hours. When I come back I expect to see you up and about, your hair washed and brushed, and you in one of the pretty outfits you have. We're going out to dinner tonight as soon as Kirby gets home.

"I've decided to take matters into my own hands now. I will bring you everywhere until you meet people and start going places yourself. I told Kirby the same thing, and he finally agrees with me. Do you want anything else before I go? I'll tell the maid to bring it up to you, but I want you up, Grace. Do you hear me? Don't just lie there staring at me as if I'm talking in a foreign language."

"Parlez-vous francais?" I asked, and laughed.

"Oh, you're so funny." She turned and started out. "I'll be back in two hours or so."

"Deux heures," I said.

"I'm glad you're finally putting your French language studies to use, but please put them to intelligent use, Grace. Go to school in France or something."

"Mais oui, Mama. Au revoir."

"Goodbye to you, too," she said, and left.

I continued to lie there, just letting my thoughts wander. I went walking through a maze of memories, sometimes seeing and hearing things that occurred when I was seven or eight and then things that had happened along the way to Joya del Mar.

It was the distinct sound of a helicopter that finally drew me out of bed and to my window. It flew low over the ocean. I knew it was owned by one of the very wealthy men or women who lived here. It wasn't military, but it still turned me into a little girl again, if only for a little while.

Later I showered and dressed and fixed my hair. I heard Mommy shouting orders at the servants below, and then I heard her coming to my room. I was ready, I thought, ready to go wherever she wanted. She opened the door, looked at the bed, and turned to see me standing by the bathroom door. For a moment I truly wondered if she saw me at all. She didn't move. She held her gaze, but her face was stiff, her lips looking like a slash of red. Finally her mouth opened and remained shaped in an O for a moment or two.

"What in hell . . ." she began, moving a step closer to me. "What are you supposed to be doing?"

"Getting ready to go with you," I sang.

"Getting ready to go with me? To what, the circus? Is this supposed to be some sick joke of yours, Grace, because it's not in the least funny."

"I'm sorry," I said. I didn't know why I had to say that, but I thought it belonged in the conversation.

"You're sorry?" She took a deep breath, looked up at the ceiling, and marched at me, seizing me at the shoulders and turning me back into the bathroom, where she held me in front of the wall mirror. "Well?" she asked.

I stared at someone. It was a young woman. She had a blue blouse on, but she wore her bra over the blouse. She was wearing a short red skirt over a pair of jeans. One side of her hair was brushed back, and the other was tied into a pigtail. The lipstick she wore was under her lower lip and over the upper, producing a crimson mustache. Small pats of rouge over her forehead and cheeks made her face look broken out in a rash. There was one long teardrop earring dangling from her left ear and none on the right.

"Who's that?" I asked.

"Really. Who *is* that? It's certainly not Grace Montgomery. Take everything off, wash your face, and go to bed," she ordered. She sighed deeply. "You win. I'm sending for the doctor. Go on," she insisted. "Do as I say, Grace."

I stood there, puzzled, but she turned and left. After she was gone I gazed into the mirror again. I brought my hands up to feel the bra and realized I wasn't looking at someone else. I was looking at myself.

What was it she wanted me to do? I wondered. *Yes, get undressed, wash my face, and go to bed. That's it.* I followed her orders. Soon she returned with our family physician, Dr. Cook. He had been Winston's doctor and had been very fond of him.

"Hello there," he said, pulling a chair up beside the bed. "What's happening with you?"

I looked at Mommy, who stood at the foot of the bed, her arms crossed under her breasts, her face in a scowl.

"We're going to dinner," I said.

"Oh, are you?" He held my wrist and took my pulse, leaned over and looked at my eyes. "Have you been taking any pills, Grace?"

"Just to sleep," I said. "I have to sleep."

"To sleep?" He looked at Mommy. She shook her head.

"I haven't given her anything, and she hasn't gone to anyone to get anything, Bob."

"Grace," he said, "where are these pills?"

I lifted my head and then the pillow. He saw the bottle and took it out to read it.

"Your prescription, Jackie Lee. From the date on the bottle it looks like a renewal."

"Grace, when did you do that?"

"I don't remember."

Dr. Cook emptied the remaining pills into his palm and counted them. He looked at the bottle again and then at Mommy.

"Considering what's missing since she got these, she's been taking at least three or four a day!"

"No wonder she's been moving around here like a zombie. I'm so disappointed in you, Grace. How could you do such a thing? It's dangerous to do that, isn't it, Dr. Cook?"

"Of course."

"I had to sleep," I repeated.

"It's better to attack whatever is preventing you from

sleeping, Grace. You're a young woman. You shouldn't need these on a daily basis," he said, pouring the pills back into the bottle and handing it to Mommy. "Do you have any pain anywhere, trouble with your eyesight, your hearing, anything?"

"No."

"Your mother says you fainted. Do you remember that?"

"No."

"Well, I'm going to have you see a neurologist," he decided, and stood up. He turned to Mommy. "I'll arrange for you to take her to see Mark Samuels tomorrow, Jackie. Let's get to the bottom of it fast."

"Thank you, Bob."

"For now I would like you to remain in bed, Grace. Have a light dinner, and just try to relax."

"Okay," I said.

"You'll be fine," he added with a smile. Then he walked out with Mommy, and they spoke in very low tones as they continued down the hallway, but I did make out the word *depression.*

The maid brought my dinner to me later. I ate most of it, and then I did try to sleep without the pills. I dozed on and off until I heard Mommy come into my room. She was returning from dinner, and I thought she looked very nice. I told her so.

"Thank you, Grace. How are you feeling?"

"Tired," I said.

"You're always tired," she complained. "Even without those pills. You don't do anything, and you're always tired." She walked to the window and looked out with her back to me. "Kirby hasn't come home, and he didn't call. He was supposed to take me to dinner. I left word for him to meet me at the restaurant, but he didn't show up, and he's still not home, and he's still not called. It was very embarrassing, sitting there in the booth by myself. I could see them all looking at me and whispering.

"All this happens at once," she moaned. Her shoulders slumped, and I felt so bad for her.

"I'm sorry, Mommy," I said.

"There's nothing for you to feel sorry about, Grace. Just get well. We're going to see the neurologist tomorrow afternoon. I was hoping Kirby would be home and be with us."

She looked at me. "Try to get some sleep, Grace," she said. She touched my cheek, leaned over, and kissed me on the forehead. "I'm going to end up taking two of those pills myself," she muttered disgustedly, and left me.

I did everything I could to fall asleep again. I even tried counting sheep, but they soon were sheep with faces of people I had known, and all that did was keep me awake. I tossed and turned and finally, just before morning, dozed off. Mommy said later that she had stopped by to see if I was ready for breakfast but had left me alone because I was sleeping so well. Finally she woke me.

"We've got to get some food into you and get you dressed to go to the doctor, Grace. Come on," she said. "Get up."

I wiped my eyes with the base of my palms and looked at her in confusion. "The doctor?"

"Oh, Grace, don't tell me you don't remember anything that happened yesterday. I had Dr. Cook here. We've made arrangements for you to see a neurologist today. Get up and get dressed normally. Do you want me to send Lourdes up here to help you?"

"No, I'll be all right," I said. I was still confused, but

I didn't want to keep telling her. I could see something else was bothering her, too.

I ate what I could, and we left for the doctor's office in West Palm Beach. He had offices at the neurological center. Everyone was very nice to us. The doctor first spoke with me for a while, and they decided to put me through some tests, which included eye exams, hearing, a brain scan, even examining my feet. I was there most of the day. In the end the doctor concluded I had no physical problems. Mommy told him she had thought so. The conclusion was I should see a therapist because my problems were mental and emotional. He suggested I see a Dr. Anderson, and Mommy made that appointment the following day.

In the meantime Kirby came home, and although they didn't argue in front of me I heard them bickering in their suite. Later that evening he came to my room to see me. I was trying to read again, hoping that it would make me tired enough to get a good night's rest. I kept thinking I had already read this book, but I wasn't positive, so I read on.

He knocked on the door and peered in. "So," he said, slipping in and closing the door softly behind him, "you haven't been feeling well, huh?"

I just looked at him without replying. He seemed very nervous, tense, his eyes shifting from one side of the room to the other and avoiding directly gazing at me. I was surprised that he looked unshaven, too. His hair wasn't its neat perfect self, and his jacket was wrinkled as it would be if he had slept in it.

"Your mother's driving me mad," he said. "All of a sudden I'm the one who's neglecting her, and it's not vice versa. Women. Can't live with them, can't live with them." He laughed.

He stole a quick look at me and walked to my vanity table, where he checked himself in the mirror. "I had a tough time getting back from Dallas. Plane delays, cancellations, slept in an airport waiting for the next flight, but does she take any of that into consideration? No. All she knows is I missed a dinner date. A dinner date, for crissakes! How important could that have been?" He turned, his arms up.

I was still staring at him. He dropped his arms to his side and looked at me askance. "What is supposed to be wrong with you? She tells me you're fine, but you fainted and did some wild off-the-wall thing with clothes and makeup." He smiled. "I would have thought you'd be more energetic, revived, ready to go out there and whip those college guys until they begged for mercy, huh?"

My silence was making him more nervous.

"Look," he said, "I heard you're going to see a psychiatrist tomorrow. You know those guys can get very nosy, poking their faces into your most intimate secrets. You be careful about that. Most of the time they're just plain pornographers, getting their kicks from their patients' exciting experiences. Understand what I'm saying, Grace? If this comes out like that, I won't be the only one with any guilt. Your mother has seen you with me. She even believes you have a crush on me and that's why you don't go out. A man can be seduced as easily as a woman. Remember that," he said in a threatening tone. "You understand what I'm telling you? Don't just sit there giving me the silent treatment, Grace. Talk."

"Je suis fatigué de parler," I said.

"Huh? What's that, French?" He tugged on his ear like Humphrey Bogart and smiled. "My French is a bit rusty. What did you say? Something about being tired?"

"Mais oui. Bon soir."

"Bon soir? What are you, dismissing me? Fine. Just remember what I told you," he said, and headed for the door, where he turned to me again. "I'm with two crazy women, if you ask me," he said, and left.

In the days and weeks to follow so much changed at Joya del Mar. Kirby's trips became even more frequent. Mommy was more and more upset about it, but I was grateful. I began my therapy with Dr. Anderson and found him to be a very nice man. Mommy began to retreat from her social committees and events. She knew she was the center of gossip again and all because of Kirby's behavior. She was doing her best to hide my condition, but with as many servants as we had and the tendency for people to gossip, that was becoming an increasingly impossible task. People like the Carriage sisters were at her, pecking and pecking in a search for new information they could gobble at their teas and luncheons.

Nearly four months later I paused in the hallway on my return from seeing Dr. Anderson because I heard the distinct sound of Mommy sobbing in the den. I hurried to the doorway and looked in at her. She was at her desk, her head lowered to her arms.

"Mommy?" I called.

Slowly, as if her head weighed a hundred pounds, she lifted it and looked at me through bloodshot eyes.

"Oh, Grace," she said, "Grace."

"What is it?" I asked her, stepping into the den.

"Kirby . . ."

"He's with another woman?" I asked quickly.

"No, worse," she said. "He's seriously depleted our

fortune with his terrible investments and ventures and heavy gambling. Our financial advisor just called to give me the very bad news. We can't keep up this estate, Grace. The best we can do is rent it out and move ourselves into the beach house. Into the beach house! Can you imagine that? Can you imagine what these people will do to us, say about us? I can't show my face anywhere in Palm Beach anymore."

"Where is Kirby now?"

"In hell, I hope," she cried, and took a deep breath. "I don't know where he is exactly. Hiding from someone he is indebted to, I'm sure. I've asked my lawyer to begin marriage dissolution activity. I've got to dissociate myself from him as quickly as I can so I can salvage something for us.

"I'm sorry," she told me. "This is all my fault. I never should have begun with him. I should have listened to wiser heads instead of my own foolish heart. Look what I have done to us."

"Oh, Mommy, you haven't done anything to us. He's done it all."

"Yes, well, he wouldn't have had the chance if it wasn't for me," she said, thumping her chest so hard with her fist it made me wince.

Then she sat straighter, flicked the tears from her cheeks, and firmed her lips. "Well, I have my work cut out for me. I might as well begin. We've been down before, and we've come back. We'll do it again," she said with determination. "As long as you're all right, Grace. As long as you get well."

I bit my lower lip.

How could I tell her now what I had been hiding? She would surely blame herself for this, too, and I feared she would blame me for something unspeakable.

I was too ashamed and felt far too guilty. Dr. Anderson
had been struggling to get me to open that final secret
door, but I had resisted even though I knew he had some
deep suspicions and would not stop until he had succeeded.

I hadn't just had sex with Kirby, my mother's husband.

Although I wasn't showing yet, I knew I was pregnant.

I couldn't be more positive about it and more terrified of revealing anything, especially to Mommy.

How many times over the next two months did I try
to convince myself it wasn't my fault? How many times
was it on the tip of my tongue to tell her everything?
Every time I thought I could do it I heard myself ques-
tioning myself. *Was it your fault? Were you flirting with
him as he had once said? Did you have to spend all that
time doing things with him? Did you have a crush on
him? Why didn't you scream more, fight more when he
kissed you like a lover kisses a woman that first time?
And if you were raped, why did you wait so long to
reveal it? Why did you let your mother sleep with the
man who had done this to you? Why didn't you have the
decency, the loyalty, to protect her? How do you look at
yourself in the mirror every day?*

Fortunately Kirby was really gone from our lives,
mostly, Mommy thought, out of fear of being chased
down by some of the more unsavory characters he was
indebted to. He put up no resistance to the legal pro-
ceedings to separate him from Mommy. Our financial
advisors and lawyers did the best they could creating
barriers to his raiding what was left of our fortune.
Once she had loved him passionately, with a young

woman's excitement, and now there was no one she hated more. And I was to tell her this person had done one more terrible thing to us?

My throat closed every time I thought I could do it, and I was too frightened and knew no one to go to who could help me find a secret way out of my dilemma. I was still barely showing, but I knew it was going to be very hard to keep my secret much longer.

While all this was going on our financial advisor had located a couple who were very interested in renting Joya del Mar, the Eatons. They had no problem about our living in the beach house and were even willing to keep on all our servants. Preparations were begun for our taking over the rear apartment in the beach house, the biggest one at least, and Mommy began to sell off whatever she could from the house to build up our bank accounts again and at least give us a sense of some security.

Mommy behaved as if someone had died the day we moved out of the main house. She would break out in quiet sobbing on and off and then suck in her breath to give the servants another order. The maids packed all our clothing and brought it to the apartment, which had no closet space in comparison. One of the bedrooms in the apartment had to be utilized for storage, and Mommy wailed about all her wonderful dresses and gowns, her pants suits and shoes that would be ruined.

Another fact of life would be the use of the servants themselves. After this day they no longer worked for us. They worked for these new people, the Eatons.

"It's been so long since I've cooked anything," Mommy complained. "We'll starve."

Her sighs were so deep and came so often I thought she would eventually crack in two. Out of the garage came our two automobiles, now to be parked on a section of the driveway.

"We'll have to sell one of the cars anyway," she concluded. I didn't really care. I had no interest in driving, going anywhere.

Just like someone who had lost her lover or her dearest friend, Mommy sat on the small loggia at the rear of the beach house. She didn't want to watch the movers bringing the Eatons' belongings. She had met the couple at our attorney's office only a few weeks ago to finalize the lease agreement, and she told me they were silly people made even more inconsequential by their apparent wealth.

"The woman giggles a lot. She insists she be called Bunny, and her husband, Asher, looks like he's never had to do anything more than lift a toilet seat his whole life."

She shook herself as if to shake off a bad chill. "Winston must be spinning in his grave. I've let him down as well as ourselves. I don't care if I never set foot off this property. I shudder to think of myself running into the Carriage sisters or any of the people I know. I swear, Grace, I'll just burst into tears the moment they say hello because I'll know just what's behind those artificial smiles. They think I deserve this. They'll all be so smug."

I didn't say anything. I listened just the way Dr. Anderson listened to me when I spoke to him in his office, my face empty of any expression that could be interpreted as some sort of judgment, while inside myself I was screaming, "It's time to tell her! It's time to tell her!"

I tried to choose the best possible moment. One night, nearly a week after we had been moved into the beach house, Mommy seemed to have come to a point where she was accepting our new status. She had successfully made one of the veal dishes Daddy used to love, and that put her in a good mood. Most of our dinner conversation was about him, or rather, I should say, most of her conversation was about him. I just sat there listening. One of her remembrances gave me the opening I needed.

She was telling me how she had revealed to him she was pregnant. "We had been trying, of course, and shortly before I had gone for an examination and test he had been shipped off for a training exercise that kept him away nearly a month. I could have written to him, but I said to myself, 'Jackie Lee, this is not the sort of thing you reveal in a letter. It's too important, and the emotion of the moment is something you want to share and remember for the rest of both your lives.'

"So I kept it a secret. The day of his arrival I went to the airport at the Navy base. They would let me, as well as other wives, go there to greet our husbands. One day a week earlier I had found this adorable baby-size Navy uniform. There was even a small cap to go with it. I bought it and put it in a gift box. There I was standing with the other women when he came down the gangway. He rushed to me and kissed me, and then I said I had brought him a present and handed him the box. I had bought him a few flamboyant shirts when we were on holiday less than a year before, and he was always teasing me about that.

" 'Not another shirt made out of someone's underwear, I hope,' he said.

" 'I don't think so,' I told him, and full of curiosity, he tore off the gift wrapping and opened the box. When he lifted out the tiny uniform his face went from surprise and confusion to utter joy."

" 'We've got it!' he cried as if we had won a prize.

" 'Yes,' I said, 'I'm pregnant,' and do you know what he did, Grace, what that big, strapping, handsome U.S. naval officer did right then and there?"

I shook my head.

"He cried," she said. "He just let his tears come, and then he wrapped his arms around me and held me as tightly as he could until he thought he was doing something that would hurt me and you and let go.

" 'I'm pregnant,' I told your father, 'but I'm not made of breakable thin china.'

"What a wonderful night that was," she said, remembering, her eyes drifting around the resurrected images.

I bit down on my lower lip and finally let my tears come unflinchingly, too. For a few moments she didn't notice, and then she blinked and looked at me.

"Oh, honey," she said, "I'm sorry. I know how much it hurts when I bring up your daddy."

I shook my head. "No," I said. "That's not it."

She held her gaze and then sat back slowly, suspicion darkening her eyes and narrowing them as well as she perused my face with a mother's intuitive observation.

"What is it, Grace? Why are you crying?"

I tried to speak, but for a moment my throat was so tight I couldn't utter a sound.

"What is it, Grace?" she asked, more demanding.

"I'm . . . I'm pregnant, Mommy," I said.

It was as if a clap of thunder had just occurred right above us. That was how my bones vibrated. She didn't move a muscle; she didn't even blink fast. Her lips trembled finally until she drew the strength to speak.

"Pregnant? How can you be pregnant, Grace? You never went anywhere, dated anyone all year."

I could feel the tears streaming down my cheeks and dripping from my chin, but I didn't wipe them off or try to stop them from coming. "He came to me one night when I was in a daze, Mommy, groggy from the sleeping pills."

Her eyes widened with the shock of her realization of just what I was telling her.

"I barely remember it, but I know he did it more than once," I said.

She was shaking her head as if to throw the words out of her ears before they could reach her brain. "No," she said, "no."

"I'm sorry, Mommy. I'm sorry."

She pushed herself up and looked down at me, her mouth twisting with the pain and the agony moving like a corkscrew through her brain and into her heart.

"No, Grace, you must have imagined it. You can't be pregnant. He's been gone for nearly five months now."

"I'm starting to show, Mommy. That's why I'm wearing these loose dresses all the time."

She stared, the reality settling in with the weight and the chill of fresh cement.

"You've known and kept it secret all this time?"

"I'm sorry, Mommy."

"Stand up," she ordered, and I did so. She came to me and ran her hands over my hips and my stomach to make the dress tighter. My bulge was clearly evident. "Oh, my God," she said, stepping back as if I was contagious. "You are pregnant, aren't you? He did this. He did this!"

She pressed her hands to her temples and grimaced with the pain, pushing so hard her face was red, her eyes bulged. Then she tore at her own hair for a moment, tugging it before releasing herself and reaching for a dish on the table. She heaved it across the small kitchen, and it smashed and splattered against the wall.

"Are you telling me that you're more than seven months pregnant?"

I barely had the strength to nod, but I did.

"Why didn't you tell me months and months ago? How could you keep this a secret, Grace? Don't you realize what you have done? Can you imagine the gossip, the disgrace? We'll be the laughingstock of the whole strip. They'll never stop talking about us now."

"I'm sorry, Mommy."

"Why didn't you tell me?" she screamed.

"I was afraid. I was afraid you would blame me," I wailed.

"Blame you? But . . ." She looked at me in a different way. "Those times, those many, many times you were alone with him, out on the sailboat, out there, or those trips you two would take, all of that, did he do anything then? Did you let him, Grace?" she asked.

I shook my head. "I don't think so, Mommy."

"You don't think so? You don't think you let him? What does that mean?"

"He said I always flirted with him, but I didn't. I didn't mean to," I moaned.

She pulled her head back and looked at me again, her eyes revealing a mixture of doubt and belief.

"He would say that," she concluded. "He *will* say that. Of course. He'll tell everyone you seduced him and not vice versa, if we let this be known."

She sank into her chair, thinking. "We can't get anyone to give you an abortion this late without chancing an even bigger scandal. What can we do? What can we do?"

I sat across from her again, and she looked at me for the longest time without speaking. I wiped away my tears and waited.

"Who else knows about this, Grace? Have you told Dr. Anderson, for example? Not that it should matter. He isn't supposed to reveal what his clients tell him."

"No, Mommy, I don't think I have."

"You don't think you have? What kind of talk is this? Don't you know if you have or haven't?"

"He gets me to say things, and sometimes I think I say things I don't mean to say."

"Who else?" she asked, sitting back.

"No one. Who else is there?"

"That's true. None of the servants, right, none of those maids who like you and whom you like to speak with, right?"

"No."

"Good. Okay. We can't let him do anything else to us," she decided. She smiled suddenly, a cold, almost evil smile. "We can, however, make him look even worse."

She pressed her palms down on the table and leaned toward me, her eyes fixed hard on mine. "You're not pregnant, Grace. Do you hear me? Do you understand?"

"No, Mommy. I am pregnant."

"No, you're not, you see. I'm the one who is pregnant. I'm the one he has left in the lurch here. Seven months is fine. I didn't show with you until the seventh month. I will start showing, and I will give out the news. In fact," she added with a wider smile, "I'll call Thelma Carriage and let it slip. That will take care of it."

"But what about me?"

"You'll stay as you do. You won't be going to your therapy for the next two months or so. I'll fix myself so I begin to show, and in a month, parading about here with a swollen stomach, I'll convince people I'm the one.

"Fortunately I haven't been out and about much, so people will accept it. I know I can depend on Dr. Cook to go along with this. When your time comes he'll deliver the baby here. We'll just say there was no time to get to the hospital. Women usually give birth easier the second time than they do the first, so people will believe it all.

"That's it, Grace. That will be our solution. Do you understand? When you start to really show, I don't want you to be visible. You'll confine yourself to indoors until I give you an all-clear, and then you can take short walks behind the beach house but never toward the main house. All we have to do is permit those silly Eaton people to realize what's what, and they'll make it the evening's headlines.

"Everyone will accept your behavior because you're practically a hermit as it is."

She paused and twisted her lips as she looked at me. "I suppose in an ironic way I should be happy about that," she said. "It makes all this subterfuge possible. Besides, I'm sure you're not the first young woman to give birth secretly in this town."

She stood up again. "Clear off the table, clean up the broken dish, and load the dishwasher," she ordered. "I'm going to look over my wardrobe and decide what I have that will work over the next two months." She smiled coldly. "What I'll do is go out and buy maternity outfits as well. That will lock up the gossip Thelma Carriage will undertake."

"I'm sorry that I've made all this trouble for you, Mommy," I said.

"I am, too, Grace. It seems that fate will not let go of us. For some reason we're a prime target for it, but we'll stand up to it as we always do," she vowed. "We really have no choice. It's either this or leaving with our tails between our legs."

She headed for her bedroom and the spare bedroom to sift through her wardrobe.

Finally the reality I had kept so well hidden began to rise to the surface of my thoughts.

And, actually for the first time, I thought about the baby inside me.

With both of us regretting my pregnancy and hating the man who had done this to me, what kind of a child would he or she be, and into what sort of a world would he or she be brought?

19

One Last Salute

When my mother was determined to do something, she devoted every last ounce of her energy toward accomplishing it. Establishing her surrogate pregnancy was no exception. She took great care in creating her physical appearance and did something I knew was abhorrent to her: She deliberately set out to gain weight, and as quickly as possible. Some days she gorged herself so much on fattening foods, especially ice cream, cakes, and cookies, that she ended up in the bathroom regurgitating for nearly half an hour. She would emerge pale and sickly, but like a stubborn and defiant prisoner of her own making she would return to the kitchen and make a milkshake. She would conquer her body, and that was that.

However, while she was doing all this I would sometimes catch her glaring at me with a glint of steel anger in her eyes. No matter what she had said or how she had

spoken about Kirby or about cruel fate, I knew she
blamed me, too. Her eyes gave me nightmares. In one
dark dream she was actually pregnant. It was as if my
pregnancy was contagious. She was screaming with
labor pains, and I was at her bedside, holding her hand,
and I was still pregnant myself! I was pleading with her
to stop, telling her she wasn't pregnant, but suddenly I
heard the sound of a baby's cry. It sent shivers through
me as I began to lift the blanket. Fortunately, before I
saw anything, I awoke, in a cold sweat and breathing so
hard I had pains around my heart.

A full month had gone by, and I had stepped out of
the beach house only twice, both times after midnight.
I was so terrified of being discovered that I couldn't
walk far, and I kept myself in the shadows like some
nocturnal creature who could be destroyed by any
light, a vampire without any strength, only the curse
upon her.

Mommy followed each step of her plan carefully.
She went to a maternity shop and bought the clothes.
She had more than one conversation with Thelma
Carriage, and during the second one she broke out in
sobs and revealed that Kirby had left her not only
depleted of her fortune but with child. She begged
Thelma not to tell anyone, which was the same as say-
ing, "Please, tell everyone in the world about me."

Some of her older acquaintances began to phone,
pretending to be concerned about her situation but
really hoping to get some new tidbit of information that
they could claim. She doled it out cleverly, sprinkling
details within the conversation. She claimed she didn't
want to know the sex of the child. She said she wasn't
sure she would keep the child. She didn't want to give
birth anywhere but in the beach house, and maybe that

way no one would be aware of the events that would follow. Mommy made each caller feel she was party to a secret, pretending to believe in the caller's oath of loyalty. She was so good and so convincing that I had to pause myself to remember it was all a ruse.

Dr. Cook came to see me once a week, Mommy again making it appear as though he was coming to see her. She was afraid one of his receptionists would find out the truth and reveal it, so she told Brenda Carriage that Dr. Cook was cooperating with her efforts and making house calls.

And then she did what I thought was the *pièce de résistance,* the crowning piece of deception. She told Thelma Carriage that she was going to try to convince people the child was mine so she would still be available for any potential new wealthy bachelor or widower. She said she was even having me wear pillows so I would appear pregnant. This would cover any possible error I would make, especially in the event someone saw me. She did this right before she invited the Carriage sisters to an afternoon tea.

By now she had managed to gain nearly seven pounds. Her face was bloated, and her disguised, imitation-pregnant figure was convincing. She told me her plan for the afternoon. I was to remain out of sight until she gave me the signal, and then I was to appear as if I didn't know they were there and quickly retreat after giving them just enough time to see me.

Afterward she was ecstatic. They had bought into it entirely, she said. I thought she was acting strangely now because she was enjoying her success too much, and then an even stranger feeling came over me. I found myself actually becoming jealous. Mommy was relishing and savoring her state of pregnancy and the poten-

tial new baby's arrival far more than I was, and my state
of pregnancy was real!

At times I thought she believed I really wasn't pregnant. She was doing that good a job of convincing herself so she could be believable to other people. A line
from a novel I read during this time came to me: "Be
careful of who you pretend to be or you'll become who
you pretend to be."

There she was straining to get up from her chair or
asking me to get her this or that. She got her waddle
walk down perfectly and moaned and sighed just like a
woman struggling with a pregnancy might. All this she
was doing without anyone else but me there! Maybe
she thought she was punishing me, getting back at me. I
was too amazed and frightened to say anything,
because when I did the first time, she turned on me, her
eyes wide with fury, and screamed, "I'm doing this for
you, you fool! I have to practice and get into the state of
mind so I don't make any mistakes when I'm in public.
How can you be so bright in college, be such an avid
reader, and be so stupid sometimes, Grace?"

I quickly retreated, my eyes clouded with tears, and
then I thought, *she's actually going through the same
mood swings I've experienced, any pregnant woman
experiences.* I even caught her in front of the full-length
mirror in her room sighing sadly about her lost figure,
the fat in her face. Surely she knew it was only for a
very short time and it was not really a result of any
pregnancy. Then, during my eighth month, she did
something that put nightmares even into my daylight
hours. She screamed for me one morning and told me to
call Dr. Cook.

"We need him right away!"

It was on the tip of my tongue to ask her why, but I

was too frightened by the look in her face. I hurried to the phone and spoke to the receptionist. She said he was at the hospital, but she would contact him and inform him. I returned to Mommy's bedroom and told her. She was lying on her side, moaning, and waved me off.

A few hours later Dr. Cook arrived, but she was there at the door to greet him before I could get there.

"Please, check her, Bob," she told him, and nodded toward me. "She was having labor pains earlier."

I stood back, astounded, but sat on my bed and waited until he came into my room and examined me.

"You're carrying very low," he said. "But I don't think it's going to be before the full gestation period. Don't worry. This sort of thing is common for first-time mothers. I'm sure you remember it well, Jackie Lee," he told her, and she nodded.

Outside my room she thanked him profusely, cried, and had him comfort her.

"Now, now," he said. "It's all going well. You'll get through this. Don't worry."

She thanked him again, and he left. Moments later she was at my door.

"You should be very grateful to that man," she said. "He's doing us a great favor. He loved Winston like a brother."

"I know," I said, my face full of questions. "But why did you have me send for him? I didn't have labor pains."

"You could have had. People would expect it. We haven't seen the doctor for a while," she said with growing impatience. "Why do you question what I'm doing? Why aren't you grateful and thankful?"

"I am, but . . ."

"Just do exactly as I tell you," she snapped, and then she went to eat one of her fattening snacks.

The last month was the worst. Whenever I had a real pain she would have to imitate it. She had become a fanatical method actor. Her screams echoed my own until I swallowed them back. The pain brought tears to my eyes, but I didn't reveal it. She even remarked about how hard the baby was kicking.

"It's difficult to get a good night's rest," she said.

There were times when I thought, *maybe she's doing this to be sure I'm really pregnant and it's not just a big tumor.* She looked as if she wanted me to confirm every symptom, every action.

And then my water broke. I was standing in the kitchen doorway watching her move with great effort to fill the dishwasher. I screamed, "Mommy!"

She turned, saw what was happening, and went to the phone to called Dr. Cook.

She helped me back to bed, muttering, "Finally, finally this will be over. Breathe," she ordered. "Remember the breathing."

She did it to demonstrate. My eyes were on her the whole time. She looked as if she felt every one of my pains, the tightening, the pressure.

Dr. Cook arrived. Mommy wasn't wearing anything under her dress by then. He hurried into my bedroom, told her what to get for him, and bore down on my delivery. It took four hours and left me so exhausted I barely acknowledged that it had finally happened. The baby's cries seemed so far off, but he showed me the infant. It was a boy.

"Fine-looking baby," Dr. Cook said. "I told you not to worry, Jackie Lee."

"Yes," she said. "He is beautiful."

"What are you going to name him?" he asked her.

I could barely breathe. He was talking to her as if the baby *really* was hers. Had everyone gone mad?

"I thought I'd name him after my grandfather, Linden," she said. She looked at me. "Linden Montgomery. We'll return to that surname, Montgomery. I don't want to even remember the name Scott. How's that sound, Grace?"

I nodded, my throat too tight to speak.

"Well, baby and mother are doing fine. I'll be back in a few days to check on you both," he said, this time looking at me.

I closed my eyes. I was expecting Mommy to put baby Linden beside me, but she left the room with him in her arms.

"We'll have to keep the bassinet in my room," she said. "Just in case. You never know. Someone could go walking by and look in our windows."

"But he'll keep you awake," I said. I wanted my baby beside me. I had an overwhelming need to have him there, to hold him.

"Grace, don't argue about the details. We're pulling this off. I've saved your reputation," she told me. "Be grateful, and don't cause any difficulties."

She had to bring the baby back to me for feeding, but she had already planned on this as well and had bought a padded bra so her own breasts would look swollen with milk. Later I discovered her lying in her bed with Linden beside her naked breast, his lips around her nipple like a baby with a pacifier in his mouth.

"He must be hungry," was all I could say.

She opened her eyes and looked at me as if I were absolutely crazy.

"Go back to bed, Grace. I know when he's really

hungry and when he's not," she said, and brought the blanket up so it covered him and her as well.

A few weeks later, after I had fed him, she came to fetch him, and I refused to give him up.

"No, Mother," I said firmly. "Just leave him be."

She looked at me, her eyes blinking quickly. "What? Why?"

"He's my baby," I said sharply.

"You can't do that, Grace. You can't say that."

"I can to you. We know the truth, don't we?"

"But if someone sees you with him . . ."

"So what if they do? I can be seen holding him. He's my half-brother, isn't he? As far as anyone else knows, that is. Besides, I'm keeping my shades down all the time, Mommy. No one can see in here."

"It's still too dangerous," she insisted. "Give him to me. I'll put him back where he belongs so he can sleep."

"No," I said.

"Grace, I have no patience for this. Look at what I've gone through to give birth instead of you! You think I want to risk ruining all we have done?"

"All we have done? All you have to do now is go on a diet, Mommy, and you'll be fine."

"Go on a diet?" She threw her head back and laughed. "That's all? What about my reputation? My life? What about the after-effects socially? I have borne the burden of it all and will forever," she said. "You can go off to college or something and find a handsome new beau and have a wonderful life. Now give me the child," she demanded, and reached for him.

I had no doubt in my mind she would tug off an arm or a leg if I held him back, so I relinquished him, and she left me sobbing in my pillow.

As the months went by and Linden grew nothing really changed. She would be the one who primarily fed him when he was off breast-feeding. She dressed him every morning, bathed him, and went shopping for his clothes. She even took him to Dr. Cook's office for a checkup. All the while I was left at home, left in the wings of her new stage show, watching like some bystander. I couldn't remember a time I felt more alone, more lost. I really did feel like some stranger, some surrogate mother who had been paid to house the fetus and had nothing more to do with him. Mommy didn't seem to notice. She was doting too much on Linden now and becoming more and more annoyed by anything I asked or did.

Meanwhile the new family in the main house, almost like a relay racer taking a baton in handoff, had continued the elaborate parties Mommy and Kirby had staged. We were always invited, but Mommy was hesitant about attending them, ashamed of where we were living and what had happened to us. The music, the laughter, even the wonderful aromas of the variety of foods reached us no matter how we closed and battened down our apartment.

"I feel like I attend anyway," Mommy muttered, and eventually got up the courage to wander over occasionally.

The Eatons had two children, a girl named Whitney and a boy named Thatcher. The little boy was handsome, adorable, but his sister was tall for her age and always looked sad and upset whenever I saw her. They rarely if ever came near the beach house. Mommy said they were probably told we were like the untouchables in India or something.

I had become so accustomed to staying at home and

so afraid of wandering too far off that I didn't meet or converse with anyone besides one of the servants for the main house. They all lived behind and above us in the beach house. I supposed I was something of a curiosity to them and especially to the Eaton children. It didn't bother me. Nothing seemed to bother me. Nothing seemed to matter anymore. I ate, I slept, I took care of Linden when Mommy would allow or be doing something, going somewhere. That was the whole of my life.

I truly felt as if the world had closed in on me, that there were no boundaries, and that even on the brightest days the rim of darkness was always there, a circle drawn around me and out of which I should never wander. Linden was walking now, and Mommy would permit me to take him on the beach and let him play in the sand.

"I'm really your mommy," I would tell him when she was out of earshot. "You're my baby."

Sometimes he looked at me as though he really understood. I so wanted him to be looking at me when he said "Mama." I repeated it many times, and even though he wasn't looking directly at me, I thought he was making the connection and would someday just start calling me Mama, and then my mother would surrender him.

It didn't happen that way, and I cried at night thinking about it. Sometimes I cried myself to sleep. I went from one kind of darkness into another. Time began to lose meaning altogether for me. There were weeks on end when I didn't know what day it was. What difference would it have made anyway? I told myself.

"You should be thinking of returning to school now, Grace," Mommy would say morning after morning. "We have a little money for that. I'm not telling you to pick some fancy college, but you have to get back out there, otherwise why did I make this great sacrifice?"

The more she pressured me to leave, the more terrified of it I became. We had long ago sold my car. I hadn't been on Worth Avenue or in a supermarket or department store for more than a year, much less mingle with people my age, but I couldn't ignore the way she was pressuring me to go. It was almost as if she wanted to be alone with Linden, and as long as I was around she couldn't be his real mother.

I really didn't know what to do. It all made me more nervous, more unsure of myself. Sometimes I would wander for hours on the beach, traipsing back and forth, walking through the edge of the incoming tide, sitting for hours and hours and looking out at the ships, moving like someone in a daze. Whom could I ask to help me? Whom could I trust?

And then, one night, he was just there.

I was standing on the dock, embracing myself and staring at a luxury liner that was close enough for me to hear the sounds of music and laughter. To me it seemed more like a ship full of people who had escaped every dark moment, every second of sadness, every worry and trouble in their lives, and now drifted in a perpetual state of happiness and excitement, drunk on the stars above them.

"I bet you wish you were on that ship, Sailor Girl," I heard, and turned to see Daddy standing there. He was in full-dress uniform, his medals gleaming in the starlight.

"Daddy!"

"Hey," he said.

I ran to him, and he held me just the way he always did.

"I'm so alone, Daddy, and so lost."

"I know," he said. "Don't worry, I'll be here for you when you need me."

"I gave birth to a little boy, Daddy, but Mommy is so possessive she won't let me be his mother even in secret."

"Give her time," he said in his usual confident manner. "We all need time."

"Why did you go, Daddy? Why did you leave us?"

"Hey, you know what it's like for an officer. When he's called, he's called. You don't question orders, Sailor Girl. You do your duty as you swore you would. You wouldn't have wanted me to go AWOL, would you? Well?"

"No, but I missed you so much, and I needed you so much. I'm tired, Daddy, tired, and I'm too young to be this tired."

He laughed. "You'll catch your breath and be strong again," he said. "Tell me about the little boy."

"He's so beautiful and clever. You should see him draw shapes in the sand. He looks at things, and then he draws them with his little finger."

"That's wonderful," Daddy said.

The luxury liner was moving farther and farther away, the laughter and the music becoming too distant to hear. The ship seemed to slip right into the darkness and take all the stars with it. I watched it disappear, and then I turned back to Daddy, but he wasn't there.

"Daddy?" I called. I started down the dock toward shore. "Daddy?"

I moved faster and called for him louder, and then I stopped at the shoreline and looked to my right and to my left and screamed for him.

"What do you think you're doing, screaming like that, Grace?"

Mommy was out on the rear loggia. She was in her robe and had her hair pinned up. The facial cream she put on her skin every night to keep it soft and youthful gleamed in the weak glow of the outside ceiling fixture just like Daddy's medals had gleamed in the starlight.

"I . . ."

"What, Grace? Well?" she demanded.

"I saw Daddy," I said. "He was right here. We spoke to each other."

"Great," she said, and turned and walked back into the apartment.

I stood there, looking down the beach and then out at the dock, but he was nowhere to be seen.

I did see him, I told myself. *I did.*

I found Mommy working on her fingernails when I entered the apartment. She looked up at me.

"If you don't start looking for someplace to go, something to do with your life, I don't know what," she said. "You sounded like a real idiot out there."

She looked at her nails again. I waited a moment and then went to bed. At breakfast she didn't mention anything about what had happened the night before. She talked about chores she had, shopping she must do.

"I'm almost afraid to leave Linden here alone with you," she finally added.

"Why?"

"You're acting strangely again. You should go back to the therapist."

"I'm fine," I said.

"I hope so," she countered in a threatening tone. Finally she left, and I took Linden to the beach as usual. It was a very quiet morning. The Eatons rarely appeared outside before one or two in the afternoon.

Mommy said that was because they partied all night into the morning. She called them the idle rich.

I didn't care. I was happy not to be bothered, not to have anyone looking at us. I sat there doing a crossword puzzle and watching Linden play.

"You were right," I heard, and looked up. There was Daddy. He was in his flight suit this time and holding his helmet under his arm. "He's a very handsome young man. A little like myself at his age," he added with a smile. "I ever show you pictures of me as a little boy?"

"Yes," I said. "I still have them in a chest."

"Well, take them out and look at them again. Show them to your mother. She is sure to get a kick out of it, out of the resemblance," he said. He looked out over the ocean. "Stiff winds today. I'm off on a mission, Sailor Girl. You take charge here, okay?"

He always used to say that to me.

"Aye, aye, sir," I said, and he smiled and gave me the two-finger salute.

I saluted back and watched him walk off. He seemed to walk right into the air and was gone.

Linden was looking up at me.

"Hey," I said. "Let me show you how to salute."

I worked on it all day and finally got him to do it. I couldn't wait to show Mommy when she returned.

"He saw Daddy do it, too," I told her, and she spun her head around at me so fast I thought she would snap her neck.

"What did you say?"

"Daddy was on the beach. He told me to dig out his old pictures, the ones of him as a little boy. He said he looked like Linden, and he said you would get a kick out of it."

She stared at me. "Why are you doing this, Grace?

Are you trying to convince me you shouldn't go back to college, or are you trying to avoid doing something with your life? Why are you doing this?"

"Doing what?" I asked.

She stared and then shook her head. "I won't play this game with you," she muttered, and went to feed Linden.

I went to the chest and found the pictures. I had them spread out on my bed when she looked in.

"See," I said, "Linden does look like him when he was a little boy."

"Put those pictures away," she ordered. "You're absolutely ridiculous."

She walked off, but I kept the pictures out for a while. I had a feeling Daddy might want to see them again, too.

Sure enough, that night I was awoken by the sound of some soft laughter and looked over to see him sitting at my desk, gazing at the pictures.

"Daddy, you were right," I said. I got up quickly and put on the lights.

"I thought I was. I like this one with me and the cat we used to have, Fluffy. I wish you could have seen that cat, Sailor Girl. She would follow me around just like a puppy dog. I ever tell you about her?"

"Yes, Daddy, many times," I said, smiling.

"Glad you dug up the pictures."

"You told me to, but Mommy didn't believe me."

"She'll come around. It takes time. Remember what I said, it takes time. Well, I have to get going. Sleep tight," he said, and walked out.

"What are you doing?" I heard. "Why are you up with the lights on? It's close to three in the morning," Mommy said from my doorway. She was holding her hands together against her chest.

"He was here looking at the pictures," I said. "He just walked out. Did you see him?"

"See who?"

"Daddy."

She brought her hands to her mouth and then walked away. "Go to sleep," she called from her bedroom door.

I put out the lights and went back to bed. When I woke in the morning, all the pictures were gone. For a moment I thought I had put them back in the chest, but when I looked they weren't there.

"Mommy," I asked, coming out to the kitchen where she was feeding Linden breakfast. "Did you see Daddy's pictures?"

"Forget about those pictures," she told me.

"But . . ."

"I said forget about them, Grace. Stop this!" she screamed at me. "Stop it now, or . . . or I'll have you sent away. I swear I will."

Linden started to cry at the sound of her anger.

"What am I supposed to stop?" I asked softly. She didn't reply. She looked as if she was going to cry instead and turned away. Then she sucked in her breath and went back to feeding Linden, comforting him.

It seemed to me that whenever I spoke to her these days Mommy got upset. It was better not to talk or to talk as little as possible.

It's part of disappearing, I thought, remembering Augustus Brewster. *First you stop talking, and then people stop hearing you, and when they stop hearing you, they stop seeing you, and soon you're gone.*

Maybe it was time to go.

*   *   *

Daddy agreed.

He came to me that night. I awoke and saw him sitting at my bedside. He was in his dress uniform again, all the medals on his chest. He was looking down, waiting for me to open my eyes. I sat up slowly.

"Daddy? Why are you here?"

He looked up slowly. "I've come for you, Grace," he said. "I received the orders just a little while ago."

"Come for me?"

"Yes, sweetheart," he said. He smiled, but it looked like a smile born from sadness, not happiness. I thought there were even tears in his eyes, and I rarely saw my Daddy cry.

"But what about Linden?" I asked.

"He'll be fine. He'll be with your mother, and she will take good care of him."

He stared hard at me a moment. "You knew I was coming for you one day, Sailor Girl, didn't you? You expected it."

"Yes, Daddy. It's just sooner than I had imagined."

"I was surprised myself," he said, "but we don't question orders, Sailor Girl. We act on them. That's what makes us successful."

"Do I need to bring anything?" I asked.

He shook his head and stood.

I threw off my blanket and stepped off my bed. "Can I at least say goodbye to Linden?" I asked.

"Sure," he said. "We'll both do that."

Moving as if we were made of air, we slipped into Mommy's room. She was fast asleep, her back to us. Linden was in his small bed beside hers, turned on his side, little lips moving ever so slightly with his breathing.

"I should kiss him," I said.

"Don't wake him," Daddy warned.

"I won't."

Ever so slowly I knelt down beside him and brought my lips to his cheek. I just held them there a second or two and then stood up again. His eyelids barely fluttered.

"Perfect," Daddy said.

I smiled, looked at Mommy, and started out of the room behind Daddy. I looked back once more before following him down the hallway to the door that opened onto the rear loggia. It was a windy evening, and the breakers were high and bone white. The sky was starless, overcast.

"Rough seas ahead," Daddy warned.

The wind rattled the shades and the blinds behind me until I closed the door. Then I followed him down the steps, and we both walked toward the dock.

"I'm a little frightened, Daddy," I said.

He stopped and nodded. "Sure you are. Why shouldn't you be? I was. Here," he said, reaching for my hand, "I'll be right beside you the whole time."

"Thank you, Daddy."

We continued toward the dock.

"You probably don't remember," he said, "but when you were very little, not much older than Linden is now, I took you down to the dock to see an aircraft carrier arriving. You thought it was going to come right on shore, and you were very frightened for a few moments. I picked you up and reassured you, and you calmed down, and then your eyes grew so big with amazement I couldn't stop laughing. There was a band there, and they were playing the Navy anthem."

"I think I remember, Daddy."

"Anchors aweigh, my boy," he sang. "You used to sing that, Sailor Girl."

"I know."

"It broke my heart to leave you behind. I know it's selfish of me, but when the order came down to get you I was happy about it. Forgive me."

"I can never blame you for anything, Daddy. Never," I said.

He smiled, and we stepped onto the dock. "Can you see the ship there, Sailor Girl?"

I started to shake my head, and then there it was, a tender to bring us out to that big beautiful aircraft carrier that waited beyond.

"Here we go," Daddy said.

We walked toward the end of the dock. I started to look back, but Daddy said, "Don't look back now, Sailor Girl. Not until you're aboard. It makes it too hard to leave."

"Okay, Daddy."

A sea gull came flying over the water suddenly and veered right over us, sailing with the wind, its beak slightly open, its eyes sewn shut.

I squeezed Daddy's hand harder, and he held mine tighter.

"Okay," he said when we reached the end. "This is it. Turn now and salute."

I did, watching him. We saluted together, two fingers, looking back at the house.

Mommy appeared to be standing there now.

"Grace!" she screamed. "What are you doing?"

"Don't answer," Daddy said. "They never want you to leave. If it was up to them we would never go on any assignments. I can't blame them, but we can't let it get to us. Let's go," he said, and we both stepped off the dock and onto the tender.

It was so cold.

"It's so cold," I said.

Daddy didn't reply.

"Daddy, it's so cold! Why is it so cold?"

Where was he?

"You fool, you damn fool," I heard, and felt an arm around my waist.

Mommy's face was beside mine, and she was struggling, spitting water, but she wouldn't let me go. The wave picked us up and tossed us both, and a moment later I felt sand beneath my feet. Mommy was tugging and screaming, and I was so confused.

Someone else was there, one of the male servants. He had his arm around my waist now and lifted me like a baby. Then he lowered me to the beach and fell beside me, breathing hard. I was coughing and spitting out sea water. Mommy was sitting there, looking so silly, I thought, her hair down, her nightgown nearly completely off, her body twisted.

"Why . . . did you do that, Grace? Why?" she demanded. I think she was crying, although it was hard to tell the difference between her tears and the sea water dripping out of her hair.

"I was going with Daddy," I said, coughing. "He had come for me." I looked out at the sea. "I don't know where he is now," I said.

The tender was gone, and so was the beautiful aircraft carrier.

He had left without me.

Once again.

He had left without me.

Epilogue

I remember thinking Mommy gets everyone to make house calls. There was my psychiatrist, Dr. Anderson, at my bedside, just the way Dr. Cook had been.

"How are you, Grace?" he asked.

I also remember thinking, *how can he be talking to me?* Surely he can't see me anymore, and surely it would do no good for me to reply. He wouldn't be able to hear me. I looked away.

"Your mother says you've been talking about your father a great deal these days."

Daddy? Yes, of course, I thought.

"You've even seen him, she says. Is that true, Grace?"

I nodded. Maybe the doctor did see me.

"You thought he wanted you to go away with him? Is that true?"

I turned back to him. "Yes," I said. I heard myself

say it and realized I could still be heard. The doctor smiled.

"I'm sure you misunderstood him, Grace. He wouldn't have wanted you to leave your mother and Linden forever, now would he?"

"It couldn't be helped. It was orders," I said.

"Well, orders can be rescinded. Just a mistake, Grace. That's all it was."

I shook my head. "No."

"She'll do it again," I heard. Mommy was standing in my doorway. "We've got to do something. I can't live with one eye open all the time. I'll be the one who needs your therapy soon."

The doctor put up his hand without turning back to her and then smiled at me.

"You just relax awhile, Grace. I'm going to speak with your mother, and I'll be back, okay?"

I didn't reply. He rose and went out with her. I heard their muffled voices, Mommy's sobbing, and then I heard the doctor go to our telephone.

I dozed off, and when I opened my eyes again Dr. Anderson was back at my bedside.

"Well now, Grace," he said, smiling, "new orders have come through."

I looked up at him. Was this true?

"You are required to go someplace where people are going to help you get well again. Your Daddy would surely like that, wouldn't he?"

I nodded.

"I want you to take these two pills, Grace. They will help you rest until it's time for you to go, okay?"

I nodded again, and he gave me the pills and some water, bracing me up with his hand as I swallowed. Then he lowered me to the pillow and smiled.

"That's fine, Grace. Good girl," he said.

I closed my eyes.

When I opened them again it was already early after-noon. One of our former house servants, Lourdes, was in the kitchen. I could hear her speaking with Mommy, who was going over a list of things she wanted her to do.

"While we're away," she repeated, practically begin-ning every other sentence with it.

Who's going to be away? I wondered. I tried to get out of bed and felt so weak my arms and legs trembled. All I managed to do was sit up.

Sitting up, I was able to see the suitcases in the hall-way just outside my bedroom doorway.

"Mommy!" I called. Was she leaving with Linden?

She came to the door.

"Well, good, you're awake. The car's coming for us in about an hour, so I'm going to have you shower and dress, Grace. Lourdes will help you if you need help," she said.

"What car?"

"The car that will take us to the airport, Grace. We have to go to the clinic where they can help you. Dr. Anderson has arranged it all. He has a friend who owns it and runs it, and he assures me his friend is the best in the profession. His name is Dr. De Beers."

"Oh," I said.

"It's for your own good, and mine too," she mut-tered. "Can you shower and dress yourself?"

"I'm not sure," I said.

I struggled a little, and Lourdes came charging in around Mommy and helped me to my feet and to the bathroom.

When I was dressed I sat on the rear loggia and

waited. I remember I was thinking it was partly cloudy with a warm breeze, but there were no sea gulls around the dock today, and there were no ships out there gliding across the horizon. The whole world seemed at pause, even the waves were gentler than usual for this time of the day. Everything was waiting for something special to happen. What was it?

Linden came out and stood there looking at me strangely. He ran his fingers over the railing and looked at me again.

"You saw my daddy, too, didn't you, Linden? You saw the naval officer, and you saw him salute, didn't you? Remember?" I said, saluting with two fingers.

He smiled, but he was more fascinated with some of the cracks that had formed in the railing. The shapes intrigued him, and he traced them and studied them as if they were the answer to some great mystery.

A man in a chauffeur's uniform appeared, and Mommy came out of the apartment quickly to give him orders.

"The suitcases are ready and waiting right inside," she told him.

He nodded, gave me a passing glance, and went inside. A moment later he was carrying them out. Linden was very curious about him. He was at the age where he was curious about everything now.

"It's time to go, Grace," Mommy said.

She was dressed very nicely in one of her designer suits and had her hair pinned up. She wore her nicest diamond teardrop earrings, too, and had her favorite cameo pinned above her right breast.

I stood up, and she took my arm and directed me toward the stairway. Lourdes came out and stood beside Linden. He watched us but said nothing.

"I should say goodbye to him," I said. "I should kiss him goodbye, shouldn't I, Mommy?"

"No," she said sharply. "You'll only make him cry, Grace. It's better if you just leave. You'll be back soon," she promised. "It's easier for everyone. Go on, walk," she ordered, and I went down the stairs.

The car was there, a black Town Car. The driver stood at the rear door that was opened and waiting for us.

"This is the car that will take us to the airport," Mommy said when I stopped walking.

"Oh." I tilted my head with confusion. "Why are we going to the airport? I forgot."

She made a face of impatience.

"We're going to South Carolina," she said slowly, pronouncing each syllable with deliberateness. "So we have to fly there. That's where the clinic is and where Dr. De Beers waits for you. You'll be fine after a while, and then you can come home," she said, but she didn't sound very sure of it. It sounded too much like a promise, and promises were more like wishes for me now.

We started toward the car again.

Linden, I kept thinking. *I'm going so far away, and I'm leaving without saying goodbye. It doesn't seem right. He'll wonder about me, and he'll be looking for me, especially in the evening. I won't be there to read him a story, and my bed will be empty. It doesn't seem right.*

At the car I paused and turned back toward the rear of the beach house. Lourdes had him in her arms and had brought him around. She was pointing toward us and telling him to wave goodbye.

"Get in, Grace," Mommy said, her voice dripping

with impatience. "We've got to go. We can't miss our flight."

Linden was looking at me so hard. My heart began to feel like a rock in my chest.

"Grace."

"Wait," I said firmly, pushing her hand off my arm.

I raised my hand slowly, bringing my two fingers to the top of my forehead.

Little Linden watched, and then he brought his hand to his, his two little fingers returning the salute.

He had seen him, I thought.

He had seen Daddy.

I would be back after all.

POCKET
BOOKS

This book and other **Virginia Andrews** titles are available from your local bookshop or can be ordered direct from the publisher.